Res...
New York ...

J.A. JANCE and
HOUR OF THE HUNTER

"Smashing good. . . . [It] begs to be compared to the
work of Tony Hillerman and Mary Higgins Clark.
J.A. Jance can stand tall even in that fine company."
Washington Times

"Chilling. . . . Satisfying. . . . A good read. . . .
It works. . . . A large cast of interesting, well developed
characters . . . a gripping conclusion. . . .
[Jance] continues to grow in her art. . . . It's no
mystery why this writer is a hit."
Seattle Times

"Jance's novel delivers suspense through richly textured
layers of flashbacks and gritty characterizations."
Publishers Weekly

"A treat. . . . Jance is a weaver, pulling anthropological
threads of Papago theology and philosophy through
a web of fear and vengeance."
Tucson Citizen

"Jance spins a good yarn. She seems to know
intuitively what an audience will go for."
Portland Oregonian

"Truly frightening. . . . If you hunger for suspense
with a Native-American background . . .
Hour of the Hunter may be for you."
Arizona Republic

Books by J. A. Jance

Joanna Brady Mysteries

DESERT HEAT • TOMBSTONE COURAGE
SHOOT/DON'T SHOOT • DEAD TO RIGHTS
SKELETON CANYON • RATTLESNAKE CROSSING
OUTLAW MOUNTAIN • DEVIL'S CLAW
PARADISE LOST • PARTNER IN CRIME • EXIT WOUNDS
DEAD WRONG • DAMAGE CONTROL • FIRE AND ICE

J.P. Beaumont Mysteries

UNTIL PROVEN GUILTY • INJUSTICE FOR ALL
TRIAL BY FURY • TAKING THE FIFTH
IMPROBABLE CAUSE • A MORE PERFECT UNION
DISMISSED WITH PREJUDICE • MINOR IN POSSESSION
PAYMENT IN KIND • WITHOUT DUE PROCESS
FAILURE TO APPEAR • LYING IN WAIT
NAME WITHHELD • BREACH OF DUTY • BIRDS OF PREY
PARTNER IN CRIME • LONG TIME GONE
JUSTICE DENIED • FIRE AND ICE • BETRAYAL OF TRUST

and

HOUR OF THE HUNTER
KISS OF THE BEES
DAY OF THE DEAD
EDGE OF EVIL
QUEEN OF THE NIGHT

ATTENTION: ORGANIZATIONS AND CORPORATIONS
Most Harper paperbacks are available at special quantity discounts for bulk purchases for sales promotions, premiums, or fund raising. For information, please call or write:

Special Markets Department, HarperCollins Publishers,
10 East 53rd Street, New York, New York 10022-5299.
Telephone: (212) 207-7528.   Fax: (212) 207-7222.

HOUR
OF THE
HUNTER

J.A. JANCE

HARPER

An Imprint of HarperCollins*Publishers*

This is a work of fiction. Names, characters, places, and incidents are products of the author's imagination or are used fictitiously and are not to be construed as real. Any resemblance to actual events, locales, organizations, or persons, living or dead, is entirely coincidental.

HARPER

An Imprint of HarperCollins*Publishers*
195 BROADWAY
New York, New York 10007

Copyright © 1991 by J. A. Jance
Excerpt from *Queen of the Night* copyright © 2010 by J. A. Jance
ISBN 978-0-06-194538-0

All rights reserved. No part of this book may be used or reproduced in any manner whatsoever without written permission, except in the case of brief quotations embodied in critical articles and reviews. For information address Harper paperbacks, an Imprint of HarperCollins Publishers.

First Harper premium paperback printing: July 2010
First Avon Books paperback printing: September 1992
First Avon Books hardcover printing: November 1991

HarperCollins® and Harper® are registered trademarks of Harper-Collins Publishers.

Printed in the United States of America

Visit Harper paperbacks on the World Wide Web at
www.harpercollins.com

HB 03.27.2024

If you purchased this book without a cover, you should be aware that this book is stolen property. It was reported as "unsold and destroyed" to the publisher, and neither the author nor the publisher has received any payment for this "stripped book."

To Bill,
who brought us "the Bone,"
and to Diana Conway,
wherever she is

ACKNOWLEDGMENTS

*T*HE PAPAGO LEGENDS used in this book are retellings of the traditional oral tales of the *Tohono O'odham*, the Desert People. These are winter-telling tales, which must not be "told" during the summer when snakes and lizards are out, for if they hear the stories, *Wamad*, Snake, or *Hujud*, Lizard, may swallow the storyteller's luck and bring him harm. There is, however, no prohibition against them in written form.

This book is set in the 1970's, long before the tribal council renamed the reservation to reflect the people's traditional name of the Desert People. References to the Papago Reservation are historically correct, although today's maps will refer to the reservation located west of Tucson as the *Tohono O'odham* Nation.

Writing this book would not have been possible without being able to use the works of Dean and Lucille Saxton as reference material: *Legends and Lore of the Papago and Pima Indians* and *Papago & Pima to English Dictionary*, both first and second editions, all three of which were published by the University of Arizona Press.

I am also indebted to the inspired retellings of some of these stories by Harold Bell Wright in his invaluable and unfortunately exceedingly rare work *Long Ago Told* (New York: D. Appleton, 1929).

Both the King County Library and Seattle Public, through their wonderfully convenient interlibrary-loan systems, supported my research by locating and helping me gain access to rare source material from libraries all over the country.

Of the "committee" who helped me on this book, I'd like to especially acknowledge Dick Sawyer, Carol and Charles Mackey, and Dan and Agnes Russell for their timely, deadline-type assistance.

In addition, I would like to say thank you to the splendid and delightfully humorous *Tohono O'odham* themselves, who, during my five years of teaching on the reservation, made me feel both welcome and appreciated, even though I'm really, as Pauline once told me, "a member of another tribe."

We are all hunters.
—Clayton Savage in *A Less Than Noble Savage,*
an unpublished manuscript
by Andrew Philip Carlisle

HOUR
OF THE
HUNTER

Prologue

*I*T IS SAID *that after that I'itoi climbed the steps of arrows and went to Eagle Man's cave. The woman was sitting there with her baby. "I have come to kill Eagle Man," I'itoi told her.*

"But you can't," said the woman. "He kills everyone."

"He will not kill me," said I'itoi, "because I have power. What time does he come home?"

"At noon."

"What does he do?"

"He eats."

"And after that?"

"He sleeps."

"And the baby?"

"He sleeps, too."

"Today, let it happen just that way," said I'itoi. "Let him come home and eat and go to sleep. Let the baby sleep with him with his head facing in the same direction."

"Where will you be?" asked the woman.

"I will turn myself into a fly and hide in that crack over there."

It happened just that way. I'itoi turned himself into a fly and hid in the crack. Eagle Man came home, ate his meal, and lay down with the baby to sleep. The baby was so small it had not yet spoken, but now it did. "Papa, somebody came," the baby said.

"What did you say?" asked Eagle Man.

"Do not listen," said the woman. "You know the baby cannot talk."

"Papa," the baby said again. "Somebody came." But every time, the woman told Eagle Man not to listen. Finally, she sang a song so the baby would go to sleep.

When they were both sleeping, the fly came out of the crack and turned back into I'itoi. He took a stone hatchet from his belt and chopped the baby's head off. Then he chopped Eagle Man's head off, too.

After I'itoi killed Eagle Man, the woman took him to a corner of the cave where there was a huge pile of bones. These were the bones of the people Eagle Man had killed.

First I'itoi woke up the people at the very top of the pile, the ones who had been dead for the shortest time. When they came back to life, their skin was a rich brown color. They were gentle and hardworking and laughed a lot.

"I like you very much," I'itoi said. "You will be Tohono O'odham, my Desert People, and live here close to my mountains forever."

The next people on the pile had been dead a while longer. When they woke up, they weren't quite so industrious, and they were a little quarrelsome.

"You're all right," I'itoi said. "You can live near me, but not too near. You will be the Pima, Akimel O'odham, and live by the river."

When the next people woke up, they were lazy and they fought a lot among themselves.

"You will be Ohb, *the Apaches," I'itoi said. "You will be the enemy and live far from here in the mountains across my desert."*

The bones at the bottom of the pile had been dead for such a long time that when they came back to life, their skin had turned white.

"I don't like you at all," I'itoi said to them. "You will be Mil-gahn, *the whites. I will give you something with which to write, then I want you to go far away from me across the ocean and stay there."*

And that, nawoj, *my friend, is the story of I'itoi and Eagle Man.*

The Indian girl staggered slightly as she sidled up to the pickup. "Mr. Ladd, are you going to the dance?"

Gary Ladd finished pumping gas into his pickup. He recognized Gina Antone, a young Papago who lived in Topawa, a village on the reservation that also housed the Teachers' Compound where he lived with his wife.

"Hi, Gina," he returned. "My friend and I thought we'd stop by for a while."

"Our truck broke down," Gina continued. She was slender and attractive and more than a little drunk. "Could you give us a ride? We've got some beer."

"Sure," Gary Ladd told her. "No problem." He hurried into the trading post to pay for the gas while a laughing group of young Papagos piled cheerfully into the back of the truck.

It was early on a hot summer's evening in June of 1968. As they settled into the bed of the pickup, the young people laughed and joked about the coming dance. None of them guessed that before the sun came up the next morning, Gina Antone would be dead, and that death, for her, would be a blessing.

The woman sat in the detective's car. He had left the engine running, so the air-conditioning stayed on. The interior of the car remained cool, even on this overheated June night. The woman listened curiously to the crackling transmissions on the police radio, but she mostly didn't understand what the voices were saying. She didn't want to understand.

Instead of getting out of the car, she sat and listened and watched. She saw the parade of flashing lights as the ambulances arrived. After that, she didn't want to see anymore. She turned away and focused instead on the luminescent hands of the clock on the dashboard as they moved from 8:00 to 8:10, from 8:10 to 8:15.

The detective hurried back to the car. "He's calling for you," the man said gruffly. "Do you want to go to him?"

"No," she said quickly. "No, thank you. I'd rather stay here, if you don't mind."

1

*T*HE ROOM WAS square and hot, and so was the man sitting at the gray-green metallic desk. Sweat poured off his jowls and trickled down the inside of his shirt. Finally, Assistant Superintendent Ron Mallory yanked open his collar and loosened his tie. God, it was hot—too hot to work, too hot to think.

Through his narrow window, Mallory gazed off across the green expanse of cotton fields that surrounded the Arizona State Prison at Florence. It was June, and irrigated cotton thrived beneath a hazy desert sky with its blistering noontime sun. Maybe cotton could grow in this ungodly heat, but people couldn't.

Ron Mallory hated his barren yellow office with its view of razor ribbon-topped fences punctuated with guard towers. The view wasn't much, but having an office at all, particularly one with a window, was a vast improvement over working the floor in one of the units. Mallory didn't complain, but all the while, he busily plotted his own escape.

Assistant Superintendent Mallory had no intention of working in Corrections forever. It was Friday. Maybe sometime this weekend he'd find some time away from Arlene and the kids to work on his book. There was a wall in Chapter 11, some kind of story-structure problem that made it impossible to move forward.

He took another swipe at his forehead with a damp paper towel and waited for a guard to bring Andrew Carlisle into his office.

"Damn legislature," he told a fly that sauntered lazily across the stacks of file folders on his desk. Why couldn't those idiots down in Phoenix find money enough to fix the prison's damn refrigeration units? The air-conditioning always went on the fritz the minute the temperature climbed above 110.

Buildings in the capitol complex in Phoenix were plenty cool. He'd damn near frozen his ass off when he'd gone there as part of the official delegation begging the legislative committee for more prison money. They'd as good as said it didn't matter if it got hot for the prisoners. After all, "Prisoners were *supposed* to be punished, weren't they?" "What about the guards?" Warden Franklin had countered. "What about the other people who work there?" "What about them?" the committee had said. They didn't give a shit about the worker bees. Nobody did.

Irritably, Mallory slapped at the fly, but it eluded him and flew over to the window just as Mendez, Mallory's assistant, knocked on the door and put his head inside the sweltering office. "Carlisle's here," Mendez said.

"Good. Send him in." Ron Mallory mopped his brow, knowing it wouldn't do any good. His face would be sopped with sweat again within moments. God, it was hot!

Ron Mallory had conducted hundreds of pre-release interviews in the time he'd held the job. There was a standard protocol. Where are you going to stay? What kind of work do you have lined up? But this wouldn't be a standard interview, because Andrew Carlisle wasn't a standard prisoner.

As soon as the guard led Andrew Carlisle into the room, Mallory noticed that even in this terrible heat the man wasn't sweating. Guys who didn't sweat usually pissed Ron Mallory off, but he liked Andrew Carlisle.

"Is this when I get the 'go-and-sin-no-more' talk?" the prisoner asked good-humoredly.

Carlisle eased himself into a chair in front of Mallory's desk without waiting for either an order or an invitation. Between assistant superintendent and prisoner, there existed a camaraderie, an easy give-and-take, enjoyed by no other inmate in the Arizona State Prison.

Ron Mallory appreciated Andrew Carlisle. Intellectually, he was several cuts above the other prisoners. Carlisle conversed about politics, religion, philosophy, and current events with equal facility and enthusiasm. Under the guise of working together as inmate clerk and warden, the two men had carried on six years' worth of wide-ranging discussions, exchanges that made Assistant Superintendent Mallory feel almost scholarly.

"That's right," Mallory responded with a chuckle. " 'Go and sin no more.' Couldn't have said it better myself. I'm sorry to see you go, though, Carlisle. Once you're gone, who's going to keep this office in order, and who'll help me finish my book? How about screwing up and coming back for a return engagement?"

"I won't screw up," Carlisle declared.

Mallory nodded seriously. "I'm sure you won't, Carlisle. You've more than paid your debt to society. As far as I'm concerned, you never should have been here in the first place. Don't quote me, but if every poor bastard who ever killed or fucked a drunken Indian got sent up here, we'd be more overcrowded than we already are. That judge in Tucson just got a hard-on for you. The important thing now is for you to put it all behind you and get on with your life. What are you going to do?"

Andrew Carlisle shrugged. "I don't know exactly. I doubt the university will take me back. Ex-cons don't quite meet the hiring and tenure guidelines."

"It's a damn shame, if you ask me," Mallory said. "You're one hell of a teacher. Look at what you've done for me. Here I am on Chapter Eleven and counting. I'm going to finish this damn book, dedicate it to you, and buy my way out of this hellhole of a dead-end job, and you're the one making it possible."

Carlisle smiled indulgently, waiting in silence while Mallory studied the contents of the file folder in front of him. "Says here you plan to go back to Tucson. That right?"

Andrew Carlisle nodded. "I'll hole up in some cheapo apartment, maybe down in the barrio somewhere."

"And do what?"

"Work. I've got a book or two of my own to write."

For most "two-for-one, early-release prisoners," the word *work* should have included an employer's name, address, and telephone number, but Mallory regarded Carlisle as an exceptional prisoner. In his case, exceptions had been made.

"What will you live on in the meantime?"

"I still have some money left from when they sold off my house to pay attorneys' fees. As long as I don't live too high on the hog, I can survive until the first advance comes in."

Ron Mallory nodded his approval. "Good plan," he said. "Hell of a plan. You'll make a fortune."

"I hope so," Andrew Carlisle replied.

Mallory pulled a small rectangular piece of shiny paper from the folder and passed it across the desk. "Here's your bus ticket to Tucson," he said. "The guard will take you to collect your personal effects and whatever money is in your account. Now get the hell out of here and knock 'em dead."

Carlisle accepted Mallory's abrupt dismissal with good grace. "I'll do that," he said, pocketing the ticket and then reaching back across the desk to give Ron's pudgy hand a firm shake. "And you keep on writing."

"I will," Mallory responded fervently. "Count on it."

Carlisle smiled to himself as he left Mallory's office. Mendez, sitting at his desk in the outer office, noticed the smile and assumed it had something to do with his release, but it was really over Ron Mallory's unfortunate choice of words. Funny that he would say it just that way—knock 'em dead.

For those were indeed Andrew Carlisle's intentions. His version of "knocking 'em dead" had nothing to do with the literary endeavor that he had already been working on in secret during his enforced six-years' worth of spare time.

He would knock a certain someone dead, all right, although he didn't yet know how. He didn't yet know where to find his intended victim, either—if she was still on the reservation, or if she'd left there and moved on. Finding her would take time, but he had plenty of that. He had all the time in the world.

A guard took him to Florence and put him on the Tucson-bound Greyhound. At Marana, he got off and walked back under the freeway to the entrance ramp on the other side. He put down his bag and stuck out his thumb, angling for a ride northbound to Phoenix.

He'd go to Tucson eventually, when he was ready, but first he wanted to talk to his mother. Myrna Louise would be surprised and happy to see him. She was always good for a handout.

* * *

Davy Ladd knew his mother was working, so he spent the morning outside, along with Bone, a scrawny black-and-tan mutt with predominantly Irish wolfhound bloodlines. The dog, fierce-looking and bristle-faced, with a squared-off, rectangular head the size of a basketball, was never far from the boy's heels.

The two of them hiked up the mountain behind Davy's house, scrambling over warm red cliffs, straying further than they should have from the house. As the hot sun rose higher overhead, both boy and dog went looking for shade. Bone crept under a scrubby mesquite, while Davy hunkered down in the narrow band of shade at the foot of a perpendicular outcropping of rock.

It was there he found the cave with an opening so small he didn't see it for a while even though he was sitting right next to it. Poking his head in, he decided it wasn't a cave after all, because caves were flat, and this one went up and down like a tall chimney in the rock. A circle of blue sky showed at the very top. He wiggled through the small opening and found that, once inside, there was barely room enough for him to stand up straight. Despite its small, confined size, the place was surprisingly cool. Davy warily checked it for snakes. People and dogs weren't the only ones who needed to escape the heat.

Suddenly, outside, Bone set up a frantic barking. Peering out, Davy saw the dog, nose to the ground, searching around wildly. Hide-and-seek was a game they played sometimes—the solitary child and his singularly ugly dog—pretending to be scouts heading off a band of marauding Apaches, maybe, or hunters stalking mule deer in the mountains.

With a joyous bark, the dog discovered the boy's hiding place. Panting, he thrust his big head into the opening and tried to climb in as well. There wasn't room for both of them to be inside at once, and Davy came out laughing. It was then he heard Rita calling him from far below.

"Come on, Bone," the boy said. "Maybe it's time for lunch."

But it wasn't. Rita Antone, the Indian woman who lived with them and took care of him, waited in the yard with both hands planted sternly on her hips as the boy and the dog returned from the mountain.

"Where were you?" she asked.

"Playing."

"It's time to come in now. I'm going to the reservation to sell baskets. If you want to go, you'd better ask your mother."

Davy's eyes widened with excitement. "I can come with you?"

"First go ask."

Worried about disturbing her, Davy crept into his mother's makeshift office. For a minute or so, the boy stood transfixed, watching Diana Ladd's nimble fingers dance across the keys. How could her fingers move so fast?

His mother's shoulders stiffened with annoyance when she sensed his presence behind her. "What is it, Davy?" she asked.

He sidled up beside her, standing with his fingers moving tentatively along the smooth wooden edge of the door that served as her desk. The child knew his mother wrote books at that desk during the summers when she wasn't teaching. He didn't know exactly what the books were about—he had never seen one of them—but Rita said it was true, so it had to be. Rita never told fibs.

She had explained that his mother's work was important, and that when she was busy at her typewriter, he wasn't to interrupt or disturb her unless absolutely necessary. This time it must be okay. Rita had told him to do it.

"What *is* it, Davy?" Diana Ladd repeated sharply. "Can't you see I'm busy? I've got to finish this chapter today."

Sometimes his mother's voice could be soothing and gentle, but not now when she was impatient and eager to be rid of him. Hot tears welled up in Davy's eyes. He stood with his face averted so his mother wouldn't see them.

"It's Rita," he said uncertainly. "She's going to the reservation today to sell baskets. Can I go along, please?"

Davy's mother seemed to exist in a place far beyond his short-armed reach. He was never exactly sure how she would react. He had learned to maintain a certain distance, to be wary of her sudden outbursts. Rita was far more approachable.

During the school year, Davy got home from school long before his mother arrived home from her teaching job on the reservation. The child spent most afternoons in Rita's single-roomed house, little more than a glorified cook shack, which was situated off the back of the kitchen of the main house. There, he ate meals at a worn wooden table, all the while devouring the stories the Indian woman told him. Often he spent hours watching in fascination while she used her *owij*, her awl, to weave intricate yucca and beargrass baskets. Other times he stood at mouth-watering attention while she patted out tortillas and popovers to cook on an ancient wood-burning range that she much preferred to the modern gas stove in the main house.

While she worked, Rita heard Davy's stories as well. Unlike his mother's writing or paper-correcting, which demanded total concentration, Rita's manual tasks were performed automatically, while her heart and mind were free with the gift of listening. Rita's heavy, stolid presence was the single constant in Davy's young life. She was the healer of all his childish hurts, the recipient of his daily joys and woes.

For once Diana Ladd broke through her own self-imposed reserve and affectionately ruffled her son's lank yellow hair.

"Rita's going to turn you into more of an Indian than she is," Diana commented with a short laugh.

"Really?" the boy asked, his blue eyes lighting up at the prospect. "Will my hair turn black and straight and everything?"

"It might," Diana returned lightly. "If you eat too many popovers at the feast tonight, it'll happen for sure."

"Feast?" Davy asked. "What feast?"

"Didn't Rita tell you? There's a feast tonight at Ban Thak. That's the other reason she's going to-day."

Ban Thak, Coyote Sitting, was the name of Rita's home village. Davy could hardly believe his good fortune. "You mean I get to go to the feast, too?"

Rita and Diana Ladd had evidently already discussed it and reached a decision, but the Indian woman always insisted that the child ask his mother, that he show her the respect she deserved.

The boy could barely contain his excitement as Diana kissed him and shooed him on his way. "Go on now. Get out of here. I've got work to do."

Davy Ladd scampered eagerly out of the room. Bone, black as a shadow and almost as big as his six-year-old owner, waited patiently outside the door. The two of them raced through the house looking for Rita. Davy was quiet about it, though. He didn't shout or make too much noise. Rita had taught him better manners than that. Children were never to shout after their elders. It wasn't polite.

He found Rita in the backyard loading boxes laden with finely crafted handmade baskets into the bed of an old blue GMC. She stopped working long enough to wipe the running sweat from her wrinkled brown face.

"Well now, Olhoni," she said, standing looking down on him with both hands folded over her faded apron. "What did your mother say?"

Only Rita called Davy Ladd by the name

Olhoni, which, in Papago, means Maverick or Orphaned Calf. That name, the one he called his Indian name, was a jealously guarded secret shared by the boy and the old woman. Not even Davy's mother knew Rita called him that.

"I can go, Nana *Dahd*," he told her breathlessly. *Dahd* was Papago for "Godmother," but the title was strictly honorary. Davy had never seen the inside of a church, and there had been no formal ceremony. Like her name for him, however, Nana *Dahd* was a form of address Davy used only when the two of them were alone together.

Davy clambered up into the truck. He helped shove the last box of baskets down the wooden floor of the short bed to where part of a livestock rack had been spot-welded to the outside wall of the cab. He held the boxes tightly while Rita used rope to lash them firmly in place.

"She says I can go to the feast too. Shall I wear my boots? Should I get a bedroll? Can Bone come?"

"Oh'o stays here," Nana *Dahd* told him firmly. "Dogs don't belong at feasts. Go get a jacket and a bedroll. Even with the fires, it may be cold at the dance. You'll want to sleep before it's over. I'll fix lunch before we go."

"Oh, no," Davy replied seriously. "I won't fall asleep. I promise. I want to stay up all night. Until the dance is over. Until the sun comes up."

"Go now," Rita urged, without raising her voice. That wasn't necessary. The child did as he was told. He sometimes argued with his mother but never with Nana *Dahd*. Finished packing, Davy stowed his small canvas bag in the cab of the truck and then made his way into Nana *Dahd*'s room.

He found her busily patting a ball of soft white dough into a flat, round cake. When the dough was stretched thin enough, she dropped it into a vat of hot fat on the stove's front burner. Within seconds, the dough puffed up and cooked to a golden brown. Meantime, Rita patted out another. Davy had often tried working the dough himself, but no matter what he did, the ball of dough remained just that—a stubborn ball of dough.

Davy hurried to his place at the bare wooden table, while Bone settled comfortably at his feet. Rita placed a mound of thick red chili on the popovers, folded them over, and brought them to the table on plates. In the center of the table sat a small bowl piled high with cooked broccoli. While Davy wrinkled his nose in disgust, Nana *Dahd* ladled a spoonful of broccoli onto his plate next to the steaming popover.

"You know I hate broccoli," he said, reaching at once for the popover.

Rita was unmoved. "Eat your vegetables," she said.

Davy nodded, but as soon as Rita turned her back, he slipped the broccoli under the table to a waiting and appreciative Bone. The dog liked everything—including broccoli.

It is said that long ago there was a woman who loved to play Toka, *which the* Mil-gahn, *the whites, call field hockey. She loved it so much that she never wanted to do anything else. Even after her child was born, she would leave the baby alone all day long to go play hockey. One day she went away and didn't come back. The women in the village felt sorry for the baby, a little boy. They fed him and took care of him.*

One day, when he was old enough, the little boy took four drinking gourds and went searching for his mother. First he met Eagle. "Have you seen my mother?" the little boy asked.

"Give me one of your drinking gourds, and I will tell you where to find your mother." The boy gave Eagle a gourd, and he said, "Go toward those mountains. There you will find her."

The boy walked until he neared the mountains. There, he met Crow. "Have you seen my mother?" he asked.

"Give me one of your drinking gourds, and I will tell you where to find your mother." The boy gave Crow a gourd, and he said, "Climb these mountains, and you will find her."

The boy climbed in the hot sun until he reached the top of the mountains. There, he met Hawk. "Have you seen my mother?" he asked.

"Give me one of your drinking gourds, and I will tell you where to find your mother." The boy gave Hawk a gourd, and he said, "Your mother is at the bottom of these mountains. Go there, and you will find her."

The boy walked until he reached the bottom of the mountains. There, he met Mourning Dove. "Have you seen my mother?" he asked.

"Give me your drinking gourd, and I will tell you where to find her." The boy gave Mourning Dove his

last gourd, and he said, "Your mother is on the other side of this valley. Go there, and you will find her."

The boy walked until he met some children playing. "Have you seen my mother?" he asked.

"Yes," the children said. "She is down on the field playing hockey."

"Go tell her that her son is here and that I want to see her." The children went to the woman and told her, but she was busy playing hockey and wouldn't come. When the children came back and told the little boy, he was very sad.

"Since my mother will not come to me, I will find a tarantula hole and go live there." He found a tarantula hole and started to go in it. Just then his mother came, but the boy was already disappearing into the ground. The mother tried to pull him back, but it was too late. The only thing left to see was a single bright feather that the little boy had worn in his hair.

The mother was very sad, and she began to cry. Ban, Coyote, was passing by, and he heard her. He went to see what the noise was all about. She told him that her son had just been buried in the tarantula's hole, and she asked Coyote to dig the child out.

When Coyote began to dig, he found that the little boy was not far underground. Coyote was hungry with all his work, and he didn't see why he should take the child to a mother who had never done anything but play field hockey, so Coyote ate the little boy. When the bones were picked clean, Coyote gave them to the mother along with the bright feather. "Someone has eaten your child," he said. "This is all I could find."

The woman was even sadder. She kept the feather,

but she asked Coyote to bury the bones of her child once more. That night she watered the ground over the bones with her tears, and in four days a green thing began to grow out of the place where the bones were buried. It was a'alichum hahshani *or Baby Saguaro, the first giant cactus in the whole world. And that is the story of The Woman Who Loved Field Hockey.*

As they neared Three Points, Rita Antone shifted down into second. The rickety '56 GMC creaked and shuddered. Like the woman who was its owner, the twenty-year-old truck was showing signs of age. Despite a serious miss in the engine, Rita had every confidence it would limp along out to Sells and back to town with no problem, but she planned to stop by the gas station and talk to her sister's boy about it.

Rita still thought of Gabe Ortiz by his boyhood name of Gihg Tahpani, or Fat Crack, but her nephew hardly qualified as a boy anymore. He was middle-aged now, a well-respected reservation businessman, with flecks of gray leaching through his straight black hair. It was Gabe's faithful mechanical ministrations that kept the old Jimmy running.

Rita knew that when Fat Crack looked at the truck, he would wipe his hands on a grease rag, shake his head sadly, and scold her because the front end was out of alignment and the tires were nearly bald, but Rita would tell him as she always did, "No tires, not now, not this time."

More than once, Diana Ladd had offered to replace the truck or fix it, but Rita always declined.

She had bought it new and kept it all those years. She didn't drive it much anymore, only a few times a year when she went out to gather the raw materials for her baskets—devil's claw from the reservation or bear grass and yucca from Benson. Then there were the anniversary trips, like this one, but because Diana Ladd didn't want to talk about that, Rita usually disguised her real intentions by saying she was going to a feast or taking her newest crop of baskets up to the top of Ioligam, the mountain Anglos called Kitt Peak, to be sold in the observatory gift shop there.

Rita was determined to drive the old truck until one or the other of them stopped dead. If the truck happened to go first, she would leave it wherever it died, parked on the side of the road if necessary.

Three Points Trading Post at Robles Junction was thirty miles west of Tucson on Highway 86, the main road leading out to the reservation. The trading post's primary claim to fame was its undisputed reputation for selling more beer on a weekly basis than all of Davis Monthan Air Force Base combined.

Charley Raymond, the most recent Anglo owner, hurried to the pumps as Rita stopped the truck. "What do you want?" he asked.

Deliberately, Rita eased her heavy frame out of the driver's seat. "Five dollars' worth of regular," she said and went inside, with Davy trailing happily along behind.

Once inside the store, Davy made a dash for the refrigerator and grabbed his favorite treat—a carton of chocolate milk. Rita went to the cooler and withdrew a single can of Coors. She didn't drink much, but the day's real task promised to be hard, thirsty work, and she would need a beer when she finished. A single beer would be welcome. It would also be enough.

Leaving the cooler, Rita steered Davy firmly past a beckoning display of Twinkies and led him to a shelf laden with plastic memorial wreaths and votive candles. He watched curiously while she selected a wreath of bright pink roses.

"This one?" she asked, holding it up for his inspection.

"It's pretty," he said with a puzzled frown, "but, Nana, why are we getting flowers?"

Shaking her head, Rita didn't answer. Instead, she took the wreath, one tall, glass-enclosed candle with a picture of the Virgin Mary on the outside, and the can of Coors, then she threaded her way through the narrow aisles up to the cash register. From behind the counter, Daisy Raymond, a narrow-faced Anglo woman, eyed Rita suspiciously.

Buying the trading post had been Charley's idea, not Daisy's. She hadn't wanted to have anything to do with it, but Charley had convinced her that running the store for a few years was a good way to finish bankrolling their retirement. Now, months later, she reluctantly agreed he was right. In beer sales alone, the place was a gold mine.

The problem was, Daisy Raymond didn't like Indians. Never had. She stood trapped behind the cash register day after day taking Indian money and trying, unsuccessfully, to conceal her dislike behind a barrage of inane chatter. Being around Daisy Raymond made Rita draw back inside herself.

"Nice day out there, isn't it," Daisy said. "Real hot for so early in the year."

"Five dollars' of gas," Rita replied, refusing to be drawn into a conversation about the weather. She placed her other selections on the checkout counter. When all the purchases were rung up and totaled on the old-fashioned cash register, Rita painstakingly counted out the exact change from her purse. People running trading posts no longer routinely cheated Indians, but Rita was careful about it all the same, especially with people like Daisy Raymond.

"Need any matches for the candle?" Daisy asked. Rita nodded.

"How come you people use so many wreaths and candles?" Daisy asked. Rita shrugged. When the Indian woman made no reply, Daisy continued on her own. She was accustomed to carrying on these one-sided conversations. "I told Charley just yesterday that we'd better order more—wreaths and candles, that is. He worries about running out of beer, and I have to keep track of everything else."

Daisy paused and looked down. Peering over the counter, she noticed Davy Ladd for the first time. He stood gazing up at her in an almost accusatory blue-eyed stare. She found the child's silence disturbing.

The Anglo woman expected that kind of behavior from the Indian kids who came through the trading post. That was bad enough, but since they came from the reservation, you could understand about their being shy and backward. With this white kid, though, it was downright impolite. Where were his parents? she asked herself. And who was going to pay for the carton of milk?

Glancing around the room, Daisy wondered if someone else had slipped into the store unnoticed, but there was no one with the boy except an ancient, withered crone of an Indian woman. It wasn't right. It just wasn't.

Daisy leaned down until her face and Davy's were on almost the same level. He looked dirty, with a ring of chocolate milk circling his mouth. The sharp odor of wood smoke emanated from his hair and clothing. Was there such a thing as a blond Indian?

"Hello there, young man. Where'd you come from?"

The woman wore bright red lipstick that made her mouth look like an angry red gash across a pale, skinny face. Her darting green eyes reminded Davy of a lizard he'd seen once.

Without answering, Davy shrank away under the woman's nosy gaze and groped behind him for the comforting reassurance of Rita's callused hand.

"He's with me," Rita said.

"Oh?" Daisy replied. "What's the matter with him? Can't he talk? By the way, you still owe for his milk."

Once more Rita counted out exact change.

Without a thank you, Daisy Raymond shoved the money into the register drawer.

"*Oi g hihm*," Rita said softly to Davy.

Literally translated, the words mean "Walk," but Davy understood the accepted current usage as "Let's get in the pickup and go."

Needing no second urging, he hurried to the door, relieved to escape the close confines of the trading post and the Anglo woman's prying eyes. He clambered up into the pickup and settled back contentedly on the frayed plastic seat. Rita opened the door. With a grunt of effort, she heaved herself into the truck.

"Are we going to the feast now?" Davy asked.

Nana *Dahd* shook her head. "Not yet. A few stops first, then the feast."

Had Pima County homicide detective Brandon Walker been a drinking man, he would have left his morning vehicular homicide investigation, stopped off at the nearest bar on his way back to town, and got himself shit-faced drunk. He hadn't, but now, back in his cubicle at the Pima County Sheriff's Department and looking at the fanfold of messages in his hand, he wished he had. Just this once.

A day earlier, Aaron Monford, a seventy-five-year-old shade-tree mechanic, had been changing a tire in his front yard when he was struck from behind by a tipsy neighbor lady on her way home from a weekly luncheon bridge game. Monford's head had been crushed nearly flat between the chrome-plated bumpers of his own jacked-up

Dodge Dart and that of the neighbor's speeding Buick. He had died instantly, without ever being transported to a hospital. The driver, drunk and suffering from chest pains, had been taken to St. Mary's Hospital.

Early that morning, Brandon had spent two hours with the now-sober driver and her solicitous and well-paid attorney. Then, from nine o'clock on, he had been in the Monfords' posh Tucson Estates mobile home listening to Aaron's devastated widow, Goldie, bewail the end of what she had expected to be their "golden years."

Low-key and polite, Brandon had worked patiently, diligently gathering the necessary information despite Goldie's periodic outbursts: How could Ari do this to her? Why had she let him go out to change the tire right then? Why hadn't he waited until evening when it was cooler like she had told him? Why had he left without giving her a chance to say good-bye?

Every time Goldie Monford opened her mouth, Brandon wanted to grab her by the shoulders and shake some sense into her head. He wanted to tell her that she should fall down on her knees and thank God that she was one of the lucky ones and so was Aaron. There was more than one way to be robbed of your golden years. In Walker's opinion, a quick death was far preferable to a slow one. Slow deaths were the real heartbreakers.

But Brandon Walker didn't berate Goldie Monford, and he didn't stop off to get drunk, either. He left the widow wallowing in her grief and drove straight back to the office. Now, standing in his dingy cubicle, he thumbed through his messages. Those ominous yellow slips of paper weighed down his soul, telling him once more that he was right and Goldie Monford was wrong.

There were six messages in all. The clerk had nodded sympathetically as she handed them to him. "Your mother," she said.

There was no written message, only a check-mark beside "Please call," but Brandon clearly read between the lines to what hadn't been said. One way or another, they were all about his father—about what Toby Walker either had or hadn't done. Brandon had learned to dread his mother's calls—hourly ones, it seemed at times—giving him constant updates on Brandon's father's latest transgressions; checks that had bounced or how Toby had once again lost his way driving home from the store—the same store they'd been going to for ten years, for God's sake! What was the matter with him? What was he thinking of?

Brandon felt sorry for both his parents. His father's erratic behavior seemed to bother his mother far more than it did Toby himself. Louella Walker was someone who prided herself on keeping things "under control." In this case, it wasn't working. She vacillated between rage and despair. Sometimes she made excuses, saying that there was nothing at all wrong with Toby, that he just needed a little extra help. If Brandon were any kind of a decent son, he wouldn't begrudge his father that much. At other times, she raged and railed that Toby was deliberately trying to drive her crazy.

If there was a middle ground in all this, Brandon wasn't able to find it. The role of parental peacemaker and crisis manager at home was a painful one. He didn't want to call home and hear either his mother's panicked tattling or her self-pitying whine. It was no surprise that Detective Walker hid out in his work. He wanted to be left alone, to go about living his life in a reasonable semblance of peace and quiet, to do an honest day's work for an honest day's pay.

The cubicle was far homier than home was. He would stay late at the office again tonight, doing whatever mundane tasks he could dredge up to do, coming home long after dinner and hopefully long after his parents had gone to bed as well. That way he wouldn't have to listen either to his mother, who talked more and more, or watch his father, who spoke less and less.

With a sigh, Brandon dropped the six messages into his trash can. Telling the clerk to hold all his calls, he pulled out the half-completed form he had started filling out earlier that morning, the one that recounted the unexpected death of Aaron Monford. Once, not so long ago, these very same reporting forms would have been anathema to him, something to be avoided entirely or put off as long as possible. Now, they were a refuge.

There were blanks on the paper—finite, measurable, boxed blanks on sturdy white paper— where clear-cut answers to simple questions were all that was required. He took more care with his penmanship these days, as though neatness and legibility were somehow next to godliness, as though his third-grade teacher might rise up from her grave and look over his shoulder again, checking the slant of each individual letter and measuring the crosses on each *t*.

Even as he was doing it, Brandon Walker was smart enough to step back and know why.

In a world where fathers become children again, writing a report is sometimes the only thing that makes sense.

2

*W*ITH A JOLT, the pickup lumbered over the rough cattle guard that marked the reservation boundary. Davy sat up straight, eager to see one of his favorite landmarks—a faded billboard advertising the tribal rodeo. Rita had taken him twice.

"Can we go again this year, Nana *Dahd*?" he asked, pointing at the sign. "It's fun."

"We'll see," she answered, shifting down while the pickup lurched drunkenly to one side.

"How come my mom stopped liking rodeos?" Davy asked. "She used to like them, didn't she?"

Nana *Dahd* looked at him shrewdly. "Why do you ask that?"

The boy shrugged and bit his lip, thinking about the picture that hung in the hallway. Smiling and surprisingly beautiful, his much younger mother was dressed up like a cowgirl with a jeweled tiara overlaying the feathered hatband of her Stetson. Looking at the picture, it was easy for Davy to imagine that long ago his mother had been a princess—a rich, happy princess. Of course, they weren't rich now, and his mother didn't seem to be very happy, either. He wondered sometimes if her unhappiness was all his fault.

"I saw her boots once," he added after a pause. "Pretty ones with diamonds on them. Bone and I found them in the back of her closet. They're gone now."

The last was said matter-of-factly, but Rita heard the hurt beneath the words. Rhinestones, she thought to herself, not diamonds, but rhinestones. And yes, the boots were gone now, put away in one of the stacked boxes in the root cellar off the kitchen where Davy wouldn't see them again and be tempted to ask more questions. Only Olhoni's impassioned pleading had spared the picture of his mother as a seventeen-year-old rodeo queen from disappearing into the same box.

Davy lapsed into uncharacteristic silence, his endless stream of questions quieted for the moment. Rita understood that many of the boy's questions were still too painful for his mother to face or answer, but it was time they were asked.

"You'll have to talk to your mother about that," Rita said.

Davy sighed. If Nana *Dahd* wouldn't tell him, he might never know. "I did ask her," he said. "She was too busy."

The truck's turn signals hadn't worked for years. Rita stuck her arm out the open window, signaling for a left-hand turn. Davy sat up straight and peered out the window. "Where are we going now?" he asked.

"Up this road," Rita replied, turning onto a

rutted, hard-packed dirt track that led off through the underbrush. Barely one car-width wide, the narrow trail wound through thick stands of newly leafed mesquite and brilliantly yellow *palo verde*, up a slight rise, and then down through a dry, sandy wash. As the tires caught in the hubcap-deep sand, the steering wheel jerked sharply to the left. Rita clung to it with both hands and floorboarded the gas pedal, barely managing to maintain the truck's forward momentum.

Engine rumbling, the pickup emerged from the wash. Ahead of them, the road gave little evidence of day-to-day use. Whatever faint tire tracks may have preceded theirs had long since been obliterated by the hoofprints of wandering herds of cattle. A second dip in the road took them through a second dry wash. Beyond that, the faded ghost of another road forked off to the left and meandered along beside an empty stream-bed through clumps of brittle, sun-dried grass and weeds.

They drove past a place where the remnants of several adobe houses were gradually melting back into the desert floor. "Did this used to be a village?" Davy asked.

Rita nodded. "It was called Ko'oi Koshwa."

"Rattlesnake Skull?" Davy asked.

The old woman smiled and nodded. The Anglo child's quick grasp of Rita's native language always pleased her.

"Where did the people go?" he asked.

"Long ago, the Apaches came here. They surprised the village and destroyed it. They took most of the women and children away, although two—a boy and a girl—escaped. They hid in a cave up there in those hills."

Rita pointed to where the base of the mountain Ioligam, Kitt Peak, abruptly thrust itself out of the flat desert floor.

"After that, people said this was a bad place, a haunted place. No one wanted to live here anymore. When they made the reservation, they left the *charco* which once belonged to the village outside the boundary."

Davy immediately began looking for the *charco*, a man-made catchbasin used by the Papagos to catch the nutrient-rich summer-rain flash floods. For centuries, water captured in these isolated *charcos* irrigated Indian fields and watered livestock.

"But why are we going to a *charco*, Nana *Dahd?* I thought we were going to a dance."

Rita stopped the truck where a barbed-wire gate barred their way. "To the *charco* first. Go open the gate," she said.

Proud to be assigned such an important task, Davy did as he was told. He stood to one side, holding the gate until Rita had driven through. Once the gate was closed and he was back in the truck, they continued to follow the faint track, stopping at last just outside a shady grove of towering cottonwoods clustered around the man-made banks of an earthen water hole.

Hard-caked mud, baked shiny by an unrelenting sun and shot through with jagged cracks and the hoofprints of thirsty cattle, was all that remained from the previous summer's life-sustaining rainstorms. It was June and hot. Both people and livestock hoped the rains would come again soon.

Davy looked around warily. For some reason he couldn't explain, he didn't like this place. "Why are we stopping here?"

"We have work to do, Olhoni. Come. Bring the rake and shovel."

Carrying the wreath and the candle with her, Nana *Dahd* slid heavily out of the pickup and trudged toward the base of the largest of the cottonwoods.

The rake and shovel, half again as tall as Davy himself, were unwieldy and difficult for a six-year-old to carry, but he struggled manfully with them, making his way without complaint over the rough track from the truck to where Nana *Dahd* stood staring down at the ground.

It wasn't until Davy reached her side that he saw what she was looking at—a shrine of sorts, although he didn't know to call it that. In the middle of a circular patch of barren ground stood a small wooden cross. On it hung a faded plastic wreath, and before it sat a smoky glass vase that had once contained a candle. Both cross and glass were framed by a broken circle of smooth white river rocks.

"What is this, Nana *Dahd*?" Davy asked. "A grave? Is this a cemetery?"

He looked up. Nana *Dahd*'s usually impassive face was awash with emotion. A single tear glistened in the corner of her eye. In all his six years,

Davy Ladd had never before seen his beloved Nana *Dahd* cry. Tears were precious and not to be spilled without good reason. Something must be terribly wrong.

"Let's go," he begged, reaching up and tugging at her hand. "Let's leave this place. It's scary here."

But Nana *Dahd* had no intention of leaving. His touch seemed to jar her out of her reverie. Patting his shoulder, she reached into the pocket of her apron and brought out a huge, wrinkled hanky. She blew her nose and wiped her red-rimmed eyes.

"I'm okay, Olhoni. We will leave, but after, not right now. First we work."

Nana *Dahd* showed Davy how animals had scattered some of the white border stones into the brush. She directed him to find and rearrange as many as he could. Meanwhile, she retrieved the hoe and began scraping the small circle clean of all encroaching blades of grass and weed. As soon as the clearing satisfied her, she carefully removed the faded wreath from the cross and replaced it with the new one.

It was summer, and the harsh early afternoon sun beat down on them as they worked. Davy rebuilt the stone circle as best he could. Rita nodded with approval as he moved the last piece of border into place.

"Good," she said. "Now for the candle."

While Davy watched, she placed the new candle before the cross, bracing it around the base with a supporting bank of rocks and dirt.

"This is to keep the candle from falling over by accident," she explained. "It would be very bad if our candle started a range fire."

Finished at last, she knelt before the cross one last time and examined their handiwork. It was good. She motioned for Davy to join her.

"Light the candle, Olhoni," she said gravely, handing him a book of matches.

Davy scratched his head in exasperation. How could grown-ups be so stupid? "But, Nana *Dahd*," he objected. "It isn't even dark yet. Why do we need a candle?"

"The light is for the spirits, Olhoni," she told him. "It's not for us."

Davy had used matches a few other times, but always in the house, never outside. It took three sputtering attempts before his small fingers managed to strike a match and keep it burning long enough to touch the flame to the wick of the candle. Nana *Dahd* watched patiently and without criticism, allowing the child to learn for himself of the need to shelter the match's faltering flame from unexpected breezes.

At last the wick caught fire. Davy glanced at Nana *Dahd* to see what he should do next. When she bowed her head, closed her eyes, and crossed herself, Davy did the same, listening in rapt silence while the old woman prayed.

To most Anglos that prayer, murmured softly in guttural Papago, would have been incomprehensible, but not to Davy, not to a child whose first spoken word, uttered almost five years earlier, had been a gleeful shout of *"gogs"*—Papago for dog—on the day Nana *Dahd* brought home an ungainly, scrawny puppy. She called the pup "Oh'o," Papago for "Bone."

From that small beginning, Davy had learned other Indian words at the same time he learned the English ones. He spoke his godmother's native language with almost the same ease as his mother's English.

Listening now, he heard Nana *Dahd*'s prayer, a fervent one, for the immortal soul of someone Davy didn't know, someone named Gina. The child listened quietly, attentively. When the prayer was finished, the old woman discovered that her legs and feet were painfully swollen. She had to ask Davy to untie her shoes and help her to her feet.

Once standing, Rita reached over and picked up the rake and hoe. "I'll take these. Get the old wreath, Olhoni. If we leave it here, hungry cattle may try to eat it."

He gathered the wreath and the empty candle glass, then followed the limping woman to the truck, straggling a few thoughtful paces behind her.

Only then, as they walked, did he ask the question. "Who's Gina, Nana *Dahd*?"

"My granddaughter, Olhoni. She died around here."

Surprised, Davy paused and looked back at the grove of trees. "Here?"

Rita nodded. "Seven years ago today. Each year, on the anniversary, I decorate her cross to let her know she's not forgotten."

"Is that why you lit the candle? Because it's the opposite of a birthday?"

It was a precocious question from a child whose mother gave him plenty of words to use but little of herself.

"Yes, Olhoni."

For a moment, Davy frowned, trying to assimilate this new and unexpected piece of information. He thought himself as much Rita's child as his own mother's. The idea that Nana *Dahd* had another child or a grandchild of her own came as an unwelcome surprise.

"What's the matter?" Rita asked.

"I didn't know you had a daughter," he said accusingly.

"Not a daughter, Olhoni, a son. Gina was my grandchild, my son's only daughter."

"She's just like my father, isn't she?" he said.

Nana *Dahd* frowned. Had Diana told Davy about the connection between the two deaths? That didn't seem likely. "What do you mean?" Rita asked.

"Gina died before I was born," he answered. "So did my father. Why did everybody have to die before I was born so I couldn't meet them?"

The question was far less complicated than Rita had feared, and so was her answer. "If you had a father, little one," Nana *Dahd* said gently, "then you wouldn't be my Olhoni. Come. We still have to go up the mountain."

When she reached the truck, Rita turned and looked back at the disconsolate child shambling behind her, kicking up clouds of dust with the scuffed toes of his shoes.

"Now what's the matter?" she asked.

"Where's my father's cross?" he demanded. "Does my mother put flowers and candles on it?"

Nana *Dahd* shook her head. She doubted it. "I don't know," she said.

It was high time the boy knew the truth about his father, but telling him wasn't Rita's place. She wouldn't tell Olhoni about that any more than she would have told him about his mother's rhinestone-studded cowboy boots.

"That's another question you'll have to ask your mother, Olhoni. Now, climb into the truck. It's getting late."

Andrew Carlisle didn't have to wait long for a ride. The fourth car to whiz past him on the entrance ramp, a green Toyota Corolla, slowed and pulled over the side to wait for him. The set of yellow lights trapped to the top told him the car was an oversized-load pilot car. The driver, a woman, leaned over and rolled down the passenger window just as he reached the car.

"Where to?" she asked.

The woman, a faded, frowsy blonde in her late thirties or early forties, was moderately attractive. She wore shorts and a halter top and held a glistening beer can in one hand while a lipstick-stained cigarette smoldered in the ashtray.

"Prescott," he said.

Over the years, lying had become such a deeply

ingrained habit that he never considered telling the truth.

She tossed her purse into the backseat, clearing a place for him. "I'm only going as far as Casa Grande," she said, "but it's a start. Get in. Care for a beer? Cooler's in the back."

Andrew Carlisle hadn't tasted a beer in more than six years. "Don't mind if I do," he said, reaching around behind him to grab a Bud from the cooler. Personally, he would have preferred Coors, but beggars can't be choosers. He took a long swig, then held the beer in his mouth, savoring the sharp bite of flavor on his tongue. Beer wasn't all he hadn't tasted in six years, he thought. Not by a long shot.

He stole a surreptitious glance at the woman. He'd heard stories about these pilot-car women, about how much they made on the job itself and how much they made moonlighting on their backs. Andrew Carlisle had spent so many years fantasizing about Diana Ladd and her swollen belly and what he'd do to her when he finally got the chance that he had almost missed this golden opportunity when it all but fell in his lap.

"Why Prescott?" the woman was saying.

"My dad's in the hospital up there," he said. "He isn't expected to make it."

The woman clucked her tongue in sympathy. "That's too bad."

"My car broke down in Lordsburg," he continued. "The mechanic said it would take at least two days to get parts and another day to put it back together. According to my mom, Dad doesn't have three days. So I decided to hitchhike there and go back for the car later."

Carlisle let his index finger stroke around and around the smooth lip of the can, sensuously wiping the beads of moisture off it and wondering how many places besides the door handle, the cooler, and the beer can he had touched. Where else would he have left prints? He would have to remember all those places later so as not to miss any when he wiped the vehicle clean.

The woman set the beer can between her legs and reached for the still-burning cigarette. A few stray ashes rained down on the seat as she took a long drag, but Andrew Carlisle was conscious only of the cool beer can resting unselfconsciously between her deeply tanned legs. Looking at it caused a sudden, insistent stiffening between his own.

"Do you do it for money?" he asked.

She looked at him and laughed. "Drive pilot cars? Of course I do it for money. Even with air-conditioning, working for mobile home-toters is a lousy job, but it's better than no job at all, which is where I was after they laid me off at Hecla."

Andrew Carlisle hadn't been talking about driving pilot cars. He had meant something else entirely. He liked the fact that she was too dumb to pick up on the *double entendre*. Women were stupid that way. Sometimes you had to hit them over the head just to get their attention.

Ahead of them, Picacho Peak loomed in the distance, its rugged gray silhouette shimmering in the heat waves that rose off the freeway's pavement. Carlisle knew the mountain's name as well as he knew his own, but he didn't let on. "What's that?" he asked, pointing.

"The mountain?" the woman asked, looking at him dubiously. "I thought you said you're from Prescott. How come you don't know Picacho Peak?"

"My dad's in Prescott," he said. "In the VA hospital up there. I'm from El Paso. I've never been here before. What did you call it, Picacho Peak? It looks steep. Do people climb it?"

"All the time. I grew up around here. The mountain's one of my favorite places. Actually, there's a rest area partway up. We could make a pit stop there if you can spare the time."

"Sure," he said agreeably. "I'd like that."

The parking lot at the rest area was totally deserted. A searing, hot wind blew down off the mountain and into their faces when they got out of the car. While the woman went to use the rest room, Andrew retrieved two more beers from the cooler and then sauntered over to a shaded picnic table. Across the desert came the whine of tires as vehicles sped along the Interstate several hundred yards away, but none of them slowed or stopped. Closer at hand there was no sign of life.

He took a leisurely sip from his second beer in six years. The alcohol was making him a little giddy, giving him a slight but pleasant buzz. He sat with his back against the warm concrete picnic tabletop and thought about taking her right there in the heat, in broad daylight, as it were.

That excited him almost beyond bearing, but there was no sense in being stupid. Carlisle looked around. At one end of the rest area, he saw a small playground. Beyond it, a trail wound off up the mountain.

When the woman emerged from the rest room, Carlisle was gratified to see that she had applied a fresh coat of vivid red lipstick. He looked forward to the taste of it, anticipating how it would feel to crush those full lips against his own. He wondered if cosmetic companies had ever considered naming their lipsticks with his kind of flavors— "Yielding Woman" would be a good one or maybe "Blood Red." Maybe he could get a job writing advertising copy.

As she came walking toward him, he again noticed the deep tan on her legs and the easy, sensuous sway of her generous hips. Not unaware of her effect on him, she seemed, in fact, to enjoy it.

He handed her a beer, which he'd already opened. "Ever make any money on the side?" he asked.

She smiled coquettishly over the top of the can, but she made no movement away from him. He caught a whiff of freshened perfume with its hint of tacit agreement. "That depends on what you have in mind," she said. "Your place or mine?"

He almost choked. She was brazen as hell. Is that what had happened to women in the six-and-a-half years since 1968 when they'd locked him up? Was that what "Women's Lib" was all about? A little reluctance might have been nice. Carlisle liked reluctance in his women. Sex was always far more interesting when the woman had to give more than she intended. This broad, for instance, thought she was in complete control. He'd be only too happy to show her otherwise.

"Right here," he said, motioning toward the picnic table behind them.

She looked at him incredulously. "Right here? In the rest area? In this heat? What if somebody comes?"

Somebody'll come, he thought. "A quickie," he said, ashamed that it sounded so much like begging.

She laughed then. Something about him struck her as funny. The muscles along his jawline tightened with sudden anger.

"Sixty-five," she said easily. "It'd be more if we had to rent a room. Let me see the money first."

Sixty-five? he thought. What kind of price was that for a piece of ass? But he counted out the bills slowly and deliberately, giving himself time to savor the sensation. He studied the fine lines of her upturned palm as he placed the money in her hand. Would a fortune-teller have been able to read the lifeline etched there and tell what was about to happen?

She took the money from him, folded it in quarters, and stuffed the wad of bills into the tight hip pocket of her shorts. "You mean right here on the table?" she asked.

"How about down the path," he suggested lamely, as though stricken with a sudden case of shyness. "Maybe far enough to be out of sight of the parking lot."

She laughed again. "So you are bashful after all," she teased.

"A little," he admitted.

Maybe he would have let her go if she hadn't laughed at him so much, but he doubted it. He knew himself better than that. The die had been cast the moment she slowed down to pick him up.

She set off at a brisk pace, leading him toward the path. Fierce heat leaped off the rocks and burned their faces.

"It may be too hot," he said, dropping back as though he had changed his mind.

"There's a spring," she said. "Water and some shade. I've been here lots of times. It's not far."

She was right, it wasn't far, but it was all uphill. About a quarter of a mile up the steep track, she swung off the main trail and followed another, fainter one off to the side. Andrew Carlisle struggled to keep up. By the time they neared the thick grove of mesquite trees, he was completely out of breath. His hard-on had melted into nothing.

He followed her as she disappeared into dappled shade. The ground beneath them seemed almost pleasantly cool compared to the overheated air and shale outside. A tiny spring sent a trickle of water down a short streambed into a rocky basin. Near the basin, someone had cleared a flat spot in the cool, shaded dirt.

Without a word, the woman kicked off her sandals and stripped out of her clothes. She wasn't wearing a bra. Her breasts sagged a bit, but her figure wasn't that bad. There were no lines or light spots in the golden tan that covered her body. She looked good for her age, and she knew it.

"Me on top or you?" she asked perfunctorily.

"Me," Andrew Carlisle said.

"It figures," she returned.

He undressed quickly, and she pulled him down on her, kissing him eagerly, letting her tongue explore his, expert fingers stroking his hard-on back to life. She was a pro who knew all the right buttons to push. They worked—all too well.

He had wanted to take his time, to savor every sensation, but his body worked against him. With a groan, it was over almost before it had begun, and she was laughing again, lying beneath him, giggling into the hot flesh of his shoulder.

"When you said quickie, you weren't kidding."

He had planned to do it anyway, but he hadn't expected the blind rage that overcame him at the sound of that laughter. It may have been funny to her, but not to him.

Steadying himself on one elbow, he shoved his thumb into the delicate hollow at the base of her throat. Her eyes went wild, first with alarm and then with abject terror when she realized the extent of her danger. She tried to cry out, but the terrible grinding pressure that starved her of oxygen also cut off her ability to scream.

Her body arched beneath him as she fought desperately to escape. She rolled from side to side and tried futilely to scoot out from under him, but he held her fast. Her sharpened, talon-like fingernails raked down his shoulders and back, but the pain that shot through him acted as a spur, exciting him, goading him. With a sense of satisfaction, he felt himself stiffen once more.

Carlisle had learned the finer points of strangling from some of the boys on Death Row at Florence. You'd think from reading newspapers that those guys never mingle with the general prison population, but Carlisle had made it his business to make contact and take lessons.

The experts all said that once you start, you can't let up or back off, and he didn't. He rode her like a rodeo bronco while she writhed and bucked beneath him, carrying them both away from the dirt clearing, scraping his knees and tearing the flesh from her naked back and buttocks as she dragged them both onto jagged, unshaded, blistering shale. He rode her and came again, semen dribbling into her pubic hair, just as the woman's eyes rolled back into her head.

He knew better than to let go too soon. He held on, lying on top of her supine body with the rocks scorching his knees and shins, until he knew for sure she would never move again.

Only then, spent and gasping for breath, did he raise up on one elbow to examine his handiwork. Her perfect pink nipple lay invitingly exposed before him, inches from his face and teeth. It was the fantasy feast Andrew Carlisle had always dreamed about from the time he began dreaming of such things, but it was something he'd only sampled once before in his life. The temptation to do it again was all too powerful.

Leaning down, he took the still-warm nipple between his lips and sucked on it thoughtfully for a moment. Then he bit it—hard, bit until the soft flesh gave way beneath his teeth and the coppery taste of blood filled his mouth. He let it linger on his tongue for only a moment before he spat it out. It was far too salty. What Andrew Carlisle really wanted right about then was another beer.

Davy loved the drive to Ioligam, as Rita called the mountain that lay like a huge sleeping lion overlooking a broad, flat valley. Nana *Dahd* had explained that *ioligam* means manzanita, a low-growing desert brush that thrives on the mountain's rocky sides. From a distance, the brush gives the mountain its bluish tint. Diana, however, always referred to the mountain by its Anglo name of Kitt Peak. Davy preferred Ioligam.

He liked the way the air seemed to clear and the sky turned bluer as they came up the slight rise near the shaded rest area and the turnoff to the village of Ban Thak where they would be going later for the feast.

"Tell me again why they call it Coyote Sitting," Davy begged. "Do coyotes really sit there?"

Rita smiled indulgently. "Only in the winter," she said, "when they tell one another stories."

As they continued on, Davy took a keen interest in the crosses that dotted the roadside here and there along the way. Like Gina's, many of them were now dressed up with vivid new wreaths and candles. In one place, four separate crosses were clustered together.

"Did four people die there?" he asked, testing the reliability of his newfound knowledge.

Nana *Dahd* nodded. "A car wreck," she answered.

She had told him they would have to hurry to get to the gift shop on top of the mountain before the road closed, but when they turned off the highway onto the much smaller one leading up to Ioligam itself, Davy puzzled over what would close it. The road with its Open Range sign seemed straight enough, at least at first, and there was nothing wrong with the weather.

Davy knew, for instance, that during heavy rainstorms, running water could sometimes fill dry creek beds and washes and make roads impassable, but on this cloudless day, that seemed an unlikely possibility. He puzzled over the question as they wound their way up the mountain. A road closing for no reason seemed as mysterious as lighting a candle in broad daylight.

Finally, he broke down and asked. "Why will the road close, Nana *Dahd*?"

"Those men up there," Rita said, nodding her head in the direction of the observatory buildings, which shone in the sunlight like so many white jewels clustered in a rough crown around the top of the mountain. "Those men who look at the stars through their big telescopes don't like light. They say headlights from cars make it so they can't see the stars."

"But doesn't I'itoi mind having all those white men living up there and making regular people stay away?" Davy asked.

The I'itoi legends were the Papagos' traditional winter-telling tales. Elder Brother stories were told only during those months when the snakes and lizards were hidden away from cold weather. It was said that if Snake or Lizard overheard someone telling an I'itoi story, the animal might swallow the storyteller's luck and bring him harm.

During the previous winter, while Diana Ladd was taking a graduate night course at the university in order to maintain her teaching certificate, Rita had entertained both Davy and herself by recounting all the traditional I'itoi tales she could remember. A few she had made up on the spot.

She had told Davy how in the old days Ioligam had been I'itoi's summer home, the place he went to relax when he left his regular home on Baboquivari, another peak many miles to the south. She had told him how, when the Anglo scientists had come to the tribe and asked for permission to build their star-gazing telescopes on the sacred top of Ioligam, the tribal council had insisted that a special clause go into the lease that declared that all caves on the mountain belonged to I'itoi. They were sacred, and not to be disturbed.

Now, though, as Davy's words slipped into her heart, Rita Antone realized that he regarded the Anglo scientists as different somehow, as a people apart from his own kind. For the first time, she wondered if she had done the right thing.

Nana *Dahd* loved her little Olhoni more than life itself, but had she gone too far? Did blond-haired Davy Ladd believe he was disconnected from "those white men" and their telescopes? Had she created an Anglo child who would always watch westerns on television and in the movies with an Indian child's inevitable dread of impending defeat?

Rita Antone had wanted desperately to pass on her legacy of wisdom, knowledge gleaned from her own grandmother, a much-respected Ban Thak wisewoman. She had expected that wisdom to flow through her own son, Gordon, to Gina, her granddaughter. But Gina had been stolen from her, and during the terrible troubles that followed Gina's death, Diana Ladd alone had been Rita's constant ally. That was a debt that demanded repayment, and she was paying it back in the only wealth she had at her disposal.

When Olhoni was born, Rita had looked at the fatherless child and had known instinctively that Diana's ability to mother the child had somehow been obliterated with the death of the child's father. So Rita had stepped into the breach, taking on the role of godmother and mentor to the little bald-headed baby. She had been happy to find willing ears into which she could pour all that she knew. The old woman had lavished on Davy the kind of love Diana Ladd couldn't wring from her own rock-hard heart.

At sixty-five years of age, Nana *Dahd* usually knew her own mind. She lived with a Papago's stolid and abiding faith in life's inevitabilities. This sudden attack of uncertainty caused new beads of sweat to break out on her forehead.

While Davy dozed contentedly in the sunlit rider's seat, Nana *Dahd* struggled with her conscience. Down by the shrine where Gina had died, Rita had crossed herself and prayed to the Anglo God, to Father John's God, her mother's God, asking for His blessing on Gina's eternal soul. But here, on Ioligam, on I'itoi's sacred mountain, the Anglo God seemed far away and deaf besides.

"*Ni-i wehmatathag I'itoi ahni'i,*" she whispered, her voice almost inaudible beneath the groaning engine of the laboring GMC. "I'itoi, help me."

But she wasn't at all sure He would.

3

*A*T *ALMOST SEVEN* thousand feet, a brisk breeze struck their faces as Rita and Davy stepped down from the GMC. After the heat of the desert floor far below, the cool mountain air felt almost chilly.

In the sparsely occupied observatory parking lot, Rita left Davy to unload baskets while she limped toward the gift shop. A little blond-haired girl sitting on sun-soaked steps regarded the Indian woman curiously as she tapped lightly on the visitor center's side entrance. At this hour, visitors inside would be watching a movie. Rita disliked walking past them on her way to the craft shop.

Edwina Galvan, manager of the shop, came to the door. Edwina, a Kiowa transplant to the Papago, had fallen in love with and married a young Papago fire fighter who now, as a middle-aged man, served as tribal-council representative from Ban Thak.

Even in her forties, Edwina's classic Plains Indian features and good looks met and exceeded all the visiting tourists' "real Indian" expectations. She augmented a stunning natural beauty with a varying wardrobe of antelope bone or squash-blossom necklaces that she wasn't shy about removing and selling on the spot if a likely purchaser showed sufficient interest.

Since coming to the Papago and assuming management of the Kitt Peak gift shop, she had developed a reputation as a shrewd and knowledgeable basket trader, one with an unerring eye for superior craftsmanship. For years, the Kiowa woman had been Rita Antone's sole customer.

Edwina smiled when she saw Rita's broad weathered face waiting outside the door. "So," she said. "If you're here, it must be June. It's sure a good thing. Your baskets are all gone."

She didn't say that because of their unrivaled superiority, Rita Antone's baskets were always the first to sell. Such high praise would be considered excessive and rude. It was enough to say that Rita's baskets were gone. The old woman nodded a brief acknowledgment of the understated compliment.

Davy appeared just then, lugging the first box of baskets. He waved at Edwina, then hurried back after the next load.

"The bald-headed baby isn't bald anymore," Edwina observed as the door closed behind him. "He's sure big. Is he in school?"

"He just finished kindergarten. He'll be in first grade next year," Rita answered.

Davy returned with the second box of baskets, smiling shyly at Edwina as he put it down on the floor. Edwina had heard all the reservation grumblings about Rita Antone, often called Hejel Wi'ithag, or Left Alone, by other Papagos. Gossips said it wasn't right for her to squander all her hard-earned knowledge on Davy Ladd, an Anglo at that—a boy whose father, convicted or not, was ultimately responsible for Rita's own grandchild's death. No one could understand why she would abandon her people to go live in Tucson with the killer's Anglo widow and her whiteskinned baby.

Edwina, still considered a reservation newcomer after a mere twenty years, accepted as a given the special bond that existed between Rita Antone and Diana Ladd. She remembered how the people had unaccountably closed ranks against the bereaved woman after Gina Antone's death, saying that the old woman was bad luck. Diana and Rita, united by nothing more than mutual grief, had been each other's strongest allies in that time of trouble. Edwina Galvan didn't fault either woman for their continuing alliance, nor did she begrudge Left Alone her devotion to the blond-haired boy. In fact, Edwina rather liked him herself.

It took Davy several more trips before all the baskets were assembled in a pile on the floor in front of the counter. By then, Rita was seated on a chair behind the counter drinking a glass of water and fanning herself while Edwina went through the boxes one by one, examining each basket in turn, writing the price on a piece of masking tape that she affixed to the bottom of each basket after first making a note in the ragged notebook that served as her master record.

"You've sure been busy," Edwina commented offhandedly as she worked. "What are you going to do with all your money?"

"Saving it for my old age," Rita answered. At that, both women laughed. Rita was sixty-five years old. Among the Papago, in a population with the highest blood-sugar count of any known ethnic group in the world, one decimated by the ravages of both diabetes and alcoholism, Rita Antone was already well into a venerated old age.

"Does she give you any of that cash?" Edwina asked Davy with a smile. He shook his head seriously. Edwina reached into her pocket and extracted a quarter. "Here, I'll give you some," she said. "Go get yourself a Coke. The machine's right outside."

Davy dashed eagerly out of the gift shop. Rita and his mother didn't let him have sodas often, so this was a special treat. He found the machine with no trouble and felt terribly grown up as he inserted the coin all by himself and pressed the selection button. A can rolled into the slot with a satisfying thunk. Grabbing it and turning at the same time, he ran headlong into the little Anglo girl who had watched him make trip after trip carrying loads of baskets. The impact of the unexpected collision knocked the soda can out of his hands. It fell to the ground and rolled away.

"Watch where you're going, dummy," he muttered. He retrieved the can, but when he opened it, half its contents blew into the air. Disappointed, he flopped down onto the steps to drink what was left. Moments later, the little girl joined him, bringing her own soda with her.

"Is that woman you're with a Indian?" she asked.

It was bad manners to ask such questions, but Davy answered anyway. "Yes."

"Are you a Indian, too?" she persisted.

"Maybe I am," Davy answered, growing surly. "And maybe I'm not, either. What's it to you?"

With that, he stomped away, not sure what about the question had made him so angry. He hurried across the parking lot to where two quarrelsome ground squirrels argued over an abandoned crust of bread. Suddenly, the automatic door of an outbuilding opened, and an ambulance eased into the sunlight.

At first Davy thought he was going to get to see it drive off with lights flashing and siren blaring. Instead, the driver parked directly outside the door, shut off the engine, then went back into the garage. He returned moments later carrying a bucket of soapy water, a brush, and a fistful of rags.

Disappointed, Davy finished what was left of his soda and went looking for Rita.

Andrew Carlisle took his time. He was in no hurry to leave the scene of his triumph and return to the car. After drinking his fill from the rocky pool, he washed the blood from his back, shins, and knees, letting the hot sun dry the moisture from his chafed skin. He took real pleasure in knowing that his victim had fought him and lost. He was a slight man, but the years of working out in prison, especially his total concentration on strengthening his hands, had paid off.

Only after he was fully dressed did he once more turn his attention to the dead woman. Andrew Carlisle was not a man accustomed to cleaning up his own messes, but in this case he made an exception. Dragging her by one arm, he hauled her into the shallow stream and washed her thoroughly, carefully rinsing off whatever traces of himself he might have left behind. Touching her now no longer aroused him, but he enjoyed looking at the ruined breast and knowing he had caused the damage. That was a trophy of sorts, something to be proud of.

When he finished cleaning her up, he dragged her back out of the water and arranged her to his liking, leaving her lying faceup in the searing sun, then he surveyed the area, gathering her clothing and sandals into a small, tidy stack. He shook an almost full package of Winstons out of the woman's shirt pocket, and was happy to see that a book of matches had been shoved inside the cellophane wrapper.

He squatted there and smoked his cigarette. Little time had passed, but already a few alert flies and ants were beginning to do what flies and ants do with dead flesh. He observed their purposeful movements with detached amusement, wondering idly how the insects knew about the unexpected bounty good fortune had laid at their doorstep. Was there some kind of secret signal, some code? Did an alert scout sound a special buzzing alarm that said, "Hey guys, follow me. Come see what I found"?

By the time Carlisle finished the cigarette, there were far more ants and flies than there had been when he first lit up. He ground out the cigarette and placed the butt along with the accumulated stack of clothing. He returned to the corpse and removed the jewelry—three rings, a Timex watch, and a single gold-chain necklace—wresting them roughly from the body not because they might be valuable or worth selling but because any delay in identifying the body would work to his advantage.

Systematically, he went through the pockets of her shorts and shirt, finding nothing but the car keys and his own sixty-five dollars. "You should have asked for more, honey," he said aloud to the dead woman as he returned the bills to his wallet. "Believe me, your pussy was worth it."

He returned to the pitiful stack of belongings and wrapped them as well as his discarded cigarette butt into a secure bundle, which he stuffed inside his shirt. The cigarettes, matches, and car keys went into a pocket. He made one last careful search of the area to make sure he had missed nothing.

Most of the terrain was rocky except for the hooker's makeshift earthen bed. With a mesquite branch, he swept the area clean of footprints, adding the branch to his bundle as well. When he was certain he had removed all visible incriminating evidence, Andrew Carlisle turned and walked away.

Welcome to the world, he thought. Payback time has started.

Diana Ladd leaned away from her typewriter and rolled her shoulders, trying to relieve the tension caused by several uninterrupted hours before her trusty Smith-Corona. The writing wasn't going particularly well, but she refused to quit.

It was probably weariness that made her drop her guard for a moment, allowing the unwelcome, errant thought into her consciousness—if only Gary were here to give her a back rub.

Disgusted with herself, she choked the thought off smothering it as quickly as she could. Seven years after Gary's suicide, her mind and body both still played those kinds of tricks on her. She felt betrayed by the treachery of her own flesh, by the aching longings that sometimes awakened her in the middle of the night. Gary was dead, dammit, and she wouldn't have wanted him around any longer even if he weren't.

When the boy was gone, Mister Bone, as Diana often called the dog, lay at her feet. As soon as the typing stopped, he raised his head, hoping Diana might throw the ball for him. When she got up and padded to the kitchen, he followed, stopping by the kitchen sink to take a long, sloppy drink from his water dish while she retrieved a pitcher of warm sun tea from the patio.

Diana Ladd knew that her friends were losing patience. One by one, they had all taken the trouble to tell her that it was high time she got over Gary's death, time that she dated someone else and found a father figure for poor little Davy. That was what they always called him—"poor little Davy." Well, she hadn't chosen very damn well the first time, and she didn't have any faith she'd do better the next time around. Besides, she had tried it—once.

She had gone out for one miserable evening with a traveling encyclopedia salesman who had made a presentation to the school faculty at Sells. He had taken her to dinner at the Iron Mask in Tucson and then to the Maverick, a country-western place on Twenty-second Street. She had done all right until the band had played "The Snakes Crawl at Night." When they did that number, she had asked him to take her home, and she'd refused to go out with him again. Months later, he still called her periodically.

Taking the glass of iced tea back to her room, Diana settled down at the desk and read through the five pages she had written since Rita and Davy had left at noon. It was tripe, she knew it, but she resisted the temptation to wad it all up into a ball and throw it in the garbage. Later, after she'd given it a rest, some of it might still be salvageable. If she was going to finish the book this summer—that was her stated goal—she couldn't afford to throw everything away.

Although she thought of the book as a novel, it was autobiographical, of course. Someone had said that all first novels are autobiographical. It was the story of a woman's attempt to go on living in the aftermath of her husband's betrayal and subsequent suicide. The problem was the main character. There was no joy in her heroine, no life.

Diana rolled another clean sheet of paper into the machine, then sat there staring at it. In the stillness of the darkened room, her parents' voices returned to haunt her. Once they started up, she had no choice but to let them play on to the end of whatever tape had surfaced in her head. All of the arguments and battles were there, preserved indelibly in her memory. The details varied occasionally, but the basic theme was always the same.

It had usually started around dinnertime when her father would come in from working in the woods near Joseph, Oregon.

"Where's that lazy daughter of yours, Iona? Why the hell isn't she down here helping you?"

Her mother's voice would come drifting up the stairs to her then—calming and soothing, as always. "She's studying, Max. Leave her alone. I don't need any help. Dinner's almost ready."

But Max Cooper was never one to be easily dissuaded. He would come to the bottom of the stairs, and his voice would boom through the house like a clap of thunder announcing a sudden storm over Oregon's Willowa Mountains.

"Diana Lee, you get your ass down here. Now!"

Knowing better than to argue or fight back, Diana would hurry downstairs. Inevitably, he would be waiting for her at the landing, swaying dangerously, hiking up his pants, tugging at his suspenders. She'd try to slip past him, but he would catch her by the braids, snapping her head back, pulling her hair until her eyes watered. She must have been twelve then, because her mother had cut off the braids right after her thirteenth birthday.

"What were you doing up there?" he demanded.

"Reading a book. For my book report."

At twelve Diana Lee Cooper hadn't known that her father was illiterate. Diana didn't find that out until much later, when her mother was dying. Max Cooper's inability to read was part and parcel of the helplessness that bound Iona Cooper to him. Aside from the fact that Diana wasn't a son, her love of reading was another reason for Max to despise their only child. Diana's love of books and schooling both mystified and infuriated him.

Diana tried to slip away, but he yanked her braids again, shaking her, lifting her off her feet. The skin all over her head smarted, but she didn't cry out. Wouldn't cry out.

"How come you've always got that snooty nose of yours stuck in a book, young lady? You get your butt out into the kitchen, girl, and learn something useful for a change."

Twenty years later, Diana Ladd could still smell his stale, beer-saturated breath and see the spikes of stiff nose hairs in his flaring nostrils.

"Once you learn how to cook and clean and please a man, then's time enough for you to sit on your ass and read books."

He had shoved her away from him then, propelling her toward the kitchen. Somehow she managed to keep her legs under her. In the kitchen,

Iona Cooper, lips clenched, bent over the stove, concentrating on stirring the gravy or mashing the potatoes, refusing to meet Diana's gaze. She never said anything aloud, never said anything her husband might overhear and use against them both, but a conspiracy of silence existed between the woman and her daughter.

Afterward, Diana Lee Ladd remembered that battle in particular and counted it as a watershed. A spark of rebellion caught fire that evening, one that Max Cooper was never able to stifle or beat out of his daughter no matter how hard he tried.

And twenty years later, Diana Lee Cooper Ladd pushed aside her typewriter, put her head down in her arms, and cried because it wasn't worth it.

What good had it done to escape her ignorant father, to flee the brutal prison that had been her home in Joseph, Oregon? There was still no joy in her life. No joy at all.

Rita carefully maneuvered the truck down the winding road. It was a thirty-minute, twelve-mile drive, most of it with the road perched precariously on the steep flank of the mountain. She kept the truck in low gear to save the brakes. While Rita drove, Davy, more quiet than usual, hunkered down in his corner of the seat.

"What is it, Olhoni?" Rita asked.

"Will I be an Indian when I grow up?"

His question mirrored her own concern, but she tried to laugh it off. "You already are," she told him.

"Really?" He brightened at once. "What kind? Papago, like you?"

Rita shook her head. "Big Toe," she said, smiling to herself because she knew the old joke would be new to Davy.

"I never heard of Big Toe Indians," he countered. "Where are they from?"

"All over," she answered.

"Are you sure?"

"They're people with so little Indian blood that the only thing Indian about them is their big toe."

"You're teasing me," he said, pouting.

She nodded. "That's one of the reasons I'itoi chose us for his people. We tease and laugh and make jokes. So does he."

"But I *still* want to be an Indian," Davy insisted.

At the bottom of the mountain, the road straightened abruptly, dropping through the foothills on a stretch of reservation-owned open range.

Rita had driven on open range all her life, and she wasn't driving fast. They were nearing the junction with Highway 86 when a startled steer came crashing up onto the roadway out of a dry wash. With no warning, there was barely enough time to react. Rita jammed on the brakes. The pickup swerved to one side, avoiding the animal by inches, but the right rear tire caught in the soft sand of the shoulder.

The GMC rolled over onto its side and then rolled again, end over end, coming to rest lying on its roof in the other lane, its hood facing in the wrong direction. Without knowing precisely what had happened or how he got there, Davy found himself standing upright in the middle of the road.

He couldn't see anything. There was a terrible shrieking noise ringing in his ears, and another noise as well—a car's horn, honking one long, terrible wail.

Davy gasped for breath and realized that the first sound came from him—his own voice screaming. He put his hands to his face and brought them away bloody, but he could see again, could see the dust still flying, the tires still spinning uselessly in the air. The engine was still running, and the horn wouldn't quit. The blaring noise seemed to be all around him, coming up out of the desert floor, raining down on him from the very sky itself.

"Nana *Dahd*," he shouted. "Where are you? Are you all right?"

There was no answer, only the horn—the terrible horn. He scrambled over to the pickup and peered inside. Nana *Dahd* lay with her body crushed against the steering wheel, which jutted far into the cab. Blood gushed from a gaping wound on her left hand.

"Nana *Dahd*!" Davy shouted again, but she didn't hear him, didn't stir.

Just then a pair of strong hands gripped his shoulders and dragged him away from the truck. Davy looked up to see that an Anglo man, a stranger, was holding him. He fought the hands with all his might, kicking and screaming, "Let me go! Let me go!" But the man held him fast.

A second man was there now, crawling on his hands and knees, peering into the truck. He reached inside across Nana *Dahd*'s still body and switched off the engine, then he tugged at some wires under the dash. The wailing horn was instantly stilled, and the sudden silence was deafening.

"Can we get her out, Joe?"

The man by the truck shook his head. "I don't think so. She's pinned. We've got to get a tourniquet on this hand, then find some help. How far back to that little trading post?"

"Three Points? A long way. What about the other direction, toward Sells?"

"Up there!" Davy told them, pointing back up the mountain, but the men didn't hear him. After all, he was only a little kid. What did he know?

"You stay with her," one man was saying to the other, letting Davy go and heading back toward his car, a shiny red Grand Prix. The two men had been traveling past the turnoff on the highway just in time to see the GMC perform its spectacular series of acrobatics.

One of the two men started toward the car, but Davy ran after him, attaching himself to the man's knee like a stubborn cocklebur. The force of his tackle almost brought both of them down.

"Up there!" Davy insisted desperately. "We've got to go up there!"

"Let go, kid. Don't waste time."

"But there's an ambulance up there. I know. I saw it!"

Finally, the boy's words penetrated. "An ambulance? On the mountain?"

"Yes. Please."

"No shit! I'm going, but you stay here. You're hurt, too."

Beating him off with a club was all that would have kept Davy Ladd from clambering into the Grand Prix. He sat in the front seat, not crying but shaking silently, his bloody face pressed to the inside of the windshield as the car raced up the steep mountain road, straightening the curves, clinging to the pavement on the outside edges.

At one point, the man tossed him a white handkerchief. "Christ, kid, use this, will you? You're getting blood all over my car."

When they reached the top of the mountain, the car screeched to a stop in the parking lot.

"Which way?"

Wordlessly, Davy pointed toward the garage. The door was closed, the now-clean ambulance inside and invisible. The man raced toward it while Davy scrambled out of the car and ran toward the gift shop. It was after four and the place was closed, but Davy pounded on the side door, the one Nana *Dahd* had used earlier. When Edwina Galvan finally opened it, he flung himself at her.

"It's Nana *Dahd*! You've got to help her. She's hurt bad."

"What happened?"

The dam broke. Suddenly, Davy Ladd was sobbing so badly he could barely talk. "A cow," he mumbled. "A cow in the road."

"Where?" Edwina demanded, but he didn't answer. She grabbed his shoulders and shook him. "Where did it happen?"

"Down on the flat. Almost to the highway."

Just then a piercing alarm sounded all over the complex at the top of the mountain. The man from the Grand Prix dashed out of the garage followed by the ambulance. Two other men appeared from nowhere and ran for the ambulance.

"It's at the bottom of the mountain," one of them shouted back at Edwina. "Radio Sells for another ambulance."

Edwina nodded and turned to go back inside. Holding Davy's hand, she intended to take him with her, but he pulled free and darted away, climbing back into the front seat of the Grand Prix just as it started out of the parking lot behind the speeding ambulance.

No matter what, Davy Ladd's place was with Nana *Dahd*.

The pain was bigger than she was and hotter than the sun. It burned through her, seared through her, until she couldn't think, couldn't breathe.

Where's Olhoni? she wondered. She had called for him, but he didn't answer. Where was he? Was he dead? No. That was impossible. That couldn't be, but where was he?

She asked the man, a man who was there trying to talk to her through the mangled window of the truck, but she could no longer translate the funny *Mil-gahn* words. The only words that made sense to her now were those of her childhood, the Papago ones. The man shook his head helplessly. He didn't understand, either.

"Where is Olhoni?" she murmured again and again. "Where is my bald-headed baby?"

There were other cars now, other people. Rita could hear them, could see feet where faces ought to be. Were they upside down or was she? What had happened? And where was Olhoni?

And then the pain. The pain that was bigger than she was grew even larger. It was a pain bigger than the stars and the sky and the universe. The pain was everything.

She heard a noise and realized that someone had cut a hole in the door of the truck. Her body was flowing out through that hole—her body and her blood.

They were moving her now, moving her out onto the ground and strapping her down to a board or a stretcher of some kind. That was when she started to fight them. The heavy white strap locked her to the board just as another strap long ago had once locked her to a bed.

She fought them like a smart cow fights when she knows she's being led to the slaughter. The pain was blinding, but she fought through it, fought beyond it. She might have won, too, but suddenly Olhoni was there, kneeling at her side, pleading with her to be still.

"Let them help you, Nana *Dahd*," he begged. "Please let them help you."

She looked up then and saw that beyond Olhoni some of the other faces swarming above her were Indian faces. She wondered where they'd come from, or if they had been there all the time.

A few of the men were trying to pick up the stretcher with her on it. She could tell from the looks on their faces that they thought she was too heavy. For some reason, this seemed funny to her, but when she tried to laugh, another searing pain shot through her.

One of the men tried to pry Davy away from her hand, but he clung to her and refused to budge.

"Let him come," one of the attendants said. "He's hurt, too."

Could that be? Olhoni hurt? Rita tried to look at him, to see what was wrong, but she blacked out then. The next thing she knew, she was riding in the ambulance, or rather on top of it. Over it somehow. She could see the two attendants huddled over a strangely familiar figure lying flat on a stretcher.

Olhoni was sitting off to one side. Rita called to him, but he didn't look up, didn't hear her. His eyes never left the face of the old woman on the stretcher. There was a bottle with some kind of liquid in it hanging above her. A plastic tube led from the bottle to a needle pressed into the flesh of the woman's arm.

Suddenly, there was a flurry of activity. "We're losing her! We're losing her!" one of the attendants shouted.

Ruthlessly, the other man shoved Olhoni aside,

pushing him roughly up into the front seat. The boy didn't protest. He went where he was told and sat there, with his hands clutching the dashboard, staring out the window in front of him.

And that was when Rita saw the buzzards, three of them, sitting in a row on three separate telephone poles, their huge wings outstretched to collect the last warming rays of sunshine. Those buzzards, their heads still naked and bloody after I'itoi scalped them in punishment for betraying him, sat there soaking up the sun on their coal-black living wing tips.

The buzzards were alive and wanted to be alive. Suddenly, so did Rita. Olhoni still needed her. I'itoi did not.

Clawing her way, hand over hand, Rita scrambled down from the roof of the moving vehicle, fought her way back inside the ambulance until she stood peering curiously down at the shrunken form still strapped to the stretcher. For some time, she gazed dispassionately at the body, amazed by how terribly ancient that old woman seemed, by how worn and wrinkled and used-up she was, but not yet ready to be dead.

With a terrifying jolt, the electrical current passed through her body, hammering her heart awake once more, and she was home.

Andrew Carlisle took his time coming down the trail. He searched back and forth, combing the mountainside until he found the two empty beer cans they had dropped on the way up. No sense in leaving a set of identifiable fingerprints.

He knew from what he'd learned in Florence that the chances of homicide cops finding a "stranger" assailant were slim as long as the stranger was reasonably smart and played it cool.

The waning afternoon sun scorched the ground around him. No one had yet ventured into the deserted rest-area parking lot by the time he returned to his victim's car. He helped himself to another beer—still cold, thank God—and started the Toyota. He turned off the air-conditioning and drove down the freeway with the windows open, letting the hot desert air flow freely over his body. It was outside air. He was free.

Fortunately, there was plenty of gas in the car, so he didn't have to stop before he got to Phoenix. He drove straight to the Park Central Mall in Phoenix proper and parked in an empty corner of the lot. There, as afternoon turned to evening, he went through the woman's purse and removed all the cash, over two hundred dollars' worth. Beneath the seat he discovered a gun, a Llama .380 automatic. He had planned to take nothing that belonged to his victim, nothing that could tie him back to her, but the weapon was more temptation than he could resist. Trying to purchase a weapon if he wanted one later might cause people to ask questions. So he pocketed the gun.

Carefully, systematically, he went over every surface in the vehicle, wiping it clean of prints. Then he did the same to the beer cans and jewelry before he took them to a nearby trash can. The clothing he ditched in another can, this one at Thomas Mall on his way to the airport.

Sky Harbor was his last stop. Once there, he pulled into the long-term lot and took a ticket. One last time he wiped down everything he remembered touching since Park Mall—the door handle, steering wheel, gearshift, window knob, and keys. Then, placing the newly wiped keys back in the ignition, he got out of the car and walked away.

It was dark by then and much cooler. In the hubbub and hurry of the airport, no one noticed him walk away. It would be a five-mile hike to his mother's new house in Tempe, but he wasn't afraid of walking. In fact, walking that far would be a real treat.

*A*ROUND SEVEN, BRANDON Walker emerged from his cubicle and ventured down the hallway hoping to bum a cigarette and some company from Hank Maddern in Dispatch.

"Who knows . . ." Brandon began by way of greeting, walking up behind the dispatcher's back.

". . . what evil lurks in the hearts of men?" Maddern finished without turning. Both men laughed.

The intro to the old radio show *The Shadow* was a private in-crowd joke, shared among the grunts of the Pima County Sheriff's Department. Professional police officers called themselves Shadows to differentiate between themselves and the political hacks who, with plum appointments, held most key jobs.

Sheriff DuShane, reelected over and over by comfortable margins, had himself one hell of a political machine, to say nothing of a lucrative handle on graft and corruption. One outraged deputy had printed up and distributed a bumper sticker that said, SUPPORT YOUR LOCAL SHERIFF.

GET A MASSAGE. He had been all too right; he was also no longer a deputy.

DuShane may have been crooked, but he was also nobody's fool. He knew the value and necessity of real cops to do the real jobs. That's where the Shadows came in. They did all the work, got none of the glory, and most of them wouldn't have had it any other way.

Hank Maddern, who had reigned supreme in Dispatch for more than ten years, held the dubious honor of being the most senior Shadow. He worked nights because he preferred working nights.

"Hey, Hank, got a smoke?" Brandon asked.

Maddern pulled a crumpled, almost-empty pack from his breast pocket and tossed it across the counter. "Didn't quit smoking, just quit buying?"

"I'll even up eventually," Brandon said, shaking out the next-to-last cigarette.

"Right. You working on a case or hiding out?" Hank Maddern knew some of what went on in Brandon Walker's home life because he often fielded Louella Walker's calls.

"Hiding out," Brandon admitted, breathing the smoke into his lungs. "Too bad it's so quiet."

"Give it time. It's Friday. Things'll heat up."

As if on cue, the switchboard buzzed, and Maddern picked up the line. Brandon, with the cigarette dangling almost forgotten between his fingers, lounged against the counter. He gazed off into space, letting his mind go blank. He wasn't ready to go back to his cubicle, and he sure as hell wasn't ready to go home.

Maddern, listening intently on his headset, made a series of quick notes. "What was that name again? L-A-D-D, first name Diana?"

Immediately, Brandon Walker's attention was riveted on Maddern. Even after six years, Diana Ladd's name was one he remembered all too well. What was going on with her now?

"The boy's name is David," Maddern continued. "Yeah, I've got that, and you're Dr. Rosemead? Repeat that number, Dr. Rosemead, and the address, too."

Maddern reviewed his notes as the doctor spoke, verifying the information he had already been given.

"Sure," he said. "I understand, it's not life-threatening, but you've got to talk to the mother. Right. We'll get someone on it right away. You bet. No problem."

He dropped the line and reached for the duty roster, running his finger down the list, checking the availability of cars and deputies.

"What's going on?" Brandon asked.

"Car accident. Out on the reservation. A kid's been hurt, but not seriously. Needs a few stitches is all. Unfortunately, they took him out to the Indian Health Service in Sells. The doc there can't lift a finger because the kid's an Anglo. They've tried reaching the mother by phone. Ma Bell says the line's off hook."

"I'll go," Brandon Walker offered at once.

"You? How come? You're Homicide. I already told you, the kid's not hurt bad."

"I'll go," Walker insisted.

"You really don't want to go home, do you? But don't bother with this. I've got a car out by Gates Pass right now."

"Gates Pass?" Brandon said. "Doesn't she still live in Topawa?"

Maddern did a double take. "You know the lady?"

Walker nodded grimly. "From years ago."

"If you want to take her the bad news, then, be my guest," Maddern continued. "But the address they gave me doesn't say Topawa. It's out by Gates Pass somewhere. The telephone number is a Tucson exchange."

The dispatcher scribbled the phone number and address on another slip of paper and handed it over to Brandon just as the switchboard lit up again. Maddern turned to answer it, waving Brandon away. "Later," he said.

Brandon Walker didn't return to his cubicle. Instead, he hurried directly out to the parking lot where his unmarked Ford Galaxy waited. It was almost dark, but the temperature inside the closed vehicle was still unbearably hot. Before leaving the lot, Walker rolled down all the windows. Switching on the air-conditioning was pointless since it didn't work. Repairs on grunts' cars got shunted to the bottom of the priority list when it came to departmental mechanics.

The air conditioner was out of order, but the high-output, police-pursuit engine roared to life as soon as Walker turned the key in the ignition. He peeled out of the parking lot in a hail of loose gravel and headed for Gates Pass, driving on automatic, his mind occupied elsewhere.

Diana Ladd. It had to be her. It didn't seem possible that there would be two women in town by that same name. She had made a big impression on him. How long ago was it? June? Jesus, it had to be almost seven years ago since the first time he saw her. He had forgotten about her between times—had forced himself to forget because some things are too painful to remember.

When had she moved to town? Not town exactly. The address on Gates Pass Road indicated an almost wilderness area well outside Tucson's city limits. She would have had more company in the Teachers' Compound in Topawa, living in the shabby mobile home where he had first met her. Had she stopped teaching on the reservation then? Maybe she had taken a job with District Number One in Tucson. God, she'd been pretty. Even six months pregnant she'd been pretty. And defiant.

He remembered the last time he saw her as though it were yesterday. They were standing in the crowded hallway of the Pima County Courthouse after the judge announced Andrew Carlisle's plea-bargaining agreement. The old Indian lady—what was her name?—was sitting on a bench off to the side. Diana Ladd came up to him, grasping his sleeve with one hand while the other rested on her bulging belly. He avoided her gaze, not wanting to see the betrayal and hurt in her eyes, but he couldn't evade the accusation in her voice.

"How could you let them do it?" she demanded, outraged, indignant. "How could you let them get away with it?"

"There was nothing I could do," he answered lamely. "I didn't have a choice."

"We all have choices," she'd returned icily.

Drawing herself stiffly erect, she marched away from him, walking with the awkward dignity of the profoundly pregnant. She went straight to the bench and helped the old Indian lady to her feet. The two women walked past him, the younger carefully leading the elder, as though the old woman were blind or crippled or both.

And Brandon Walker, left alone in the midst of a milling crowd, looked after them and wondered what he could have done differently. Of course, that was years ago now. He was no longer as green, as naive. He knew now that Diana Ladd had probably been right all along. There were things he could have done, arms he could have twisted, debts he could have called that might have made a difference.

A golden sliver of moon peeked over the jagged-toothed canyon as he drove the winding road to Gates Pass. He had no delusions that Diana Ladd would appreciate his coming to find her and tell her the news. Hearing about the accident from someone she knew, even someone she didn't like, would be less hurtful than hearing it from a complete stranger.

In his gut, he understood that, but Brandon Walker wasn't looking forward to the meeting.

He knew Diana Ladd hadn't forgiven him for what had happened, and that was no surprise. He hadn't forgiven himself.

At that time, long ago, Rattlesnake's bite had no poison. The children laughed at him and played with him and tossed him in the air. Sometimes, for a joke, they would pull out all his teeth. This made Ko'oi, Rattlesnake, very unhappy.

One day Ko'oi went crying to First Born. "The children are always teasing me and making me miserable. Please change me so I can go live somewhere else and be happy."

First Born had already changed many of the animals, so he took Rattlesnake, pulled out all his teeth, and threw them away. They fell in the desert, and overnight grew into the mountains we call Ko'oi Tahtami, or Rattlesnake's Tooth.

In the morning, First Born gathered up a few small, sharp rocks from these mountains and threw them into some water. They grew sharp and white and long, just the way rattlesnake teeth are today. First Born gave them to Rattlesnake and said to him, "Here. Now the children will no longer torment you, but from this day on, you will have no friends. You must crawl on your belly and live alone. If anything comes near you, you must bite it and kill it."

And that, nawoj, *my Friend, is the story of how Ko'oi, Rattlesnake, got his teeth.*

In a lifetime of serial matrimony, Myrna Louise Spaulding had worked her way through a list of last names far too numerous to remember. Like overly zealous Chicago voters, she cast her ballot in favor of marriage, voting early and often. She always married for love, never for money. She always divorced for the same reason—true love— which may have been true at the time but never lasted long. Myrna Louise wasn't a risk-taker. She never slipped one wedding band off her much-used ring finger without having a pretty good replacement prospect lined up and waiting in the wings.

Her son, Andrew Carlisle, found his mother's peculiar penchant disturbing at first, humorous later, and ultimately boring. In his opinion, if Myrna Louise had been any good at the game, she would have seen to it that she picked up a few good pieces of change here and there along the way. But no. With one minor exception, she always targeted bums and ne'er-do-wells who were far worse off mentally and financially than she was.

Her last husband, Jake Spaulding—who also happened to be her late husband—had managed to roll over and die before the divorce was final. Much to her stepchildren's dismay, Jake died without first revising his will. He left Myrna Louise in sole possession of the little family house on Weber Drive.

As a neighborhood, Weber Drive didn't have much to recommend it, unless you liked the multi-colored jack-in-the-box on the corner, but the house constituted a roof over Myrna Louise's head for a change. On her meager pension and with the widow's mite she had lucked into after Jake Spaulding's timely death, she figured she'd barely be able to cover both taxes and utilities.

A bit down-at-the-heels, Weber Drive still managed to be respectable enough, and even a bit self-righteous. Myrna Louise had made tentative overtures of friendship toward some of the neighbors. She was determined to fit in here, to really belong someplace at last. Her son's unexpected arrival was a definite fly in the ointment. Those very same neighbors might well pull the welcome mat right out from under the mother of an ex-con.

"Why, what in the world are you doing here?" a stunned Myrna Louise demanded, covering her dismay as best she could when the opened door revealed her son waiting on her doorstep.

"I came to see my mama," he said with a smile. "I thought you'd be glad to see me after all this time."

"Oh, I am. Of course I am. Come in. Come in here right now. But why didn't you let me know you were coming?"

"Because I didn't know, not for sure, anyway. They like to keep people guessing until the very last minute. It makes for better control."

She dragged Andrew into the living room and stood looking fuzzily up at him. Myrna Louise should have taken to wearing glasses years before, but she usually couldn't afford it, and besides, she was far too vain. A driver's license might have forced her into glasses earlier, but she'd never owned a car, not until now. Jake's car was still out in the garage. She planned to sell it if money ever got really tight.

"So are you out on parole, or what?" she asked petulantly.

"I'm out period, Mama. Free as a bird."

"Good," she said. She paused uncertainly. "Andrew, I'd really like it if the neighbors didn't find out. About where you've been, I mean. Not that I'm ashamed or anything, it's just that it'd be easier . . ."

"I'm still your son," he began.

"Don't let's be difficult. You see, you've been having all that mail sent here, all those things for Phil Wharton, whoever he is. I've been saving them, keeping them here for you just like you said. Who is he anyway, a friend of yours or what?"

"It's a pen name, Mama. I couldn't very well send things out with my own name on them, now could I."

"Thank goodness," she said.

"What do you mean?"

"Well, that's sort of what I've been pretending. That you were him, or at least that Phil Wharton was my son."

"You've been telling your friends that I'm Phil?"

Myrna Louise cringed at the hard edge of anger in his voice. "I didn't mean any harm, Andrew. One of the ladies was here when the mail came one day. She saw it on the table and asked about it. I told her that you're a journalist who's been out of the country working on assignment and that you'd be home soon."

"So you've lied to them?"

"Please, Andrew, I . . ."

Andrew had her dead to rights, but the idea of his mother making up that kind of whopper was really pretty funny. He decided to let her off the hook. After all, it was his first night home.

"It's okay, Mama. The name's Phil, remember?"

Breathing a sigh of relief, Myrna Louise smiled gratefully. He was going to go along with it and not embarrass her in front of her friends. She wouldn't be expelled from the morning coffee break after all.

At once she switched into full motherly mode. "Have you had any dinner? Are you hungry?"

Sure he was hungry. Why wouldn't he be hungry? It had been a busy day, a trying day. Besides, hiking up and down mountains always gives a man one hell of an appetite.

Diana waited until the sun went down before she tried going up on the roof to work on the cooler. No wonder people called them swamp coolers. The thick, musty odor was unmistakable, gagging. Diana climbed up the ladder armed with a bottle of PineSol. She raised one side of the cooler and poured several glugs of powerful disinfectant into the water. The oily, piny scent wasn't a big improvement, but it helped.

After returning the side of the cooler to its proper position, Diana stood for a few moments on the flat, graveled roof to survey her domain. The wild and forbidding front yard remained much as it had been when she first bought the place. An overgrown thicket of head-high prickly pear cast bizarre, donkey-eared shadows in the frail moonlight. She had spent far more effort in back, where both yard and patio were surrounded by a massive six-foot-high rock wall. The end result was almost a fortress. Inside that barrier, she felt safe and protected.

The house and outbuildings, sturdily constructed in the early twentieth century and lovingly remodeled during the twenties, had originally belonged to one of Pima County's pioneer families. When family fortunes fell on hard times and when surviving family members dwindled to only one dotty eighty-year-old lady, most of the land, with the exception of the house, cook shack, and barn, had been deeded over to the county as payment for back taxes. That had been during the late forties. The old lady, who wasn't expected to live much longer anyway, had been allowed lifetime tenancy in the house, with her estate authorized to sell off the remainder after her death.

The old lady confounded all predictions and lived to a ripe 101, refusing to leave the walled confines of the compound until the very end, but letting the place fall to wrack and ruin around her. She died, and the wreckage went up for sale at almost the same time Gary Ladd's life-insurance proceeds came into Diana's hands.

After spending her entire childhood in housing tied to her father's job, Diana Ladd wanted desperately to escape the mobile home in the

Topawa Teachers' Compound housing, to bring her baby home to a house that belonged to her rather than to her employer. She jumped at the chance to buy the derelict old house.

The realtor had done his best to dissuade her, patiently pointing out all the things that were wrong with the place. It was full of garbage—of dead bread wrappers and empty tin cans and layers of old newspapers six feet deep. The plaster was falling off the lath in places, windows were cracked and broken, the roof leaked, and the toilet in the only bathroom had quit working. Throughout the house, failing wiring was a nightmare of jury-rigged repairs, but Diana Ladd was not to be deterred. She bought the place, warts and all, and she and Rita Antone set about fixing it up as best they could.

Six years later, the remodel was stalled for lack of money. To solve that problem, Diana had temporarily set aside home-improvement projects in favor of finishing her book. Writing it was pure speculation, of course. She had made some preliminary and reasonably favorable inquiries, but the book wasn't sold yet. She hoped that when she did sign a contract, she'd be able to hire a contractor to complete some of the heavier work.

Standing on the roof, she watched the approach of an oncoming pair of headlights on the road overhead. Approaching her driveway, the vehicle slowed to a crawl and the turn signals came on. As the unfamiliar car turned off the blacktop, Diana Ladd suffered a momentary panic. For years, she had steeled herself against the possibility of

Andrew Carlisle's coming after her in the same way she had prepared herself for the possibility of a snakebite. With Carlisle, as with the neighborhood's indigenous snakes, you assumed a certain amount of risk and did what you could to protect yourself.

Rattlesnakes rattle a warning before they strike, and so had Andrew Carlisle. The last time she had seen the man in the hallway at the courthouse, he had mouthed a silent threat at her when his accompanying deputy wasn't looking. "I'll be back," his lips had said noiselessly.

Over the years, she had learned to live with that threat, treating it seriously but keeping her fear firmly in the background of her consciousness. Most of the time, anyway, but the arrival of unfamiliar cars always brought it to the forefront.

The tires bounced down the rough, rocky road, and the headlights caught her in a piercing beam of light, blinding her, trapping her silhouetted against the night sky. She stood there paralyzed and vulnerable, while fear rose like bile in her throat.

From near the base of the ladder, she heard Bone's low-throated warning growl. The urgency of the sound prompted her to action, jolted her out of her panic. The headlights moved away. In sudden pitch darkness, she scrambled clumsily toward the ladder.

"Bone," she called softly, hoping to reach the ground in time to catch the dog's collar and keep him with her, but the tall, gangly hound didn't wait. Still growling, he raced to where the rocky, six-foot wall with its wooden gate intersected the corner of the house. The wall would have stopped most dogs cold, but not the Bone, a dog with the size and agility of a small mountain goat. Bounding from rock to rock, he scrambled up several outcroppings to the top, then flung himself off the other side.

As the car pulled to a stop in the front drive, the dog hurled himself out of the darkness toward the car, lunging like a ferocious, tooth-filled shadow at the front driver's side tire. Using the dog's attack as cover, Diana slipped into the house unnoticed. She was already in the living room when the trapped driver laid on the horn.

Cranking open the side panel of the front window, she called, "Who is it?"

The driver must have rolled down his window slightly, because the dog left off attacking the tire and reared up on his hind legs at the side of the car, barking ferociously.

"Call off this goddamned mutt before he breaks my window!" an outraged voice demanded.

"Who is it?" Diana insisted.

"Detective Walker," the voice answered. "Now call off the dog, Diana. I've got to talk to you."

As soon as she heard the name, Diana recognized Brandon Walker's voice. A sudden whirlwind of memory brought the buried history back, all of it, robbing her of breath, leaving her shaken, unable to speak.

His voice softened. "Diana, please. Call off the dog."

She took a deep breath and hurried to the door. "Oh'o. *lhab*," she ordered in Papago, stepping out onto the porch. "Bone. Here."

With a single whined objection and a warning glare over his shoulder at the intruding car, the dog went to her at once and lay down at her feet.

Brandon Walker switched off the headlights and the engine. Cautiously, he opened the door, peering warily at the woman and dog waiting on the lighted porch.

"Are you sure it's all right? Shouldn't you tie him up or something? That dog's a menace."

"Bone's all right," she returned, making no move to restrain the animal. "Why are you here? What do you want?"

"I've got to talk to you, Diana. There's been an accident."

"An accident? Where? Who?"

"Out on the reservation. Your son David's been hurt. Not bad, but . . ."

"Davy? Oh, my God. Where is he? What's happened?"

Hearing the alarm in Diana's voice, the dog rose once more to his feet with another threatening growl. Diana grabbed Bone's collar and shoved him into the house, closing the door behind him.

With the dog safely locked away, Brandon Walker moved closer. "It's not as bad as it sounds," he reassured her quickly, "but the Indian Health Service doctor can't do anything about either treating him or letting him go until they talk to you. Your phone isn't working."

Diana's hand went to her throat. She looked stricken. "I forgot to put it back on the hook when I quit working." She started toward the house, leaving him standing there.

"Wait. Where are you going?"

"To call the hospital and get my car keys," she said. Two minutes later, she emerged from the house and headed toward her car, a tiny white Honda.

"Why don't you let me drive," Brandon offered, motioning toward the far more powerful Galaxy. "We'll make better time, especially if we use the lights."

She wavered for a moment, vacillating between driving herself and accepting his offer of help.

"What did the doctor say?" Brandon pressed.

"That Davy will have to go on into Tucson for stitches."

"See there? Let me drive. That way, you can take care of the boy."

The detective's good sense overcame Diana Ladd's stubborn independence. Without another word, she headed for his car.

Later, as the Ford roared down the highway, lights flashing overhead, Diana noticed she was still holding the partially full bottle of PineSol. She clearly remembered putting it down when she used the phone, but in her frantic rush to leave the house, she must have unconsciously picked it up again. As unobtrusively as possible, she slipped the offending bottle out of sight under the seat of the speeding Galaxy. Diana Ladd was upset, and she didn't want the detective to realize exactly how upset she was.

Fat Crack Ortiz owned the only gas station in Sells. He also owned the only tow truck. Consequently, he was the first member of Rita Antone's family to be notified of the accident on Kitt Peak Road.

After towing the demolished Jimmy back to the station, he hurried straight to the hospital. One of a handful of Christian Scientists on the reservation, Fat Crack subscribed to neither medical doctors nor medicine men, but he was prepared to be open-minded as far as other people's beliefs were concerned.

As soon as he turned up in the emergency-room lobby, one of the nurses, Effie Joaquin, recognized him. "Is it serious?" he asked.

Effie nodded. "It sure is. She's ruptured her spleen and broken some ribs and one arm. There may be other internal injuries as well. She went into cardiac arrest in the ambulance. Do you want to see her before she goes into surgery?"

"If I can," Fat Crack said.

The nurse ushered him into the emergency room. Rita, looking pale and shrunken, lay on a gurney with an IV bag draining into her flaccid right arm. The other arm was swathed in bulky, bloody bandages. He walked over to the gurney and bent close to Rita's head.

"*Ni-thahth?*" he whispered gently in her ear,

speaking the traditional words for his mother's elder sister.

Her eyes fluttered open, darted around wildly for a moment, then settled on his face. *"Ni-mad,"* she returned. "Nephew."

"I will pray for you," he said, reaching out and touching her grasping fingers, feeling his own power flowing into her. His auntie did not believe according to his lights, but Fat Crack's faith was strong enough for both of them.

"Olhoni," she whispered.

Her nephew had not heard the name before. At first he didn't understand what she was saying. He thought she was still worried about the spooked steer that had caused the accident.

"He's fine," Fat Crack reassured her. "You didn't hit him at all."

Rita shook her head impatiently and wet her parched lips. "The boy," she said. "Davy. He's outside. Stay with him. Until his mother comes."

"Sure, *Ni-thahth,*" he told her. "I will see that he isn't left alone."

Rita's eyes closed then as Effie came to get the gurney. "The operating room is ready now," she said. "You'll have to wait outside."

"Yes," Fat Crack said. "I will wait."

Myrna Louise fixed her son a quick dinner of scrambled eggs, bacon, and toast, washed down with a tumbler of her own rotgut vodka, then she showed him into the tiny second bedroom.

"Jake's clothes are still in the closet there," she

said. "I haven't gotten around to calling Goodwill to come pick them up. Maybe some of it will fit."

Andrew Carlisle waited until his mother left the room and closed the door behind her before he hurried over to the bed. He groaned with disappointment. Three large self-addressed envelopes lay there on the chenille bedspread—manuscript-sized envelopes—each address, written in his own clear hand, said *Mr. Philip Wharton.*

Damn! So none of the three so-called literary agents had had balls enough to take it. He ripped open the envelopes one by one. A copy of his manuscript, *A Less Than Noble Savage*, was in each, along with three separate form letters saying thanks, but no thanks. For obvious reasons, he hadn't used his old agent, but these jerks were treating him like a rank amateur.

Damn them all straight to hell anyway! Who the hell did they think they were, turning him down with nothing more than a form letter? Not even a personal note? They didn't know what they were missing—who they were missing—but he'd show them.

Hands trembling with suppressed rage, he tore each of the rejection slips into tiny pieces and threw the resulting confetti into the garbage. Those stupid bastards didn't know good writing when they saw it. They were too busy selling the public on half-baked, vapid fantasy/mysteries written by limp-wristed creeps who never once bloodied their own hands.

What had Andrew Carlisle always drummed

into his students' heads? Write what you know. If you want to know how it feels to be a murderer, try choking the life out of something and see how hard it is, how much effort it takes, and see how you feel about it afterward.

He felt a sudden stirring in his groin as he remembered Margaret and how it had felt to drain the life out of her. He knew now, from going through her purse and car, that the blonde's name was Margaret, Margaret Danielson—Margie for short.

The pulsing urge came on him suddenly. He forced himself to undress and lie on the bed and just think about her. He allowed himself to masturbate until he found release, because it was far too soon for him to do anything else.

Rita opened her eyes. A brilliant white light was shining above her. Around the periphery of her vision, several people in green caps and face masks stood over her. All she could see were eyes—eyes and a few anxious frowns, no one she recognized, no one she knew.

A man leaned over her. She smelled the sharp, pungent odor of aftershave. He patted her arm gently. "It's going to be fine, Rita. Everything's going to be okay."

Dr. Rosemead meant his reassuring touch and softly uttered words to offer his patient some comfort. They had exactly the opposite effect. She shrank away from his fingers, her whole body convulsing and struggling against the restraints that bound her to the operating table even though every movement sent sharp stabs of pain through her body.

"Anesthetic!" Dr. Rosemead ordered sharply. "For God's sake, give her something!"

Davy sat quietly in the busy waiting room next to the mountain of a man he knew to be Nana *Dahd*'s nephew. The cut on his head had mostly stopped bleeding, although his hair was still sticky in spots where more blood had oozed out since the last time someone had cleaned it off. One of the nurses had said he would probably need stitches. He wondered if they used a sewing machine or maybe just a needle and thread.

His head ached, and when he tried to move around, he felt dizzy, so he sat still. The man next to him spoke to him briefly in Papago when he first sat down, then he seemed to go away completely. His body was there, but his mind seemed far, far away. It made Davy think of the way his mother was sometimes when she was working, so he contented himself with sitting and watching.

Being in that room was almost like being invisible. The people around him glanced at him and then looked quickly away. They spoke to one another in Papago, and the things they said made him realize they didn't know he understood what they were saying. They called Rita by another name, Hejel Wi'ithag, which means Left Alone. They called him by another name, too— Me'akam Mad, or Killer's Child. He couldn't understand why they called him by such a strange, mean name, or why they seemed not to like him.

Davy was tired, and his head hurt. He wanted Rita, but the nurses said she was in surgery. They said she was badly hurt. And where was his mother? Why wasn't she here? Just thinking about it made fat tears try to leak out the corners of his eyes. He squinted hard to keep that from happening. He sighed and tried to swallow the huge lump in his throat.

For the first time in more than an hour, the huge man next to him stirred and looked down at the little boy. Then, raising his broad, bare arm, he pulled Davy against him.

At first Davy started to resist, but only when he was resting against the enveloping warmth of the man's massive chest did the boy realize how cold he was and how tired. He stopped struggling and let his eyes close.

Pillowed against Fat Crack Ortiz's massive bulk, Davy Ladd fell fast asleep.

5

THE CAR WINDOWS were open, allowing in the cool night air as well as a noisy, windy roar that made conversation impossible. That was fine with Diana. She had no desire to talk to Brandon Walker, whose very presence unleashed the disturbing flood of memories now surging through her awareness. Blind to the nighttime desert flowing by outside the speeding Ford, Diana was totally preoccupied with pieces of the past that jerked like disjointed figures caught in the brilliant flashes of a strobe of recollection. The spinning figures danced in her mind's eye without order or definition.

Diana Lee Cooper was hard at work in the ditto room that Friday morning when the news came. Everyone in the English Department was so stunned that they all abandoned ship without anyone thinking to come tell her, and she was far too busy to notice.

In addition to the regular batch of departmental quizzes and outlines, Dr. Hunsington, the diminutive head of the English Department, had a twenty-five-page syllabus to put out—seventy-five copies of each. Once she finished running off Halitosis Hunsington's syllabus, it had to be collated and stapled.

Well after noon, she finally completed the last of the stapling and emerged into a strangely deserted hallway. Laden with an armload of slippery paper, she was surprised to find the door to the English Department closed and locked. A hastily hand-penciled note tucked in one corner of the darkened window announced, CLOSED UNTIL MONDAY. H. F. HUNSINGTON.

"Closed?" she demanded of the inexplicably darkened window and empty hallway. "What do you mean, closed?"

Diana looked around and found herself absolutely alone. Where had everyone gone? Her first reaction was that maybe her father's dire predictions of nuclear holocaust had come true, and everyone had disappeared into bomb shelters, but she quickly talked herself out of that one. Had nuclear warfare broken out, surely she would have heard sirens or some other kind of audible warning. There had been nothing.

As a dollar-an-hour, fifteen-hour-a-week work-study student, Diana Cooper had no key to the University of Oregon's English Department office. What was she supposed to do with all the dittos she had run off, she wondered, take them home with her? On her bike?

That was crazy. The office had been full of people earlier when she left for the ditto room—

Dr. Hunsington, his secretary, the receptionist, and a whole collection of professors, instructors, and teaching assistants, all milling around the receptionist's desk, waiting to collect their daily quota of departmental mail to say nothing of their semimonthly pay checks. So where were they now?

She started to leave the dittoed papers by the locked door while she went to find someone with a key. She quickly discarded that idea. Several exams had been entrusted to her for dittoing purposes that morning. Diana took her charge of exam security very seriously, and she was unwilling to let the tests out of sight for even a moment. Taking the entire stack with her, she started down the hall.

Halfway down the long corridor, she heard the echo of solitary footsteps coming up the stairs at the far end. Diana was immensely relieved when Gary Ladd, one of the teaching assistants, materialized out of the stairwell. He turned immediately and started toward his office in the T. A. bullpen at the far end of an adjacent wing.

"Mr. Ladd," Diana called. "Yoo-hoo."

He stopped, turned, and came back toward her, his head cocked questioningly to one side. "What are you doing here?" he asked. "I thought everybody went home."

Garrison Walther Ladd, III, was by far the best-looking male teaching assistant in the English Department's stable. With aquiline, tanned good looks and lank blond hair, he wore expensive but rumpled clothing with offhand, upper-class ease. Garrison Ladd knew he was hot stuff. Breathless coeds who came within his sphere of influence found him irresistible. They tended to hie themselves off in search of obliging physicians willing to issue prescriptions for birth-control pills.

This was Diana's second year as an undergraduate student assistant in the English Department at the U. of O. During that time she, too, had admired Gary Ladd, but only from afar. For one thing, she had convinced herself that someone from Joseph, Oregon, could never be in Gary Ladd's league. For another, he was a graduate student while she was only a lowly sophomore.

He looked at her now with his tanned brow furrowed into a puzzled frown. "Why didn't you go home when everybody else did?"

"I'm working," she said. "At least I'm trying to work. I've got this whole stack of papers to deliver, but the door to the office is locked. Do you have a key? Where'd everybody go?"

Gary Ladd reached into a jacket pocket, extracted a key ring, then took two steps down the hallway before stopping and turning on Diana. "Nobody told you, did they?"

"Told me what?" she returned. "I've been in the ditto room. When I came out, everything was closed up. Even the classrooms are empty. What's going on?"

"Somebody shot President Kennedy."

"No!"

The very idea was incredible, unthinkable. Assassinations happened in other parts of the world—wild, terrible, jungle-filled places like South America or Africa—but not here in the good old U.S. of A. "Where?" she managed to stammer. "When?"

"This morning. In Dallas. They already caught the guy who did it."

"Is he all right?"

Garrison Ladd looked mystified. "He's fine. They've got him in jail."

"No, not him. I mean President Kennedy. Is he all right?"

Gary Ladd shook his head, while his gray-blue eyes darkened in sympathy. "He's dead, Diana. President Kennedy is dead. They just swore in LBJ on the plane headed back to Washington. Come on. Let's go drop off your papers. They must be heavy."

An Indian Health Services nurse hovered over Rita's bed-bound form, but the old woman's mind was far away in another time and place.

Dancing Quail hid behind her mother's full skirts as the horse-drawn wagon pulled up beside the low-slung adobe house. It was the end of *Shopol Eshabig Mashad*, the short planting month. For days the children of Ban Thak had worried that soon Big Eddie Lopez, the tribal policeman, would come to take many of them away to boarding school.

Seven-year-old Dancing Quail didn't want to leave home. She didn't want to go to school. Some of the other children had told her about it, about how they weren't allowed to speak to their friends in their own language, about how they had to dress up in stiff, uncomfortable clothing.

Her parents had argued about school. Alice Antone, who sometimes worked for the sisters at Topawa, maintained that education was important. Joseph Antone disagreed, taking the more traditional view that all his daughter really needed to know was how to cook beans and make tortillas, how to carry water and make baskets—skills she would learn at home with her mother and grandmother and not at the boarding school in Phoenix.

But when Big Eddie's horse plodded into Ban Thak, Joseph Antone was miles away working in the floodplain fields. Big Eddie came over to the open fire where Alice stirred beans in a handmade pottery crock.

He wiped the sweat from his face. "It sure is hot," he said. "Where is your husband?"

"*Gan,*" Alice said, nodding toward the fields. "Over there."

"Will he be home soon?" Big Eddie asked.

"No," she answered. "Not soon."

"I have come for the children," Big Eddie announced. "To take them to Chuk Shon to catch the train."

Dancing Quail had been to Tucson once with her mother and had found the town noisy and frightening. They had gone to sell her grandmother's *ollas*—heavy, narrow-necked pottery crocks that kept water sweet and cool even through the heat of the summer. Alice had walked the dusty streets carrying a burden basket piled high with *ollas*, while Dancing Quail had trailed along behind. Once home in Ban Thak, the child had not asked to go again.

Quietly now, Dancing Quail attempted to slip away, but Alice stopped her. *"Ni-mad.* Daughter, come back. Go quickly and get your other dress. You are to go with this man. Hurry. Do not make him wait."

The huge policeman looked down at Dancing Quail with considerable empathy. He, too, had been frightened the first time he left home for school. Dancing Quail was one of those children who would have to be watched closely for fear she might run away before they could put her on the train. It would be better if Dancing Quail weren't the first child he loaded into the wagon.

"Give her something to eat," Big Eddie said. "I will go get the others. It won't be so bad if she's not the only one."

He climbed back into the wagon and urged the waiting horse forward. Alice turned to her daughter, who still hadn't moved. "Go now," she said. "Roll your other dress in your blanket."

"Ni-je'e," Dancing Quail began. "Mother, please . . ."

Alice stopped her with a stubborn shake of her head. "The sisters say you should go. You will go."

Dejectedly, but without further argument, Dancing Quail did as she'd been told.

Her grandmother, Oks Amichuda, which means Understanding Woman, had lived a full, busy life before coming to live, in her old age, with her son and daughter-in-law. No longer able to work and cook, Understanding Woman, like other old women, had taken to sitting, either in the shade or the sun, depending upon the weather, and making pottery and baskets, which Alice was able to sell or trade.

From her pottery-making place, Understanding Woman had seen and heard all that was said. Oks Amichuda sided with her son on the subject of Dancing Quail's education, but an old woman who lives under her daughter-in-law's roof must be circumspect. She got up and hobbled after her grandchild. In the shadowy adobe house, she went to the storage basket in which she kept her few treasures. Understanding Woman extracted something and brought it to where Dancing Quail was rolling her dress into the blanket.

"He'eni," the old woman said urgently. "Here! Take it."

Dancing Quail looked up. Her grandmother was holding out a small, tightly woven medicine basket.

The child's eyes grew large. *"Ni-kahk,"* she said, shaking her head. "Grandmother. Not your medicine basket."

"Yes," Understanding Woman insisted, "to keep your spirit safe."

So the medicine basket went into the bundle. When Dancing Quail emerged from the house, Alice handed her a rolled tortilla filled with beans. Soon Big Eddie returned, bringing with him five other children from the village. Bravely, Dancing

Quail climbed into the wagon behind him. She didn't look back. She didn't want her mother to see that she was crying.

Brandon Walker found the noisy silence in the car disturbing. His mother, Louella, who had never suffered an introspective moment in her whole life, spoke at tedious length about anything and everything. Women who didn't talk made the detective nervous.

What was Diana Ladd thinking about as she sat there wordlessly on the far side of the car with the wind whipping long tendrils of auburn hair around her face? She seemed oblivious to it and made no effort to brush it away.

Finally, he could stand it no longer. "When did you quit teaching on the reservation?" he asked.

She didn't answer, and he glanced in her direction, thinking she had drifted off to sleep, but no, her eyes were open. He tried again, almost shouting to be heard above the rushing wind.

This time Diana turned toward him in acknowledgment. "I didn't quit," she replied. "What made you think that?"

"You're living in Tucson," he returned. "I thought you had free housing with the district as long as you taught out there."

"I wanted a house of my own," she said, and turned her face away from him, effectively cutting off all further conversation.

In 1943, long before the era of sanitary landfills, garbage dumps were still called garbage dumps and bums still scrounged through the accumulated trash, living on whatever crumbs they could scavenge. It was then that the moderately progressive town fathers of Joseph, Oregon, bought the old Stevens place down by the creek to use as the town dump. Through a fluke, the ramshackle old house came with the deal. Initially, the intention was to tear the house down, bulldoze it into the ground, but then someone came up with a better idea.

Everyone in town knew that Iona Anne Dade had made a terrible mistake in marrying Max Cooper—everyone, that is, except perhaps Iona herself, who by then was already alarmingly pregnant with her daughter, Diana. In those days, when good Catholic girls made matrimonial mistakes, they had no choice but to stand pat and make the best of a bad bargain.

So when Max Cooper—an indifferent, sometime logger—was offered the position of garbage-dump caretaker in Joseph, Oregon, it was more as a humanitarian gesture toward his pregnant young wife than it was a vote of confidence about Max's own dubious job skills or work ethic. And when the Stevens house, such as it was, got thrown into the bargain, it was out of deference to Iona's daddy, the late Wayne Dade, who had spent many years loyally serving on the town council.

The ladies of Joseph in a rare show of true Christian charity, for once put aside their differences in creed, rolled up their sleeves, and went to work on the place. Baptists did most of the scrubbing and cleaning, Methodists painted, and Catholics sewed curtains. Even stand-offish Mormons signed on to braid rag rugs for the bare linoleum floors.

From the time Max and Iona Cooper moved into their newly refurbished quarters, Max was known in the town of Joseph as the Garbage Man. In the winter when it was too cold to work in the woods and in the summer when it was too hot, or when he wasn't down at the tavern too drunk to walk, Max Cooper minded the gate, collected the dump fees, and kept the riffraff out. The rest of the time his wife handled it.

Iona Cooper did her housework or gardening, all the while listening for the bell over her kitchen sink that announced someone's arrival at the garbage dump's locked gate. Rain or shine, summer heat or bitter winter's cold, she would drop what she was doing and hurry across the field.

People knew that she was the person who usually opened the gate, who collected the fees, and who returned the change, but no one ever thought of Iona Cooper as the Garbage Woman. She was always Iona Dade Cooper, Wayne's daughter, the lady who sold milk and eggs, who pickled tomatoes and canned peaches, and who always could find some little something in her pantry for the hungry bums who invariably turned up on her doorstep. She baked wedding cakes for hire and sewed matching bridesmaid dresses. And everybody respected her for what she did, because if you were married to a worthless oaf like Max

Cooper, that's what it took to keep a roof over your head.

Nobody ever once mentioned the word *divorce*, least of all Iona Dade Cooper.

Brandon Walker slowed the car when they came onto the open-range part of Highway 86. He knew that in the cool of the evening, livestock would be making its nightly way to water and forage. He didn't want to take any chances.

What was she thinking about, huddled over there against the far door? Was she just worried about her son, or was she thinking about something else—about that time seven years ago when their lives had collided once before, about how he had told her back then that she should trust the system? Diana Ladd had been naive back then. So had he.

Driving along, Brandon himself rehashed the entire case in his head, how Gina Antone—he remembered her name now—was found floating facedown in a retention pond after an all-night rain dance at San Pedro Village. Initial presumption was death by drowning, but subsequent investigation indicated murder. Not only murder, but mutilation and torture as well.

The water hole where the body was found was outside reservation boundaries, so the Pima County Sheriff's Department was called in on the case. Dead Indians didn't count for much around Jack DuShane's Sheriff's Department. As a result, the case was delegated to the newest kid on the block—Brandon Walker, recently returned from Southeast Asia.

Even a novice like Walker found it simple to follow the trail that led to Garrison Ladd, who had been seen at the dance in the company of both the dead woman and a man named Andrew Carlisle, a professor of creative writing from the University of Arizona. As soon as the long arm of the law threatened to close in on them, Gary Ladd took himself out to the desert and put a bullet through his head, leaving his buddy Carlisle to take the rap for both of them.

Under questioning, Carlisle maintained that the two men were just out to have a little harmless fun. "You know how things get out of hand at rain dances," he told the investigators. He maintained the girl was already drinking when they picked her up at Three Points. The three of them went to the dance, sat in the circle, and drank the cactus wine. Afterward, at the girl's insistence, they left the village and stopped off at the water hole to polish off a few beers.

Carlisle claimed that he passed out only to waken later and be unable to find Ladd or the girl anywhere. He made his way back to the pickup and started it up, planning on driving home. He was still so smashed that he didn't realize Gary Ladd had, for some unaccountable reason, tied a rope around the girl's neck and fastened the rope to the bumper of the truck.

After driving only a few feet, he was startled to find Ladd, who had passed out in the bed of the truck, pounding frantically on the window, motioning for Carlisle to stop. Too late they hurried back to check on the girl; Gina Antone was already dead.

Still drunk, the men took her back to the water hole and sat there, drinking warm beer and talking about what to do. Carlisle claimed to know nothing at all about what had happened to the girl's breast. Carlisle took no responsibility for anything else that might have transpired between Gary, Ladd and Gina while he himself was asleep. Carlisle's claim of drunken innocence galled the detective, but without contradictory testimony, he couldn't shake the story.

Throughout the questioning process, Carlisle maintained that they put the body in the water, hoping no one would notice for a while, and that when they did, people would assume Gina had drowned. Things didn't work that way. As soon as the girl's grandmother reported her missing, the people of San Pedro remembered the two drunk *Mil-gahn* who had escorted Gina Antone at the dance. Word was passed along, first to the tribal police, and later to Brandon Walker of the Sheriff's Department.

Much to his dismay, Sheriff DuShane found himself stuck with a solved murder and a very prominent murderer—a University of Arizona professor, no less. Those were complications DuShane hadn't counted on when he assigned Brandon Walker to the case. Offending the university community didn't bode well for DuShane's political future. Several pointed damage-control suggestions were made to Detective Walker advising him to back off. Rather than quitting, Walker renewed his efforts.

He called on Diana Ladd in the aftermath of her husband's suicide. "What about the bite on Gina's breast?" a tearful Diana had demanded when he questioned her not only about the suicide, but also in regard to Gina Antone's death. Word of the grisly mutilation had somehow found its way into newspaper accounts of the murder.

"What about it?" Brandon asked.

"Gary would never do something like that. Never. Isn't there some way to check it, to do an impression of the bite mark and compare it with Gary's dental records? They won't be the same, I know they won't."

Of course, the one ghoulishly mutilating bite wasn't all Gina Antone had suffered, not by any means. There were burns and cuts and signs of innumerable forced entries. But the bite itself could have provided the most telling testimony had Brandon Walker been able to check it, but pertinent information about the bite somehow had disappeared from Gina Antone's file. For years now, that missing piece of paper had haunted Brandon Walker. Would the outcome have been different had it been found?

There was no way to tell for sure, but without it, Andrew Carlisle's lawyer managed to plea-bargain the more serious charges down to one of second-degree rape and voluntary manslaughter. The judge on the case, hard-nosed Judge Clarence Barker, took an immediate and intense dislike to Andrew Carlisle. Barker threw the book at Carlisle anyway, handing out eight years. That much of a stretch was a long time for a first-time offender, especially when the perpetrator was an Anglo and the victim was an Indian, but Barker made it stick, and no amount of appealing changed it.

For some reason Brandon Walker could never fathom, during the legal maneuverings, Diana Ladd became Rita Antone's constant companion and champion. All the while maintaining her own husband's innocence, she made it her business to see that Andrew Carlisle got what was coming to him. She was outraged by the plea-bargaining arrangement. From her point of view, eight years in Florence was a mere pittance of punishment, almost as good as Carlisle getting off scot-free.

Years later, Walker could see that Gary Ladd hadn't exactly got off, either. Dead by his own hand, he went to his grave under a cloud, convicted of suicide and innocent of murder and rape only by the narrow technicality of never having come to trial. Walker considered both Ladd and Carlisle guilty as hell. Both were equally despicable, but most of the burden for their crimes had fallen on Diana Ladd's narrow shoulders.

Justice really was blind, Walker thought humorlessly. Gary Ladd was dead, but his widow was still paying.

Back in the deserted English Department office, standing with his arms crossed, Garrison Walther Ladd leaned against the receptionist's desk regarding Diana's fetching backside with considerable interest while she distributed the packets of dittoed material to the various mailboxes. Knowing he was looking at her made her nervous. A deep flush spread up her neck and across her cheeks, not stopping until it reached the roots of her auburn hair.

"You're serious about what you do, aren't you?"

"Why wouldn't I be?" After what Garrison Ladd had just told her, what else could he expect?

"Most girls your age are more . . . well, light-hearted, I suppose."

She resented his making small talk. After all, the president was dead. Shouldn't they be talking about that? "Most girls don't have to pay their own way," she returned.

"Do you? Really? Pay your own way, I mean."

"No," Diana answered bitterly. "I'm just working to wear out my new clothes."

Garrison Ladd laughed then, blue eyes twinkling with hearty merriment, white teeth flashing in the fluorescent lighting. "You're something else!" he said. "You really are."

She wished he would go away and let her be, but he probably didn't want to be responsible for leaving her alone in the office after the place had been closed up and secured for the weekend. She had wanted to work all five of her scheduled hours that morning and afternoon. Her budget was so tight that she couldn't afford to miss work from any of her three jobs. She only had a few more paychecks to accumulate enough money to pay off next semester's tuition and books.

She finished distributing the dittos and checked the empty box where instructors sometimes left typing for her.

"So what are your plans for the afternoon?" he asked.

She shrugged. "Go back home, I guess. Nobody left any typing for me."

"Want to stop by the I-Hop for a cup of coffee?" he asked. "I don't much feel like working, either."

Diana wanted to point out that not wanting to work and not being able to were two entirely different things. "Sure," she said. "Why not?"

He offered her a ride, but she insisted on bringing her bike. "The I-Hop puts me partway home," she told him. "No point in having to come all the way back here."

"You mean you live off campus and you don't have a car?"

She nodded.

"Like I said before, you're something else."

The gurney wheeled Rita down the hallway from the recovery room. When the movement stopped, Dancing Quail was standing beside a wagon in the broad, dusty street. She watched fearfully as a strange-looking *Mil-gahn* woman— the outing matron—moved toward the children. She was tall and thin with short, bright-colored curls the color of red hawk's tail. Indian hair was usually long and black and glossy, like a horse's tail. Not only was the outing matron's hair red, it was curly, too. She peered sternly down at the children through two round pieces of glass that somehow stayed perched on her nose.

Big Eddie ordered the children out of the wagon. One by one, they tumbled down, taking their small bundles of belongings with them. They lined up alongside the wagon and waited expectantly while the outing matron examined each of them in turn. The woman stopped in front of Dancing Quail and glared down in disapproval. Dancing Quail shook under the white woman's fierce gaze. She stared at the ground, wondering what was the matter. What had she done wrong?

Beside her, some of the other children giggled and whispered. "Dancing Quail has no shoes," one of them said.

Instantly, the woman shushed the speaker, but by then Dancing Quail, too, knew what was wrong. Looking up and down the line, she could see that from somewhere in their bundles, all the other children had managed to find shoes. They were scuffed and ragged, but of all the children, only Dancing Quail still stood with her bare toes poking holes in the soft, dusty ground.

The woman spoke sharply in a strange language.

"She wants to know your name," Big Eddie said in Papago.

Dancing Quail swallowed hard. "E Waila Kakaichu," she began, but the woman cut her off saying something Dancing Quail didn't understand.

"Your papers at the agency say your name is

Rita," Big Eddie explained. "Here in Tucson and in Phoenix, that is your name."

Dancing Quail swallowed hard and tried not to cry. She didn't want another name. She liked her old name.

"Rita," someone was saying. "Rita. Wake up."

The old woman battled Effie Joaquin's summons. She didn't want to wake up. It would have been easier to stay where she was, back in that hot long-ago summer day with her toes warm and bare in the sandy dirt. Rita's throat hurt. She felt sick. One arm wouldn't move at all. It dangled uselessly above her head on some kind of rope and pulley.

"Wake up now. Would you like some ice?"

Effie held up a teaspoon filled with crushed ice and ladled some of it into Rita's mouth. The cold slivers of ice felt good as they slithered down her parched throat.

"Davy . . ." she whispered.

"He's all right," Effie assured her. "Dr. Rosemead is with him right now. So's his mother. She just got here a few minutes ago. They'll take him to a hospital in Tucson for stitches."

"He's not hurt bad?"

"No." Effie smiled. "Not nearly as bad as you."

Rita Antone breathed a huge sigh of relief. The pain it caused in her broken ribs brought tears to her eyes, but she didn't care. Davy was all right. Olhoni was all right.

Dancing Quail's long-ago tears, and Nana *Dahd*'s

new ones, coursed in matching tracks down Rita Antone's weathered cheeks.

When Dr. Rosemead took Diana and David Ladd into an examining room, Brandon Walker made his way to the pay phone in the corner. It was almost nine, but even so, he had to wait his turn before he could use the phone. There were two Indians in line ahead of him.

His mother's answering voice was sharp and angry. He knew he was in trouble as soon as she picked up the phone.

"Hi, Mom," he said brightly. "How's it going?"

"Why did you take so long to call back?" Louella demanded.

"I couldn't help it, Mom. I'm at work. We've been busy."

"When will you be home?"

"That's hard to say. I'm out at Sells right now."

"Sells! Out on the reservation? Are those Indians busy killing one another again?"

"It's a car accident," he explained patiently. "I'm just helping out."

"Well, it's great that you have time to help those Indians. What about your parents?"

"That's why I'm calling. What do you need?"

"Five checks are missing from the checkbook. I've asked your father what he did with them. He says he doesn't know."

"Is it possible that you wrote checks and forgot to write them down?"

Louella Walker's response was as predictable as it was arch. "Certainly not! I don't *forget* to write down checks. You know me better than that."

"Maybe you should take my advice and close that account."

Brandon and his mother had had several heated arguments about his parents' joint checking account since the previous month, when it had been seriously overdrawn by several checks. Without consulting anyone else, Toby Walker had made a number of wild purchases, including an even dozen Radio Flyer wagons and two new couches and chairs. Sending back the couches and chairs had been easy. Returning wagons to a mail-order house had been far more difficult.

"You know I can't do that," Louella countered. "I couldn't possibly do such a thing to your father."

Then you're going to have to suffer the consequences, Brandon felt like saying. Sometimes his mother seemed like a willful child—both his parents did—and he was losing patience.

"Write down the missing numbers," he said. "We'll call the bank in the morning and put a stop-payment on them."

"But that'll cost too much money."

"Not as much as sending back another set of wagons."

"All right," she agreed reluctantly. "When will you be home?"

"I don't know," he answered. "Late probably."

"Should I leave your dinner out on the counter?"

"No," he told her. By the time he got home, Brandon Walker didn't think he'd be hungry.

* * *

Andrew Carlisle waited until he thought his mother was asleep. Then, clad in Jake Spaulding's red flannel robe, he tiptoed back down the short hallway to the cluttered bathroom. He rummaged through a drawer until he found what he needed—a pair of scissors as well as a razor and a new package of blades.

One careful handful at a time, he began cutting off his hair, shearing it off as close to his scalp as he could. He didn't hear or see his mother come up to the open doorway. The option of leaving even a bathroom door open behind him was still a sensation worth savoring.

"Andrew," Myrna Louise said with a frown. "What in the world are you doing?"

"Cutting my hair."

"I can see that, but it's terrible. It's all clumpy."

"This is just the top layer. When I finish with the scissors, I'm going to shave the rest of it off with a razor."

"Why?"

"Because I want to be Yul Brynner when I grow up. Don't all women think Yul Brynner is sexy?"

"I don't. I don't like bald men."

"But you'll still like me, won't you, Mama?"

"I suppose," she sighed.

He returned to the haircut while she continued to watch. "You know, I still have it," she said musingly, almost dreamily.

"Have what?"

She hesitated before answering. "Your baby

curl. From your very first haircut. I've kept it in my music box all these years. No matter where I've lived, I've always kept that curl with me."

This revelation surprised Andrew Carlisle. "No shit," he said.

"Why, Andrew!" Myrna Louise exclaimed indignantly. "You know better than to speak to your mother that way."

"Sorry," he returned. "After a while, you get used to not having a mother around."

He hadn't deliberately set out to hurt her feelings, but instantly her eyes filled with tears.

"You know I would have come to see you if I could have. Florence is so far away from here, and you know how I hate to ride buses. Besides, tickets cost so much."

She was crying now, leaning against the doorjamb and sobbing brokenly.

Andrew went to her and took her in his arms. "It's all right, Mama. I didn't expect you to show up there. It was a terrible place. It would have given you nightmares."

"It did anyway," she responded. "I had nightmares the whole time you were gone."

6

*T*HIS IS DETECTIVE Walker, Davy," Diana Ladd said, introducing her son to Brandon when the session in the Indian Health Service examining room was finally over. "He's giving us a ride back to Tucson."

"Detective?" Davy asked. He looked warily up at Brandon Walker through long blond lashes. "Are you a real policeman?"

"Yes, I am." The detective nodded. Little kids were usually dazzled once they understood they were talking to the genuine article. As far as children were concerned, detectives were something rare and wonderful who existed only in the exotic worlds of television or the comics.

"Not only that," Walker added with a grin, "you're going to get to ride back to Tucson in a real police car."

David Ladd's reaction was diametrically opposed to what Walker expected. The child scuttled away from both the detective and his mother, pausing only when he had planted himself firmly beside a bemused Dr. Rosemead, who was still standing in the doorway of the examining room.

"No," Davy declared adamantly. "I don't want to."

"We have to," his mother said. "You heard the doctor say you can't stay here."

Davy had listened while Dr. Rosemead explained why non-Indians couldn't be treated by the Indian Health Service. The boy couldn't understand why Big Toe Indians didn't count since that's what Rita said he was, but right then being a Big Toe Indian wasn't his biggest worry. The alarming presence of a detective was.

"I'll go in Rita's truck," Davy insisted. "I'll go with my mom."

"Rita's truck is broken, remember?" Diana explained patiently. "And I didn't bring my car."

The boy glared up at the tall detective with the funny short red brush of mustache marching across his upper lip. "Are you going to take us to jail?" Davy asked.

"To jail? Of course not," Brandon Walker answered. He wondered where Davy Ladd would have got such a strange idea.

Diana Ladd laughed outright. "Come on, Davy, don't be silly. Detective Walker's just going to give us a ride back home, then I'll take you to the hospital in Tucson for stitches."

Davy didn't care about stitches. He remembered what the Indian women had said about him, speaking in Papago when they thought he didn't understand. If it was true, if he really was

Killer's Child, then his mother must be a killer. This tall, scary detective was probably going to arrest her, take her away to jail, and keep her forever. If his mother went away, what would happen to him? Other kids had two parents. Davy didn't. With his father dead and Nana *Dahd* hurt, how would he live? What would he eat? How would he take care of Oh'o?

Davy stood his ground, shaking his head and refusing to budge. Diana lost all patience. "Come on," she ordered. "Now! It's late, and I'm tired. This has gone on long enough."

She held out her hand. Rita had taught Davy never to disobey an adult's direct command. One tiny, reluctant step at a time, he inched toward her outstretched hand.

Dr. Rosemead smiled and nodded. "Good," he said. "I'm sure he'll be fine, but if you're worried about a possible concussion, Mrs. Ladd, you can always wake him up every hour or so for the next twenty-four, just to be on the safe side. We'll call on ahead so the doctors at St. Mary's are expecting you."

Diana and Davy led the way to the car, but Brandon could see that the boy was hanging back. He was clearly frightened, although the detective couldn't imagine why. It offended him for little kids to be afraid of cops. Didn't they teach kids that policemen were their friends? Wasn't there some project called Officer Friendly working in the schools these days?

As he opened the car door, the detective tried

once more to smooth things over with the boy. "Do you want to sit in front?" he asked.

"No," the boy asserted stubbornly, shying away from the detective's outstretched hand. "I'll ride in back."

Myrna Louise couldn't stand to stay there in the hallway and watch the entire hair-cutting process. It was too hard on her, brought back far too many painful memories. Even though Andrew was almost fifty—he would be in a few months since she had already turned sixty-five—she still thought of him as her little boy, her baby.

All her husbands had said she spoiled Andrew rotten, except the last one, Jake. He'd never met Andrew. They'd fallen in love and married and almost got divorced while Andrew was—away. That's how she always thought of it—away. She never allowed herself to think about Andrew's last seven years in anything other than the vaguest of terms.

On reflection, she supposed it was true—she had spoiled Andrew, whenever she got the chance. That was her one regret in life, that she had seen so little of him after she lost custody. She'd never forgiven her first mother-in-law for that, for encouraging Howie Carlisle to go to court to take her little boy away from her, to have her—Myrna Louise—declared an unfit mother. That was still a terrible blow even though the judge had softened it some by agreeing to let her see Andrew sometimes. When she had a decent place to stay, she'd been able to have him with her during the summers for as long as a month or so and maybe again around Thanksgiving or Christmas, but that was all. In her mind, she'd never functioned as a real mother.

Myrna Louise leaned back in her rocker and closed her eyes, remembering Andrew as he had been when he was little—so cute, so smart, so mischievous. "Full of the devil," is what Howie used to call it.

Because of the tufts of soft gray hair spilling in a heap onto the bathroom floor, Myrna Louise recalled as if it were yesterday that long-ago time when Roger, her second husband, took her little boy to have his first haircut.

Roger was offended by Andrew's headful of adorable blond curls. He insisted it was time the child have a real boy's haircut, that the curls made him a sissy. Before the two of them left for the barbershop, Myrna Louise took her son aside and talked to him, telling him how he should behave.

"You mind your uncle Roger," she said. "You do everything he tells you."

"He's not my uncle," Andrew muttered stubbornly under his breath.

"What did you say?"

"He's not my uncle. Granny said so."

Any mention of her former mother-in-law threw Myrna Louise into unreasoning rage. "He most certainly is, too," she insisted, "and that's what you're going to call him."

"No," Andrew said.

"Yes," she returned.

"Say 'Uncle.' "

"Uncle," Andrew replied sullenly.

"Say 'Roger.' "

"Roger."

"Now say 'Uncle Roger.' "

"I can say 'Uncle,' " her son responded, "and I can say 'Roger,' but I can't say 'Uncle Roger.' "

And he never did. Not once.

Without humidity to hold it back, the heat peeled away from the desert floor like skin from a sun-ripened peach. Brandon and Diana tried driving with the Ford's windows wide open, but it was too chilly on Davy, who had stretched out lengthwise in the backseat and fallen sound asleep, so they rode with the front windows barely cracked, making conversation possible.

"Davy's a cute kid," Brandon offered tentatively. Riding with this strangely silent woman still made him uncomfortable.

Diana nodded. "He takes after his dad."

Walker had noticed Davy's physical resemblance to his father, but he hadn't wanted to mention it. The boy's wide-set blue-gray eyes and blond good looks were a long way from his mother's brown-eyed, dark-haired features. Brandon hoped, for Davy's sake, that looks were all he'd inherited from his father. If genetics were destiny, then David Ladd was doomed.

"Sometimes he does funny things, bizarre things," Diana mused, "and I wonder if it's anything like the way his father was when he was a child, but I don't have any way of knowing."

"You don't see your in-laws?"

Diana shook her head. "They wanted me to come back to Chicago and live with them, but I wouldn't do it."

"Why not?"

"Rita," Diana answered simply. "They didn't understand about Rita. Since I couldn't bring her along, we didn't go."

Diana's in-laws weren't the only ones who didn't understand about Rita, Brandon Walker thought, about the strange bond that existed between the young Anglo woman and the much older Indian. It didn't make sense to him, either.

"Davy's grandparents don't stay in touch?"

"They send Christmas presents. That's about all."

"That's too bad."

"It's their loss," Diana added.

Garrison Ladd told Diana Cooper about his parents that very first November afternoon during their three-hour coffee marathon at the I-Hop. "I don't like them much," he said. "Especially my dad."

This was something about Garrison Ladd that Diana Lee Cooper could relate to. She knew all there was to know about hating your own father. "What's wrong with him?" she asked.

"He's brilliant for one thing, and expects everyone else to be the same. He's worked his way up to being a big-cheese executive with Admiral back in Chicago. He started out in electrical engineering between the wars after graduating from the Armour Institute of Technology, with honors and two degrees. He was determined that I follow in his illustrious footsteps."

Diana Cooper would have loved to have a father who was undeniably brilliant, someone who would encourage her to go on to school of any kind rather than being, like Max Cooper, a solid wall of resistance.

"Your father doesn't sound so bad," she ventured.

"Oh yeah? This man doesn't understand the word *vacation*. All he does is work, work, work, and make money. He's probably richer than Midas by now. He and my mother live in this fantastic house on the shores of Lake Michigan. They have all these smart friends, but they're boring as hell, and they don't have any fun. They don't know how."

"That still doesn't sound so bad," Diana ventured.

"Why? What does your father do?" Gary Ladd asked, leveling that disconcerting blue-eyed gaze of his on her.

Diana flushed, both because he was looking at her and because of the question. She knew that particular question would come eventually, and she dreaded it. When she told him about Max, would Gary Ladd stalk out of the restaurant and leave her to pay for her own coffee? Sick at heart but incapable of doing anything else, Diana felt obliged to answer straight from the hip. If, after she told him, Garrison Walther Ladd, III, walked out and left her sitting there alone at the table, then all she'd be out was a single cup of I-Hop coffee.

"He's a garbageman," Diana replied.

Garrison slammed his cup into the heavy china saucer, slopping coffee. "You're kidding!"

"No."

"This is a joke, right?"

"It's no joke. My dad runs the garbage dump in Joseph, Oregon."

"Joseph? Where's that?"

"In the Willowa Mountains. On the other side of the state, a town at the end of a road. You might say I'm a dead-end kid."

It was easier for Diana to make fun of herself and Joseph first, rather than waiting for other people to do it. From his initial reaction, she couldn't tell if Garrison was making fun of her or not. He seemed intrigued.

"Fascinating. How many people live in Joseph?"

"Eight hundred, give or take."

"My God! That's amazing."

"What's amazing about it?"

"Look, I'm from Chicago. When I came here, I thought Eugene was small, but eight hundred people? Jeez, that's wonderful."

"It doesn't seen particularly wonderful to me."

"Just think about it," Garrison Ladd continued, his face alight with enthusiasm. "It's hard to believe that there are still places like that in this country, wide-open spaces."

"It's wide open, all right," Diana returned dryly. "It's so open there's nobody there."

"So what do people do?"

"For a living? Farming, ranching, logging."

"No mining?" he asked.

"No mining."

Garrison Ladd folded his arms across his chest, shook his head, and grinned at her. He had a very engaging grin. "Too bad," he said.

"What do you mean?"

"Did you ever listen to *Stella Dallas*, or are you too young?"

"Who's Stella Dallas?"

"That's what I get for messing around with younger women. *Stella Dallas* used to be on the radio back in Chicago when I was growing up. They said she was a girl from 'a small mining town in the West.' I always told my mother that Stella Dallas was the kind of girl I was going to marry. Right up until you told me there was no mining in Joseph, I thought maybe I'd marry you."

At that preposterous statement, Diana Lee Cooper burst out laughing. She couldn't help it. The few other patrons in the restaurant that afternoon, the ones who weren't at home glued to their television sets, regarded her disapprovingly. This was a day of mourning, a day of national tragedy, as citizens of the country, regardless of political leanings, began to come to grips with the bloody drama playing itself out in Dallas. It was not a time for levity, but Diana laughed anyway.

Kennedy was dead, Johnson was president, and Diana Lee Cooper was falling in love.

Rita slept, and so did most of the Indian children, stacked like so much cordwood on the sweltering, screened-in wooden porch of the outing matron's red brick home. The children had been there for varying lengths of time, from several days to only one or two, while Big Eddie completed his annual boarding-school roundup. The children from Coyote Sitting were the last to arrive. They lay in a miserable huddle at the far end of the long room.

As before, it was noisy in Chuk Shon, far too noisy for Dancing Quail to sleep. Just then another huge *wainomi-kalit* rumbled down the metal tracks a few blocks away. The whole house shook, and Dancing Quail did, too. She shivered and clutched her grandmother's precious medicine basket close to her chest. The sound terrified her. The other children had told her that the monster was called a train and that the next night they would travel to Phoenix riding on that huge, noisy beast.

To calm herself, she slipped her fingers inside the basket. On the way to Chuk Shon, Dancing Quail had examined each of the precious items in Understanding Woman's basket. For the *Tohono O'odham*, four is a powerful number, and there were four things in the basket—a single eagle feather, a shell Understanding Woman's dead husband had brought back from his first salt-trading trip to the sea, a jagged piece of pottery with the sign of the turtle etched into the smooth clay, and half a round rock that looked like a broken egg.

The outside shell of the rock was rough and gray, but inside it was alive with beautifully colored cubes. The cubes reminded Dancing Quail of the sun setting behind dark summer rain clouds that sometimes wrapped themselves around Ioligam.

Now, as the iron beast's whistle once more screeched through the night, Dancing Quail's groping fingers closed tightly around the rock. She held it and willed herself not to cry. Gradually, a feeling of calm settled over her. Somehow she knew that this mysterious rock was the most important gift in Understanding Woman's basket. Nothing on the coarse gray outside hinted at the beautiful secret concealed within. That was her grandmother's secret message for her—to be like the magic rock, tough on the outside but with her spirit hidden safely inside.

No matter what the stern, tall woman with her fiery red hair said, no matter what strange name the *Mil-gahn* woman called her, Dancing Quail would still be Dancing Quail.

With the geode clutched tightly in her fingers, the child drifted into a fitful sleep.

"Look," Brandon said, as they sped around the long curve at Brawley Wash just before Three Points. "Why go all the way out to the house for your car? You'll have to drive on into town by yourself. I'd be happy to drive you to the hospital and bring you back home afterward."

"You've done enough already," Diana responded. "More than you should have."

But Brandon Walker didn't want the evening to be over, didn't want to go home to the house where his father, who didn't have a brain tumor and who didn't have anything definite wrong with him that the doctors could point to, sometimes didn't recognize his own son's face.

"The boy's asleep," Brandon continued. "If you change cars, you'll wake him up."

"I'll have to wake him up in half an hour anyway. That's what the doctor said."

"By then we'll already be at the hospital. Besides, you must be worn out."

Diana surprised herself by not arguing or insisting. "All right," she said, leaning back in the car and closing her eyes. It felt good to have someone else handling things for a change, to have someone taking care of her. That hadn't happened to her for a long time, not since her mother died.

With her daughter away at school, Iona Dade Cooper avoided telling anyone she was sick. Once Diana found out about it, Iona brushed aside all alarmed entreaties that she go someplace besides La Grande for tests, that she utilize one of the big-city hospitals in Spokane or Portland with their big-city specialists.

"Too expensive," Iona declared firmly. "Besides, I wouldn't want to be that far away from your father."

Diana had bitten back any number of angry comments. As usual, her father was a bent reed, not strong enough for anyone else to lean on. Max Cooper had refused to come to the little community hospital in La Grande the night before his wife's exploratory surgery, claiming that being around hospitals made him nervous.

"Well, stay here then!" Diana had flared at him. "For God's sake, don't go out of your way!"

In the old days, Max would have backhanded his daughter for that remark, but not with Gary, his brand-new son-in-law, standing there gaping.

"I have an idea, Mr. Cooper," Gary Ladd said soothingly, stepping into the fray.

Max loved the fact that his son-in-law insisted on calling him "Mr. Cooper." No one in Joseph accorded the Garbage Man that kind of respect.

"Diana can go down to La Grande to be with Iona tonight, and I'll stay here. That way, neither one of you will be alone."

Max nodded. "I appreciate that, Gary. I really do."

So Diana spent the night in the hospital with her mother, sitting on a straight-backed chair near the bed, talking because her mother was too frightened to sleep despite the doctor-ordered sleeping pills.

"You'll look after your father when I'm gone, won't you, Diana?" Iona asked.

"Don't talk that way, Mom. It's going to be fine. You'll see."

But Iona knew otherwise. "He'll need someone to take care of the bills. No matter what happens, as soon as you get back to Joseph, go down to the bank and have Ed Gentry put you on as a signer on both the checking and savings accounts."

"That's crazy, and you know it. Daddy'll never agree to having me as a signer on his bank account."

"He'll have to," Iona replied. "He'll need someone to write the checks for him."

"Write the checks?" Diana echoed stupidly.

"Your father doesn't know how to read or write, Diana," Iona explained. "He never learned. He never wanted you or anyone else to know, but if something happens to me, if I die, he's going to need someone to look after him."

Diana was dumbstruck. "Daddy can't read?"

"I tried to teach him years ago when we first got married, before you were born, but the letters were always jumbled and funny. He couldn't do it."

"If he can't read, how did he keep his job all these years?"

"He's always been able to do math in his head, so nobody ever knew. When there were receipts that had to be written up or reports of some kind, I always handled those."

"Will he lose his job?"

Iona nodded. "Probably, and the house, too. I'm worried about what will happen to him."

"I'll take care of him," Diana promised. "I don't know how, but I will."

Iona lapsed into silence. For a while, Diana thought maybe her mother had fallen asleep. Diana sat there stunned, still grappling with the sudden knowledge that her father was illiterate.

She remembered his angry tirade when she had told him she was going to go to the University of Oregon to learn how to be a writer.

"A writer!" he had roared. "You, a writer?"

"Why not?" she had spat back at him, daring him to hit her but knowing that he wouldn't because the rodeo was just days away. Max Cooper couldn't afford to give his daughter a black eye just before the Chief Joseph Days Parade and Rodeo.

"I'll tell you why not. You're a woman, that's why not."

"What does that have to do with it?"

"Was Shakespeare a woman?" he demanded. "Were Matthew, Mark, Luke, and John women? I'll say not. They were all men, every last one of them, and let me tell you, sister, they're good enough for me!"

She remembered the conversation word for word, and all the time that lying bastard had been berating her about how good Matthew, Mark, Luke, and John were, he couldn't read a one of them. Sitting there in the darkened hospital room, Diana felt doubly betrayed, not only because her father had fooled her, but because her mother had helped him do it.

"I'm glad you married Gary," Iona said at length. "He seems like a very nice boy."

"He's not a boy, Mom. He's twenty-five, five years older than I am."

"Well, I just wish you'd start a family soon. I so

wanted to have grandchildren." Iona's eyes filled with tears, which she wiped away with a corner of the sheet.

Diana didn't have the heart to tell Iona that her good Catholic daughter was a mortal sinner who had been taking birth-control pills for a year now, ever since the first week of December of 1963. Gary had just happened to know of a doctor who wasn't averse to giving single girls prescriptions for the Pill.

Now that they were married, she and Gary had agreed it wasn't time yet for them to consider starting a family, especially not until he finished his master's degree. He was thinking about applying for a creative-writing program in Arizona. Diana still had two more semesters to go before she'd have her teaching credential.

"He's a lot like your father, isn't he?" Iona said.

Diana was offended by the question and didn't answer. Gary wasn't at all like her father. She'd gone to great lengths to find someone as different from Max Cooper as he could possibly be. Gary was smart. He had a good education and a sense of humor, and he had never once raised a hand against her in anger. Maybe he was a little lazy. If there was a right way to do something and an easy way, Gary would choose the easy way every time. Maybe in that regard there was a certain similarity between her husband and her father, but other than that, Garrison Walther Ladd was as different from Max Cooper as day from night.

"Does he treat you nice?" Iona asked.

"He treats me fine, Mom. Don't worry."

Relieved, Iona Cooper finally relaxed enough to fall asleep. They did the surgery early the next morning. When the doctor came looking for Diana in the small waiting room, his shoulders sagged under the weight of the news. As soon as she saw the haggard look in his eyes, Diana knew the prognosis wasn't good.

"How bad is it?" she asked.

He shook his head. "Very bad, Diana. I'm sorry. It's already metastasized. Completely inoperable. There's nothing to do but take her home and make her as comfortable as possible."

"How long does she have?"

"I don't know. A few months maybe. A year at the most."

Iona was still under sedation and wasn't expected to come out of it for several hours. In tears, Diana fled the hospital and drove like a maniac along the twisting road from La Grande to Joseph, wanting to fall into Gary's arms, to have him hold her and tell her that everything would be fine.

But when she got home, the house was deserted. She couldn't find the men anywhere. After waiting one long half hour and doing two days' worth of dirty dishes that had been allowed to accumulate in the kitchen sink, she finally thought to go check the bomb shelter behind the house. Dug into a hillside, the shelter was Max Cooper's pride and joy. He had built it himself, cinder block by cinder block, with plans he had ordered by mail and which his wife had patiently helped him decipher.

And that was where Diana found them, both

of them, father and husband, passed out cold on two of the three army cots. A litter of empty beer bottles covered the floor around them.

Sick at heart and without waking them, Diana turned on her heel and drove back to La Grande. She never told Gary she'd seen them like that, and if either one of them noticed that someone had come into the house and done the dishes while they were drunk and passed out, no one ever mentioned it.

"We're here," Brandon said quietly, pulling up under the brightly lit emergency-room canopy at St. Mary's Hospital. Diana jerked awake from an exhausted sleep. She started to waken Davy, but Brandon stopped her.

"You go on inside and start filling out paperwork. I'll park the car and carry Davy in. He's way too heavy for you."

The detective eased the child out of the backseat, hoisting him up to his chest and wrapping his arms around the narrow, bony shoulders. The child stirred enough to look at him once, but he was far too tired to object. With a weary sigh, Davy snuggled his head against Brandon Walker's neck. Scents of an improbable mixture of hospital disinfectant and wood smoke drifted up from Davy's sweaty hair, reminding Brandon of something missing from his own life—little boys and Cub Scout camp-outs.

Battling the lump in his throat, the detective carried Davy Ladd inside and sat with the boy cradled in his arms while Diana talked to the emergency room clerk. Walker missed his own boys right then with a gut-wrenching, almost physical ache. He could count on one hand the number of times he'd actually held either Tommy or Quentin like this.

The boys were tiny when he went off to Nam, and Janie had taken them with her when she moved out and divorced him four years ago, claiming she was tired of playing second fiddle to the Pima County Sheriff's Department. Louella Walker had raised her son right. Brandon was only too happy to sop up all the guilt Janie dished out. He agreed completely that the failure of their marriage must have been all his fault, accepting as gospel the idea that he had somehow let Janie and the boys down.

That, of course, was before he heard about the new addition his former wife was expecting, about his own sons' soon-to-be half brother, Brian, a nine-pounder who was born a scant six months after Janie left home. Brian's birth was also a full year and a half after Brandon Walker's vasectomy. Later, when he was back at the house getting it ready to sell, a neighborhood busybody had told him that Janie and her second husband had been playing around the whole time Brandon had been off doing his duty to God and country in Vietnam.

He saw Tommy and Quentin sometimes, but not often enough. Eight and nine years old now, they barely knew him. He was the obliging stranger who showed up on the front porch periodically to take them to ball games or movies or to the Pima County Fair. Now that little Brian was old enough, he wanted to go along, too.

At first Brandon said absolutely not. No way! He did his best to hate the little bastard, but he wasn't able to keep that up forever. The sweet little sad-eyed guy, left crying on the porch once too often, had worn down Brandon's resistance. More of Louella Walker's guilt, perhaps, but after all, it sure as hell wasn't the kid's fault that his parents were a matched pair of creeps. So lately, Brian was usually the fourth member on the infrequent Saturday afternoon outings.

Afterward, Brandon would sometimes kick himself for being a patsy, for being too goddamned easy, but that's just the way he was. Besides, Brian appreciated going to ball games even more than Tommy and Quentin did.

When Andrew Carlisle finished shaving his head, his tender scalp was screaming at him, but as he examined himself in the mirror, he knew a sore head was well worth it. He looked like a new man, felt like somebody else completely. He'd have to be careful to wear a hat the next few days so he didn't blister his bare head, but no one would put this smooth-headed man—Phil Wharton, Andrew told himself—together with the bushy-haired Andrew Carlisle who had been released from prison early that afternoon. The previous afternoon, he corrected, glancing at his watch—Jake Spaulding's watch, which was his now.

He went into the living room and checked on

his mother. Myrna Louise was sound asleep in the rocker, head resting on her chin, mouth open, a thin string of spittle dribbling from one comer of her mouth. He waved his hand in front of her face to be sure she was asleep, then he went back into the bathroom and shaved his legs.

When he finished with that, he returned to his room and retrieved the gun, Margaret Danielson's automatic. Long ago, Myrna Louise had been known for going through her son's things. Andrew didn't want to take any chances.

Besides, she had given him the keys to Jake's old Valiant. She told him the tags were still good and he was welcome to use it anytime he wanted. He went out to the little one-car garage and slipped the gun under the base of the jack in the trunk's spare-tire well. That way it would be safely out of the house should he need it.

The other key his mother had given him was to his storage locker, the place where he had directed her to leave all his furniture and belongings once she emptied his house in Tucson before selling it. At the time, Myrna Louise had questioned what he was doing with all that camping equipment in storage and what did he keep in the huge metal drum? He had reassured her that his survivalist gear was nothing more than a harmless interest in camping, a hobby he might want to take up again once he got out.

Andrew was reasonably certain all his equipment was there, at least most of it. He'd have to go down to Tucson as soon as possible and do a thorough inventory to make sure everything he needed was in good working order. Once he finished that, he'd be ready to go hunting again.

He could hardly wait.

After what she'd been through with her mother, the last thing Diana Ladd expected to happen in the emergency room was for her to get queasy when the doctor started to put stitches in Davy's head. The doctor asked her if she'd be all right, and she confidently assured him that she would be, but that was before she knew that they wouldn't be able to deaden it, that the stitches would have to be done with only ice cubes as anesthetic.

As Davy winced and cried out under the needle, she felt herself getting weak-kneed and woozy. A nurse helped her from the room. While she sat in the lobby with her head dangling between her knees feeling both foolish and helpless, Brandon Walker hurried into the emergency room and held Davy Ladd's hand while the doctor sewed the little boy's scalp back together.

It didn't seem like that big a deal, really, but when Brandon Walker carried a wide-awake Davy back out of the emergency room and delivered him into his mother's waiting arms, Diana's tearful gratitude warmed his heart. No matter what Louella said, maybe Brandon wasn't such a poor excuse for a human being after all.

He waited patiently while Davy proudly showed his mother the shaved spot on his head and the straight line of caterpillar-leg stitches that marched from his temple down one cheek.

"Ready?" Brandon asked at last.

"Yes," Diana said. "Would you mind carrying him again? You're right. He really is too heavy."

"I can walk all by myself," Davy said. "The doctor said I was real brave. I was, wasn't I?" He looked up at Brandon for confirmation.

"Yes, you were. You barely cried at all."

They walked to the waiting Ford three-abreast, with the boy between them holding each of their hands.

"Can I sit in the front now?" Davy asked, while they waited for Brandon to unlock the door.

"You bet," Brandon Walker replied. "Any kid with twelve stitches in his head ought to get to ride in the front seat."

In La Cantina, a dive of a bar in Rocky Point, Mexico, the driver of a red Grand Prix was sipping tequila and telling a buddy of his about the tough little boy he'd met earlier that day after a spectacular auto accident.

"That kid was something else," the man was saying. "Here he was with all kinds of blood pouring out of his head, but all he could think about was this poor old Indian broad who was still pinned in the truck. I was about to take off in the wrong direction to get help, but he wouldn't let me. He kept dragging on my leg and insisting there was an ambulance up on top of the mountain, for Chrissakes. Damned if he wasn't right. If we hadn't gone up the mountain after it right then, I don't think she would have made it. Maybe she didn't, for that matter."

"You say the woman was an Indian and the kid was an Anglo?"

"A regular towhead," the man answered. "And cute as a button."

"I wonder if there isn't a story in this," his buddy said. "You know, human interest. I'll talk to my features editor about it when I go back tomorrow. Maybe it's something we can use next week. Once it gets hot around here, feature stories are tough to come by."

The speaker drained his shot glass, licked a patch of salt off his hand, and took a bite from the lime on a napkin on the bar in front of him. "Ready for another?"

"You tell me. Is the Pope Catholic?"

7

*B*RANDON WALKER, STRETCHED out full length on Diana Ladd's long but sagging couch, wasn't sure which of the two woke him—the boy or the dog. When the detective opened his eyes, a pajama-clad Davy Ladd sat cross-legged on the floor next to the coffee table, munching on a rolled-up flour tortilla and sharing an occasional bite with a grateful, tail-thumping dog. Bone lay with his bristly, spike-haired head resting comfortably on the child's knee. Both the boy and the dog were staring intently, watching Brandon Walker's every move.

"Did your mom let you sleep over?" Davy asked.

The question brought Brandon Walker fully awake and put a rueful smile on his lips. "Not exactly."

By now, his mother would have discovered her thirty-four-year-old son's overnight absence and would be absolutely ripped. Louella had never come to terms with the idea that her son was a fully grown man.

Brandon had returned to the family home as a

temporary measure in the bleak financial aftermath of his divorce. Because of his father's failing health, that stopgap measure had stretched
into a more or less permanent arrangement. There
was no longer any discussion about Brandon
moving into his own place, and most of the time
he didn't mind. After all, his parents needed
him—his physical presence as well as his regular
financial contributions. The only major draw-
back was the fact that his mother continued to
treat him like an errant teenager.

"If your mom didn't let you, how come you're
here then?" Davy asked thoughtfully.

"Because of your mom," Walker answered.
"She was worried about you and asked me to
stay."

Just then the tiny travel alarm clock Diana
had placed on the coffee table beside him went
off with a shrill jangle. Brandon quickly silenced
it, hoping not to waken Diana. They'd both had
very little sleep.

"What's the clock for?" Davy asked.

"To wake me up," Brandon replied. "So I could
wake you."

The detective sat up and put both feet on the
floor. At once Bone raised his head and regarded
the man warily. Remembering the dog's violent
attack on the Galaxy, Brandon reminded himself
not to make any sudden or unexpected moves.

"Why?" the boy asked. "I'm already awake."

"I noticed," Brandon Walker responded, struck
by Davy's precociousness. The boy had to be
around six, but he sounded older. His long, lank

hair, so blond it was almost white, flopped down over one eye in sharp contrast to the other side with its round pink patch of bare skin and ladder of stitches. The combination gave him an almost comic appearance, but the expression on his face was serious.

"How come you did that?"

"Did what?"

"You and Mom, woke me up all night?"

"The doctor said not to let you sleep too long, or you might not wake up."

"He was wrong," the boy pointed out. "Are you hungry? There's tortillas in the kitchen."

"Sure," Walker told him. "A tortilla sounds great."

The boy and dog trotted off to the kitchen, while Brandon Walker stumbled into the bathroom to splash cold water on his face. He was happy not encountering Diana anywhere along the way. He was puzzled by what had happened between them during the night, and he wasn't sure what to say to her when next they met.

Davy was back in the living room sitting on the couch with the dog at his feet when Brandon returned from the bathroom. A rolled tortilla on a paper towel lay on the coffee table.

"Hope you like peanut butter," Davy said. "That's what I like for breakfast. Tortillas with peanut butter."

Brandon tried a bite. The tortilla—delicious, delicate, and thin—was as transparent in spots as a piece of tissue paper.

"Will Rita be okay?" Davy asked.

Brandon tried to answer, but the very first bite of peanut butter had glued itself to the roof of his mouth. At the same time, a stony-eyed Diana Ladd entered the room on her way to the kitchen. "Coffee?" she asked on her way past.

Much to his dismay, all Brandon Walker could do was nod helplessly and point to his mouth. There's nothing like making an awkward moment impossible, he thought miserably. Nothing like it at all.

When Hunter returned, once more looking like a human being, the people were afraid of him. For a time, Hunter and his sister lived together in peace, but then the people went to Wind Man, a powerful medicine man, and asked him to do something to Hunter. Wind Man blew and blew until he made a mighty dust devil.

Hunter's sister was out gathering firewood when Wind Man's dust devil caught her and took her far away. Hunter waited for his sister for a long time. Finally, he went looking for her, but he couldn't find her anywhere.

Hunter called to his uncle Buzzard for help. Buzzard looked for her for four days. He couldn't find her either, but he told Hunter that he had heard something strange up on Cloud-Stopper Peak, which the Mil-gahn call Picacho.

The next day Hunter and Buzzard together went to the mountain. The woman was up there, but she was crying. The mountain was very steep, and she didn't know how to get back down. When he heard that, Buzzard remembered that there was a medicine man in the east who was good at getting women. He flew off and returned with Ceremonial Clown.

Clown called to the woman. He looked so funny and said such funny things that the woman stopped crying and started laughing. Then Clown got some seeds out of his medicine bag, planted them, and he began to sing. While he sang, the seeds began to grow into a gourd plant, which grew up the side of the mountain. After four days, when it was tall enough, Clown climbed up it and carried the woman down.

So Hunter had his sister back, and the people who hated them stayed away. But one day Hunter said, "Let's go far away from this place. I will become Falling Star. When people see me, the earth will shake, and people will know something terrible is going to happen."

His sister agreed. "I will be Morning Star, and come up over there in the east. If people are alert and industrious, they will be up early enough to see me and say to each other, 'It is morning. Look, there is the morning star.' "

And that, my Friend, is the story of Falling Star and Morning Star.

Like Margaret Danielson, Ernesto Tashquinth had been laid off six months earlier from the Hecla mining operation on the Papago Reservation southwest of Casa Grande. The bottom had dropped out of the copper market. Mines all over Arizona were closing for good.

From the time he was a baby, Ernesto's mother, a Papago married to a Gila River Pima from Sacaton, had called her son S-abamk or Lucky One.

Stories about Ernesto Tashquinth's continuing good fortune followed him everywhere—through his sojourn at the Phoenix Indian School and during his stint in the army. That luck was once again holding true back home on the reservation.

Ernesto had been laid off from the mine along with many others at a time when job opportunities were scarce, but he had somehow managed to finagle his way into a position with the Arizona Highway Department. It wasn't a particularly wonderful job by some standards, but it paid reasonably well, and the work was steady. With truck and tools provided for him, Ernesto's job was to clean rest rooms, tidy up the grounds, and empty trash cans at rest areas along I-10 between Tucson and Cottonwood.

Ernesto much preferred this kind of solitary work to the dusty hubbub of the open pit mine. He enjoyed being by himself and setting his own pace. Of all the rest areas on his route, he liked the one at Picacho Peak best. For one thing, it was off the road by a few hundred yards. Without such easy access, it was usually less crowded than the others. Occasionally, the parking lot stayed empty the whole time Ernesto was working there. When that happened, he was free to let his mind wander back through the old stories his great-grandfather used to tell him, especially tales about Cloud-Stopper Mountain.

During those hot early summer days, while cleaning up other people's garbage and wiping down the shit they sometimes smeared on restroom floors and walls, Ernesto Tashquinth was dealing with some pretty heavy shit of his own. Straight out of high school, he had been drafted into the army and shipped off to Vietnam as an infantryman. The fact that he had returned home without so much as a scratch on his body had also been attributed to his incredibly good luck.

Unlike some of his buddies, Ernesto hadn't been physically hurt, but he had seen plenty. His scars, none of which were visible, came in part from luck—from being one vital step away from the land mine that had blown away his best pal's limbs and life. They came from seeing a tiny dying child, enemy or not, burned to a crisp by napalm. They came from the sounds and smells of a faraway war that still haunted his dreams and disturbed his sleep.

As the year's summer sun warmed the Arizona desert, it warmed Ernesto as well—cleansing him somehow, driving the horrors he had experienced out of his heart and mind, gradually singing his spirit back to life. There was much to be said for the old ways his great-grandfather had told him about, and much to be learned from them as well.

By midmorning that June Saturday, Ernesto finished cleaning the two rest rooms and was coming outside to empty the trash when he saw a pair of buzzards circling high over one of the springs near the base of the mountain. As his desert forbears would have done, Ernesto wrinkled his nose and sniffed the air. If something was dead or dying up there on the mountain, the odor had not yet reached the picnic area. That was good. It would be better for him to go investigate now, to find whatever it was and get rid of it right away, rather than waiting until someone told his supervisor about it.

Assuming the carrion to be from a dead animal, Ernesto armed himself with a shovel and a large plastic trash bag. He had played on this mountain as a child, and knew the series of hidden springs that dotted Picacho Peak's forbidding and seemingly barren flanks. He hurried to the concealing grove of trees with no trouble. Reaching them, he was surprised to find there was still no identifiable odor.

That told him the kill was relatively fresh. If the putrid odor of dead flesh had permeated the hot desert air, those buzzards would no longer be circling.

The first thing Ernesto saw through the sheltering curtain of mesquite trees was a glimpse of bare, sunburned leg. Thinking he'd stumbled upon a devoted sunbather, Ernesto's first instinct was to turn quickly and go back the way he'd come, but something about the leaden stillness of that bright pink leg told him otherwise.

"Hello?" he called. "Anybody here?"

There was no response, no answering movement. Puzzled, he pushed his way through the leaves until he could see more clearly. A naked woman lay faceup on the rocks before him, empty eyes open to the sky, her skin burned a fierce red by the blistering sun.

In a rush, all the horror of Vietnam flooded back over Ernesto Tashquinth. Sickened, he wasn't able to look again for several long moments. When he did, he found himself unable to turn away. He moved toward the body like a sleepwalker—staring, mesmerized. Not only was she sunburned, her whole body was a mass of wounds. Industrious ants crawled across her, following orderly, seemingly well-marked trails like hordes of tiny cars negotiating rush-hour freeway traffic. Flies swarmed and hovered in the heavy air above her, hoping to find some appropriately still-damp place in which to lay their eggs.

But what fascinated and at the same time appalled Ernesto Tashquinth, what held his eyes hostage, were the naked, sunburned, upturned breasts, especially the right one. Something was wrong with it. He moved closer until he saw that the entire right nipple was missing—not missing exactly, but hanging loose, attached to the body by a single shred of flesh and skin.

The gray shadow of a soaring bird glided overhead, an ominous cloud passing between Ernesto and the sun. A buzzard had done that to her, he assumed at once, looking up at the patiently circling bird. A buzzard had inflicted that gross indignity on the dead woman's body.

Ernesto was grateful that he had arrived in time to interrupt the grisly process. There was nothing to be done about the flies and ants, but he could keep the birds away. Whoever she was, at least he could spare her that.

Bent on protecting the body, Ernesto tore the

trash bag open until he had a flat strip of black plastic three feet wide and eight feet long. He covered her feet first, using rocks to hold the corners of the plastic in place. It wasn't until he approached the woman's crimson face that he realized he knew her, that she was someone he had worked with at the mine.

Margie Danielson, one of the white ladies at Hecla, had worked in payroll. She had given him his pink slip only two weeks before issuing her own.

After he recognized her, Ernesto Tashquinth knelt there silently for a moment before covering her face. His mother was right after all, he decided. He really was lucky. Ernesto Tashquinth was still alive and kicking. Margie Danielson wasn't.

In Rita's leaden dream it was night, and the train station was hot and dusty. It should have been dark, but the wavering gas lights of downtown Chuk Shon gave everything an eerie glow. Thirty or so Indian children stood huddled together in a silent, apprehensive group at the far end of the platform.

Under one arm, Dancing Quail carried a blanket with her clothing and Understanding Woman's precious medicine basket rolled safely inside. In her other hand, clutched tightly in a sweaty fist, she carried her magic rock. The little girl stood with the others, her feet blistered and sore in the stiff secondhand or thirdhand leather shoes the outing matron had given her.

The train pulled into the station, causing the very ground to tremble. Dancing Quail looked to the sky. Falling Star always signaled the shaking of the earth, but above her the sky was hazy with Chuk Shon's dust and smoke. If Falling Star tried to warn them just then, no one could have seen him.

The youngest child in the group, Dancing Quail watched in amazement as people climbed down from the train using steps a man had placed in front of the doors. They emerged carrying small cases and boxes. They looked all right. Dancing Quail had worried that whoever stepped inside that huge, smoking iron monster would be instantly devoured, eaten alive, but these people hadn't been. Maybe she wouldn't be, either.

Other people came out on the platform now and began boarding the train, taking the places of those who got off earlier. Soon it would be Dancing Quail's turn. She clutched her magic rock and asked I'itoi for courage.

At last the outing matron motioned the children to move out, but not toward the doors of the train through which the other people had disappeared. Instead, they were herded back along the platform almost to the end of the train, where they were ordered up a straight metal ladder on the outside of one of the cars.

Faced with the unfamiliar ladder, Dancing Quail drew back in dismay. She knew how to climb rocks and cliffs, but she had never seen a ladder before. She watched while one of the older boys pulled himself up it. How could she climb that way and still hold on to her rock and her blanket? Dancing Quail edged her way to the back of the line, hoping to escape notice. With the other children all on top of the car, Dancing Quail found herself being pushed forward by the outing matron.

There was no alternative. Dancing Quail stuck the magic rock in her mouth and gripped it between her teeth while she started up the ladder. She was terrified climbing up, and even more terrified once she reached the top and looked back down. The ground was far away. What would happen to her if she fell?

Following the example of the other children, she dropped to a sitting position just as the whistle shrieked and the train lurched forward. Wrapping her legs around the rolled blanket, she held on to a metal rail with both hands. Wind whipped her hair across her face, blinding her. At first she was afraid the wildly rushing air would pry her loose. It was a long time before she dared let go with one hand long enough to remove Understanding Woman's precious rock from her mouth.

Afraid to sleep for fear of falling off, Dancing Quail tried to stay awake, but eventually the rhythmic racket of metal on metal lulled her eyes closed.

"Rita!"

Someone from far away was calling her by that other name, the same name the outing matron had used.

"Rita," the voice called again, more firmly this time.

Dancing Quail didn't want to answer. She didn't want to wake up because she knew when she did that it would be the same as it had been that long-ago morning when the train finally reached Phoenix. The sun would be bright overhead, and Understanding Woman's magic rock would be gone forever. Sometime during the night it had slipped from her grasp and fallen from the swaying boxcar.

More than half a century later, Dancing Quail still mourned its loss.

Juanita Ortiz rose stiffly from the uncomfortable chair where she had spent the night at her sister's bedside. She went to look out the window, while the nurse woke Rita to take her pulse and temperature.

Gabe hadn't come by the BIA compound to summon his mother until late, not until after Diana Ladd had picked up Davy. Fat Crack had given Juanita some lame excuse about promising Rita not to leave the child alone. His mother didn't approve. It wasn't right that Gabe should have waited with the little white boy all that time without coming to tell his own family about Rita's injuries. How could an Anglo's needs come before those of Gabe's own family?

Looking out the window, Juanita Ortiz shook her head in frustration. There was much she didn't understand about her son, and she understood her sister even less.

Of all the people on the reservation, only a few—Juanita Ortiz among them—still remembered that, as a child, Rita Antone had once been called Dancing Quail. And only Rita remembered that their father's pet name for baby Juanita had been S-kehegaj, which means Pretty One. That was all a long time ago. Dancing Quail no longer danced, and no one had called Juanita pretty in more than forty years.

With chart in hand, the nurse left the room. Juanita went back over to the bed. Dr. Rosemead had told her that Rita's injuries weren't nearly as serious as he had at first supposed, but that if she hadn't been in the ambulance when her heart stopped, she surely would have died.

"*Ni-sihs,*" Juanita said softly. "Elder Sister, how are you?"

"Thirsty, *ni-shehpij,*" Rita answered, opening her eyes and speaking formally to her younger sister. "I sure am thirsty."

The nurse had left a glass newly filled with crushed ice on the nightstand. Juanita ladled a spoonful of ice into Rita's parched mouth.

"I must see S-ab Neid Pi Has," Rita whispered as soon as she could speak again after swallowing the ice.

Instantly, Juanita Ortiz's eyes hardened. S-ab Neid Pi Has, Looks At Nothing, was an aged, blind medicine man who lived as a hermit in Many Dogs, an almost-abandoned village just across the Mexican border from the rest of the reservation. He was a man who lived according to the old ways, who long ago had divorced himself from white man's liquor, whose lungs smoked only Indian tobacco.

Juaníta had converted from Catholic to Presbyterian as a young woman when she married Arturo Ortiz. She heartily disagreed when her son, Fat Crack, went off and joined the Christian Scientists, but at least, she conceded, he was Christian. Juanita staunchly drew the line at the idea of summoning a medicine man.

"Ni-sihs," Juanita scolded disapprovingly. "Sister, you are in a hospital. Let the doctors and nurses take care of you."

But Rita still remembered those three huge buzzards sitting with outstretched wings on the row of passing telephone poles. The Anglo doctors with their bandages and thermometers could fix her broken body perhaps, but those three ominous buzzards represented Forebodings, something that required the ministrations of a medicine man. They were symptomatic of a Staying Sickness—a disease that affects only Indians and one that is impervious to Anglo medical treatment with its hospitals, operating rooms, and bottles of pills.

"I must see Looks At Nothing," Rita insisted stubbornly. "Please ask Fat Crack to go get him and bring him here."

When Andrew Carlisle told his mother that he was going to Tucson to check on his storage locker, Myrna Louise wondered if he might go away and not come back. She made him a huge jar of sun tea and iced it down in a Thermos. Andrew always liked to do that, she remembered, to travel with lunches and drinks packed from home rather than stopping off someplace to buy meals. It made sense to travel that way, with prices in all the restaurants higher than a cat's back.

She made him a good breakfast, too—toast and coffee and eggs over easy. He said he'd seen nothing but scrambled for years. Powdered scrambled. Those couldn't be any too good.

He didn't talk while he ate, and he didn't look at her. Myrna Louise didn't know what to do or say, so she hovered anxiously in the background, pouring more coffee into his cup long before it was empty, offering to make more buttered toast or fry a few more eggs.

"Look," he said crossly, pushing his cup away before she could fill it again. "Don't fuss over me, Mama. I can't stand it when you fuss."

Myrna Louise's eyes clouded with tears, and she hung her head. "I was only trying to help," she said, her voice quavering. "I mean, I don't know how you expect me to act."

He turned on the charm at once, a trick he'd been able to perform at will since childhood, forcing his mother to smile through her tears in spite of herself.

"Treat me like I just got back from Istanbul, Mama."

"But I don't know anything at all about Istanbul."

He laughed. "Believe me. They probably don't have over-easy eggs there, either."

Diana brought a mug of coffee into the room and slammed it onto the coffee table in front of

Brandon Walker. Davy, always attuned to his mother's moods, looked at her guardedly.

"Are you mad, Mom?" he asked.

"I'm not mad at anybody, Davy," she said, her tone contradicting the words. "Go get dressed. We'll drive out to Sells and see how Rita is."

Davy hurried away with the dog padding behind him.

"I'm sorry about last night, Diana," Brandon began. "It's just that, under the circumstances . . ."

"Forget it," she snapped, cutting him off in mid-apology. "It doesn't matter."

But it did matter, at least to him. It had been late at night, some time after they came back from getting Davy's stitches. Davy was asleep in his bedroom, but the grown-ups were wide awake. They were sitting on the couch drinking lemonade and talking when the calm after the storm was suddenly too much. Diana dissolved into an unexpected squall of tears. It was natural for her to fall against Brandon Walker's shoulder, natural for him to put a comforting arm around her. The electricity had been there for him from the first moment he laid eyes on the woman. Holding her that way brought it all back to him in a rush.

He wanted her. God, how he wanted her, just like he'd wanted her years earlier when he was still married and she was pregnant as hell. The sweet, clean, smell of her hair filled his nostrils. The touch of his fingertips on bare, smooth skin stirred his whole body and aroused a part of Brandon Walker that he kept on a very short leash.

He wasn't sure when the comforting arm he'd draped around her shoulder evolved into a caress, or when exactly he began to kiss that soft, sweet-smelling hair, but he was painfully aware of her abruptly sitting up straight and pushing him away.

"No," she said. "I'm sorry. I didn't mean it. Go now, please. Just go away."

He was almost glad she'd stopped it when she did, before things got out of hand. He wanted her, but not like this, not when she was at the end of her emotional rope. Brandon Walker wanted her, and he wanted Diana Ladd to want him back.

But in the aftermath of that one unexpected kiss, she was overtaken by a sudden fit of unaccountable fury. She accused him of taking unfair advantage and ordered him out of the house. Walker simply refused to leave. Telling her he wasn't going to leave her alone with an injured child no matter what, he kicked off his shoes and stretched his long frame out full length on her living-room couch. Short of using a gun, that didn't leave Diana many options. Still angry, she stalked off to bed.

During the night, they reached a truce of sorts. He insisted on getting up with her every time she went to check on Davy anyway. Finally, at five in the morning, she knuckled under and gave him an alarm clock. Now, though, awake and sipping coffee, she seemed angry again, and Brandon didn't know what to do about it.

He looked around the room with its freshly stuccoed walls and open-beam ceilings, searching for a reasonable topic of discussion that would keep the conversation out of harm's way.

Hanging on the wall behind the couch was a basket Brandon recognized as a Papago maze with I'itoi standing in the cleft at the top of the design. He had seen Papago baskets like that before, but this one was unusual in that the design work was done in red rather than the traditional black.

"Great basket," he said.

Diana nodded. "It was a housewarming present from Rita when we first moved in here."

"I've never seen a red one before."

"They're fairly rare," she told him. "The color isn't dyed; it comes from a yucca root. Killing live yuccas to make baskets doesn't go over too well these days."

"It suits the room," he said stupidly, groping for something to say. "It goes with the rest of the house."

Brandon Walker knew he must sound like a complete jackass, but talking about the basket seemed to have blunted the worst of Diana's anger.

"You should have seen it when we first moved in," Diana said. "It was awful. Rita was a huge help. Between the two of us, we managed to make the place habitable."

Brandon changed the subject. "I heard Davy telling the doctor that you're writing books. Is that true?"

Diana flushed. "I'm trying," she said. "Nothing published yet, but I'm working at it."

Brandon frowned as a trace of memory surfaced. "Isn't that what your husband . . . ?"

He broke off the question as soon as he saw the pained expression on her face, but it was too late. The damage was done. He berated himself for blundering and making things infinitely worse rather than better.

"Yes," she said. "That's what Gary was studying before he died. Writing. As a matter of fact, he told me that on our very first date. That he was going to write the great American novel someday."

Brandon Walker thought he already knew the answer, but he asked the question anyway, just to be polite. "Did he?"

Diana Ladd stood up abruptly and swept both coffee cups off the table.

"No. Gary never finished anything he started," she said bitterly, heading toward the kitchen. "He had a very short attention span."

They were still in the booth at the I-Hop, drinking their eighth or ninth cup of coffee. The waitress was growing surly.

"You're shitting me!" Gary Ladd exclaimed in delight. "You're going to be a writer, too?"

After hearing about Gary Ladd's Pulitzer Prize ambitions, Diana Lee Cooper shyly mentioned her own interest in writing. "It's what I've always wanted to do," she added, surprised to find herself confiding in this semi-stranger.

Diana's desire to write wasn't something she confessed to others openly or often. People in Joseph, Oregon, laughed uproariously at the very idea. Here at the university, she always felt unworthy, underqualified. But Gary Ladd didn't seem to share that opinion.

"Hey, that's great," he said, giving Diana's shoulder an encouraging pat accompanied by one of his engaging grins. "What say we do it together—matching typewriters on a single table, right?"

She laughed and nodded. "Right."

From near the cash register, the waitress glared at them pointedly. Garrison Ladd grabbed Diana's hand. "Come on," he said. "Let's go before they throw us out."

On the way outside, Diana glanced down at her watch. "Oh, my God," she said in dismay. "I'm late." She started for her bike with Garrison Ladd right behind her.

"Late for what? Where are you going?"

"Ushering. I have to get home, change, and get back down here in less than an hour."

"Ushering?" he asked. "What's this about ushering?"

"At Robinson Hall. It's my second part-time job," she explained. "I make three dollars a night."

November's early darkness was settling over Eugene, bringing with it a chill winter rainstorm as she knelt on the wet ground and struggled with the stubborn lock on her bicycle chain.

"Wait a minute. Let me get this straight. You work in the English Department fifteen hours a

168 — J. A. Jance

week, and you usher in the auditorium as well. Do you have any other jobs I don't know about?"

"Only the newspaper," she told him.

"What newspaper?"

"*The Register-Guard.* I deliver ninety-six papers during the week and a hundred-ten on Sundays."

"When do you find time to eat and sleep?" he asked.

"When I can. I told you, I have to pay my own way. This is what it takes to stay in school."

"That may be, but you sure as hell don't have to ride that thing home in this downpour. Don't be stubborn. Let me load it into my van."

She accepted gratefully. The radio was on as they drove toward the rambling house off Euclid where Diana lived in a tiny apartment over a garage. They were almost there when the local announcer began a public-service listing of all the functions for that evening that had been canceled or postponed in a show of respect for the slain president. Among them was the performance of the Youth Symphony scheduled for Robinson Hall.

"Damn." Diana bit her lip in disappointment and fought back tears. There went another three bucks she wouldn't have come next payday. Along with the other two she had missed by not working all afternoon at the department, payday would be very short indeed in a budget that was already tight right down to the last nickel. At this rate, how would she ever accumulate enough money to buy next semester's books?

"That means you're off tonight?" Garrison Ladd was saying.

Not trusting herself to speak, Diana nodded.

"What will you do instead?"

"Study, I guess," Diana answered bleakly. "I've got some reading to do."

"How about dinner?"

"Tonight? Isn't that . . ."

"Tacky?" he supplied with a wink. "You think just because somebody knocked off the president, the rest of us shouldn't eat?"

"It does seem . . . well, disrespectful."

"From what I hear about JFK himself, he'd be the last one to want us missing out on a good time. Come on. I'll take you someplace special. How about the Eugene Hotel? They have terrific steaks there."

Diana found herself salivating at the very mention of the word *steak*. She hadn't tasted one since the previous summer's rodeo-queen supper. Her school budget seldom made allowances for hamburger, let alone steak. She let herself be enticed.

"All right," she said. "But I've never been to the Eugene Hotel. What should I wear?"

"We'll manage," he said.

Despite Iona's warnings about not inviting men up to her room, it didn't seem polite to leave Garrison Ladd waiting outside in the cold car while she went up to change. After all, he was an instructor at the university. Surely, someone like that was above reproach.

She started having doubts though when, after

closing the apartment door behind him, he stopped just inside the threshold and didn't move.

Diana turned back and looked at him. "Have a seat," she said. "I'll go into the bathroom and change."

He studied her curiously. The undisguised appraisal in the look made her nervous. "What's the matter?"

"Come here," he said, crooking his finger at her.

"Why?"

"Just come here."

Against her better judgment, she did as she was told, walking toward him slowly, woodenly. What was going on? she wondered. Maybe her mother was right. Maybe she shouldn't be here in her room alone with this man.

Diana stopped when there was less than a foot between them. "What?" she asked.

"Has anyone ever told you how lovely you are?"

"Come on," she said, shaking her head. "Don't give me that old line."

She started to move away from him, but he caught her wrist, imprisoning her hand in his and drawing her closer. With his other hand, he brushed the hair back from her face and then traced the slender, curving jaw with a gently caressing finger.

"It's not a line," he said. "You're beautiful."

"People in Joseph don't talk to the garbage-man's daughter that way," she said stiffly. Tentatively, she tried to free her hand, but he didn't let it go.

No doubt about it. Her mother *was* right. She'd

made a serious mistake in inviting him up here, and she didn't know how to get rid of him. She tried again to loosen his grip on her wrist, but he held firm.

"They don't? How do they talk to her?"

Now Diana was genuinely scared. Her apartment was a long way from the main house. If she yelled for help, no one would hear her.

"Let me guess," Garrison Ladd continued, still holding her captive. "They'd probably say something gross, like 'Fall down on your back, honey, and spread your legs.' "

At once hot, humiliating tears stung Diana's cheeks. This was the very thing she had hoped to escape by running away from Joseph, by running away from home. Those words, those exact same words, were ones her father had shouted at Iona in one of his drunken, raging tirades when neither one of them knew their daughter was in the house.

Too young to realize what was going on, Diana knew no words for what her father had done to her mother. She had hidden in the closet and waited until it was over, crying and praying that her father would die, that God would strike Max Cooper dead on the spot, but, of course, He hadn't.

And now, here she was faced with those very words again, and with whatever else came with those words. She squared her shoulders and prepared to fight. Running away hadn't done her any good if the words had found her anyway, searched her out here in Eugene in her own apartment. Maybe destiny wasn't something you could escape by running from one end of the state to the other, but she sure as hell didn't have to go quietly.

"Let me go," she snapped. "You're hurting me."

"Not until you kiss me, Liza."

Liza! She felt as though he'd slapped her. Who the hell was Liza? An ex-girlfriend maybe? Had Gary Ladd mixed her up with someone else?

"My name's not Liza. Let me go!"

He smiled and effortlessly pulled her to him until her taut body was against his chest. "Haven't you ever heard of Liza Doolittle, Liza? She's a garbageman's daughter, too, you know. And my name is Henry Higgins, so what are you going to wear to the ball, my dear?"

He kissed her then, quickly, briefly—a brotherly kiss not even a garbageman's daughter could fault him for—and led her to the closet, where he began rummaging through her clothing, looking for an appropriate dress.

The rush of relief and gratitude that swept over Diana almost brought her to her knees. He hadn't meant her any harm. It had all been a game, genuine teasing. She wasn't used to that, and she didn't know how to handle it.

"Here we are." He held up the blue taffeta semiformal Diana's mother had made for her to wear to the prom. "This should do nicely."

Gathering everything she needed into a bundle, Diana hurried into the bathroom to change, while Garrison Ladd lounged comfortably on her bigger-than-twin-but-less-than-full-sized bed. The idea of him sitting there big as you please made her blush. Her mother had warned her about that, too, about letting men sit on your bed, but then what did her mother know?

As soon as Diana was dressed, they drove to Garrison's place, a two-bedroom apartment with a pool, emptied now for the winter. He invited her up, but she wasn't taking any more chances. She stayed in the car while he went inside to change. He came out wearing a tuxedo—his very own tuxedo. Except for Walter Brennan, maybe, no one in Joseph, Oregon, owned his own tuxedo.

They went to the hotel for a dinner of medium-rare steaks, lush salads, and huge baked potatoes complete with sour cream and chives. Feeling like Cinderella, Diana couldn't help noticing that Garrison Ladd paid more for that single steak dinner than she'd earn from a full week's worth of work, but that didn't keep her from enjoying herself.

They laughed at anyone and everyone, including one tearful waitress who acted as though it were inappropriate for anybody to be out on the town having such a gloriously good time with John F. Kennedy not yet in his grave.

Diana Lee Cooper didn't know when she'd ever had so much fun. She laughed until she cried, and then she laughed some more, and all the while the part of her that had never laughed before was falling more and more in love by the minute.

Finally, at midnight, she'd had enough. "I've got to go home and get some sleep," she announced. "I've got newspapers to deliver in the morning."

"No way," he told her. "I'm not letting you out of my sight. We'll stay up all night. When it's time to deliver your damn newspapers, I'll help you. How does that sound?"

At five o'clock in the morning, in a driving rain, the two of them delivered the black-banded newspapers that announced President John F. Kennedy's death. Garrison Ladd drove her around the route in his VW-Bus. Diana, barefoot but still wearing her blue dress, hopped in and out of the bus to send the papers sailing through the air. Gary Ladd was impressed that she never missed a single porch.

Afterward, back in her apartment, cold and wet and still laughing, she let him help her out of her soaked clothes. The wet taffeta was ruined, but Diana didn't care. She didn't look at it as he unzipped it and let it slip to the floor in a sodden heap. Nothing mattered except this wonderful man she was with who had the ability to make her laugh and feel beautiful at the same time.

She barely noticed as he unfastened her bra and slipped her garter belt and panties down to the floor. She stepped delicately out of them and stood naked before him while he wrapped his arms around her, holding her close.

"You're shivering," he said. He kissed her once, a long, lingering kiss, and she responded eagerly. Playfully, he nibbled at her ear. It tickled, and she giggled, but then she caught herself. She realized what was happening and tried to pull away.

"Don't tease me," he whimpered urgently. "Please don't tease me."

She closed her eyes and let herself melt against him while the room whirled around her. She tried to block out the sickening memory of her father's drunken voice, but it was all there again in her mind, not only the night she'd spent in the closet but also that other terrible long-ago night after the first pre-rodeo dance.

A few of the boys took her out behind the school and offered to show her exactly what she'd have to do to win. They told her that any girl who came from the wrong side of the tracks wasn't going to make it to the top any other way. Somehow she escaped them. She ran all the way home, arriving in tears with her clothes half torn off.

And just when she got inside, closing the door behind her, just when she thought she was safe, Max Cooper materialized behind her and switched on the light. Drunk, he was enraged when he saw her clothes. "Slut!" he shouted. "You worthless, no-good slut! What the hell have you been up to?"

Desperate to get away, she darted past him up the stairs. The booze slowed him down, and she got away clean, but Max plowed up the stairs after her. Upstairs, she locked herself in the bathroom and was sick, vomiting into the toilet. He banged on the door a couple of times. She heard him distantly, over the sound of her own retching. At least he didn't break the door down. The wooden door kept his fists at bay, but his words found their mark all the same.

"You're a bitch, Diana Lee Cooper! A no-good bitch of a prick-tease!"

She was washing her face by then, staring at her ashen face in the bathroom mirror. She wouldn't be that, she vowed into the mirror. No matter what he called her, no matter what it was, she wouldn't ever be that.

"What did you say?" she asked vaguely.

She stood with her head thrown back, her wet hair dripping on the floor behind her. Without her being aware of it, Garrison Ladd had kissed his way down her yielding neck and across the gentle swell of her breast. He closed his lips around one delicate, upright nipple. She moaned with pleasure as wild sensation shot through her body.

Reluctantly, he let the nipple go. Straightening up, he crushed her against him while his breath came in short, harsh gasps. Through the confines of his trousers, she could feel his urgent hardness straining against her. She pulled back from him again for a moment, far enough away to look up at his face and see the blazing intensity in his eyes.

That was when the second realization hit her— Garrison Ladd wanted her. Diana Lee Cooper was stunned by the unbridled passion in his wanting. How had she allowed it to happen? How had she let him go this far? Because it was too far—too late to tell him no, too late to make him stop. She remembered the promise she'd made, a sacred vow spoken to the frightened face of a girl reflected back in a pockmarked bathroom mirror while her father pounded on the door. There could be no turning back.

She reached up with both hands and pulled Garrison Ladd's face down until his lips once more grazed hers.

"I won't tease you," she whispered fiercely. "Not ever."

And she kept her word.

8

*I*T IS SAID that from then on the people were very
jealous of Little Bear and Little Lion. They wanted
the boys' beautiful birds to use the feathers on their
own arrows. One night the boys' grandmother warned
them, "Tomorrow the people will come here. They will
kill me and try to steal your birds. You must take the
birds far away from here and throw them off the mountains in the east."

The next morning, it happened just as she said. The
people came to the house and killed Wise Old Grandmother, but Little Bear and Little Lion escaped, taking
their beautiful birds with them. Back then, the people
had not yet lost the ability to follow tracks, so they followed the two boys across the desert.

As Little Bear and Little Lion started up the far
mountain, they heard the angry people close behind
them. Little Bear was too tired to go on. "Here," he said
to his brother. "You take my bird as well. I will wait
here for the people. They may kill me, but at least the
birds will be free."

And that is what happened. Little Bear kept the
people with him long enough for Little Lion to throw

*the beautiful birds with their multicolored feathers off
the mountain. And that,* nawoj, *is the story of how
Sunrise and Sunset got their colors.*

They say a certain type of criminal always re-
turns to the scene of his crime, and Andrew
Carlisle fit that mold. He was curious. He wanted
to know if anyone had discovered Margaret Danielson's body yet; not that he would actually have
gone up the mountain to see for himself, but he
couldn't resist pulling off into the rest area at
Picacho Peak since it was on his way. He was re-
warded by the collection of law-enforcement vehicles parked haphazardly around the picnic and
playground area, which told him what he needed
to know.

The highway patrol had cordoned off almost
half the rest area, but a few tables were still available. He took his Thermos to one of those and
settled down to watch the fun, which included
several milling television cameramen, some re-
porters, and a few stray newspaper photographers.

"What's going on?" Andrew asked a man who
came by lugging a huge television-equipment suitcase.

"An Indian killed a woman up there on the
mountain," the guy said. "They're just now bringing the body down."

An Indian? Carlisle thought. No kidding. They
think an Indian did it? He couldn't believe this
stroke of luck. For the second time in as many
chances, fate had handed over the perfect fall
guy for something Carlisle himself had done,

someone to take the blame. Sure, he'd gone to prison for Gina Antone, mostly because the cops thought he'd driven the truck that had inadvertently broken her neck. They had never suspected the real truth, not even that wise-ass of a detective, because if they had, it would have been a whole lot worse. Now, here he was again with somebody else all lined up to take the rap.

One thing did worry him a little. It hadn't taken long for the cops to find her. He hadn't expected them to work quite this fast, but he was prepared for it anyway. He was glad now that he'd taken the time to clean the bits of his flesh from under her fingernails. With something like that, you couldn't be too careful. His mentors in Florence had warned him not to underestimate cops. The crooked ones had a price—all you had to do was name it. Straight ones you had to look out for, the ones who were too dumb to take you up on it when you made them an offer they shouldn't refuse.

"Mom, if Rita dies, will we put a cross on the road where she wrecked the truck?"

They had just driven by the Kitt Peak turnoff on their way to Sells. With all the emergency vehicles gone, there was no sign of the almost-fatal accident the previous afternoon.

"Probably," Diana answered, "but Rita isn't going to die. I talked to her sister this morning. She'll be fine."

"Does my daddy have a cross?"

The abrupt change of subject caused Diana to

swing her eyes in her son's direction. The car almost veered off the road, but she caught it in time. "Why do you ask that?"

"Well, does he?"

"I suppose. At the cemetery. In Chicago."

"Have I ever been there?"

"No."

"Is that where he died?"

"No. Why are you asking all these questions?" Diana's answer was curt, her question exasperated.

"Did you know Rita puts a new wreath and a candle at the place where Gina died? She does that every year. Why don't we?"

"It's an Indian custom," Diana explained. "Papago custom. Your father wasn't a Papago."

"I thought you said I was going to turn into an Indian."

"I was kidding."

Davy fell silent for several miles, and his mother was relieved that the subject seemed closed. "Did you ever kill anything, Mom?" he asked at last. "Besides the snake, I mean."

Jesus! She had almost forgotten about the snake. It was two years now since the afternoon she was inside and heard Bone barking frantically out in the yard. Alarmed, she hurried out to check.

She found all three of them—boy, dog, and snake—mutually trapped in the small area between the side of the house and the high patio wall. The rattlesnake, a fat four-footer, had been caught out in the open sunning itself.

It's said that the first person can walk past a sleeping rattlesnake but a second one can't. Davy had walked past the drowsing snake unharmed and was now cornered on the rattler's far side. Bone, barking himself into a frenzy, was smart enough not to attempt darting past the now-coiled and angry snake.

Diana Ladd was usually scared witless of snakes. As a mother, this was her first experience in dealing with a life-or-death threat to her child. Instantly, she became a tigress defending her young.

"Don't move, Davy!" she ordered calmly, without raising her voice. "Stand right there and don't you move!"

She raced back to the garage and returned with a hoe, the only weapon that fell readily to hand. She had a gun inside the house, a fully loaded Colt .45 Peacemaker, but she didn't trust herself with that, especially not with both Davy and the dog a few short feet away.

She had attacked the snake with savage fury and severed its head with two death-dealing blows. Only after it was over and Davy was safely cradled in her arms did she give way to the equally debilitating emotions of fear and relief.

"How come your face's all white, Mom?" Davy had asked. "You look funny. Your lips are white, and so's your skin."

"Well?" Davy prompted once more, jarring Diana out of her reverie. "Did you?"

"Did I what?"

"Ever kill anything besides the snake?"

"No," she said. "So help me God, I never did."

As the sun rose above her hospital room window, Rita's life passed by in drowsing review.

Traveling Sickness came to Ban Thak the year Dancing Quail was eight and again away at school. The sickness crept into the village with a returning soldier, and many people fell ill, including all of Dancing Quail's family, from her grandmother right down to little S-kehegaj.

Desperately ill herself, but somewhat less so than the others, Understanding Woman sent word to the outing matron asking that Dancing Quail be brought home from Phoenix to help. Understanding Woman also sent for a blind medicine man from Many Dogs village, a man whose name was S-ab Neid Pi Has, which means Looks At Nothing.

At fifteen, Looks At Nothing left home to work in Ajo's copper mines. Two years later, he was blinded by a severe blow to the head during a drunken brawl in Ajo's Indian encampment. The other Indian died. Looks At Nothing, broken in body and spirit both, returned home to Many Dogs Village. The old medicine man there diagnosed his ailment as Whore-Sickness, which comes from succumbing to the enticing temptations of dreams, and which causes ailments of the eyes.

First Looks At Nothing was treated with ritual dolls. When that didn't work, singers were called in who were good with Whore-Sickness. For four days, the singers smoked their sacred tobacco and sang their Whore-Sickness songs. When the singing was over, Looks At Nothing was still blind, but during the healing process he came to see that his life had a purpose. I'itoi had summoned him home, demanding that the young man turn his back on the white man's ways and return to the traditions of his father and grandfathers before him. In exchange, I'itoi promised, Looks At Nothing would become a powerful shaman.

By the time Understanding Woman summoned him to Ban Thak, Looks At Nothing, although still very young, was already reputed to be a good singer for curing Traveling Sickness. He came to Coyote Sitting, sang his songs, and smoked his tobacco, but unfortunately, he arrived too late. Dancing Quail's parents died, but he did manage to cure both Understanding Woman and Little Pretty One. Looks At Nothing was still there singing when Big Eddie Lopez, dispatched by the outing matron, brought Dancing Quail home from Phoenix.

Riding to Chuk Shon inside the train rather than on it, Dancing Quail was sick with grief. With both her parents dead, what would happen if she had to live without her grandmother and her baby sister, too?

Soon, however, it was clear that Understanding Woman and Pretty One would recover. Dancing Quail was dispatched to pay Looks At Nothing his customary fee, which consisted of a finely woven medicine basket—medicine baskets were Understanding Woman's specialty—and a narrow-necked *olla* with several dogs representing Many Dogs Village carefully etched into the side.

Dancing Quail approached the medicine man shyly as he gathered up his remaining tobacco and placed it in the leather pouch fastened around his waist. At the sound of her footsteps, he stopped what he was doing. "Who is it?" he asked, while his strange, sightless eyes stared far beyond her.

"Hejel Wi'ikam," she answered. "Orphaned Child. I have brought you your gifts."

Looks At Nothing motioned for her to sit beside him. First she gave him the basket, then the *olla*. His sensitive fingers explored each seam and crevice. "Your grandmother does fine work," he said at last.

They sat together in silence for some time. "You are glad to be home?" he asked.

"I'm sorry about my parents," she said, "but I'm glad to be in Ban Thak. I do not like school or the people there."

Looks At Nothing reached out and took Dancing Quail's small hand in his, holding it for a long moment before nodding and allowing it to fall back into her lap.

"You will live in both worlds, little one," he said. "You will be a bridge, a *puinthi*."

Dancing Quail looked up at him anxiously, afraid he meant Big Eddie would take her right back to Phoenix, but Looks At Nothing reassured her. "You will stay here for now. Understanding

Woman will need your help with the fields and the baby."

"How do you know all this?" she asked.

He smiled down at her. "I have lost my sight, Hejel Wi'ikam," he said kindly, "but I have not lost my vision."

Fat Crack drove his tow truck south past Topawa on his fool's errand. Rita had told him that Looks At Nothing still lived at Many Dogs Village across the border in Old Mexico.

The international border had been established by treaty between Mexico and the United States without either country acknowledging that their arbitrary decision effectively divided in half and disenfranchised the much older—nine thousand years older—Papago nation.

Because Many Dogs Village was on the Mexican side, Fat Crack would have to cross the border at The Gate—an unofficial and unpatrolled crossing point in the middle of the reservation. Once in Mexico, he would have to make his way to the village on foot, or perhaps one of the traders from the other side would offer him a ride.

Supposing Fat Crack did manage to find the object of his search, how would he bring the old man back to Rita's bedside in the Indian Health Service Hospital? According to Fat Crack's estimates, if Looks At Nothing were still alive, he would be well into his eighties. Such an old man might not be eager to travel.

The Gate was really nothing but a break in the

six-strand border fence surrounded by flat open desert and dotted, on both sides, with the parked pickups of traders and customers alike. Owners of these trucks did a brisk business in bootleg liquor, tortillas, tamales, and goat cheese, with an occasional batch of pot thrown in for good measure.

Fat Crack approached one of the bootleggers and inquired how to find Looks At Nothing's house. The man pointed to a withered old man sitting in the shade of a mesquite tree.

"Why go all the way to his house?" the man asked derisively. "Why not see him here?"

Looks At Nothing sat under the tree with a narrow rolled bundle and a gnarled ironwood cane on the ground in front of him. As Fat Crack approached, the sightless old man scrambled agilely to his feet. "Have you come to take me to Hejel Wi'ikam?" he asked.

Fat Crack was taken aback. How did the old man know? "Hejel Wi'ithag," he corrected respectfully. "An old widow, not an orphaned child."

Looks At Nothing shook his head. "She was an orphan when I first knew her. She is an orphan still. *Oi g hihm*," he added. "Let's go."

Fat Crack helped the wiry old man climb up into the tow truck. How did Looks At Nothing know someone would come for him that day? Surely no one in Many Dogs owned a telephone, but the old man had appeared at The Gate fully prepared to travel.

Devout Christian Scientist that he was, Fat Crack was far too much of a pragmatist to deny, on religious grounds, that which is demonstrably obvious. Looks At Nothing, that cagey old shaman, would bear close watching.

Brandon Walker dreaded going home. He figured that after he'd spent the whole night AWOL, Louella would be ready to have his ears. He stopped in the kitchen long enough to hang his car keys on the pegboard and to pour himself a cup of coffee, steeling himself for the inevitable onslaught. Instead of being angry, however, when his frantic mother came looking for him, she was so relieved to see him that all she could do was blither.

"It's a piano, Brandon. Dear God in heaven, a Steinway!"

"Calm down. What are you talking about?"

"Toby. I worry about buying food sometimes, and here he goes and orders a piano. For his sister, the concert pianist, he told them. His sister's been dead for thirty-five years, Brandon. What is Toby thinking of? What are we going to do?"

"Did the check clear?"

"No. Of course not. Do you know how much Steinways cost? The store called me and said there must be some mistake. I told them it was a mistake, all right."

"Where's Dad now?"

"Inside. Taking a nap. He said he was tired."

"Let's go, Mother," Brandon ordered. "Get your car." This time he wasn't going to allow any argument.

"The car? Where are we going?"

"Downtown to the bank. We'll have to hurry. It's Saturday, and they're only open until noon. We're closing that checking account once and for all."

Louella promptly burst into tears. "How can we do that to your father, Brandon, after he's worked so hard all these years? It seems so . . . so underhanded."

"How many Steinways do you want, Mom?" His position was unassailable.

"I'll go get my purse. Do you think he'll be all right here by himself if he wakes up?"

"He'll have to be. There's no one else we can leave him with. We'll hurry, but we've both got to go to the bank."

It wasn't until he was left alone with the young deputy that Ernesto Tashquinth realized exactly how much trouble he was in. Come to think of it, the Pinal County homicide detective had been asking him some pretty funny questions: Why did he go up the mountain to check the spring in the first place? What was the woman's name again? How long had he known her? How well did he know her?

Ernesto tried to be helpful. He patiently answered the questions as best he could. The buzzards, he told them. He had seen the circling buzzards, and he was afraid if something was dead up there, the smell might come down to the picnic-table area and get him in trouble with his boss.

But now the detective had gone up the mountain to oversee the removal of the body, and Ernesto was left with a young hotshot deputy who couldn't resist swaggering.

"How come you bit that poor lady's boob off, Big Man? Do you know what happens to guys like you once you're inside?"

Ernesto didn't need the deputy to draw him any pictures. He remembered all too well a former schoolmate from Sacaton who, accused of raping a white woman, had turned up dead in a *charco*, suffocated on his own balls.

"I want a lawyer," Ernesto said quietly. "I don't have to say anything more until I have a lawyer."

"The judge will be only too happy to appoint you one, if you live that long," the deputy told him with a leering grin. "He'll do it by Monday or Tuesday at the latest, but it's a long time between now and then, chief. If I were you, I'd be good—very, very good."

They brought squares of Jell-O for lunch, and Juanita tried to feed them to her, but Rita shook her head and closed her eyes once more.

The next years passed happily for Dancing Quail, although no one called her that anymore. She became Understanding Woman's *ehkthag*, her shadow. Dancing Quail kept busy caring for her little sister, looking after the fields, and helping her grandmother make baskets and pottery. At age six S-kehegaj herself went off to school, taking her turn at riding to Chuk Shon in Big Eddie's wagon. Pretty One thrived in the new environment. She returned home the following summer wishing to be called only by her new Anglo name, Juanita, and refusing to part with her stiff leather shoes.

When Dancing Quail's young charge went off to school, no one thought to send her. People forgot that Dancing Quail was little more than a child herself. By then, her grandmother was so frail that she needed someone with her most of the time. Dancing Quail was happy to be that someone. She spent all her waking hours with Understanding Woman, caring for her and learning whatever lessons her grandmother cared to teach.

Dancing Quail was fourteen and had passed her first menstruation with all due ceremony the summer Father John rode into her life. He had hair the color of autumn grass and funny red skin that sometimes peeled and flaked off in the hot sun.

Father John came to Ban Thak because the sisters at Topawa had sent him. They worried that Alice Antone's orphaned daughter was growing up too much under her grandmother's pagan influence. The girl never came to church anymore, not even at Christmas and Easter. The sisters sent Father John in hopes that by offering the girl a cleaning job at the mission in Topawa, they might also coax her back into the fold.

Father John, fresh out of seminary, was an earnest young man on his first assignment. When he saw Rita with her long black hair flowing loose and glossy around her shoulders, when he saw her dancing brown eyes and bright white teeth against tawny skin, he thought her the loveliest, most exotic creature he had ever encountered. He was intrigued by the fact that, despite the heat, she didn't wear shoes. When he rode into the village in his dusty, coughing touring car, she ran beside it barefoot, along with the other village children, laughing and making fun of him because they could run faster than he could drive.

He spoke to Understanding Woman that afternoon as best he could. Unable to communicate in a common language, they were forced to call upon Dancing Quail to translate in her own inadequate English. She giggled as she did so.

Father John trotted out all his best arguments, including the one he thought would make the most difference. "If you work at the mission," he said, "the sisters will pay you money so you can buy nice things for yourself and for your grandmother."

"Where?" she asked. "Where will I buy these things? The trading post is far from here. I have no horse and no car."

"I could give you a ride sometimes," he offered.

"No," Dancing Quail said decisively. "I will stay here."

"What did he say?" Understanding Woman asked anxiously. There had been several exchanges during which Dancing Quail had translated nothing.

"He wants me to work at the mission. I told him no. My place is here with you."

"Good," Understanding Woman said, patting her young granddaughter's hand. "It is better that you stay in Ban Thak."

A Mormon missionary, dressed in a stiffly pressed white shirt and wearing a carefully knotted tie, brought word to Rebecca Tashquinth that her son, S-abamk, the Lucky One, was being held in the Pinal County jail in Florence and that he would most likely be charged with the brutal murder of Margaret Danielson. It was thought, the missionary reported dutifully, that the woman had been raped as well, but no one knew that for sure. Not yet.

Rebecca was well aware of the kinds of lawyers local judges appointed for Indian defendants, particularly those accused of serious crimes against Anglos. She didn't waste time on a useless trip to Florence. The guards at the jail wouldn't have let her see her son anyway. Instead, she got in the car and drove to Ahngam, Desert Broom Village, to speak to her father.

Eduardo Jose was a man of some standing in the community, a man with both livestock and a thriving bootleg-liquor business. Eduardo knew how to deal with Anglos. He had even hired himself an Anglo lawyer once to help him when the cops had caught him transporting illegal tequila across nonreservation land to the annual *O'odam Tash* celebration in Casa Grande.

If anyone could help her son in all this, Rebecca's father was the man who could do it.

* * *

Diana was still angry with Rita when she got to the hospital. She resented Davy's questions about his father, questions he had never asked before. She blamed Rita for bringing all that ancient history back to the foreground, but when she saw the old woman, seemingly shriveled in the bed and swathed in bandages, she forgot her anger.

Rita's sister, Juanita, was sitting by the bed when Diana entered the room, but she rose at once and went out into the hallway. Diana knew Juanita didn't like her, and she had long since ceased worrying about it. If Gary's parents didn't understand why she and Rita were inseparable, why should Rita's relatives do any better?

Rita opened her eyes when Diana stepped to the head of the bed and touched her good hand.

"How's Davy?" Rita asked.

"He's fine. He has a few stitches in his head, that's all."

"Is he here? Can I see him?"

"The doctor won't let him come into the room. He's too young. You have to be sixteen."

Rita reached for her water glass and took a tentative sip through the straw. "Yesterday was the anniversary," she said quietly. "Davy went with me. He may ask questions."

Diana laughed uneasily. "He already has, Rita. It's all right. I'm getting a lot closer to being able to answer them."

"He'll want you to put up a cross. For his father, I mean. A cross with a wreath and some candles."

"I can't do that."

In Diana Ladd's mixed bag of fallen-away Catholic religion, suicides were never accorded full death benefits. She had told Gary's parents to bury him wherever they liked, but as far as she was concerned, Garrison Ladd still didn't qualify for a memorial wooden cross and never would.

"Why didn't you tell me you were a virgin?"

"You didn't ask."

Diana Lee Cooper and Garrison Ladd cuddled together on Diana's narrow three-quarter bed nestled like a pair of stacked teaspoons. With his back pressed against the wall and his head propped up on one elbow, Gary's other hand glided up and down Diana's slender back. He liked the feel of smooth skin stretched taut over backbone and rib and the gentle curve of waist that melted into the small of her back. He liked fingering the matching indentations of dimples that marked the top of her buttocks. Most of all, he liked the fact that she didn't warn his hand away from places most other girls wouldn't let him touch.

Diana Lee Cooper lay on her side, head on a pillow, with one arm dangling loosely off the edge of the bed. Unsure of herself, Diana worried that perhaps it hadn't been all Gary had expected. "Was I all right?" she asked.

Garrison Ladd laughed out loud. "It was more than all right." He kissed the back of her neck. "The boys in Joseph must not have been paying attention."

"The boys in Joseph called me names," Diana replied grimly.

"You're kidding."

She shook her head. The boys had called her names, but they were pikers compared to her father. Max Cooper was the champion name-caller of all time.

She turned so she could look Gary Ladd full in the face. Maybe this man who, like her, also hated his father, could help her decode her own, help her understand that looming darker presence who even now reached out across the state and attacked her with bruising words far worse than his punishing fists.

"My father was the worst," she said, carefully controlling her voice. " 'Cunt' happened to be his personal favorite."

Gary Ladd shook his head in disbelief. "Your father called you that to your face?"

"Yes."

"Why?"

"I don't know."

She suspected it was because calling her that robbed her of her books and dignity and cut her down to size. While she still mulled the question, Gary Ladd lost interest in the conversation. He rolled Diana over on her back so he could caress her full breasts and run his hands up and down the ladder of ribs above her smoothly flat abdomen. He twisted the curly auburn pubic hairs around the tips of his fingers and touched what lay concealed beyond those curiously inviting hairs.

He waited to see if she would object and move his probing fingers away. Some girls did, even after screwing their brains out, but Diana didn't. She lay with her eyes closed, her body quiet and complacent beneath his touch. Diana Ladd was the girl of his dreams. How could he have been so lucky?

"What brought you to Eugene?" he asked, wanting to delay a little before taking her again. "How'd you get here?"

"By horse," she answered.

He checked her expression to see if she was joking, but her face was unsmiling, impassive.

"Come on. You're kidding. You rode all the way across Oregon from Joseph to here on a horse?"

"My mother got me the horse, a beautiful sorrel quarter horse," she said. "His name was Waldo. Waldo was my ticket out of town."

Diana came home from school carrying an armload of books, half of them textbooks and the others from the library. She found old Mr. Deeson's pickup, with horse trailer attached, parked in front of their house. The presence of a neighbor's pickup wasn't particularly unusual. Chances were, Mr. Deeson had stopped off to unload some garbage, and her mother had invited him in for a cup of coffee or freshly baked cookies. She often encouraged customers to stop by for half an hour or so in order to stave off her ever-present loneliness.

Diana hurried past the trailer with its stamping load of horseflesh. In the kitchen, she found

George Deeson and her mother chatting over coffee, just as she'd expected. What she hadn't expected was the sudden silence occasioned by her arrival.

"There you are," Iona said eagerly. "We've been waiting for you to come home. I've got a surprise for you."

"What kind of surprise?"

"Out front. I thought you'd want to unload him yourself."

For a moment, Diana wasn't sure she'd heard correctly. "Unload him?" she repeated. "You mean the horse? That's the surprise?"

"Your Granddaddy Dale did me a favor once way back when," George Deeson drawled. "I never did quite get around to paying him back once I got on my feet. My brother gave me this here horse out yonder, and Waldo—that's his name by the way—was just standing around in my pasture, taking up room and eating my hay.

"The girl who had him before, my niece, I'm sorry to say, didn't do justice by him a'tall. All she ever did was race barrels. Take him out, run him around those barrels hell-bent-for-election, and then lock him right back up in his stall. A good horse needs more than that, needs some companionship, needs some time off. Know what I mean?"

Diana nodded, but she didn't understand, not really. George Deeson continued on as though she did.

"It occurred to me that maybe you folks could

make good use of him. What do you think, girl? Would you like a horse?"

Diana staggered to the table and put down her load of books. She had long ago shed the childish dream of ever having a horse of her own. The Coopers simply didn't have the money. Not only was there the initial purchase price, there was also the ongoing expense of feed and upkeep and tack. In addition, Max Cooper had told his daughter over and over again that he didn't like horses and wouldn't ever have one on his place.

"We can't afford it, can we, Mother?"

"I already told you, girl, that there horse is free," George put in. "You don't have to pay a dime for him. I've got the papers right here in my pocket, all ready to sign over to you."

"We'll manage," Iona told her daughter firmly. "You just sign the papers and don't worry about it."

"But what'll Daddy do? He always said . . ."

"Never mind what your father said," Iona countered. "I'll handle him. You go ahead and sign the papers."

Within minutes, the bill of sale was signed, and Waldo, a registered quarter-horse gelding, belonged to Diana Lee Cooper.

"I reckon we'd otta go unload him now," George Deeson said. "He'll ride in a trailer all right as long as it's movin', but he don't much like standin' around being cooped up in 'em for very long afterward. Me neither, if you know what I mean, missus."

George Deeson picked up his battered straw

hat from the floor next to his chair and led the way out to the pickup and trailer. Waldo came complete with a whole set of tack-horse blankets, two saddles, and several bridles, all of which George Deeson unloaded in a heap on the Coopers' front porch.

"Are you sure all this comes with the horse?" Diana asked.

"Sure, I'm sure," he told her. "Now your mama said we should take Waldo and all his stuff out to the old barn. She says she's fixed him up a stall."

George eased the horse out of the trailer and handed the reins over to Diana. "You'd better try leadin' him. He'll need to be gettin' used to you, and you'd better plan on spendin' plenty of time with him, too."

Diana led the way around to the old barn where a newly cleaned stall was waiting. When had her mother had time to do so much extra work along with all the other things that demanded her attention?

"Know anything about takin' care of horses?" George Deeson asked.

"Not very much. I've never owned one before. Some of my friends have horses, but I don't get to ride very often."

"Reckon I'll be over of a Saturday mornin' to give you a lesson or two as long as your mama throws in some of her coffee and homemade biscuits."

"How come, Mr. Deeson? I don't understand."

"How come? Why, girl, hasn't your mama told

you yet? Me and her's gonna turn you into a rodeo queen."

"Me?" Diana asked in stunned disbelief.

"Yup, you. You're how old now? Thirteen?"

Diana nodded.

"It'll take around four years, I reckon, give or take." He leaned over and studied Diana's face.

"Yup," he said, "this girl's got good bones. She'll do just fine, but take it from me, missus, them braids gotta go. Braids don't win no prizes these days, although they used to. They sure enough did, and not so very far back, neither."

That evening, after supper, Iona cut off Diana's braid. The following day, when school got out, Iona drove Diana to the drugstore in La Grande and bought her rollers, hair spray, combs and brushes, and makeup. When Diana came downstairs the next morning wearing her first tentative attempt at makeup, she waited for her father to say something, but he was strangely silent on the subject, almost as though he didn't notice.

The next Saturday morning and for almost every Saturday morning that followed during the next four years, George Deeson appeared at the Coopers' house bright and early to spend hours working with Diana and Waldo. When it was too cold to be outside, they worked in the barn. He taught her saddling and bridling and grooming. Together, Waldo and George Deeson taught Diana barrel racing. George taught her how to sit astride the horse so girl and horse were a single, symbiotic unit. He taught her how to read Waldo's moods, how to calm him down during rumbling thunderstorms and barrages of exploding fire-crackers, how to coax him in and out of unfamil-iar horse trailers.

George Deeson taught Diana self-reliance, en-couraged her to take Waldo off on long, solitary trail rides to one of the fifty-two alpine lakes in the Willowa Mountains surrounding Joseph, Oregon. There, with only her horse and her books, alone sometimes for days at a time, Diana could read and fish and care for her horse far away from Iona and Max Cooper's day-to-day conflicts. And those trips weren't good only for Diana, either. Starved for human companionship by his previ-ous owner, Waldo thrived on the generous doses of attention Diana lavished on him.

But more than all that, George Deeson edu-cated Diana Lee Cooper in something she never could have learned from her own mother. George Deeson taught Diana presence, schooled her in how to carry herself. He tutored her in the art of smiling and helped her master the rodeo-queen wave. Most of all, he infected her with his un-shakable belief that one day she really would be queen of the Chief Joseph Days Rodeo.

George Deeson taught Diana all that and more. It didn't dawn on her until years later that he never told her why.

And she didn't ask.

9

*L*OOKS AT NOTHING rode in the truck with-out saying a word, offering no explanation and asking for none. Fat Crack did the same.

Halfway back to Sells, a call came in from Law and Order on the truck's two-way radio. The tribal-police dispatcher told Fat Crack that he was needed near the Quijotoa Trading Post, where an Anglo lady's Winnebago had broken down on her way to Rocky Point. She wanted a tow back home to Casa Grande.

Fat Crack was disappointed. He had wanted to go along to the hospital and watch the old medi-cine man strut his stuff. Now, that would be im-possible.

In the early afternoon, Fat Crack came through the low pass outside Wedged Turtle Village, which Anglos call Sells. As the truck slowed for the cattle guard marking the village boundary, Looks At Nothing held out his hand. "Stop here," he said.

"My aunt is in the hospital," Fat Crack ob-jected. "Let me take you there."

"No," Looks At Nothing responded. "I will go to her later. Not now. Let me out."

Fat Crack stopped, and Looks At Nothing climbed down.

"But there's nothing here," Fat Crack said through the open window. "At least let me take you to the trading post."

Looks At Nothing shook his head. "I have what I need," he said. "I will wait under a tree until it is time."

As Fat Crack drove away, he glanced back in the rearview mirror. Looks At Nothing, shimmering like a ghost in the rising midday heat, poked around with his cane in the nearby dirt and loose gravel. Then, after locating the soft shoulder of the road, the old man carefully made his sightless way down the steep embankment, heading unerringly toward the shade of a small grove of trees.

Fat Crack shook his head. Some things defied explanation. This was certainly one of them.

Long ago, a medicine man raised his daughter alone. She was good and beautiful and hardworking. The wise man taught his daughter that she must not laugh at silly things, or men would think she was too easy.

When the girl grew up and was ready to marry, her father said she would marry whoever could make her laugh. First Coyote tried, and then Whippoorwill, and even Horned Toad, but none of them could make her laugh.

One day Coyote was sitting on a hill when he saw the girl he still wanted to marry. She was walking around gathering wood, and her burden basket was walking behind her. Burden baskets never walk on their own sticks, but, as I told you, the girl's father was a very powerful medicine man.

Coyote kept watching. The girl gathered a large stack of wood and loaded it into the basket, and still the burden basket followed her. As she started back to the village, Coyote came down to where she and her basket were walking.

"So," Coyote said. "Your basket walks around."

As soon as he said that, the basket stopped walking and turned into a mountain—Giwho Tho'ag or Quijotoa, as the whites call it.

And that, nawoj, *is the story of Burden Basket Mountain.*

Early afternoon passed with no word from Fat Crack and Looks At Nothing. Worrying that perhaps the medicine man would not come, Rita closed her eyes once more.

By age sixteen, most Papago girls were married. With the outing matron's help, educated girls could now find domestic jobs in Tucson, Phoenix, and even California. Girls like that were especially prized wife material on the cash-poor reservation, but Dancing Quail was no prize. No one wanted to marry her.

Earnings from domestic service were far more than Dancing Quail made selling baskets and *ollas*. Not only that, anyone marrying Hejel Wi'ikam, as people now called her, would assume the added burden of her ready-made family—a blind, useless old grandmother and an arrogant younger sister named Juanita.

Once more the determined Franciscan sister saw a chance to redeem Alice Antone's elder daughter. Once more they sent Father John to carry their message.

"Come to Topawa and work in the mission," he said. "The sisters will teach you how to clean houses so that one day you, too, will be able to work in Phoenix or Tucson."

For the first time, even Dancing Quail saw her lack of education as a liability. "But what of my grandmother?" she asked. "I can't leave her here alone in Ban Thak."

For this, Father John had a prerehearsed answer. "Bring her along. There's a little house near the mission where you can both live. She won't be far away. You'll be able to care for her and still work and earn money."

Dancing Quail considered the offer for several long moments. Without men to look after their fields and livestock, she and Understanding Woman had struggled desperately just to survive. White man's money was the key, and the girl knew it.

"How would I get her there?" she asked. "My grandmother is old. It's a long way from Coyote Sitting to Burnt Dog Village."

"Don't worry," Father John told her. "Pack your things. In two days, I'll come back and take both of you in my car."

Dancing Quail was dubious. "What if she won't go?"

But the old woman surprised everyone and voiced no objection. It was time her granddaughter married. Burnt Dog Village offered far more potential suitors than Coyote Sitting.

With Dancing Quail's help, Understanding Woman began to pack. One by one, she gathered her possessions and placed them in two old-fashioned crossed-stick burden baskets. The most treasured item was Understanding Woman's only remaining medicine basket, the last one she had made before her eyesight failed.

"*Ni-ka' amad,*" Understanding Woman said. "Granddaughter, do you still have the medicine basket I gave you that time?"

Dancing Quail hung her head in shame, grateful for once for her grandmother's blindness. She had never admitted to anyone how she had lost Understanding Woman's beautifully colored spirit rock or how the school attendants had taken the medicine basket away from her as soon as they found it rolled up in her blanket. They had confiscated it, and she never saw it again.

"No, *ni-kahk,*" Dancing Quail said softly. "No, Grandmother. I lost it long ago."

She was afraid her grandmother would think she hadn't appreciated the gifts, hadn't treated them with proper respect.

"The rock, too?" Understanding Woman asked.

"The rock, too."

For a time, the old woman sat fingering that final medicine basket. It wasn't nearly as well made as earlier ones had been. The seams were crooked. Some of the weaves were as rough-edged as if the work had been done by a rank beginner. Rough or not, though, this had been her own special basket, the one she had kept entirely to herself. Instead of packing it along with her other household goods, she placed it on the ground beside her.

"It does not matter, *ni-ka' amad*," Understanding Woman said. "I will teach you to make another."

The next day, when Father John drove up in his spindle-wheeled touring car, the two women waited outside their adobe house with two fully loaded burden baskets standing between them.

"Ready?" he said.

In the two years since first coming to the reservation, Father John had learned to speak some Papago. He sensed that the old woman had never ridden in an automobile before and that she was anxious about it.

Dancing Quail went to load the burden baskets while Father John eased Understanding Woman to her feet and helped her to the car. "Are you afraid, Grandmother?" he asked.

The old woman shook her head. "No," she answered, although her voice quivered. "I am not afraid."

Just then something slipped from her hand. She gasped and bent to retrieve it, but the small basket rolled out of the car onto the ground, spilling as it fell.

Father John quickly gathered the fallen basket and its scattered contents, scooping things back into it almost without looking—a tiny straw doll with a strange clay face, a small fragment of broken geode, and something that looked like a hank of human hair, a chipped arrowhead. The old woman's hands were still desperately searching the floorboard of the car when Father John placed the restored basket safely under them.

"Is this what you're looking for?" he asked.

Understanding Woman nodded gratefully and clutched the basket to her shriveled breast as though it were a precious newborn baby.

"Yes," she murmured, settling back. "Thank you."

Rita had no idea Juanita had gone home. When she opened her eyes, she saw a brown-robed figure sitting there in her sister's place, head bowed in the afternoon sun. She knew at once who it was, although she hadn't seen him for twenty years. In the mid-fifties, she had gone to San Xavier for a Saint Francis feast and run into him by accident not realizing that after years in California, he had transferred back to the Papago.

Unaware she was awake, Father John's beads clicked quietly in liver-spotted hands as he intoned a whispered rosary in her behalf. Silently, she examined every minute detail of him— parchment-like skin stretched across bony knuckles, sparse hair white now rather than the color of dried grass. Like his hands, the bald place on his head was dotted with large brown spots. Underneath the brown cassock, he was precariously thin.

He's old now, too, Rita thought. We're both old. She said, "Are you still trying to save my soul?"

Father John's head jerked up at the sound of her

voice. "And mine," he answered quietly. "Yours and mine."

She turned her face to the wall, surprised that after all this time unbidden tears still sprang to her eyes at the mere sound of his voice. What was he doing here in the hospital room with her? How had he found her? She had never asked for his help. Who had called him?

"Your sister called me," he said, answering the unspoken question. "After what happened to Gina years ago, I asked Juanita to let me know if anything . . ."

"Go away," Rita said, refusing to turn and face him again.

"But . . ."

"Go away," she insisted.

She heard the heavy swish of his robe as he rose to his feet. Beads rattled when he dropped them into a pocket.

"If there's ever anything I can do . . ."

Still she didn't look at him.

"*Ni-gm hu wabsh oan*," he began. "Forgive me. Dancing Quail, please forgive me."

Rita didn't answer. Father John left, closing the door gently behind him. Afterward, Rita tried to blot him from her mind, but he wouldn't leave. He was there, walking around in her soul, not as he was now, old and liver-spotted, but young again, tall and straight, with a headful of palomino-colored hair.

Before he visited the storage locker, Andrew Carlisle stopped at Woolworth's and bought himself a long blond wig, a selection of makeup, and some suitable women's clothing, including a frilly blouse, an obscenely padded bra, and a pair of thongs. He had concluded it would probably be best if a woman showed up at the locker, and the clothing would come in handy for his private fund-raising program later on in the day.

The wig served a dual purpose. It concealed his newly achieved baldness, and it also protected the tender, underexposed skin from the glaring June sun. The few minutes he'd spent outside at Picacho Peak had given him a good start on a painful sunburn.

He used a discreet stop at a gas station to change clothes. He went into the men's room as a man and came out as a woman. Fortunately, no one was watching, but when he arrived at U-Stor-It-Here off Fort Lowell and Alvernon, Andrew Carlisle almost laughed aloud at his having taken such elaborate precautions. The woman in the RV-turned-office waved him through the open gate without a second glance, no questions asked.

Carlisle enjoyed the anonymity of being a nameless, faceless woman as he sorted through the locker and inventoried his own equipment. It was almost as if he were someone else checking through a stranger's possessions.

The survival gear was all there. He opened the hasp-held lid on the metal fifty-five-gallon drum and looked through the freeze-dried food he kept there as well as the water-purification equipment and tablets. He had no intention of allowing the adventure of a lifetime to be short-circuited by a raging case of diarrhea brought on by drinking giardia-contaminated water.

Other than noticing his survival equipment and commenting on it, his mother hadn't messed with any of it. Carlisle was grateful for that. Good for Myrna Louise. Maybe she was actually getting a little smarter with age, although he doubted it.

Andrew had always been a bright boy—he took after his father, Howard, in the brains department. He aced his way through every private school in which his ambitious grandmother had enrolled him. He knew he was smart, and he knew equally well that his mother wasn't. Her overwhelming stupidity was always both a shameful burden and a mystery to him.

While still a child, he wondered how his father had ever become involved with fifteen-year-old Myrna Louise in the first place. Only in adulthood did he finally conclude that basic good looks and raw sex appeal were his mother's main assets. Were in the past and remained so in certain geriatric quarters. After all, she had reeled Jake Spaulding in without the least difficulty. Myrna Louise's big problem was always keeping a man once she got him.

In addition to stupidity, that was Myrna Louise's major flaw—she had never learned the meaning of power or how to use it. Her son had, certainly not in his undergraduate days at Southern Cal and not in the rarefied and surprisingly easy Ph.D. program at Harvard, either, a school where he once again took top honors. No, Andrew Carlisle learned the basics of power, about the granting and withholding of favors, about exploiting both the weak and the powerful, during his years in prison at Florence, during his post-Ph.D. program, as he called it.

Nobody really expected that he'd be sent to prison. That didn't usually happen to educated white men no matter what their crime, but go to prison he did. He left the courthouse with the searing image of an awkwardly pregnant but triumphant Diana Ladd burned into his memory. If she had dropped it, if she hadn't kept pressing the cops and the prosecutors, no one would have given a damn about Gina Antone. Diana Ladd was the one person who had cost him those precious years out of his life. He would see that she paid dearly for it.

At first he merely wanted her dead, her and the child she carried as well. He employed vivid fantasies of what he'd do to her in order to dull the pain of what was happening to him during his own brutal initiation to prison life.

Over the years, he'd refined his thinking about exactly what he wanted from Diana Ladd. The Margaret Danielsons of the world were useful in the short term, good for immediate gratification, but they afforded little genuine satisfaction. Real vengeance, authentic eye-for-an-eye-type vengeance, demanded more than that. Whatever price he exacted from Diana Ladd would have to be equal to that required of him by those thugs in the prison—absolute submission and unquestioning obedience, no more, no less. The key to that would be her child. . . .

With some difficulty, Carlisle roused himself from contemplation. He wondered uneasily how long he'd been standing, lost in thought, in that overheated storeroom. Slipping in and out of his imagination like that was dangerous. He would have to pay more attention, keep a better grip on what he was doing. The ability to deliberately disassociate himself from reality was a necessary survival skill in prison, but letting it sneak up on him unawares on the outside could cause trouble.

Even so, thinking about Diana Ladd was sensuously seductive, irresistible. Knowingly now, he let himself slip back into the dream. Where would he take her? he wondered idly. Where would he have the time—it would take some time, of course—to do all he wanted, to bring the bitch to her knees?

The answer came in such a brilliant flash of inspiration that it seemed he must have known it all along. Thinking about it made him giddy. It was so right, so perfectly appropriate to go back to the place Garrison Ladd had shown him, to use the man's own pitiful excuse at research to destroy his entire family, both widow and child. How wonderfully appropriate.

Carlisle took one last careful look around the storeroom. He had moved all the necessary equipment into one corner so it would be easily accessible and could be gathered at a moment's notice, but except for a hunting knife, he didn't take any of it along with him in Jake Spaulding's Valiant. Not right then. It wasn't time yet.

He went out and closed the door behind him, locking it with a real sense of purpose and anticipation. All he had to do now was find Diana Ladd and that lump of a baby of hers. The child must be six years old by now. Once he did that, the rest would take care of itself. All things come to them who wait.

Dr. Rosemead said you had to be sixteen years old to visit with the patients in their rooms. While his mother was down the hall in Rita's room, Davy waited in the busy lobby. He watched with interest as a very sunburned white man came in through the doors and hurried to the desk. A thick curtain of silence fell over the room.

"I'm looking for a patient named Rita Antone," the man said loudly, glancing down at a small notebook he carried.

"Who?" the Indian clerk asked.

"Rita Antone," he repeated. "An old lady who was hurt in a car wreck yesterday."

"I don't know her," the clerk said.

Davy couldn't believe his ears. This was the very same clerk who had, only minutes before, given his mother the number to Rita's room.

"They told me she came here by ambulance. Did she die?"

"I don't know," the clerk repeated blankly.

With an impatient sigh, the man gave up, stuffed the notebook back in his pocket, and retreated the way he had come. Almost without realizing what he was doing, Davy followed the man outside and caught up with him as he climbed into his car.

"I know Rita," Davy said.

Surprised, the man swung around and looked down at him. "You do? Really?"

Davy nodded. "That woman in there told a lie. Rita is too in there. My mom's with her."

The hot sun shone on Davy's stitches, making them itch. Unconsciously, he scratched them.

"Wait a minute," the man said suspiciously, kneeling and staring at the sutured wound. "Wait just one minute. What happened to your head?"

"I cut it. Yesterday."

"How?"

"When the truck turned over, I guess."

"Rita Antone's truck?" the man asked.

Davy nodded, wondering how the man knew about that.

"So you must be the boy who told my friend about the ambulance on the mountain?"

"You know the man in the red car?" Davy returned.

"As a matter of fact, I do," the man said with a smile. "You're actually the person I wanted to see. Let's go over there in the shade and talk." They left the man's car and headed toward a mesquite-shaded concrete bench just outside the hospital door. "What's your name?"

"Davy."

"Davy what?"

"Davy Ladd."

"And where do you live, Davy?"

"In Tucson."

"What's your mother's name?"

"Diana."

The man had taken the notebook back out of his pocket and was scribbling furiously in it. Now, he paused and frowned, cocking his head to one side. "What's your daddy's name?"

"I don't have a daddy," Davy told him. "My daddy's dead."

"I'll be damned!" the man exclaimed. "You're Garrison Ladd's son, aren't you!"

Davy could hardly believe his ears. He knew from his grandmother's Christmas letters that Garrison was his father's name, but he had never heard it spoken by anyone other than his mother when she was reading those letters aloud. His blue eyes grew large.

"You mean you knew my daddy?"

"I sure did," the man answered. "We had a class together at the U back when I still thought I was going to be a novelist when I grew up. I guess Gary did, too. We were both wrong."

"You mean my daddy wanted to write books?"

The man looked startled. "Sure. Didn't you know that?"

"I don't know anything about my daddy. He died before I was born."

For a moment, the man's eyes grew serious, and then he nodded. "I'll tell you what, Davy, you tell me what you know about Rita Antone, and I'll tell you what I know about your father. Deal?"

He held out his hand, and the boy placed his

own small one in it. "Deal," Davy said gravely, and they shook on it.

Louella Walker sat up straight and chatted almost hopefully as they returned from their brief trip to the bank. The lady there had been most helpful.

"The same thing happened to my grandmother," Anna Bush had said sympathetically, when they explained the situation. She graciously made arrangements to drop service charges on the bounced Steinway check.

"The only sensible thing to do is to start a new account with just your signature and your son's on it, if that's all right."

In the end, that's what they did.

"She was very nice," Louella was saying to her son as they drove home, "although I still feel a little underhanded. It's like I'm robbing your father of his dignity."

She said that as they turned off Swan onto Fifth and came within sight of their own driveway three blocks away. Brandon saw the problem long before Louella did.

"Oh, my God!" he muttered grimly.

"What's the matter?"

"My car," he said. "The department's car. It's gone."

As a homicide detective, he took his county-owned vehicle home in case he was called to a crime scene over the weekend when the department was seriously understaffed. For years, everyone in the family had hung car keys on a kitchen pegboard upon entering the house. Pure reflex, it was a habit no one thought to change in the face of Toby Walker's failing mental capacity.

"Your car?" Louella asked, puzzled, not yet grasping the seriousness of the situation. "Wherever would it be?"

When Diana came down the hall from Rita's room, Davy wasn't waiting in the lobby. She found him outside, drinking a forbidden Coke. He seemed distant, uncommunicative.

"What's the matter?" she asked.

"Nothing," he said.

"Are you worried about Rita?"

"I guess," he told her.

"Well, don't be. Dr. Rosemead says she's going to be fine."

Diana was tired when she and Davy got back home. She put the boy down for a nap and decided to take one herself. Locking the door to her room, she stripped off her clothes and lay naked under the vent from the cooler, letting the refreshing, slightly PineSol-scented air blow across her body.

She was tired, but she couldn't sleep. Instead, she lay there and castigated herself for her unreasonable outburst at Brandon Walker. After all, she was the one who had started bawling on his shoulder. What red-blooded American male wouldn't have got the wrong idea? It was just that she didn't want this particular male anywhere in her vicinity. His presence brought up too many unpleasant memories, reminded her of a time in her life that she wanted to keep buried far beneath the surface of conscious thought.

So, of all possible people in the world, why had she chosen Brandon Walker's shoulder to cry on? She realized now that she was lonely for male companionship, but was she so desperate that she would throw herself at the first available man who chanced across her path?

But then, what was so new and different about that? she asked herself grimly. Nothing at all. The loneliness had always been there, for as long as she could remember, and it had always made her do stupid things—Garrison Ladd being a prime case in point.

They'd been inseparable that first weekend, and he had insisted on helping her with her Sunday papers. Then, after the paper route, they'd eaten bacon-and-egg breakfasts at the Holiday Inn before going back to his apartment, where, he told her with a guilty grin, he happened to have a real, full-sized double bed.

"I'll only be a minute," he said, leaving her in the doorway of his book-lined living room. "Wait right here."

She was sure he wanted to straighten the room and make the bed before he invited her into it, which she was equally certain he was going to do. Diana Lee Cooper didn't object. Going to bed with him was a foregone conclusion, the reason she'd agreed to come to his apartment in the first place.

She knew he wanted her again, that he couldn't

get enough of her, and Diana Lee Cooper was willing. In fact, she was more than willing.

As she meandered around the room, looking through the collection of books—volumes of poetry and philosophy, a Middle English version of *The Canterbury Tales* complete with margins full of carefully handwritten notes—she realized that she'd do whatever it took to capture and keep this Garrison Ladd.

Here was someone she wanted—a man of intellect, a man of some refinement and grace, a man she could respect, who was, as far as she could tell, as different from her own backwoods father as he could possibly be. That difference was exactly what she'd been searching for—someone not the least bit like Max Cooper.

And if "spreading her legs," as her father would have said, was all it took to win him, then bring on the double bed and spread away. She knew what those words meant now, and she was beginning to have some sense of her own power. She'd show her father, all right. If sex was the bait and Gary Ladd was the prize, she'd screw until Garrison Ladd couldn't walk or talk or see straight, if that's what he wanted. She'd do whatever he asked and more besides.

As she stood there in the apartment's small living room waiting for him, Diana Cooper couldn't see that the furnishings were relatively cheap. Compared to what she knew from Joseph, it was palatial. What she saw convinced her that she'd found the man of her dreams, one worthy of her undying loyalty, someone she could afford to lavish her love on, someone who would give her love and laughter in return.

She was so smitten, so convinced by her own initial, naive assumptions, that it was years before she began to question them. By then, it was too late.

"You can come in now," he called.

As she'd suspected, the bed had been hastily made, with lumpy covers pulled up over pillows but not properly tucked in. He was closing the closet door when she walked into the bedroom.

For the first time, Garrison Ladd seemed slightly unsure of himself. "The couch isn't very comfortable," he said hesitantly. "I thought we could lie here and watch television or something."

The fact that he seemed nervous filled her again with that headspinning, newfound sense of power. Without a word, she kicked off her shoes, slipped out of her jeans, and peeled the University of Oregon sweatshirt off over her head. When she looked up from unfastening her bra, Garrison Ladd was still standing with his hand frozen to the knob on the closet door. He stood unmoving, his eyes feasting hungrily on her nakedness.

"Well?" she said airily, moving toward the bed and turning down the covers. "Are you coming or not?"

He jumped away from the closet.

"You didn't want us to watch television with our clothes on, did you?"

"No," he said with a startled laugh. "No, I guess not."

He hurried out of his own clothes then, dropping them on the floor as he went, and flipping on the switch of the tiny television set as he came to the bed. Gradually, the picture appeared, but the sound stayed off.

Laughing, Garrison Ladd fell across the bed and landed on top of Diana, knocking the breath out of both of them, making them both laugh some more. He kissed her once and then settled his head on the pillow beside her.

"You know," he said thoughtfully, "the 'Playboy Advisor' always said there were girls like you in the world, but I never believed it. Not for a minute."

"Girls like what?" Diana asked, feigning innocence, as though she had no idea what he meant. She wanted to hear him say the words.

"Girls who like *doing* it," he returned.

She bit him gently on the exposed side of his neck, and was gratified to feel under her fingertips the fine layer of gooseflesh that rose at once on the bared skin of his chest.

She remembered how, during one of their Rodeo Royalty weekends in Pendleton or Omak or one of those places, her attendants had explained to her in gory detail exactly how biting affected men, how it turned them on. It was one of those all-night gabfests with the chaperon fast asleep in the motel room next door when Diana finally confessed to the others that the current year's queen of the Chief Joseph Days Rodeo was still a virgin. Shocked runners-up Charlene Davis and Suzanne Lake took it upon themselves to give Diana Lee Cooper the benefit of their own somewhat wider experience.

"If you really want to drive a man crazy," Charlene said, "you bite him all over. Most men can hardly stand it if you do that."

"Or lick 'em," Suzanne added mysteriously. "Like an all-day sucker."

The other two girls rolled on the bed with laughter, although Diana didn't quite understand what was so funny.

"And then . . ." Suzanne said, still laughing and gasping for breath, ". . . and then . . . when they're all excited, you leave 'em high and dry. I did that to stupid Joe Moore, remember him? I'll never forget. His little prick was standing straight up in the air, waving like a rabbit's ear. When I got out of the car, he started to cry, I swear to God. I mean, he was literally bawling like a baby. He came after me and begged me to get back in the car and finish it, and I said to him, 'I don't know what kind of a girl you think I am.' "

And Suzanne and Charlene laughed some more. Diana joined in, but only half-heartedly. It wasn't so funny to her, because she knew then for the first time what her father had meant when he called her that—a prick-tease. Once more she swore to herself that she wouldn't be that. If she teased a man, it would be because she intended to do something about it.

She bit Gary Ladd again, harder this time, just at the base of the neck, her sharp teeth leaving a line of small indentations in the smoothly tanned skin. He groaned above her, and she could feel the hardness of him pressing at her through the covers.

He pawed at the sheet and blanket and pulled them away from her, then he fell on her, burying himself deep inside her body. Bruised and sore, she nonetheless raised welcoming hips to meet him, while behind them, on the silenced television set, Jack Ruby mutely gunned down a handcuffed Lee Harvey Oswald.

It was a weekend where no one got quite what they bargained for—not Ruby, not Oswald, and certainly not Diana Lee Cooper.

Because Toby Walker had essentially stolen a county car, Brandon was reluctant to report it through regular channels. He called Hank Maddern at home and asked for advice.

Maddern's suggestion was succinct. "Report it," he said at once. "That'll get word out to the cars so everybody's looking. In the meantime, I'll come over and we'll see what we can do."

Leaving Louella with strict instructions to remain by the phone, Brandon escaped from the house and his mother to the relative sanity of Hank Maddern's Ford F-100. Maddern drove through the neighborhood in ever-widening circles while the younger man brimmed over with self-reproach.

"It's all my fault," he fumed. "All of it. I never should have left the damned keys there in the first place, but I just didn't think about it. In our house, car keys have been kept on that pegboard for as long as I can remember."

"He's never done anything like this before?" Hank asked.

"Never."

"There's always a first time," Maddern said with a shrug.

One-handed, he shook two cigarettes out of a pack, passed one to Brandon, and then punched the lighter. "And for Chrissake, forget about whose fault it is. Fault doesn't matter. By the way, what was your old man wearing when he took off?"

"Pajamas," Brandon answered. "Red-and-white-striped cotton pajamas."

"Somebody dressed like that shouldn't be too tough to find. How were you fixed for gas?"

"Gas? Almost empty, actually. I should have filled before I left the office yesterday, but I didn't want to take the time. I drove all the way out to Sells and back last night."

"And didn't come home until late, either," Hank added with a mischievous wink. "Did you get lucky?"

"Look, Hank, it wasn't anything like that," Brandon said quickly. "Diana Ladd needed help with the boy, that's all."

"Until five o'clock in the morning? According to Tom Edwards, five was the last time your mother called looking for you."

"Great," Brandon muttered, shaking his head. "That's just great. A little privacy might be nice."

Maddern heard the edginess in Brandon's voice and dropped the subject. "Does your dad have money?"

"With him? A little, maybe, but not much."

"What kind of credit cards? Any bank cards?"

"No. Mom took those away. The department-store cards as well. He probably has a Chevron and a Shell. Maybe a couple of others."

"That's where we'll start then, with gas stations."

They headed north on Swan, stopping at every gas station along the way where Brandon knew his father had a working credit card. They went west on Broadway and south again on Alvernon. At a Chevron station on Alvernon south of Twenty-second Street, they finally hit pay dirt. The young Mexican kid tending the pumps remembered Toby Walker well.

"Hey, man, I thought it was crazy. This guy comes in wearing pajamas and no shoes, driving a county car, and wanting to know how to get to Duluth. Where the hell is Duluth?"

"Minnesota," Brandon said quietly.

"Duluth," Maddern repeated. "Why Duluth?"

"It's where he grew up. On a farm outside Duluth."

The attendant thumbed through the credit-card receipts. "Here it is. Tobias Walker. He took 15.9 gallons of premium and said something about a farm, about going there for dinner. He asked me how to get back over to I-10, and I told him."

They drove to where Alvernon intersected with the freeway. "Which way?" Walker asked. "He's got plenty of gas. He could drive two hundred and fifty miles in either direction without having to stop for more."

"At least we know what to do now," Maddern said.

"What's that?"

"Call the Highway Patrol. If your dad's out on the freeway, it's not just our problem anymore."

Public transportation as known in the Anglo world was nonexistent on the reservation. Hitch-hiking was the alternative.

As Fat Crack left Casa Grande for Sells late in the afternoon, he stopped for a hitchhiker just inside the reservation boundary. Fat Crack could tell from the way the man shambled after the truck that he was drunk, but he offered a ride anyway. "Where to?"

"The Gate," the man said. "I just got outta jail, and I want to get drunk. It sure was bad in there."

For an Indian, this was a talkative drunk. Fat Crack found himself hoping his rider would pass out and sleep until they reached Sells.

They drove past the turnoff to Ahngam. "Do you know Eduardo Jose?" the rider asked.

Fat Crack nodded. Eduardo Jose's bootlegging exploits were legend.

"His grandson's sure in big trouble," the man continued. "They brought him in to the jail this morning. For raping and killing a white lady."

"That's too bad," Fat Crack told him.

They drove for several more miles in stony silence. Both of them knew full well that Indians who went to jail for raping white women didn't generally live long enough to see the inside of a courtroom, let alone a penitentiary.

"He bit her," the man said much later. "What kind of a sickness would make him do that?"

But a stunned Fat Crack didn't answer right away. "You say he bit her?"

The man nodded. "Her *wipih*," he said. "Her nipple. Almost off. One of the deputies told a cook, who told some of the others."

The hairs on the back of Fat Crack's neck stood erect under his gray Stetson. He had heard once before about someone who did that to women, a killer who bit off his victims' nipples. It had happened to Gina, his cousin. Supposedly, Gina's killer was dead.

The cab of the tow truck was suddenly far too small, and the hot air blowing through the opened windows took Fat Crack's breath away.

Just as Looks At Nothing, despite his blindness, had known unerringly where to find the shady grove of trees, Fat Crack knew at once, despite the fact that Gary Ladd was dead, that there was some connection between this dead woman at Cloud Stopper Mountain and his cousin, found murdered in the *charco* of deserted Rattlesnake Skull Village seven years earlier.

Unable to do anything else about it, Fat Crack tightened his grip on the steering wheel, and he began to pray.

Diana must have slept. When she woke up, it was early evening. She dressed hurriedly and guiltily, worrying about what Davy was up to.

She found him on the living-room couch. She could see his head over the back of the couch and see Bone's long, curving tail sticking out from in front of it.

"Are you hungry?" she asked, pausing in the doorway.

Davy didn't look up. He was working on something in his lap, staring down intently, lips pursed, shoulders hunched, brow furrowed.

"What are you doing?" Diana asked when he didn't answer.

She walked up to him and peered down over his shoulder. His lap was full of whitened yucca leaves. In his hand was the small awl Rita had given him for his birthday.

"What in the world are you doing with Rita's yucca?" Diana demanded. "You know you're not supposed to touch those."

Davy looked up at her, his eyes filling with tears. "I'm trying to make her a basket," he said. "But I don't know how to do the center."

10

WHEN HE LEFT the storage unit, Andrew Carlisle took with him only the hunting knife. The blade had been honed to a razor sharp edge, which years of careful storage hadn't dulled. The knife was big enough to be deadly, but small enough to conceal in the brightly colored summer bag among his other purchases.

Back in the Valiant, he drove to the Reardon Hotel off Fourth Avenue. He had checked his bank balance and found that he didn't have as much cushion as he wanted. Once finished with Diana Ladd, he would disappear. He needed cold hard cash, running money. He wanted it quickly and from a quarter where no questions would be asked.

When it came to not asking questions, the seedy Reardon suited his purposes admirably. Carlisle had heard about the hotel and bar and its singular clientele from some of the other residents of the joint.

Joint. Thinking about Florence in that jarring bit of jargon always brought a mental smile to

Carlisle's Ph.D.-trained ear. Phraseology wasn't all he'd picked up in prison, not by a long shot. There were always lessons to be learned in that all-male, survival-of-the-fittest environment where sex was a valuable commodity, a bargaining chip. It was a milieu that regarded small men as prized possessions, and Andrew Carlisle was a small man.

Once he understood that exploitation was inevitable, he surrendered willingly and made himself available to the highest bidder, to partners who could make the physical pain and mental degradation most worth his while. He closed his mind to the reality of it even while it was happening, and learned to stand outside himself during the blowjobs and the rest, to calmly total up the privileges each encounter would give him, all the while keeping score of what the outside world would owe him once it was over—the world in general, and Diana Ladd in particular. Every blowjob, every bloody submission, had its price.

Carlisle registered at the Reardon Hotel under an assumed name. The guys in Florence claimed the queers at the Reardon to be easy pickings for an apparently willing stranger. Prison gossip suggested that the closeted homos who frequented the place were always interested in a new piece of tail. Male-to-male prison trysts were a necessary evil, but legitimate fruits, people who lived that way because they chose to, were looked down on with absolute contempt by the convicted felons in the Arizona State Prison.

Carlisle had listened avidly to tales about the

Reardon and other such places. He listened and drew his own conclusions, deciding how such men might fit into his long-term planning. Now, he was ready to transform plan to action.

He dressed carefully, applying makeup and adjusting the wig in a practiced manner. He'd done it before, in Florence, at the behest of one of the prison's head honchos, a man the inmates called PS, short for Peeping Supervisor. PS, a voyeur par excellence, enjoyed arranging private amateur theatricals. Scripts usually called for an ersatz conjugal visit in which inmates played both female and male roles. Brutally forced sex often came into play in these dramatic sketches, with PS and his buddies gaping from the sidelines.

PS was high enough in the prison hierarchy to be able to make suitable arrangements for the shows, including times, places, and appropriate costumes for all performers. Since PS was also in charge of inmate work assignments, plums of which were handed out on a strict patronage basis, his presentations never lacked for volunteer performers.

Carlisle, lusting after a choice inmate-clerk assignment that would give him access to both typewriter and postage, auditioned for PS in private. His enthusiastic performance allowed him to be drafted into the ensemble. Due to small stature, which made costuming him as a woman fairly easy, Carlisle was typecast in female roles. He enjoyed himself immensely. Not the sex per se. Women characters were, by definition, victims. What happened to the "wife" was often physically unpleasant, but Carlisle managed to discover certain psychic rewards.

One was a sense of kinship to his scholarly roots. He had always been struck by Elizabethan drama, by the complex female roles that, during Shakespeare's time, were performed by male actors. Carlisle considered himself capable of doing justice to *King Lear*'s Regan or to Lady Macbeth. He shrugged off typecasting ragging from other inmates because he saw his performances as a challenge. It wasn't his fault that those other ignorant bastards were too dumb to realize he was playing a part in an ancient and ongoing tradition.

His relationship with PS and his theatrical accomplishments provided the cushy job as Mallory's inmate clerk that had been his initial objective, but there was one additional benefit as well. Seeing the effect the playacting had on PS and his like-minded cronies gave Andrew Carlisle a powerful sense of validation. He found it amusing to observe the audience's reactions, to see the rapt attention on their stupid faces and hear their ugly sounds of approval. They liked seeing someone stripped and brutalized before their very eyes. They probably would have liked doing it themselves if they'd just had guts enough, which they didn't.

And that was where the validation came in—from knowing there was no difference between him and those bastards in the audience, between the jailer and the jailed, between the acknowledged perpetrators of crime and violence and those who, theoretically, were dead set against it.

Not all the corrections folks were like PS and his pals. Compared to PS, Mallory was a damned Eagle Scout, but between the bad apples and the criminals, there was hardly an iota of difference. If anything, the inmates maybe had a bit more guts since they had demonstrated the courage of their convictions and had balls enough to act on their baser impulses. But then again, they were also dumb enough to get caught.

Dumb enough to get caught once, Carlisle added to himself as he examined the effect of his cross-dressing in one of the Reardon's deteriorating bathroom mirrors. Once; but not twice. He'd see to it.

For almost an hour, Diana joined Davy on the couch, and the two of them tried to pull together the center coil of Davy's basket, but the slick pieces of cactus sprang apart again and again. Diana had been in the same room while Rita started hundreds of baskets. Now, the Anglo woman berated herself for not paying closer attention. When Rita did it, the process seemed totally effortless. Finally, Diana gave up.

"How about some dinner?" she asked, stretching.

"What kind?" Davy asked. "The tortillas are gone. I already checked."

"Rita's not the only one who can cook around here, you know," Diana told him.

"Can you make tortillas?"

"No."

"Popovers?"

"Well, no."

"See there?" Davy returned glumly, and went back to working on the elusive basket.

Chastened, Diana retreated to the kitchen. Davy was right, in a way. She had got out of the habit of cooking. That was something Rita handled, and the older woman was much better at it than she was. There didn't seem to be any sense in rocking the boat.

Now, though, she looked through her larder, surprised by some of the things she found there. She settled on hot chocolate. She remembered hot chocolate as a cold-weather drink, one her mother would make for wintertime Sunday-night suppers. Iona Cooper had served steaming mugs of hot chocolate accompanied by slices of toast slathered with homemade jam. There were always hunks of sharp cheddar cheese sitting on a platter in the middle of the table. Iona Dade Cooper's hot chocolate, cocoa as she called it, had been anything but ordinary. It wasn't remotely related to the new versions that came dried and in envelopes.

One at a time, Diana gathered the necessary ingredients—chocolate syrup, sugar, salt, canned milk, and vanilla—mixing them as her mother once had, with a glob of this and a pinch of that. When the ingredients were all in the saucepan, she stood stirring it absently over the gas burner, remembering the sudden role reversal after her mother's return from the hospital. She remembered the myriad cups of hot chocolate she had made for her mother, for both of them, in those last few months before the cancer had cheated Iona Dade Cooper of even that small pleasure.

After Iona's diagnosis, Gary returned to Eugene, while Diana dropped out of school—temporarily, she thought—to stay home and care for her dying mother. Someone had to do it, and Max wasn't up to it. The process had taken two full semesters.

At first Gary came over on weekends to spell her a little, but that happened less and less often as the months wore on. It was too long a drive, he said. It took too much time away from his work. And Max Cooper didn't hang around much, either. On those rare occasions when he was there, Diana resented his being in the way and underfoot. When he started staying away, Diana barely noticed his increasingly prolonged absences. She was only too happy to have him out of the way.

Gradually, Diana's world shrank until it encompassed only her mother's room with its hospital bed and cot, the bathroom, and the worn path in the linoleum that led from the bedroom to the kitchen. The days and nights became almost interchangeable except that sometimes, during the day, the endless hours were punctuated by someone from town stopping by with a covered dish.

Iona Cooper had always been a private person, but now the barriers between mother and daughter melted away, leaving them far more intimate than either of them wanted. The forced intimacy deprived them both of dignity as Diana learned to do things she never thought herself capable of—giving shots, caring for her mother's most basic needs, cleaning her, feeding her.

Pain, her mother's enemy, became Diana's mortal enemy as well. She fought it with whatever puny medications the doctors allowed her. Hollow-eyed from lack of sleep, she battled the pain by engaging her mother in countless hours of conversation. Sipping hot chocolate, Diana and her mother talked for months, weeks, and days on end while the blessed periods of respite between one dose of pain medication and the next grew ever shorter and shorter.

"Why?" Diana asked one day. She had heard Max come in and stumble his way upstairs to his own room, bouncing off first one wall and then another, cursing drunkenly under his breath.

Iona's eyes opened and fixed on Diana's face. "Why what?" She had heard her husband, too. The lines of communication between them were all too open. Both mother and daughter knew what the other meant.

"Why did you stay all these years? Why didn't you leave?"

Iona shook her head. "Couldn't," she said.

"Why not?"

"Damaged goods," Iona answered. Turning her face to the wall, that was all she would say, and since turning away was all she had left, her only shred of privacy or self-determination, Diana respected the gesture. She didn't intrude, and she didn't ask again.

An orderly brought dinner. Rita ate a few spoonfuls of watery vegetable soup before drifting back into her reverie.

The little adobe house the sisters made available to Rita and her grandmother was just outside the mission compound. One of the older nuns, Sister Mary Jane, set about teaching Rita the rudiments of *Mil-gahn* housekeeping, but the instruction process was hampered by Rita's poor grasp of English. Sister Mary Jane also worried about the Indian girl's lack of formal religious training. When apprised of the situation, Sister Veronica, the sister in charge, declared Rita far too old to be placed in one of the mission's elementary classrooms or in one of the regular catechism classes, either. She enlisted Father John's aid.

As early summer came on, Rita spent an hour with him each afternoon. During the worst heat of the day, his office was cool and quiet. Rita was happy to be there. She loved smelling the strange odors that emanated from his skin. She loved listening to the rumbly, deep voice that reminded her of late summer thunder on distant Ioligam.

At school in Phoenix, Rita Antone had been a miserably homesick, indifferent pupil, but in the mission at Burnt Dog Village, under Father John's tutelage, she made swift progress.

Understanding Woman was the first to notice the change in her granddaughter, the way she chattered constantly about Father John and all that he said or thought or did. The older woman warned Dancing Quail to stay away from the priest, that thinking about him so much violated a dangerous taboo, but her wise counsel fell on deaf ears. Dancing Quail wasn't listening.

Sister Mary Jane wasn't far behind the old Papago woman in developing her own misgivings. It was probably nothing more than a harmless schoolgirl crush, she decided, but in time her concerns were passed along to Father Mark, Father John's superior at San Xavier. Father Mark promised to address the situation as soon as he got back out to the reservation. He would be there, he said, in time for the rain dance at Vamori.

Unfortunately, he was one rain dance too late.

The Arizona Highway Patrol located Brandon Walker's car abandoned in a rest area in Texas Canyon east of Benson. The ignition was on, but the engine wasn't running. The car was totally out of gas when someone finally noticed it. Tobias Walker was nowhere in evidence.

Hank Maddern drove Brandon to the scene. Around them, huge bubbles of boulders loomed round and gray in the moonlight like so many fat, unmoving ghosts. The Cochise County Sheriff's Department was summoned. The on-scene deputy reassured Brandon that a search-and-rescue team complete with bloodhound was en route as well.

Searching the car for clues, Hank came up with a partially used bottle of PineSol. "Why do you suppose he brought this along?"

"Beats me," Brandon returned. "I can't imagine."

An hour later, the dog and his handler arrived. The hound picked up a trail almost immediately, and led off through the ghostly forest of rocks over rough, rocky terrain. The handler had ordered everyone to stay behind for fear of disturbing the trail. Brandon stood there in the shallow moonlight, listening for the dog and wondering what to do now. After this stunt, when they found his father, the consequences would be far more serious than just taking his name off the checking account.

At last the hound bayed, and a signaling pistol cracked through the night. They had found him. Sick with relief, Brandon took off in the direction of the sound, but he met the handler hurrying toward him.

"Where is he?" Brandon demanded. "Did you find him or not?"

"I found him, but you'd better send for an ambulance."

"He's hurt? Did he fall?"

"Probably. He may have had a stroke. He's paralyzed."

Without a word, Brandon turned and sprinted back toward the rest area. He wanted to sit down and weep, but of course he couldn't. There wasn't time.

Little Bear and Little Lion were dead, but the spirit of Wise Old Grandmother called them home. She told them where to find her body and what they should do with it. They found it just where she said it would be, and they buried her in a dry, sandy wash the way she had told them.

Four days later, they went back to the place and found that a plant had grown up out of her grave, a plant with broad, fragrant leaves that we call wiw and that the Mil-gahn call wild tobacco. Little Lion and Little Bear cut the leaves and dried them, just the way the Wise Old Grandmother had told them.

The people were worried when they saw the two boys they had killed were back home and living in their house just as they always had. The people called a council to figure out what to do. They did not invite Little Bear and Little Lion, but the boys came anyway and sat in the circle.

Coyote, who was also at the council, sniffed the air. "I smell something very good," he said. "What is it?"

He went over to the boys, and Little Bear showed him some of the rolled-up tobacco. He lighted it and offered it to the man who was sitting next to him, but the man refused to take it.

Coyote crept close to Little Bear and said in the language of I'itoi, which all the animals and people used to speak, "Offer it to him again," Coyote said, "only this time say, 'nawoj,' which means friend or friendly gift."

Little Bear did as Coyote said, and once more offered the tobacco to the man sitting next to him. This time the man accepted it. He took a smoke and then passed it along to the man next to him, saying "nawoj" as he did so.

And so the tobacco went all the way around the circle. When it was finished, the people decided that Little Lion and Little Bear had brought them a good gift, this *tobacco, and that they should be left to live in peace to raise it.*

And that, nawoj, *is the story of the Ceremony of the Peace Smoke, or the Peace Pipe, as some tribes call it, for the* Tohono O'odham, *the Desert People, do not use pipes.*

Effie Joaquin waited until after nine when both Dr. Rosemead and Dr. Winters went home to their Saturday night poker game in the hospital housing compound. Only then did she go get the medicine man. With younger Indians, it usually didn't matter, but with older ones, people who still clung to the old ways, if the medicine man wasn't summoned, the patients might simply give up and not recover.

Effie didn't much believe in all this singing of songs and shaking of feathers, but her elderly patients did. If they wanted a medicine man, she saw to it that one came to the hospital. Usually, he arrived late enough at night that the doctors didn't notice. Effie was always careful to air out the acrid smell of wild tobacco before the doctors came back on duty the next morning.

Effie drove her pickup as far as the grove of trees where she knew Looks At Nothing would be waiting.

"*Oi g hihm,*" she said to the old man, opening the door. "Get in and let's go."

She drove back to the hospital and steered him down the hall. Letting him into Rita Antone's room, she left him there, closing the door behind him.

Looks At Nothing had been in hospital rooms before, but this one was worse than most. As always, he was shaken by the sharp, unpleasant odors assailing his nostrils. *Mil-gahn* medicine was not pleasing to the nose, but in this room there was something more besides—a sensation so fraught with danger that it filled the old man's heart with dread.

"*Nawoj*," he said softly, testing to see if Hejel Wi'ithag was awake. "Friend."

"*Nawoj*," she returned.

Guided by the sound of her voice and tapping the ironwood cane, he made his way to the bed. When he was close enough, she reached out and grasped his hand.

"Thank you for coming."

"It is nothing," he said. "I am always happy to help little Dancing Quail. I know you are troubled."

"Yes," she responded. "Would you like a chair?"

Looks At Nothing pulled his hand free from hers and felt behind him until he located the wall. "There are no other patients in this room." It was a statement, not a question.

"Two other beds," Rita told him, "but no one is in them. We're alone."

"Good." Looks At Nothing eased his wiry frame down the wall. "I will sit here on the floor and listen. You must tell me everything."

And so she did, a little at a time, from the car wreck to the buzzards. Looks At Nothing opened the leather pouch he wore around his scrawny waist and smoked some of the hand-rolled wild tobacco cigarettes he carried there. Gradually, the pleasant Indian smoke overcame the *Mil-gahn* odors in the room. He listened, nodding thoughtfully from time to time. When Rita finished, he sat there in silence and continued to smoke.

"Tell me about this Anglo boy," he said at last, "the one you call Olhoni."

Rita told him about Davy then and about Diana Ladd, a mother who, like the Woman Who Loved Field Hockey, was so busy that she neglected her own child. As the hours went by, she told the medicine man everything she could remember, weaving together the threads of the story in a complicated pattern that had its beginnings with Gina's murder.

At last there was nothing more to tell. Exhausted by the effort, Rita closed her eyes, while Looks At Nothing staggered unsteadily to his feet.

"Where does your nephew live?" the old man asked.

Rita frowned. "Fat Crack? He lives behind the gas station in one of those new government houses. Why do you ask?"

"I must go see him," Looks At Nothing said. "Together we will decide what to do."

Johnny Rivkin, the well-known Hollywood costume designer, was slumming. Fresh off the set in Sonoita, he had come to Tucson to have some fun R & R over the weekend. Hal Wilson, the director, had warned him that Johnny's particular brand of entertainment wouldn't be tolerated by the locals in the several small southern Arizona towns where they were filming Hal's latest Americanized spaghetti western. A search for other outlets brought Johnny straight to the Reardon Hotel.

Larry Hudson, Johnny's lover of some fifteen years' standing, had recently thrown him over in favor of a much younger man. Johnny's ego damage was still a raw, seeping wound. In public, he tried to shrug it off, to act as though it didn't matter, but it did—terribly.

For years, Johnny Rivkin had successfully negotiated the treacherous costuming end of the movie biz, but despite having a name for himself, he was still basically shy. He didn't like the meatmarket pickup scene. He didn't like shopping around, making choices, and maybe being turned down. He still looked good. He had the plastic-surgeon receipts to prove it, but truth be known, the hunks were all out looking for younger stuff these days.

This is Tucson, he reminded himself, trying to ward off discouragement. He hoped that since the place was a real backwater, maybe he'd be able to find someone not quite so jaded as those back home in L.A. Maybe one or two—two would be much nicer than one—would be dazzled enough by Johnny Rivkin's name and connections that they would follow him anywhere, opening up the possibilities for a long-term *menage à trois*. That was what he wanted—the illusion of permanence with a little excitement thrown in for good measure.

Outside the Reardon, Johnny paused at the

bar's dismal entrance with its broken neon sign. No one would ever mistake the place for a Hollywood glamour spot. From inside, he heard the sound of intermittent laughter, smelled the odor of stale smoke and the sour stench of spilled beer.

For the hundredth time, or maybe the thousandth, Johnny Rivkin cursed Larry Hudson for throwing him out for forcing him back into the open market. Johnny was too old to be out making this scene again, to be playing the game, searching for warm bodies. He wanted his old life back—his comfortable, boring, settled life. This was too much effort.

Steeling himself for the ordeal, Johnny pushed open the door. The bar was long and smoky and dimly lit. A series of shabby booths lined one side of the room. All occupied, they were filled with small groupings of men in twos, threes, or fours talking in low voices. A televised baseball game flitted across the color screen above the bar, but the sound was off. No one except the bartender was paying any attention to it.

When the door opened, an uneasy silence filled the room as the regulars noted and evaluated the newcomer. Was he one of them or not? Had a straight arrow mistakenly wandered into their midst? That happened occasionally, often with disastrous results.

The roomful of men gauged everything about Johnny Rivkin, from the quality of his expensive but casual clothing and his seasoned California tan to the several gold chains peeking coyly out from under an artfully unbuttoned collar. Johnny had dressed carefully for the occasion, calculating exactly the kind of impression he wanted to make, but he loathed the unabashed scrutiny of strangers. Unfortunately, in places like the Reardon, that was always the real price of admission.

Eventually, with a collective shrug, the regulars looked away. The inspection was over, and Johnny Rivkin had passed. He belonged.

Relieved, Johnny made his way down the crowded bar. The only unoccupied stool was halfway down the room next to the only woman in the place. That was too bad. It might give people the wrong idea, drive away some of the most likely prospects. The pickup process was painful enough without people jumping to erroneous conclusions.

He settled onto the bar stool and ordered a Chivas on the rocks, which he paid for out of a good-sized roll of bills. He didn't like showing that kind of money. Some people said it was dangerous, but at his age, money—lots of it—was often the only insurance against ending up alone.

Next to him, the blonde bestirred herself and ordered a whiskey sour. As soon as she spoke, Johnny realized she was a he in drag, a man almost as old as Johnny himself. Doing a quick professional evaluation of the blonde's clothing, the costumer almost choked on his drink. The outfit was appalling. The shoes and purse were worse. Rivkin didn't know where or when he'd seen such cheap, ugly stuff. If you're going to go to the trouble of dressing up, he thought, why not put on something decent?

The bartender brought the whiskey sour, and

the blonde paid for it, pocketing every penny of change. Johnny Rivkin felt a faint tweak of sympathy. He still hadn't forgotten his own impoverished early days. The blonde was someone for whom money, or the lack of it, was a major issue. You had to feel pretty damned poor to stiff the bartender out of his tip. Maybe abject poverty explained the awful clothing as well.

Sipping his drink, the blonde stared straight ahead toward the ranked bottles standing at attention behind the bar. There was an almost palpable sadness about the drag queen, a loneliness and despair that matched Rivkin's own and touched a chord of sympathy in him.

Johnny had never been a particularly good conversationalist where strangers were concerned. He didn't mind being in groups of people he knew, but with strangers, instead of talking, he froze up and contented himself with making up imaginary scenarios about the people around him. Now, he found himself wondering if the blonde, like him, hadn't been recently thrown out of a long-term relationship with nothing more than the clothes on his/her back. Johnny knew how that felt. It wasn't any picnic.

"Mind if I smoke?" Rivkin asked.

The blonde looked up, seemingly noticing Johnny for the first time. "No. Go right ahead."

Johnny opened his gold cigarette case, took out a cigarette, and offered one to the blond. "Thanks," she said, taking it. "Are you new to town?"

"Just passing through, really," Johnny answered. "I'm working on that new Hal Wilson film. We've been on location in Sonoita all week. That place is a hellhole."

Dropping Hal Wilson's name didn't seem to have any visible effect. Maybe the blonde wasn't into films.

Johnny polished off his drink, probably sooner than he should have, but being in a dump like the Reardon made him nervous. He wanted to make a connection and get the hell out of there.

"May I buy you a drink?" he asked, when the bartender responded to his signal.

"Sure," the blonde said without enthusiasm. "That would be nice."

Johnny believed in his intuition, in his ability to read other people. He decided in this instance to put it to the test.

"If you don't mind my saying so, you look like you just lost your best friend."

The blonde met Johnny's gaze with a rueful shake of blonde mane. "It shows that much, does it?"

Johnny raised his glass. "It takes one to know one."

"Really. You, too?"

Rivkin nodded. "After a mere fifteen years."

"I guess I got off lucky," the blonde said. "For me, it was only six."

"Cleaned you out?"

For the first time, the blonde smiled and then laughed aloud. "You could say that. I got away clean but broke."

Mentally, Johnny patted himself on the back.

He had been right all along. He returned the smile over his glass.

"So misery loves company," he said in his best imitation New York accent. "Maybe we could cheer each other up later, in my room, make a little revenge."

The blonde looked at him quizzically. "Here?"

"Are you kidding? In this flea trap? Not on your life." Johnny picked up the blonde's cigarettes, deftly placed his room key under it, and slipped the package and key down the bar.

"The Santa Rita. Room 831. In about half an hour."

"Sounds good to me," the blonde said.

Relieved to have scored with so little wasted effort, Johnny got up to leave. "By the way, do you like champagne?"

The blonde nodded.

"Good. I'll have a bottle on ice by the time you get there. Don't be late."

"I won't," the blonde told him with another brave smile. "I have a feeling my luck just took a turn for the better."

When Looks At Nothing left Rita's room, Effie Joaquin expected to take him back to his camp near the outskirts of town. He thanked her for the offer and said he'd find his way alone.

"But it's dark out there," Effie objected.

The old man smiled. "Darkness is my friend," he told her.

Effie considered herself personally responsible

for bringing the old man to the hospital. She didn't want anything to happen to him on his way home.

"It's just that other people might not be able to see you," she snapped impatiently.

"Don't worry," he said. "It isn't far."

Keeping to the shoulder of the road, Looks At Nothing made his way to the gas station. At once a dog began to bark. The old man followed the sound, making the dog bark even louder.

"Who is it?" a woman's voice demanded from inside the house.

"Looks At Nothing," the medicine man answered. "I'm looking for Fat Crack."

"Just a minute," she said. "I'll get him."

Moments later, a door opened. "What do you want?" Fat Crack asked.

"To speak to you," Looks At Nothing answered. "About your aunt. She needs your help."

"My help? I thought she wanted your help. After all, you're the medicine man."

Looks At Nothing settled cross-legged on the ground, took a cigarette out of his pouch, lit it, and offered it to Fat Crack. *"Nawoj,"* he said.

"Nawoj," Fat Crack returned, accepting the cigarette gracefully because it would have been rude to do otherwise. "What's this all about?"

"Sit," Looks At Nothing ordered. "We must not rush."

Reluctantly, Fat Crack did as he was told. Although his heavy body was much younger than the gaunt old medicine man's, it wasn't nearly as agile. Fat Crack was used to chairs. Sitting on the hard ground was uncomfortable.

"You are a man of great faith, are you not?" Looks At Nothing continued.

Fat Crack was taken aback by the directness of the medicine man's question. "Yes," he said. "I suppose so. Why?"

"Your aunt is in grave danger," Looks At Nothing said.

Fat Crack nodded. "I know," he said.

Somehow he had known that from the moment she asked him to go get the medicine man. From the way she acted, he knew there was something more serious at stake than just the physical damage from an automobile accident.

"You are very still," Looks At Nothing observed.

"I'm thinking," Fat Crack said. "I'm wondering what this danger to my aunt could be and why you need my help."

"Sit here with me for a while," Looks At Nothing said. "Smoke with me. The two of us will hold a council and let the sacred tobacco smoke fall upon our words. In this way, we will decide what to do."

Part of Fat Crack, the Christian Scientist part of him, began to buck and balk. Talk of sacred tobacco smoke didn't sit well with the teachings of Mary Baker Eddy. Still, the gentle power wielded by the medicine man didn't seem inherently evil.

"Gabe," the woman called impatiently from the

doorway of the house. "Are you coming back inside?"

"After," Fat Crack replied. "I will come in after, but first this old man and I are going to talk."

11

*H*OW DID MY daddy die?" Davy asked.

Diana Ladd was tucking her son into his bed when he asked the direct, awful question she had dreaded for years. Always before, during oblique conversations, she had skirted the issue, promising herself that if he ever asked straight out, she would be forced to respond in kind. Wanting to protect him, she had rehearsed countless carefully nonjudgmental answers, in hopes that one day Davy would grow up and form his own opinions about his father.

Diana sat down on the edge of the bed and placed one hand on Davy's chest. In the soft glow of the night-light, his eyes were luminous dark pools gazing up at her. She swallowed hard.

"He committed suicide," she said.

Davy frowned. "Suicide. What does that mean?"

"Your father killed himself," Diana answered. "With a gun."

"Why? Didn't he love us?"

Davy's ingenuousness wrung at Diana's heart.

She fought back tears, and bitter answers as well. "He didn't know you," she said gently. "You weren't even born yet."

"Well, why did he do it then?"

"He was scared, I guess."

"About what?"

"About what was going to happen to him. You see, there had been a . . ." She paused, losing heart, unable to say the word *murder* aloud. "There had been an accident," she finished lamely. "Your father was afraid of getting into trouble."

"Did he kill someone?"

Stunned, Diana wondered if Davy had somehow learned the truth. How else could his questions cut so close to the bones of truth? None of this was going the way she'd planned. "Is that what someone told you?" she asked.

Davy shrugged. "Not really. I just wanted to know why they called me that."

"Called you what?"

"Me'akam Mad," he replied.

Diana Ladd knew some Papago, but not nearly as much as Davy. This she didn't recognize at all. "What does that mean?"

"Killer's Child," Davy whispered.

Instantly, Diana was outraged. "Who called you that?"

"Some of the Indian ladies. At the hospital. They thought I didn't understand."

Not trusting her ability to speak, Diana got up and paced to the window. She stared out at a star-studded sky over the jagged black shadow of mountain. Even with the cooler running, the house was warm, but she felt suddenly chilled.

"Is it true?" Davy insisted. "Did my father kill somebody?"

"Yes," Diana answered at last, abandoning all pretense. Davy had to be told.

"Who?"

"Her name was Gina, Gina Antone."

"Rita's granddaughter?"

Diana nodded. "Yes."

"But Rita loves us. Why would she if . . ."

Diana turned decisively from the window. "Davy, listen to me. Your father was there when Gina died, but he didn't do it, and he didn't remember anything that happened. He fell asleep, and when he woke up, she was dead. Another man was there with them—a friend of your father's, a man named Andrew Carlisle. He tried to put all the blame on your father."

"What happened to him?"

"The other man? To Carlisle?" Davy nodded. "He went to jail, finally. The state prison. Rita and I saw to it."

"But he didn't die?"

"No."

"People still think my father did it."

"Probably. He wasn't alive to defend himself."

"And the other man was?"

"Yes, and he hired expensive lawyers. He was an Anglo, a well-known one, a teacher from the university, and the dead girl was only an Indian. Everybody acted as though it didn't matter if an

Indian got killed, as though she weren't important. With your father dead, it was a terrible time for me, but it was worse for Rita. She didn't have anyone to help her, so I did—with the police, with Detective Walker and the prosecutor. If I hadn't been there, Carlisle never would have gone to jail."

Most of Diana Ladd's impassioned explanation fell on deaf ears. Davy plucked out only one solid fact from the raging torrent of words. "Detective Walker? The man who was here this morning? The one who took me for my stitches?"

"Yes."

"He knew about my father, too?"

"Yes."

Abruptly, Davy flopped over on his side, turning away from her and facing the wall. "I don't want to talk anymore."

"But, Davy . . ."

"I'm going to sleep."

Drained and rejected, Diana started to leave the room, but Davy called to her before the door closed. "Mom?"

"What?"

"How come everybody knew about my father but me?"

The hurt and betrayal in Davy's voice squeezed her heart. "It was a terrible thing," she told him. "You weren't old enough to understand."

"I'm old enough now," he muttered fiercely into his pillow when the door clicked shut. "I am too."

But he wasn't. Not really. He lay awake for a long time after his mother left him, trying to understand why his father would have wanted to be dead so soon, why he hadn't wanted to wait around long enough to meet his own son.

Davy wished he could have asked him. He really wanted to know.

Looks At Nothing was gone, leaving Rita alone with her memories of that long ago, fateful summer. Homesick, Understanding Woman had wanted to return to Ban Thak. It was too hot in Burnt Dog Village. She longed to be in Coyote Sitting where it was cool and where she would be among old friends for the coming rain dance. Hearing this, Father John generously offered a ride. They would leave one day and return the next. Surely, the nuns could spare Rita for that long.

When the big day came, Dancing Quail was excited to be going home for the first time since she had moved to Topawa earlier that spring. She wore new clothes, which she had purchased from the trading post with her own money. She looked forward to seeing other girls her age, to being included as one of them.

By now Dancing Quail had ridden in Father John's touring car more than once. She was totally at ease. While Understanding Woman drowsed peacefully in the backseat, Rita chattered away in her much-improved English, pointing out the various sights along the way, telling Father John the Papago words for mountains and rocks, plants and animals, and reciting some of the traditional stories that went along with them.

Father John had offered a ride, but he wasn't pleased to be going to the rain dance, and he didn't much like the stories, either. On a professional basis, he disapproved of the annual midsummer rain dances, thinking them little more than orgies where people got so drunk on ceremonial cactus wine that they vomited into the dirt. Ancestral Papago wisdom dictated this was necessary to summon back Cloud Man and Wind Man who brought with them summer rains, the lifeblood of the desert. Father John thought otherwise.

When he first arrived on the reservation, the priest's initial impulse had been to preach fiery sermons and forbid his parishioners' attendance at the dances altogether, but Father Mark, his superior, had counseled otherwise. He said the church would be better served if Father John attended the various dances in person, putting in goodwill appearances at each. He advised the younger man to do what he could to keep his flock in line, but not to turn the dances into forbidden fruit. After all, Father Mark explained, forbidden or not, the Papagos would go anyway.

Dutifully, Father John attended, but he didn't think it did any good. He was beginning to realize that the Papagos were an exceedingly stubborn lot and almost totally impervious to the influence of outsiders. They listened politely enough. As succeeding waves of Anglo missionaries washed across their austere corner of the world, the *Tohono O'odham* accepted and incorporated some new ideas while blithely casting off the rest.

Father John suspected that Papago acceptance of any external religion, his included, was only skin deep. The Bible with its Old and New Testaments got layered in among all the other traditional stories, ones about I'itoi and Elder Brother. In this regard, his young charge Rita was no different from the others. She listened attentively during weekly catechism sessions, answering questions dutifully and well, but he worried that just beneath the surface of Dancing Quail's shiny Catholic veneer lurked an undisturbed bedrock of pagan beliefs.

"What are you going to do at the dance?" he asked. At sixteen, Rita seemed much too young to sit in the circle and drink the cactus wine. He worried about that as well.

She laughed and tossed her head. "I think I'll find myself a husband. Did you know that during a rain dance the woman may choose? The rest of the time, the men do the choosing."

"I hope you choose well," Father John said seriously.

He had seen several instances of unwise choices. Young women with their newfound jobs and independence were finding partners for themselves rather than following the old ways and letting their families do the negotiating. As a result, there was a growing problem with out-of-wedlock pregnancies. In addition, there were more and more cases where young fathers simply walked away from familial responsibilities.

"Maybe I'll choose you," Rita said with a mischievous smile.

Father John flushed. Dancing Quail always laughed at him when his ears turned red like that.

"I've already explained that to you," he said seriously. "Priests don't marry."

"But what about that new priest, the Pre . . . pre . . ." She stumbled over the long, unfamiliar word.

"Presbyterian?" Father John supplied.

"Yes. What about that new Reverend Hobson? He's a priest with a wife and three children."

"He's not a priest," Father John explained. "He's a pastor—a Protestant, not a Catholic. Pastors marry. Priests don't."

"I don't understand," Rita said with a frown. "You're all from the same tribe, aren't you?"

Father John had never before considered the issue in quite those terms. "Yes," he answered. "Yes and no."

The first giant cactus, Hahshani, *was a very strange thing. Growing up over the spot where Coyote had buried the little boy's bones, he was tall and thick and soft, shooting straight up out of the ground until he finally sprouted arms.*

The people and animals were curious, and they all came to look at him. The children played around Hahshani *and stuck sticks into him. This hurt Giant Cactus, so he put out long, sharp needles to keep them away. Then the children shot arrows into him. This made* Hahshani *very angry, so he sank into the ground and went away to a place where no one could find him.*

After Giant Cactus disappeared, the people were sorry and began looking for him. Finally Crow, who was flying over Giwho Tho'ag or Burden Basket Mountain, came back and told the people he had found the cactus hiding in a place where no animals ever went and where no people hunted.

The people called a council. Afterward, the chief told the people to prepare four large baskets, then he told Crow to take the baskets and fly back to Hahshani. When Crow reached Giant Cactus, Hahshani was covered with red, juicy fruit. As the chief had directed, Crow loaded the fruit into the baskets and took it back to the people. Crow placed the fruit in ollas that were filled with water, and then the ollas were set on the fire, where they were kept boiling from sunrise to sunset.

For four days, they cooked the fruit, and when it was finished, the chief told the people to prepare for a great wine feast. The people were puzzled because they had never tasted wine before. So all the people—Indians, animals, and birds—gathered around to drink the wine.

At the feast, everyone drank so much that they began to do silly things. Grasshopper pulled off one of his legs and wore it as a headdress. Nighthawk saw this and laughed so hard that his mouth split wide open. Since then, Nighthawk is so embarrassed by his big mouth that he only flies at night. Some of the other birds were so drunk that they began fighting and pulling out each other's feathers. That is why some of them still have bloody heads to this day.

When the chief saw all this fighting, he decided that there would be no more wine feasts, so he carefully gathered up all the Giant Cactus seeds and gave them to a messenger to take far away. The people didn't like this, so they sent Coyote after Messenger.

Coyote asked Messenger to show him what was in his hand. Messenger said no, but Coyote begged for one little peck, and finally, after much coaxing, Messenger gave in. He opened his hand, just the slightest bit. As soon as he did, Coyote struck his hand, and the seeds of Hahshani flew far into the air.

The wind was coming from the north. Wind caught Hahshani's seeds and carried them up over the mountaintops, scattering them on the south sides of the mountains.

And that is why, to this day, Giant Cactus grows only on the south sides of the mountains. And since then, every year, the people have held the feast of the cactus wine.

The night was cooling fast. In the desert outside Sells, a coyote howled and was answered by a chorus of village dogs. It was a pleasant, peaceful sound that made both Papago men feel relaxed and at home.

For some time, Looks At Nothing sat smoking the *wiw,* the wild tobacco, and saying nothing. Fat Crack admired the old man's concentration and stubbornness. He had heard stories about how the injured Looks At Nothing, returning to the reservation from Ajo, had shunned the white mans' ways, including alcohol and store-bought tobacco and cigarettes. The only alcohol the medicine man consumed was the cactus wine made once a year from fruit of the giant cactus. He smoked only the native tobacco, gathered from plants growing wild in the sandy washes. The single exception, his post-World War II Zippo lighter, was more a concession to old age than it was to the *Mil-gahn*.

As the burning sticks of rolled tobacco moved back and forth between them, and as the smoke eddied away from them into the dark sky, Fat Crack could see why this particular tobacco smoke might still retain some of its ancient power.

"What do you believe caused the accident?" Looks At Nothing asked at last.

"A steer ran across the road in front of the truck," Fat Crack answered. "When she tried to miss it, the tire caught on the shoulder and the truck rolled. That's what Law and Order told me."

"That may be how the accident happened," Looks At Nothing said, "but it's not what caused it. Do you know this Anglo child Hejel Wi'ithag lives with, the one she calls Olhoni?"

Fat Crack nodded. "Davy Ladd. His mother is a widow. Rita lives with them and looks after the boy. What about him?"

"The boy is the real cause of your aunt's accident."

"Davy Ladd? How? He's only six. He was at the hospital. He sure wouldn't hurt her. They say he saved her life."

Looks At Nothing's cigarette glowed softly in the night. He passed it back to Fat Crack. "The boy is unbaptized. His mother was born a Catholic, but he himself has never been inside a church. Do you know the old priest from San Xavier?"

It took a moment for Fat Crack to follow what seemed like an abrupt change of subject, but finally he nodded and smiled. Looks At Nothing and Father John were contemporaries, but the medicine man thought the Anglo was old.

"Yes. My mother told me about him. He's retired now, but he still helps out sometimes."

"He was once a special friend of your aunt's. We must go to him tomorrow, in Tucson. We will tell him about this problem and ask his advice. I will call for singers to treat the boy in the traditional way, but Father John must do the other."

This is crazy, Fat Crack thought. He was familiar with the old superstition that claimed being around unbaptized babies was dangerous and caused accidents, but supposedly only Indian babies were hazardous in this fashion. That's what he'd been told.

"Why are you doing this?" he asked. "Why bother with two kinds of baptism when the boy isn't even Indian? Besides, the accident already happened."

"The boy is a child of your aunt's heart," Looks At Nothing said softly. "It doesn't matter if he's *O'odham* or not, and the accident isn't the only danger."

"It isn't?"

"While she was in the ambulance, Hejel Wi'ithag saw buzzards, three of them, sitting sunning themselves in the middle of the afternoon, not in the morning like they usually do. It is bad luck to see animals doing strange things. It means something bad is coming, something evil.

Not only is it dangerous for your aunt, but for two other people as well."

The old man paused to smoke, and Fat Crack waited. "There is something very puzzling in all this," Looks At Nothing continued finally. "The evil seems to be *Ohb*, and not *Ohb*, Apache and not Apache."

Fat Crack was struck by the medicine man's use of the old-fashioned word that means, interchangeably, both Apache and enemy.

"Yes," Fat Crack murmured under his breath, agreeing without knowing exactly why. "You're right. It is *Ohb* or at least *Ohbsgam*, Apachelike."

"You believe this to be true?" Looks At Nothing demanded.

Fat Crack stared up at the sky. Here was an undeniable answer to his earlier prayer for help. He hadn't expected it to come this soon, and certainly not in the guise of an old, blind medicine man, but surely the connection he had felt that afternoon was here again and stronger than ever.

"Do you remember my cousin, Gina, Rita's granddaughter?"

Looks At Nothing nodded. "The one who was murdered?"

"Yes, near the *charco* of old Rattlesnake Skull Village."

"I remember."

"There were two men involved, two *Mil-gahn*. One of them was the little boy's father, Olhoni's father. He committed suicide afterward. The other man went to jail." Fat Crack paused briefly.

"Go on," Looks At Nothing urged.

"One of the men bit off Gina's *wipih*, her nipple. At the time it was said the dead man did it, that he was the one who bit her, but now I don't believe it. The same thing has happened again, just yesterday, to another woman at the base of Cloud-Stopper Mountain."

Both men were silent for some time, listening while the coyotes and dogs passed another series of greetings back and forth, sharing the night in a way not unlike the two men sharing their wild tobacco.

"Is it possible that the spirits of the dead Apaches invaded this *Mil-gahn*'s spirit, making him *Ohbsgam*, so he is Apachelike without being Apache?"

"Yes," Looks At Nothing agreed, impressed by Fat Crack's intuition. "Is it possible that this other man is out of jail?"

"After six years," Fat Crack replied, "it's possible."

"We must find out."

"I know the detective," Fat Crack said. "I met him. He was with the boy's mother when she came to the hospital last night. Perhaps he will help us."

"You will speak to him at once," Looks At Nothing ordered.

"All right," Fat Crack nodded. "Tomorrow. When we go to see the priest, I will also speak to the detective."

"Good," the medicine man said. "That's good."

Evidently, the council was finished, because Looks At Nothing snuffed out his cigarette and stood up. "It is late. We should get some rest. Come for me at my camp beside the trees in the morning. We will go together to Chuk Shon."

Fat Crack stood up as well. One of his feet had fallen asleep. He almost fell.

"Wait, old man. I'll go get the truck and give you a ride."

"No," Looks At Nothing said. "Show me where the road is. I can find my way from there."

They flew Toby Walker to Tucson Medical Center in a helicopter. Meanwhile, Hank Maddern and Brandon Walker tried to deal with the problem of the Pima County sheriff's car. Initially, the Cochise County detectives were determined to impound it. Eventually, though, after a late-night sheriff-to-sheriff call, it was decided to let Brandon take it back to Tucson. Even when committed by an elderly father, joy-riding was, after all, nothing but a misdemeanor.

"This isn't the last we're going to hear about this," Maddern warned as he helped siphon gas into the bone-dry Galaxy. "DuShane's going to be pissed as hell about this, and he'll make your life miserable. You'll wind up directing traffic at the Pima County Fairgrounds before he's through."

Brandon thought about his unconscious father, helpless and strapped to the stretcher, being loaded into the waiting helicopter. The medics said it looked like a massive stroke.

"Let him do his worst," Brandon said. "Who gives a shit?"

"Good boy," Maddern told him. "Don't let the turkeys get you down."

Using siphoned gas, they got as far as Benson, where they filled up both vehicles. "You turn on your lights and get your ass to the hospital," Maddern ordered. "I'll pick up your mother on the way and meet you there as soon as we can."

"Thanks," Brandon said.

He appreciated having a little extra time before facing his mother. No doubt Louella Walker would take the position that her son had failed again, as usual. Regardless of what happened, Louella could always twist it into being his fault.

Brandon found Toby Walker in the intensive-care unit hooked up to a bank of machines. The doctor he spoke to was grave.

"Don't get your hopes up," he said. "The next twenty-four hours are critical. We're dealing with not only a severe stroke, but also a severe sunburn. He's badly dehydrated. What was your father doing out in the desert alone like that?"

"He was going to Duluth," Brandon said.

"Duluth? That's in Minnesota."

"I know," Brandon replied, "but that's where he told the gas-station attendant he was going in nothing but a pair of pajamas."

"Your father was senile then?" the doctor asked.

"How could he be? He's not that old."

"You'd be surprised," the doctor said. "We're seeing more and more cases like this all the time.

They seem to be getting younger instead of older. Even without the stroke, you'd soon find he wouldn't be able to care for himself."

"And with it?"

"It's not good," the doctor said, shaking his head. "Not good at all."

He walked away just as Louella surged into the room on Hank Maddern's arm and rushed up to Brandon. "How is he?" she demanded. "Can I see him?"

Brandon nodded. "You can see him once every hour for five minutes at a time."

"Tell me. Is he going to be all right?"

"Of course, Mom," Brandon told her. "He's going to be fine."

But with any kind of luck, Brandon thought, by morning Toby Walker wouldn't be alive.

Diana couldn't sleep. The rooms of her house were too small, too confining. With Bone at her side, she left the house and paced the yard, remembering how it had been that morning when Gary came home. He had been out all night, and she had spent the night consumed with alternating bouts of rage and worry, sure at times that he was dead in his truck somewhere, and convinced at others that he was out with another woman, just like before.

Why had she believed him when he said all that was behind him? She had trusted him enough, had enough faith in the future of their marriage, to stop taking the pill at last, to start trying to get pregnant. How could she have been so stupid?

All that long night Diana had sat in the living room, an unread book open on her lap, listening for Gary's truck, watching for his headlights. By morning she found herself hoping that there had been an accident, that he'd wrapped himself around a telephone pole somewhere, so she wouldn't have to face what her woman's intuition warned her had happened, so she wouldn't have to *do* anything about it, so she wouldn't have to make a decision.

It was long after sunrise before he came home. Her heart pounded in her throat when she heard his inept fumbling at the lock. She didn't wait long enough for him to come inside and close the door. She didn't care if she woke up the neighbors, if all the other teachers in the compound heard every word.

"Where were you?"

"Out."

"Damn you. Where?"

"The dance. At San Pedro. I told you I was going there."

A cloud of alcohol-laden breath surrounded him, filling her nostrils and wrenching her gut, reminding her of her father.

"I thought they drank wine at the dances, cactus wine. I didn't know they served beer."

Not looking at her, he started toward the bedroom. "Please, Diana. Drop it. I've got to get some sleep."

"Sleep!" she screeched, heaving the book across the room at him. Her aim was bad. The book hit the wall three feet behind his head and fell to the floor with an angry thud.

"You need sleep?" she raged, getting up and coming across the room after him. "What about me? I've been up all night, too, up and worried sick!"

He turned to face her, and the ravaged, stricken look on his face brought her up short. Something was terribly wrong, and she couldn't imagine what it was.

"I said drop it!"

The quiet menace in his words took her breath away. She had heard those very same words countless times before, spoken in just that tone of voice and with just that shade of meaning, but always before they had come from her father, always from Max Cooper. Never from her husband, never from Gary.

Without another word, he disappeared into the bedroom and closed the door behind him. For minutes afterward, she stood in the middle of the room staring at the door, too frightened to move, too sick to cry.

Room 831 in the Santa Rita Hotel was a reasonably plush two-room suite. The bottle of champagne was on ice, and Johnny Rivkin had donned a blue silk smoking jacket by the time his expected guest turned the key in the lock. The blonde came in looking even more bedraggled than Johnny remembered. The dim light in the bar of the Reardon had been very kind.

"Welcome," Johnny said with a smile. "I'm glad you decided to come."

"I almost didn't," the blonde returned. "I don't remember how to do this anymore."

"Come on." Johnny did his best to sound cheerful and encouraging. "It'll all come back to you. The two of us will have some fun. If you like dressing up, you might check out the closet in the other room. I work in the movies, you see. I always keep a few nice things on hand just in case."

The blonde disappeared into the other room while Johnny busied himself with opening and pouring champagne. His hands shook some. He didn't know if it was nervousness or anticipation, maybe both. An unknown assignation was a lot like diving into an ice-cold swimming pool. Once you were in, everything was fine, but getting in required nerve.

The blonde came back out wearing a long silk robe with nothing on underneath, walking with shoulders slouched, hands jammed deep in the pockets. His obvious nervousness made Johnny feel that much better.

"Here," he said, passing a glass. "Try this. It'll be good for what ails you."

The blonde settled in the other chair, primly crossing his ankles, pulling the robe shut over his knees.

"Take off the wig," Johnny ordered. "It's dreadful, you know. I'd like to see you as you really are."

"Are you sure?" the blonde asked.

"I'm sure."

When the wig came off, Johnny found himself faced with a totally bald fifty-year-old man still wearing the garishly madeup features of an aging woman. The effect was disconcerting, like looking at your own distorted face in a fun-house mirror.

"What's your name?" Johnny asked.

"Art."

"Art what?"

"Does it matter?"

"Only if I want to call you again."

"Art Rains."

"And what do you do, Art Rains? For a living, I mean."

Johnny was beginning to enjoy himself. Here was someone who hated small talk almost as much as he did, someone else who wasn't any good at it. Knowing that made Johnny feel in control for a change, something that didn't happen to him very often.

"Believe it or not, for the past six years, I've been a housewife." Art ducked his head as he made this admission, as though it were something he was ashamed of.

"I believe it all right." Johnny got up and poured two more glasses of champagne. "Here. Have another. It'll take your mind off your troubles, Art. You need to relax, lighten up, have some fun."

"What did you have in mind?"

Johnny shrugged. He was enjoying the *tête-à-tête*. It was a shame to rush into it. "I don't know. Not something terribly energetic. We're both a bit old for that sort of thing. Maybe start out with a nice massage. I have some lovely oils in the other room. Larry always said that I'm very good with my hands."

Art smiled sadly. "That's something else we have in common."

"Well, come on, then. Shall we flip a coin to see who goes first? Although my mother always said company got to choose."

"I'll do you first," Art said, "unless you'd rather . . ."

"Oh, no, by all means. Suit yourself."

Trembling with anticipation, Johnny took his glass and the almost-empty bottle of champagne and led the way into the bedroom. He set the bottle and his glass on the bedside table and stripped off his jacket and trousers. If Art had been much younger, Johnny might have worried more about how his body looked, but Art Rains wasn't any spring chicken, either.

Before Art had arrived at the hotel, Johnny had turned down the covers on the bed. Now, he lay facedown on the cool, smooth sheets and waited. He sighed and closed his eyes. This was going to be delightful.

"Mind if I turn on the radio?" Art asked.

"Not at all."

Soon KHOS blared in his ear. Johnny didn't much like country-western, but it was a good idea to have some background music. After all, if this was very good, there might be a few inadvertent noises. A Holy Roller family might be next door.

A moment later, Johnny was surprised when, instead of a pair of well-oiled caressing hands touching his back or shoulders, he felt the weight of a naked male body settle heavily astride his buttocks. He didn't worry too much about that, though. There was certainly more than one way to do a massage. Johnny had heard the Japanese actually walked on people's backs.

Suddenly, a rough hand grabbed a fistful of hair and jerked his face off the pillow.

"Hey," Johnny said. "What's this . . . ?"

The sentence died in the air. Johnny Rivkin never saw the hunting knife that cut him. In fact, he hardly felt it at first. He tried to cry out for help, but he couldn't, nor could he free his flailing arms from the powerful hands that held him fast.

Rivkin's body leaped in the air, jerking like a headless chicken while Glen Campbell's plaintive "Wichita Lineman" lingered in the air and the almost-empty champagne bottle and glass fell to the carpeted floor but didn't break.

Johnny Rivkin's death was much bloodier than Margie Danielson's had been. Andrew Carlisle was glad he'd taken off all his clothes, glad he'd be able to shower and clean himself up before he left the room.

He had planned to let things go a little further, indulge in a little more foreplay, but buggering an aging queer didn't have much appeal. Besides, Carlisle was impatient. He wanted to get on with it.

He waited out the ride, which wasn't that different from the other, although it seemed to take quite a while longer before Johnny Rivkin's gurgling struggles ceased. Fortunately, the hotel mattress was easy on Andrew Carlisle's sore knees. They still hurt from the scorching rocks at Picacho Peak.

12

*I*T WAS LATE when Diana fell asleep, and even later when she woke up on Sunday morning. With Rita gone, the house seemed empty, and prospects for breakfast weren't good.

On her salary, eating out wasn't something Diana could afford often, but that Sunday morning seemed like a time to splurge. Both she and Davy had been through enough of a wringer that a special treat was in order. They drove to Uncle John's Pancake House on Miracle Mile and waited through the Sunday morning crush.

Over brightly colored menus, Diana explained that Davy could choose from any number of *Milgahn* foods—eggs and bacon, buttermilk pancakes, Swedish pancakes, German pancakes—but popovers with honey or tortillas with peanut butter weren't an option.

The waitress, a crusty old dame from the eat-it-or-wear-it school of food service, arrived at their table pad in hand. She fixed her eyes on Davy. "What'll you have, young man?"

Shyly, he ducked his head. "Swedish," he said in a strangled whisper. "With the red berries."

"And what to drink?"

"Milk."

"How about you, ma'am?"

"German pancakes and coffee."

The waitress nodded and disappeared, returning a few moments later with coffee and milk. She put the milk in front of Davy. "How'd you get all those stitches?" she asked.

Davy blushed and didn't answer. "He was in a car accident," Diana explained, speaking for him. "Out on the reservation."

The waitress frowned at that, but she left the table without saying anything more. A few minutes later, she was back, carrying a section of the Sunday paper. "This you?" she asked, holding the paper up so Davy could see it.

Davy looked at the picture and nodded. "What's that?" Diana asked.

The waitress looked at Diana in surprise. "You mean you don't know about it?"

Handed the paper, a stunned Diana Ladd found herself staring into the eyes of a clearly recognizable picture of her son, complete with stitches.

"Your breakfast's on me this morning, sweetie," the waitress was saying to Davy. "You sound like a regular little hero to me, saving that old woman's life. Wouldn't you like something else along with your pancakes, a milk shake maybe?"

"No," Davy said. "Thank you. Just milk."

The waitress left, and Diana turned on Davy. "How did your picture get into the newspaper?"

Her son glanced nervously at the paper. Next to his own picture was a smaller one, a head shot of the man who had spoken to him the previous afternoon. "The man had a camera. He took my picture yesterday while you were inside the hospital with Rita."

"You talked to a reporter?" Diana demanded, her voice rising in pitch. "You let him take your picture?"

Davy squirmed lower in his chair until his eyes barely showed above the top of the booth. "Yes."

"Why didn't you tell me?"

"He was a friend of my father's," Davy told her. "I was afraid you'd get mad."

And, of course, he was right.

From George's Beat, a biweekly column by George O'Connell in the *Arizona Daily Sun*, June 14, 1975:

Seven years ago Friday a young Papago woman died brutally in the desert west of Tucson. Two men were eventually implicated in the death of twenty-two-year-old Gina Antone. One of them was a student of creative writing at the University of Arizona. The other was the English professor in charge of that same program.

The professor, Andrew Carlisle, was eventually convicted of voluntary manslaughter and second degree rape. He was sentenced to serve time in the Arizona State Prison at Florence, while his student, Garrison Ladd, committed suicide rather than face arrest and conviction.

Now, seven years later to the day, two of the families involved in that earlier tragedy are once more linked together in the news, only this time with a far different result.

On Friday, Rita Antone, the slain girl's sixty-five-year-old grandmother, was severely injured in an automobile accident on Highway 386, forty miles west of Tucson. Mrs. Antone now makes her home in Tucson with Diana Ladd, Garrison Ladd's widow, and her son, David.

Medics from the scene report that Mrs. Antone would probably have died without reaching the Indian Health Service Hospital in Sells had it not been for the quick-witted thinking of six-year-old David, who was himself injured in the accident.

One of the first to arrive on the scene after the single-vehicle rollover accident was Joe Baxter, a Tucson resident on his way to Rocky Point for the weekend. Baxter said that it was David Ladd's firm insistence that there was an ambulance available at the Kitt Peak Observatory that prompted him and a traveling companion to seek help there. Aid summoned from either Sells or Tucson probably would have arrived too late to save Mrs. Antone's life.

Years ago, when I was finishing my graduate degree in English at the University of Arizona, I was enrolled in a literature class with David

Ladd's father, who, like many of our classmates, had delusions of being the Great American Novelist and creating a heroic masterpiece to leave as a legacy.

Mostly those dreams were just that—all dream and no action. However, I'm realizing now that there's more than one kind of masterpiece. Garrison Ladd's son, reticent about his own brave behavior despite injuries that required twelve stitches, is that heroic masterpiece, but he's certainly not the only hero in the drama.

Talking to him, I learned that Rita Antone, grandmother of the girl whose murder was linked to Garrison Ladd, is now a well-loved member of the Ladd family.

It strikes me as ironic (and more than a bit inspiring) that these two women, Diana Ladd and Rita Antone, an Anglo woman and an Indian, whose lives were first linked by death and mutual tragedy, have gone on to forge a relationship based on love and mutual respect.

It is an atmosphere in which two courageous women are raising a very responsible young man, one who in no way can be regarded as a chip off the old block.

In a world where bad news usually outweighs the good, where there are always far more questions than there are answers, it's refreshing to know this kind of thing can happen.

Long ago, Evil Siwani, a powerful medicine man, became jealous of I'itoi. Three times the medicine man and his wicked followers killed I'itoi, and three times

I'itoi came back to life. The fourth time, when morning came, I'itoi was still dead.

"That's all right," his followers said. "In four days, he will come back to life." But on the morning of the fourth day, I'itoi was still dead.

Many years passed. One day some children from a village found an old man sitting next to a charco near where I'itoi's bones had been left to dry in the sun. The old man was making a belt to carry an olla. "What are you doing, old man?" the children asked.

"You must watch carefully," he said. "Something surprising is going to happen."

So the children went home and told their parents. All the people from the village came to see the old man. They found him filling his olla with water. The people knew at once he was I'itoi grown to be very old. They wanted to talk to him, but before they could, he picked up his olla and started off toward the east.

There were many people along the way, but I'itoi knew these were the S-ohbsgam, the Apachelike followers of Evil Siwani, so he didn't speak to them. When I'itoi arrived at the village in the East he asked to see the chief, then he sang his song and told them he was I'itoi, who had made them. He told them how the Ohb, the Enemy, had killed him four times, and how each time he had come back to life. The chief of the East listened to I'itoi's song. When it was finished, he said, "I may not be able to help you, but go to my brother in the West. Tell him your story. I will do whatever he says."

I'itoi traveled far until he found the chief of the West. He sang his song that told about how the medicine man and his followers, the S-ohbsgam, had killed him four times and how each time he had come back to life. The *chief of the West shook his head. "I don't know if I can help you. Go to my elder brother, chief of the North, and ask him. I will do whatever he says."*

So I'itoi went to the chief of the North, who listened to his song. "I do not know if I can help you," the chief said. "Go to my elder brother, chief of the South. I will do whatever he says."

Once more I'itoi traveled a long, long way, and once more he sang his song, about how Evil Siwani and the S-ohbsgam had killed him four times and how he had come back to life. As soon as the chief of the South heard this, he sent a messenger to the villages of all his brothers.

"Come," he told them. "Whoever wants to prove his manhood must come with me. This man has suffered much at the hands of Siwani and his S-ohbsgam. We must go and help him."

And this, my Friend, was the beginning of the final battle between Evil Siwani and I'itoi.

Morning came and so did breakfast. Rita lay with her eyes closed, but she didn't sleep.

Understanding Woman went to the circle to visit with her friends while Dancing Quail gravitated to the younger women. Unfortunately, her new clothing and job at the mission didn't purchase what she wanted most—respect and acceptance from her peers. To the others, she was still Hejel Wi'ikam, still Orphaned Child. Girls who worked in Tucson still looked down on her.

Laughing easily, they gossiped endlessly about the latest one of their number who had "done bad" and been shipped home in disgrace. They giggled about exploits from their latest day off and speculated about who would marry next. On the fringes of their laughter, Dancing Quail had nothing to say. Several girls who were planning weddings were younger than she. Finally, one of them turned on her, a mean girl she had known briefly in Phoenix.

"What about you?" the girl asked. "Who will marry you?"

"I don't know," Rita answered despairingly, ducking her head.

The other girl giggled. "Since you already live with the sisters, maybe you should be one of them. If no *O'odham* will have you, maybe you should be a Bride of Christ."

At that, all the girls broke into gales of laughter. Ashamed, Dancing Quail took her sleeping mat and blanket and fled into the night, far from the fires and songs of the feast, far from the other girls' deriding laughter. She stumbled up the mountain to a place where she had played and hidden as a child. There, she lay down and wept.

Much later, long after she'd quit crying, Dancing Quail heard someone calling her name. Worried when he found her missing from the group, Father John came looking for her.

"Here," she called in answer.

"What's wrong?" he demanded, blundering into the clearing. "Why did you run away? Is someone here with you?"

"I am *hejelko*," she answered. "I am alone."

"But why? What's wrong?" He knelt beside her. As he reached out to touch her face, the tears started again.

"I'm not brave enough to choose for myself. The girls say no one will choose me."

"Nonsense." Father John gathered her into his arms. "You're young and beautiful, strong and healthy. Of course someone will choose you."

Despite his intention of making only an obligatory appearance at the dance, it had been necessary, in order to be polite, that Father John drink the thick, pungent wine. He had sat in the circle while servers had come around several times, dispensing wine from ancient, wine-stained baskets. Without his being aware of it, the volatile drink had overtaken him. The comforting, fatherly caress with which he intended to console Dancing Quail soon evolved into something quite different.

The mutual but unacknowledged attraction between them had long been held at bay by sobriety and by the singular force of Father John's convictions. Now, those convictions crumpled. What passed between them then was as unanticipated and electrifying as a bolt of lightning on a clear, still night.

It happened once and only once, but as is so often the case, once was more than enough. The damage was done.

Again Andrew Carlisle took his time at the scene of his latest triumph. He treated himself to a luxurious bath—Johnny Rivkin's bathroom held numerous wonderful bath potions. Finished bathing, Carlisle meticulously removed all body hairs from the drain and flushed them down the toilet. He went through the room, looting it at leisure, taking all the cash, leaving everything else, and thoroughly cleaning each surface as he finished with it.

The closet was another matter entirely. There were some things in there that he simply couldn't bear to leave behind, including a loose-fitting lush pink silk pantsuit that fit him perfectly. Two more wigs, these of much better quality than the one he had purchased, some underwear, and two pairs of hooker-heel shoes that might have been made for him. After choosing some items to wear, Carlisle stowed the rest, including the clothing he'd worn into the hotel, in one of Rivkin's monogrammed Hartmann suitcases.

He took more than usual pains with his makeup, so that shortly after six that Sunday morning, when a well-dressed woman walked through the lobby carrying a suitcase, nobody paid the slightest attention to her. She paused outside the door long enough to pull a Sunday edition of the *Arizona Daily Sun* out of a vending machine, but nobody noticed that, either.

Three blocks away, totally out of sight of the Santa Rita, Andrew Carlisle climbed back into Jake Spaulding's waiting Valiant. As he drove north, he took perverse pleasure in anticipating the kind of effect his costume would have on his mother. Myrna Louise had never approved of him dressing up, not even when he was little.

Oh, well, he thought, dismissing her. Other than packing his lunch and maybe washing a few clothes now and then, what had Myrna Louise ever done for him?

Driving home from breakfast, Diana seethed with anger. Some of it was aimed at Davy, but most was reserved for that damn full-of-business columnist. It was despicable for him to have taken advantage of an innocent child, to interview him and pry out information. Not only that, what, if anything, had he told Davy about his father? How much did George O'Connell know to tell?

Not as much as I do, Diana thought, with her whole body aching from the pain of remembering. Not nearly as much.

Garrison Ladd had slept the entire day away while Diana waited with her stomach roiling inside her. She wanted him to wake up and talk to her.

Feeling so physically ill bothered Diana. It wasn't like her to be sick. Since she wasn't feverish, she chalked it up to lack of sleep and a bad case of nerves. She steeled herself for what she regarded as the worst it could be—another other woman, she supposed. The very thought of it sent her spinning into a dizzying wash of memory, of coming home to Eugene from Joseph unexpectedly one weekend during her mother's final illness, of walking into her own house and finding Gary in bed with one of the female teaching assistants.

Already worn by the constant strain of caregiving, Diana snapped, turning into a wild woman and running raving through the house. She screamed and threw things and broke them, while the terrified T.A. cowered naked behind a locked bathroom door. Gary followed Diana from room to room, trying to keep her from hurting herself, pleading with her to listen to reason.

Reason! He had balls enough to use the word *reason* on her, as though she were a child pitching a temper tantrum. Still raging, she left the house vowing divorce. She went straight back to Joseph and to caring for her mother. What else was there to do?

Predictably, Gary appeared in Joseph two days later, bearing flowers and candy and gift-wrapped apologies. He begged and cajoled. He hadn't intended for it to happen, but he was so lonely with Diana gone all the time. It never would have happened if he hadn't missed her so much. He'd change, he promised. As soon as Diana got her undergraduate degree, they'd leave Eugene, whether he was finished with his Ph.D. program or not. They'd go somewhere else and start over, if she'd please just take him back.

Christ! she thought, waiting for him to wake up and fighting back a wave of nausea. How could I have been so dumb? How could she possibly have believed him? she wondered, and yet she had. Why? Because believing was easier than admitting you were wrong, easier than telling your dying Catholic mother that her only daughter was getting a divorce. But most of all, because believing was what Diana Ladd had wanted to do more than anything else. In spite of everything that had happened, she loved Garrison Ladd. She wanted him to love her back with the same unreasoning devotion.

At four that afternoon, Gary got up and came out into the living room of their shabby, school-owned thirteen-by-seventy-foot mobile home. "Hello," he said sheepishly.

"Hello," she returned. "How are you?"

"Hung over as hell. That cactus wine is a killer." Gary had uttered the words without even thinking, and then, as they registered, he turned ashen gray.

Diana didn't understand what was happening at the time, but she remembered the incident later with terrible clarity as the nightmare of Gina Antone's death began to unfold around her. What he said was nothing more than a slip of the tongue, but it was a clue. If she had paid attention, it might have warned her of what was to come, but she wasn't smart enough to pick up on it, and what difference would knowing have made? She couldn't have prevented what happened any more than she could have hoped to stop a speeding locomotive bare-handed.

She remembered Gary groping blindly for the back of a chair and dropping heavily into it. He had buried his face in his hands and wept. It was the first time Diana ever saw her husband cry.

Her own nausea totally forgotten, she hurried to comfort him and to bring him a glass of chilled iced tea. Whatever was wrong, she would do her best to fix it for him. Whatever it was, she would somehow smooth it over. After all, she had Iona's shining example to follow, didn't she? That's exactly what her mother would have done, had done for all those years, all her life. Smoothed things over. For everyone.

Fat Crack's tow truck looked at home among the others parked in the dusty San Xavier parking lot. Many of the vehicles had out-of-state licenses or rental stickers, but by far the majority were beat-up old pickups, station wagons, and sedans that belonged to the regular parishioners. Hard as it was for out-of-state guests to fathom, the musty-smelling mission still functioned as a church, with a regular schedule of well-attended masses.

While Looks At Nothing stayed in the truck, Fat Crack went to the door of the church and waited for Father John to come out. He did at last, accompanied by a somewhat younger-looking priest.

"Father John?" Fat Crack asked tentatively.

"Yes."

"My name is Gabe Ortiz, Juanita's son, Rita Antone's nephew."

A concerned frown furrowed the old man's forehead. "I hope your aunt's all right."

Fat Crack nodded. "She's fine. She's in the hospital, but fine. I have someone over here who needs to speak to you."

"Of course," Father John said, excusing himself from his colleague.

Fat Crack led the way. They entered the row of

parked cars a few vehicles away from the tow truck just as Looks At Nothing climbed down from his seat. The old medicine man stood leaning on his cane. He seemed to stare right through them with his glazed and sightless eyes.

Father John stopped abruptly. "This is . . ." Fat Crack began.

"S-ab Neid Pi Has," Father John supplied, speaking Looks At Nothing's Indian name in perfectly accented Papago. "This old *siwani* and I have met before," he said.

Father John stepped forward, reached out, took Looks At Nothing's gnarled old hand, and shook it. "*Nawoj*," he said. "Welcome."

Brandon Walker was worn out with trying to find a comfortable position on the post-modern waiting-room furniture, but he had nonetheless managed a few catnaps during the early morning hours while his mother came and went from brief visits with her husband. It was just like when President Kennedy died, Brandon thought. The doctors didn't tell everything they knew all at once for fear of starting a panic. Brandon suspected they had known last night that there was no hope of recovery for Toby Walker, but they wanted to give the family a chance to adjust to the situation. Brandon took the news as a direct act of mercy from a God he was surprised to learn he still believed in. Louella might continue to insist it wasn't true, couldn't possibly be true that Toby was dying, but her son knew better.

Each time a pale and shaken Louella emerged from the room, she was that much more entrenched in her disbelief. "I want a second opinion," she announced at last.

Brandon rubbed his forehead. "What's a second opinion going to buy you except another doctor bill?"

His question provoked Louella to outrage. "How can you mention money at a time like this? That man in there, that so-called doctor, says we should turn off the respirator. Just like that. As though it's nothing."

"Pop's not there, Mom," her son said gently. "He hasn't been for a long time, really. Turning off the machine would be a blessing."

He started to add "for us all," but thought better of it.

"No! Absolutely not. I won't have it."

"If he lives, he'll be a vegetable, Mom. He won't know either of us. He won't be able to eat on his own or stand or breathe."

"But he's still *alive!*" his mother hissed. "Your father is still alive."

Too tired to argue anymore, Brandon capitulated. "I'll go talk to the nurse about a second opinion," he said.

He went to the nurses' station and asked to speak to the head nurse.

"She's on her break," the clerk said.

He nodded. "That's all right. I'm going to the cafeteria for some coffee. I'll talk to her when I get back."

He walked down the long breezeway to the

cafeteria. It was mid-morning now and hot, but he felt chilled inside and out. The air-conditioning seemed to have settled in his blood and bones.

How would he ever make Louella see reason? She was his problem now and no one else's. Toby was still breathing with the help of his respirator, but he was really out of the war zone. It didn't seem fair for the focus of the battle to be immune to it.

Brandon took his cup of muddy coffee and a cigarette—he had finally bought a pack of his own—to a table in the far corner where someone had left most of a Sunday paper lying strewn with a layer of toast crumbs and speckles of greasy butter.

He started to toss the paper aside, and then stopped when he recognized Davy Ladd's serious picture staring out at him from the top of the page. He read the article through twice before his weary brain fully grasped the material.

Why in the world would Diana Ladd have permitted Davy to be featured in the paper like that? He would have thought she'd want to preserve her privacy. After all, if she had an unlisted phone number, why go advertising her location on the front page of the second section of a Sunday paper?

Shaking his head, he tore out the page and stuffed it in his pocket. Brandon Walker was the very last person to pretend to understand why women did some of the crazy things they did. If, prior to the fact, Diana Ladd had asked his advice, he would have counseled her to keep Davy's name and picture out of the paper at all costs. You could never tell what kind of fruitcakes would be drawn to that kind of article or how they would behave.

But the truth of the matter was, Diana Ladd hadn't asked his advice, so MYOB, buddy, he told himself. You've got trouble enough of your own.

The three men wandered over to one of the many ocotillo-shaded food booths that lined the large dirt parking lot. In each shelter, two or three women worked over mesquite-burning fires, cooking popovers in vats of hot grease, filling them with chili or beans, and then selling them to the hungry San Xavier flock, churchgoers and tourists alike.

Father John led them to a booth where he evidently had a charge account of sorts. The women took his order and quickly brought back three chili popovers on folded paper plates and three cans of Orange Crush. No money changed hands.

"Shall we go into my office to eat?" Father John asked. "It's much cooler in there."

They went to a small office hidden behind the mission bookstore where Father John was obliged to bring in two extra chairs so they could all sit at once. While eating his own popover, Father John observed the fastidious way in which the medicine man ate. Chili popovers are notoriously messy, but Looks At Nothing consumed his meticulously, then wiped his entire face clean with a paper napkin.

Father John flushed to think that there had

once been a time when he would have thrown a visiting *siwani* out of the mission compound, especially this particular *siwani*. He had learned much since those early days, not the least of which was a certain humility about who had the most direct access to God's ear. Over the years, he had come to suspect that God listened in on a party line rather than a private one.

Patiently, although he was dying of curiosity, the old priest waited to hear what Looks At Nothing had to say. Father John knew full well that it was the medicine man and not Fat Crack who was the motivating force behind this visit. And he knew also that whatever it was, it must be a matter of life and death. Nothing less than that would have forced stiff-necked old Looks At Nothing to unbend enough to set aside their ancient rivalry.

It was August, hot and viciously humid. The summer rains had come with a vengeance, and the Topawa Mission compound was awash in thick red mud. As Father John picked his way through the puddles from rectory to church, the Indian materialized out of the shadow of a nearby mesquite tree. He moved so easily that at first the priest didn't realize the other man was blind.

"Understanding Woman has sent me," the man said in slow but formal English. "I must speak to you of Dancing Quail."

Father John stopped short. "Dancing Quail. What about her? Is she ill? She missed her catechism lesson yesterday."

The other man stopped, too, unexpectedly

splashing into a puddle. As he struggled to regain his balance, Father John finally noticed that his visitor couldn't see.

"Dancing Quail will have a baby," he said.

"No! Whose?"

For the first time, the blind man turned his sightless eyes full on the priest. Without being told, Father John understood his visitor must be the young medicine man from Many Dogs Village, the one people called Looks At Nothing.

The blind man faced the priest, but he did not answer the question. He didn't have to, for under the medicine man's accusing stare Father John knew the answer all too well. His soul shriveled within him. His fingers groped for the comforting reassurance of his rosary.

"How far along is she?"

"Since the Rain Dance at Ban Thak, she has missed two *mash-athga*," Looks At Nothing said, "two menstrual periods."

"Dancing Quail has told you this?" Father John managed.

"Dancing Quail says nothing. It is her grandmother who has sent me. We who have no eyes have other ways of knowing."

"I will quit the priesthood," Father John declared. "I will quit and marry her."

"No!" Looks At Nothing was adamant. "You will not see her again. She is going far away from here. It is already arranged with the outing matron. She will go to a job in Phoenix. You are not to stop her."

"I'll speak to Father Mark, I'll . . ."

"You will do nothing. A man who would break one vow would as easily break another." An undercurrent of both threat and contempt permeated Looks At Nothing's softly spoken words. "Besides," he added icily, "Father Mark has already been told."

"You want her for yourself!" The accusation shot from Father John's lips before he had time to think.

Looks At Nothing recoiled as though he'd been slapped. In his earlier, hotheaded days, such an insult might have merited a fight to the death. The man he had killed in Ajo had died for much less, but now the medicine man simply stepped back, putting a yard or so of distance between them.

"I am *mahniko*," Looks At Nothing said slowly and with great dignity, "a cripple, marked by I'itoi as a holy man. You would do well to be the same." With that, he turned and walked away.

Determined to plead his case to his superior, Father John left at once for San Xavier. Father Mark refused to consider the idea of the younger priest renouncing his vows to marry the girl.

"What's done is done," he said. "She's gone. Forget about her. You have a vocation."

Father John returned to Topawa to find that both Dancing Quail and Understanding Woman had disappeared from the mission compound. He heard that the old woman died the following year, alone in her hut in Ban Thak. Father John didn't see Dancing Quail again for almost thirty years, but he prayed for her daily, for her and for her child as well.

Looks At Nothing pulled a cigarette and lighter from the cracked leather pouch he wore around his waist. Father John watched with some admiration as the blind man, with steady hands, used a Zippo lighter to fire the ceremonial cigarette, the Peace Smoke, as the Papagos called it.

The medicine man took a long drag and then passed it to the priest. "*Nawoj*," he said.

"*Nawoj*," Father John returned. He had never learned to appreciate the sharp, bitter taste of Indian tobacco, but he inhaled without betraying his opinion. He passed the cigarette along to Fat Crack, who took his turn.

"We are here to talk about the boy," Looks At Nothing announced.

"What boy?" Father John asked, confused by the medicine man's statement. Who was he talking about?

"His name is Davy Ladd," Looks At Nothing continued. "He is the son of the woman Dancing Quail lives with."

Rita Antone's old name spun out of the past in a whirlwind of memory that gathered both old men into its vortex while Fat Crack was left temporarily mystified. Dancing Quail? Who was that? It was a name he'd never heard before.

Father John caught himself. "Oh, yes," he said. "Davy Ladd. I remember now. What about him?"

"He is unbaptized," Looks At Nothing answered.

For a moment, nothing more was said as the cigarette once more made the rounds. "Unbaptized in both the *Mil-gahn* way and the *O'odham* way. He is a danger to himself, to his mother, and especially to Dancing Quail."

"Why do you tell me this?" Father John asked. "What does this have to do with me?"

"His mother was once a child of your church, your tribe. She has fallen away and has never taken her baby to the church. You must fix this."

Father John's first impulse was to laugh, but he had long since learned to suppress those inappropriate inclinations.

"*Siwani*," the priest said placatingly. "Baptism is a complicated issue. I can't just fix it, as you say."

Looks At Nothing rose, and for a moment stood over the other two men, leaning on his cane like a strange three-legged bird.

"You must," he said in a matter-of-fact tone that brooked no argument. "You must, or Dancing Quail will die."

With that the old medicine man turned and made his way out of the room, while Fat Crack followed closely behind.

13

THEY SAY IT *happened long ago that some quail were out eating during the harvest, Coyote crept up on them and ate them all except for one small quail who hid himself under the thick flat leaves of* Ihbhai, *of Prickly Pear. The frightened quail waited while Coyote ate up all his brothers and sisters. When it was safe, Quail ran home crying, "Coyote has eaten us all. He has eaten all my brothers and sisters."*

One wise old quail heard this and decided to get even. He waited until one day when Coyote was sound asleep. He cut Coyote open and took out some of his tail fat, then Quail sewed him back up, filling the empty space with rocks. After that, Quail flew off somewhere, started a fire, and began roasting the fat.

Coyote woke up and sniffed the air. "I smell something good," he said. He started to follow the smell, but as soon as he moved, all the rocks inside him began to rattle. The sound made Coyote very proud. "That is the sound of my medicine drum," he said.

Rattling all the way, Coyote walked until he found the place where the quail were having their feast. "Your food smells good, Little Brothers. Let me have a taste."

They gave him some, and Coyote liked it. "Where did you get this meat?" he asked.

"Way over there," Quail said. "Beyond the mountains. Baskets are traded for it."

Coyote set off to go get some meat of his own, but as soon as he left, he heard the quail laughing and saying, "Look, Coyote has eaten his own tail fat."

Coyote came back. "What did you say?" he asked, but the quail wouldn't answer. Just then a cottontail came running by. "What did the quail say?" Coyote asked.

"They said, 'Coyote has eaten his own tail fat.' "

As soon as he heard this, Coyote knew he had been tricked, and he was very angry. He chased after the quail, who disappeared down a hole in which they had hidden a cactus all wrapped in feathers.

Coyote dug in the hole after them. When he pulled out the first quail, he asked, "Did you do this to me?"

"No," the quail answered. "It wasn't me."

Coyote dug further and pulled out another quail.

"Did you do this to me?"

"No," the second quail answered. "It wasn't me." And so it went until he pulled out the very last one.

"Did you do this to me?"

But the last quail didn't answer. "Ah-ha," said Coyote, "since you don't answer me, you must be the one," and he bit hard on the quail, but he only hurt himself because that last quail was really the cactus.

And that, nawoj, is the story of how Quail tricked Coyote.

Andrew Carlisle was in no hurry to get home. Avoiding the freeway, he drove up the back way from Tucson to Tempe, coming into town through Florence junction and Mesa. He stopped at the Big Apple for a late breakfast. As usual, the previous night's exertions left him feeling wonderfully alive and ravenously hungry.

He had been out of prison for only two days. Already two people were dead. One a day, sort of like multiple vitamins, he thought. It was only fair. He'd been saving up for a long time, but Margie Danielson and Johnny Rivkin had been mere appetizers, something to hold him until the main course came along.

Thinking about Margie Danielson made him remember the newspaper waiting in the car. He asked the waitress for one more cup of coffee and went out to retrieve *The Arizona Sun*. It was important to stay abreast of how the Picacho Peak investigation was going. If the cops suddenly moved away from their Indian suspect, if they somehow stumbled on a lead that would point them in the right direction Andrew Carlisle needed to know at once so he could take appropriate countermeasures.

He turned to the second section, the local news section, and the name Ladd jumped off the page at him. How lucky could he get? There he was, Garrison Ladd's own kid, complete with a picture and more than a few helpful details. Hardly able to contain his excitement, Carlisle read through the column. The names were all there, ones he'd thought he would have to search out, one by one, over a lengthy period of time—Rita Antone, Diana Ladd, and David Ladd. If the boy had been in a car accident, his name and address were now part of an active police report. Carlisle knew from personal experience that, for a price, almost everything in the Pima County Sheriff's Department was up for sale. Cash on delivery. Discretion advised.

Jubilant, he paid his bill, adding in an extra tip, and headed for Weber Drive. Maybe he'd take his mother out to celebrate that night. She wouldn't have to know exactly what they were celebrating. He'd spend some of Johnny Rivkin's cash and take her someplace nice like Casa Vieja in old Tempe or maybe little Lulu's just up the street.

Myrna Louise was sitting in her rocker when he came into the house. Fortunately, he had left the Hartmann bag in the car. His mother sniffed disapprovingly when she saw the pink pantsuit. "You shouldn't dress like that, Andrew. What will people think? Roger was right. You should have had that first haircut much sooner."

Carlisle felt far too smug to let Myrna Louise draw him into that decades-old argument. "Don't look so upset, Mama. Your neighbors won't even notice. They'll think your sister came to visit, or your cousin from Omaha."

"I don't have a cousin in Omaha," Myrna Louise insisted.

"It was just a figure of speech," Andrew Carlisle told her. "I don't know why this disturbs you so. It's like wearing a disguise. Maybe you should try it sometime. It's fun, like playing dress-up. Didn't you play dress-up when you were a child?"

"When I was a child," she replied stubbornly, "but not when I was fifty years old."

Carlisle went into his bedroom. He saw at once that the stack of manuscripts was missing from the bookshelf. Turning on his heel, he charged back down the hall to the living room.

"Where are they, Mama?" he demanded.

"Where are what?"

"Don't give me that. You know what I mean. Where are my manuscripts, the ones that came in the mail?"

"I burned them," she replied quietly. "Every single page."

Carlisle's jaw dropped. "You what?"

"Outside. In the burning barrel. I burned them all."

Andrew Carlisle went livid, his hands shook. "What the hell do you mean, you burned them?"

"They were trash, Andrew. Smutty, filthy trash. You have no business writing such terrible things, about all those people killing and being killed. It made my blood run cold. Wherever do you get such terrible ideas!"

Andrew Carlisle sank into a chair opposite his mother, hoping she was lying, knowing she wasn't.

"Mama," he croaked. "Do you have any idea what you've done? Those were my only copies of *A Less Than Noble Savage*. I'll have to rewrite it from scratch."

"I'd set about getting started then, but try to write it a little nicer this time, Andrew. And leave out the woman who gets burned up, the one who gets set on fire with paint thinner. That was horrible. It reminded me of the Harveys' cat."

Even now she could remember the agonized screams of that poor dying cat, her next-door-neighbors' cat, after Andrew and some of his friends had lit it on fire with paint thinner and matches. Over the years, she had almost managed to forget about it, but reading the manuscript had brought it all back in vivid detail.

The remembered sound in her head had kept her awake for hours. Temporary relief had come when, around midnight, she had donned a robe and gone outside to burn the book. It had taken a long time. Hours even. Myma Louise had wanted to be sure that each page was properly disposed of, with every shred of it reduced to crumpled ash, so she had fed the manuscripts into the flame one typewritten page at a time.

The problem was, after she was finished and when she went back inside, the sound came back anyway. It was screaming in her head even now as she sat staring at this stranger in the pink silk pantsuit who was supposedly her son.

Yes, the cat was back with a vengeance, and Myrna Louise was afraid it would never go away again.

They took away the breakfast tray without Rita's noticing.

This time Understanding Woman took her concerns straight to the convent's superior. After hearing what the old Indian woman had to say,

Sister Veronica made arrangements for a hasty trip to San Xavier, where they spoke at length to Father Mark. He listened gravely and agreed to take immediate action.

The next afternoon while Dancing Quail was busy with her endless dusting, she heard visitors being ushered into the convent. Soon Sister Mary Jane came looking for her. "Someone is waiting to see you, Rita."

Dancing Quail was thunderstruck when she came to the arched doorway of the living room and found her grandmother sitting on the horsehair couch with Sister Veronica. Across a small table, in matching chairs, sat Father Mark from San Xavier and the BIA outing matron from Tucson; Dancing Quail stood transfixed for a moment, looking questioningly from face to face.

"Good afternoon, Rita," Father Mark boomed heartily. "Come in and sit down."

Dancing Quail slipped warily into the room. She made for a small footstool near Understanding Woman. When she sat down next to her grandmother, she looked to the old woman's weathered face for answers, but Understanding Woman made no acknowledgement.

"We're here about you and your baby," Father Mark said brusquely.

Father Mark's loud, forthright ways were often offensive to the politely soft-spoken Papagos who made up his flock. At this frontal attack, Rita's features darkened with shame, but she made no attempt at denial.

"You must go away at once, of course," he continued. "Your staying here is entirely out of the question. To that end, I have contacted Mrs. Manning here. Between us, we've made arrangements for you to have a position with a good family in Phoenix. Isn't that right, Lucille?"

Over the years, the outing matron's once-red hair had faded to a muddy gray, but Dancing Quail still remembered the withering look the woman had given her years before when the *Mil-gahn* woman discovered that the little girl from Ban Thak had no shoes.

Lucille Manning nodded. "They are a very respectable family in Phoenix. Under most circumstances, they wouldn't consider taking someone in your . . . in your condition. But Adele and Charles Clark are old friends of Father Mark's. They're also very interested in Indian basketry. When I told them you were a basket maker, they decided to make an exception."

"I don't understand . . ." Rita began.

The priest cut her off. "Of course you do, girl! You're not stupid. It would be very bad for Father John if you stayed here to have this baby. It would drive him out of the priesthood, destroy him completely, leave him to rot in hell. You wouldn't want to do that, now would you?"

"No, but . . ."

"And we've found a place where you can go. It'll be a good job, one that pays more than the sisters can."

"But what about my grandmother?" Dancing Quail asked. "What will happen to her?"

"I will go home," Understanding Woman said,

speaking for the first time. "I will go home to Ban Thak and wait to die."

Father Mark told Rita to pack her things, that the outing matron would leave shortly to take her to Tucson and the train. The girl left the convent with Understanding Woman.

"Please, *ni-kahk*," Dancing Quail begged. "Grandmother, please don't send me away."

Understanding Woman was adamant. "You must go," she said firmly. "To lead a holy man or a priest away from his vows is very bad luck, for you and for him as well. You must go far away and never see him again."

Without further argument, Dancing Quail gathered her things. This time she didn't use a burden basket. The girls who worked in town said that burden baskets were old-fashioned and clumsy. One of the nuns had given her a cast-off leather case. Into this battered relic, she put her own meager possessions.

She was about to strap the case shut when Understanding Woman appeared at her side. "*Ni-ka'amad*," the old woman said. "Granddaughter, here. This basket is not as good as that other one. Be careful not to lose it this time."

Tentatively, Dancing Quail picked up Understanding Woman's medicine basket, the last one the old woman ever made. She opened the top and peered inside. There were the things she remembered—a clay doll, another fragment of the same beautiful spirit rock, an arrowhead, and a hank of long black hair. Tears streamed down the young woman's face as she replaced the lid and carefully wedged the basket in one corner of the case.

Because of Father John, her grandmother was sending Dancing Quail away, but with her blessing rather than without. The old woman's puny medicine basket could offer only the slightest protection against the outside world, but it was far better than no protection at all. Besides, it was the only gift Understanding Woman had to give.

The two Indians left San Xavier and drove to the Pima County Sheriff's Department. Fat Crack had been here on business numerous times, and he knew his way around. He also understood the kind of treatment they could expect.

"I want to speak to Detective Walker," he said, going up to the glass-enclosed cage that separated clerk from waiting room.

"He's not in," the clerk said.

"Can you call him?"

"He's not on duty today."

"I need to talk to him."

"I'm telling you, he's not in."

"We'll wait," Fat Crack said, and showed Looks At Nothing to a chair. An hour later, they were still there.

Sheriff DuShane didn't usually come in on weekends, but he had forgotten his golf clubs at the office, and he needed them now. He was surprised to find two Indians seated stolidly in the front waiting area. There were usually plenty of Indians in the cell-block, but not that many out front.

"What's with the powwow in the lobby?" he asked.

The clerk shrugged. "Who knows? They want to talk to Walker. I told them plain as day that it's his day off."

"Like hell it is," DuShane growled. "You call him and tell him to get in here to take care of it. I don't need a bunch of Indians sitting around stinking up the place."

"But he's at the hospital with his father . . ."

"I don't give a rat's ass where he is. You get him on the horn and tell him to take care of it. Brandon Walker's in deep shit with me about now. He'd by God better not drag his heels."

Brandon Walker was both mystified and relieved by the departmental phone call that summoned him from Tucson Medical Center. The relief came from having a legitimate reason to abandon his distracted mother who was still waiting for the appearance of the second-opinion doctor, a process that Brandon could neither stop nor speed up. He wondered why two reservation Indians would insist on seeing him this ragingly hot Sunday afternoon.

In the waiting room, he immediately recognized the younger of the two as the person looking after Davy Ladd in the hospital at Sells. The old man, blind and bent, leaning on a gnarled ironwood cane, was a complete stranger.

"Would you like to come back to my office?" Walker asked.

Fat Crack translated Brandon's words. The old

man shook his head emphatically, speaking rapidly in Papago.

"He wants to talk outside," Fat Crack explained. "He wants to smoke."

The crazy old coot could smoke in here where it's cool, Brandon thought, but he shrugged his shoulders in compliance and followed the other two men outside into the ungodly heat. Fat Crack led them to a small patch of shade under a thriving mesquite tree. The old man sat cross-legged on the ground and opened the flap of a leather pouch that he wore around his waist. Removing a homemade cigarette, he started to light up. Brandon reached for his own cigarettes, but the younger man stopped him.

"Looks At Nothing would like you to join him," Fat Crack said, sitting down next to the old man.

Obligingly, Walker left his package of filter-tips where they were. He squatted down close to the other two and waited. He tried unsuccessfully to estimate ages. The younger man was probably in his mid-to-late forties, but the older one's sundried, weathered skin defied categorizing.

After deftly lighting his cigarette with a worn brass lighter, the old man puffed on it in absorbed concentration. He reminded Brandon of the aged Vietnamese villagers he had seen during the war, venerated old wise men who had seen one regime topple after another, and who had waited patiently for the inevitable time when the Americans would disappear as well.

At last the old man turned his sightless eyes in

Brandon's direction. He held out the cigarette, offering it to the detective. *"Nawoj,"* he said.

Brandon's first inclination was to say thanks but no thanks, that he'd have one of his own, but instinct warned him that there was more at stake here than just refusing a certain brand of cigarettes, homemade or not.

"Take it," Fat Crack urged. "Say *'nawoj.'"*

"Say what?"

"Nawoj," Fat Crack repeated. "It means 'friend' or 'friendly gift.'"

"Now-witch," Brandon said hesitantly, mimicking the strange sounding word as best he could. He accepted the cigarette and took a deep drag while Fat Crack nodded approval. The smoke was far stronger than the white man had anticipated. He managed to choke back a fit of coughing.

"Indian tobacco," Fat Crack explained as he in turn took the cigarette.

This is crazy, Brandon thought. What if someone sees me? But just then the old man started speaking in Papago. For a gringo, Brandon Walker was fairly fluent in Spanish, but this language wasn't remotely related to that. He couldn't understand a word. When the old one stopped speaking, the younger one translated.

"He says he's sorry about your father, but that sometimes it is better to die quick than to be old and sick."

Brandon's jaw dropped. How did this aged Indian know about Toby Walker? "How does he . . . ?" Brandon sputtered, but the old man spoke once more. Again Fat Crack interpreted.

"He's sorry to bother you like this, but we must speak to you about my cousin, about Gina Antone, who was murdered years ago."

The blind man's mysterious knowledge about Toby Walker was forgotten as Brandon's finely honed detective skills took charge. "Gina Antone? What about her?"

"We want to know about the other man, the one who went to jail."

"He's still in prison. In Florence."

"Are you sure?"

"Of course I'm sure."

"We would like you to check." This time Fat Crack spoke on his own without waiting for the old man.

"When? Now?"

Fat Crack nodded. The Indians showed no inclination to move. Shaking his head in exasperation, Brandon Walker rose to his feet and went back inside. He was gone a long time, fifteen minutes, to be exact. During that time, Looks At Nothing and Fat Crack sat smoking in the shade in absolute silence.

Finally, Brandon Walker returned. He stood over the other two men for a moment, examining each enigmatic face. Finally, he squatted back down next to them.

"I just talked to the records department in Florence," he said. "Andrew Carlisle was released on Friday. Now tell me, what's this all about?"

Once more the hairs on Fat Crack's neck stood up straight beneath the weight of his Stetson.

"Do you remember when my cousin was killed?" he asked.

"Yes."

"Do you remember her *wipih*, her nipple?"

"I remember," Walker said grimly. It was something he had never forgotten. "But the man who did that is dead," Brandon added. "He committed suicide."

"He is not dead," Fat Crack declared quietly. "It has happened again, just like that. On Friday, near Picacho Peak. The sheriff has arrested an Indian, but an *O'odham* wouldn't do this, wouldn't bite off a woman's nipple. Neither would a dead man."

A spurt of adrenaline surged into Brandon Walker's system, but his face betrayed nothing. "How do you know about this?" he asked.

"From an Indian who was in jail in Florence," Fat Crack answered.

"And why did you come to me? Why not go to the sheriff in Pinal County? They're the ones who have jurisdiction in the case."

"Because," Fat Crack said simply, looking at the second Indian. "My friend here is an old man. He doesn't like to travel so far."

To release her anger, Diana's first impulse on arriving home was to clean her house from top to bottom. Not that the house was dirty. She had to find something to occupy her hands and body. She swept and mopped and scrubbed. She even ventured into the root cellar behind a door she seldom opened where she still kept all those packed boxes—Gary's stuff and her mother's stuff—sitting there like ticking time bombs of memory, filled with things she couldn't throw away because she couldn't stand to sort them.

Against one wall were Gary's boxes. Rita had packed those for her. It was the first thing Rita had done for Diana, packed Gary's belongings into tidy stacks of boxes during the three days Diana was in University Hospital having Davy. And across the narrow room, stacked against another wall, labeled in Diana's stepmother's bold, careless printing, were the boxes that held all that remained of Iona Dade Cooper's worldly possessions.

The last month and a half, Iona Cooper was in the hospital in La Grande. During that time, Diana's world shrank even smaller. Sympathetic nurses brought Iona's food and looked the other way when Diana ate it, not that she ate much. She was listed as a guest in the La Grande Hotel, but she went there only to shower and change clothes. Most of the time she slept sitting up in a chair beside her mother's bed.

The two women spent most days entirely alone, with sporadic interruptions by passing doctors and nurses. Max Cooper came by a few times during the first week or so, then he disappeared and didn't return. Iona asked for him sometimes, but Diana refused to call him and beg him to come. If he couldn't come on his own, the hell with him.

There was nothing Diana could do except be there with a comforting word and touch during Iona's occasional lucid moments, whatever hour those increasingly rare moments surfaced. The rest of the time, Diana's sole function and focus was as her mother's advocate, as an insistent voice in the bureaucratic wilderness, demanding medication and attention from busy nurses and attendants whose natural tendency was to ignore an uncomplaining patient.

During the last week, Diana prayed without ceasing for the struggle to be over, for it to be finished. The afternoon before Iona died, Diana went back to the hotel to shower and change clothes. She checked for messages, as she always did. There was one: *See the manager.*

Mr. Freeman, the manager, a bespectacled older gentleman who had always treated Diana with utmost kindness, came out from his little office behind the desk. He was carrying a check that Diana recognized instantly as one she had written only the day before.

"I'm very sorry, Mrs. Ladd, but there seems to be some problem with the check."

Diana was mystified. "How could there be a problem?" she asked. "There's plenty of money in the account."

Constantly worried about money, her mother had waited far longer than she should have before agreeing to go to the hospital, but then she maintained that her daughter and son-in-law shouldn't have to shoulder any additional expenses on her account including Diana's bill at the hotel.

Since Iona's initial hospitalization, Diana had been a signer on her parents' checking account. Iona insisted Diana use that account and no other each week when she paid her hotel bill.

Tentatively, apologetically, the manager handed over the offending check. Stamped across the face of it in screaming red letters were the words ACCOUNT CLOSED!

"I don't know how this can be, Mr. Freeman. I'll have to check on it later. I need to get back to the hospital right now."

"Of course, Mrs. Ladd. Don't you worry. Later will be fine."

That afternoon, before the bank closed in Joseph, and while nurses were busy changing Iona's bedding, Diana called Ed Gentry. He was full of apologies.

"Your father came in and closed that account two days ago. Since he's a bona fide signer, there wasn't a thing I could do about it. If you're short, Diana, I'll be happy to advance you some cash."

"No," she told him. "I'm fine."

The next morning, when it was finally over, Diana prepared to have it out with Max Cooper. He hadn't even bothered to come tell his wife good-bye. She tried calling, but no one answered. Finally, after paying the bill with her own money, she checked out of the hotel and drove back to Joseph. She'd done what she could, but all other arrangements would have to wait until her father arrived in La Grande with his new checkbook.

Driving up to the house, Diana tried the door, but it was latched from the inside. She knocked, only to have the door opened by a complete stranger. The last thing Diana expected was to find a strange woman ensconced in her mother's place, someone Diana didn't recognize and who didn't know Iona's daughter, either.

"Yes?" the woman said tentatively, as though Diana were some kind of suspicious door-to-door salesman.

Something about the possessive way she opened the door warned Diana this wasn't some thoughtful neighbor come to help out in time of trouble.

"I live here," Diana said, pushing her way into the kitchen. "Who are you?"

Just then Max came into the room from the living room. One thumb hooked under his suspenders, he carried a can of beer in his other hand. At nine o'clock in the morning, he was already swaying slightly from side to side. "What's going on here?" he demanded.

Diana looked at him with absolute loathing. "Who is this?" she spat, pointing at the woman.

"Francine. Francine Duncan. You mean you two haven't met? Francine, this is Diana."

"Oh," Francine said.

"And where were you?" Diana demanded furiously, moving past Francine to stand directly in front of her father. "Where've you been for the last month and a half?"

"Busy," he mumbled. "I been real busy around here. Besides, like I told you and your mother both, I can't stand hospitals."

"You won't have to worry about it anymore," Diana said. "It's over. She's gone."

Max Cooper sank to the floor as though someone had suddenly lopped him off at the knees. Francine rushed to his side. "Oh, Max, I'm sorry. I'm so, so sorry."

"You stay out of this," Diana snapped. "Nobody asked you."

She left Joseph that afternoon and never went back. The boxes came two months later, a week after Max and Francine's handwritten, after-the-fact wedding announcement. Diana came home from school and found the boxes sitting waiting for her on the patio of the apartment in Eugene. A note on the top one said, *Your mother's things*.

Ten years later, Diana had yet to crack the masking tape on even one of those boxes. Knowing Francine had packed them had somehow desecrated Iona Dade Cooper's possessions. Diana didn't know if she'd ever be able to bring herself to touch them.

Andrew Carlisle had looked down on Myrna Louise for as long as he could remember, but this was the first time he ever remembered hating her. He went to the tiny, spartan bedroom assigned to him in his mother's house and fell onto the narrow bed while his whole body throbbed with abhorrence.

How could she have done this to him? How could she?

A *Less Than Noble Savage* was gone, completely gone. Oh, he still had a rough, rough draft, but six years of refinements had been obliterated. It was as though Myrna Louise had amputated a part of his body. This was his baby, his creation, something he'd nurtured and suckled throughout the endless days in prison.

At times, polishing the exploits of his main character was all that had kept him sane. Carlisle had liked his brute of a protagonist, Clayton Savage, had related to him both as a man and as a character. This modern-day, self-appointed, bloodthirsty renegade had only one objective while slicing and dicing his way through 643 double-spaced manuscript pages—making sure *Custer Died for Your Sins*, that powerful Native American polemic, was more than just a catchy title.

And now the new and revised Clayton Savage was lost to him, another sin to lay at Diana Ladd's door. Something else for which that bitch would be held accountable.

Practicing biofeedback, a trick they'd taught him in the Joint, Carlisle managed to get his breathing back under control. Don't get mad—get even, he told himself. That was the secret.

Finally, with the embryo of a plan forming in his head, he got up and went over to the dresser. Deliberately, he felt along the front of it until he found a loose piece of fascia board. He tugged at it until it broke off in his hands, then he went out into the living room still carrying the broken piece. He walked past his mother, who had not yet moved from her rocker.

"Where are you going?" She asked the question mechanically, strictly out of habit, even though she didn't want to. She had no need to know where her son was going or what he would do, but she was unable to change a lifetime's worth of asking.

"To the lumberyard," he said. "I need some glue. A piece of wood broke off the dresser in my room."

Away from the house, away from her, he was able to think more clearly. He bought the glue for the dresser. He also bought some caulking compound and a caulking gun. He told the man at the check stand that he was installing a tub in an add-on bathroom.

By the time he came back home, Andrew Carlisle was his old self again, his old charming self.

"Sorry I was so upset earlier, Mama," he said. "It's not that big a deal, really. Besides, you're right. It probably wasn't all that good a book in the first place."

"You're not mad at me anymore?"

"No," he lied. "Not at all. How about going out to dinner? We could go someplace special, for a steak or whatever you like."

Myrna Louise's eyes lit up. She was always game for going out to dinner. "I really like that place over in the shopping center," she said. "Lulubelle's or whatever. They have good ribs."

"That settles it," her son told her with an easy smile. "That's where we'll go then, and tomorrow, if you like, we could ride down to Tucson together. I have a few more errands to run. It's a long drive. It would be fun to have some company."

Late in the afternoon, Diana and Davy drove out to Sells. Right after they arrived, Diana took Davy around to the side of the building and held him up so he could speak to Rita through the open window. Then, warning him not to talk to anyone else in her absence, Diana left him in the lobby and went down the hall to Rita's room.

"Davy sure looks good," Rita said. "The cut on his head isn't too bad?"

"No. It's fine. He's proud of all his stitches."

The two women were quiet for a moment. Over the years, they had spent so much time alone together that long silences between them were not unusual. There was nothing in the older woman's placid countenance to warn Diana that a storm was coming.

"My nephew was here earlier," Rita said at last. "He came to give me some news."

"Oh? What's that?"

"Carlisle."

At the sound of the name, Diana's heart caught in her throat. "What about him?"

"He's out."

"When?"

"Friday. Already he has killed again."

"No. Are you serious?"

Rita nodded. "Fat Crack told me. They have arrested an Indian, but it was Carlisle who did it. He bit her."

"My God," Diana breathed. "I'll have to get in touch with Detective Walker right away and let him know."

"No," Rita said. "Detective Walker already tried with Carlisle, and he failed. Gina is dead. Your husband is dead, and now Carlisle is free. We will not give Detective Walker another chance."

"What are you saying?" Diana asked. She knew what Rita was thinking, but she didn't dare put it into words.

"I remember what he said in the hallway," Rita continued slowly. "When the deputy's back was turned and when he thought no one else was looking. He said he would come for you, for us. Let him."

"Let him? Do nothing and wait for him to come after us?"

Rita nodded. "That's right. I have one very old friend who is a powerful medicine man. He and my nephew will help us."

An involuntary shiver ran up and down Diana's spine. "You're saying we should take care of Carlisle ourselves?"

"Yes."

"But how can we when we don't even know where he is?"

"He will come to us. We must let him."

"And then what?"

Rita considered her words carefully before she spoke. "The *Tohono O'odham* only kill to eat or in self-defense. If Carlisle comes after us, then it is self-defense, isn't it?"

It wasn't as though Rita Antone was attempting to talk Diana Ladd into something she had never considered on her own. Selling the idea wasn't necessary. For almost seven years now, Diana had longed to throttle Andrew Carlisle with her bare hands.

"How do we find him?" Diana asked.

"We don't," Rita answered. "Windmill doesn't go looking for Wind Man. Neither will we. While we wait for him to come, we have much to do."

14

*I*T IS SAID that long ago a young woman from the Desert People fell in love with a young Hiakim, a Yaqui, and went to live with his family far to the south. The mother of the girl, Old White-Haired Woman, loved her daughter very much and missed her. Every evening she would go out to the foothills and call to her daughter's spirit, and every night there was an answer. One night, though, she heard nothing.

That night she went to her husband and said, "My daughter needs me. I must go to her."

Her husband, who was also old and lame besides, shook his head. "You are a bent old woman, and the Hiakim live far from here. How will you find your way?"

"The Little People will help me," she said. So the next morning she got up and called to Ali Chu Chum O'odham, the Little People, in their own language, for Old White-Haired Woman still remembered how to speak to them. As soon as they heard her call, the animals came right away.

"What do you want, Old Mother?" the Little People asked.

"My daughter's spirit is calling me from far away in the land of the Hiakim. I must go to her, but I am old and do not know the way."

"We will help you, Old Mother. We will help you go to your daughter."

And so the birds brought Old White-Haired Woman seeds and grain to eat along the way. The bees brought her honey, and Coyote, who had once been in the land of the Hiakim, guided her footsteps. After many, many days, they reached the village where Old White-Haired Woman's daughter lived with her husband and her baby, but the bent old woman found that her daughter was very sick.

"Mother," the girl told Old White-Haired Woman, "my husband's people are waiting for me to die so they can take my baby off into the mountains and teach him to be a warrior. I want you to take him back home to the Tohono O'odham, so he can grow up to be kind and gentle. You must leave tonight. Tomorrow will be too late."

Old White-Haired Woman was tired and wanted to rest, but she knew her daughter was right. Late that day, she loaded the baby into her daughter's burden basket and went through the village, this way and that, so people would think she was gathering wood. Then, when she was out of sight, she started back north.

Once more the Little People came to help her, but the next morning she could hear that a band of Hiakim warriors were following her trail. When they were almost upon her, she called out to I'itoi for help. He sent a huge flock of shashani, blackbirds, who flew around and around the Yaqui warriors' eyes until they could see nothing. Meanwhile, I'itoi led Old White-Haired

Woman and her grandson into a wash that became a canyon. In this way, they went north toward the land of the Tohono O'odham.

But Old White-Haired Woman was very tired after her long journey. Finally, one day, she could go no farther. "I must stop here," she said. So I'itoi took the boy the rest of the way home. When he came back, he found that the old woman's feet had grown underground and all that was sticking up were two sticks of arms.

"You are a good grandmother," I'itoi said. "You may stay here and rest forever, but once a year, you will be the most beautiful flower on the earth." He touched the sticks. Wherever he put his fingers, beautiful white flowers grew. "Once each year," I'itoi said, "during the night, Wind Man will be heavy with your perfume, but when the sun comes up in the morning, you will be gone."

And that, nawoj, *is the story of Old White-Haired Woman and the beautiful flower that the* Mil-gahn *call the night-blooming cereus. The Desert People call it* kok'oi 'uw, *which means ghost smell, or* ho'ok-wah'o, *which means witch's tongs.*

Brandon Walker never clocked in, but he worked all afternoon Sunday just the same. Trying to get a lead on Andrew Carlisle, he finally was put in touch with Ron Mallory, at home, taking the frustrated assistant superintendent away from his typewriter.

"My name is Brandon Walker," he said by way of introduction. "I'm a homicide detective with Pima County."

"What can I do for you, Detective Walker?"

Mallory asked cordially enough, but all the while he was wondering who the hell had given this joker his home telephone number.

"I'm trying to locate Andrew Carlisle. Your records department couldn't give me a current address."

Carlisle! Mallory thought, alarm bells chiming in his bureaucratic, cover-thine-ass mentality. Carlisle had only got out on Friday, and somebody was already looking for him?

"He's in Tucson somewhere," Mallory answered. "I can probably have an address for you next week. What's this all about?"

The slight hesitation in Walker's answer alerted Mallory that everything wasn't entirely as it should have been.

"I was the arresting officer on that case years ago," Walker said. "I'm concerned about him being released into the same area where some of the witnesses still live. He may go after them."

Mallory took a deep breath and used his shirt-sleeve to wipe the beads of sweat that suddenly dotted his forehead. "Look, Detective Walker," he said, all trace of cordiality disappearing. "Andrew Carlisle was an exemplary prisoner. He never made a bit of trouble. He was released after paying his debt to society for that particular crime. It sounds to me as though you're out to harass the poor guy."

"Harassment's got nothing to do with it," Brandon Walker countered. "I'm not the only one who'll be looking for him."

"What do you mean?"

"When they come asking," Brandon added, "I'd have that address handy."

He put down the phone and then sat there looking at it. He had wanted to have some solid information before he called Pinal County. He wondered how his information would be received once the homicide detectives knew it had been gleaned from some aging Indian medicine man over a ceremonial smoke of native tobacco.

Brandon had already looked up the phone number and even partially dialed it twice, hanging up each time before the connection was made. This time, he dialed and let it ring. When the call was answered, he asked to speak to the detective in charge of the Picacho Peak case. It was Sunday. Walker guessed correctly that the detective assigned to that case would be hard at work.

"Detective Farrell," a voice said gruffly into the phone.

"My name's Walker," Brandon told him. "Detective Walker from Pima County, just down the road apiece."

"What can I do for you?"

"I'm calling about your Picacho Peak case. I may have some relevant information."

"Shoot."

"I was the arresting officer years ago on a homicide that happened out near the reservation, the Papago. A young Indian woman was murdered. Two Anglos were the perpetrators." Brandon Walker paused.

"So?" Farrell prodded.

"That case may be related to the new one."

"What makes you think that?"

"The young woman's breast was bitten. One nipple was completely severed."

Walker could hear the other man shifting in his chair, sitting up straight, coming to attention. "Wait just a god-damned minute here!" Farrell exclaimed. "We haven't released one particle of information about that. How the hell do you know about it?"

"That's not important," Brandon said. "How about if we meet and exchange information."

"Where?"

"The coffee shop at the base of Picacho Peak. I'd like to look over the crime scene if I could."

Farrell drew back. "That's a little irregular. Are you working a case?"

"The bastard already went to prison for my case. At the time, most of the blame was passed along to somebody else who happened to be dead. Material evidence about the bite that would have linked this joker to that part of it mysteriously disappeared between the crime lab and the evidence room. It was never found again."

Detective G. T. (Geet) Farrell was nobody's dummy. "I see," he said after a short pause. "You think this is the same guy, but because of double jeopardy, you can't lay a glove on him for the other case."

"You've got it."

"I'll meet you at Nickerson Farms in one hour," Farrell said. "Bring everything you've got. We'll compare notes."

"Right," Brandon Walker said. "I'll be there."

* * *

Coming back from visiting Rita in Sells with Davy asleep in the backseat, Diana Ladd pulled into the driveway of her house and felt a sudden knot of fear form in her stomach. For the first time, she was daunted by the isolation, by the vast distance—two miles or more—from her house to that of her nearest neighbor. It hadn't seemed nearly so far with Andrew Carlisle locked safely away in prison, but now that he was out . . . Bone's welcoming woof came from just inside the door. The sound made Diana feel much better.

Davy sat up. "We're home already?" he asked.

"We're home," Diana told him, but without the internal thrill those words still sometimes gave her. Knowing Andrew Carlisle could come looking for her any time made the house seem less a refuge and more a trap—a trap or a battle-ground.

But then Andrew Carlisle had been a battle-ground from day one, from the moment she first heard his name. She had almost finished earning her bachelor's degree by then. Carrying extra loads and going to summer school she had graduated only one semester late. Gary was eager to get out of Eugene. He said he was only keeping his promise about going elsewhere and starting over. She found out much later that he had nearly come to blows with his adviser over plagiarism in his dissertation. If he hadn't left the University of Oregon voluntarily, he would have been thrown out.

Gary was the one who first heard about the creative-writing program being offered in Arizona. He claimed that a similar one being offered in Eugene wasn't nearly as good. Both Diana and Gary had applied, but only one was accepted. Diana still smarted at Gary's words the day the two matching envelopes came. They matched on the outside, but the contents differed. One said he was in while the other announced that she wasn't.

"I guess there's only going to be one writer in our family," Gary had said with that infuriating grin of his, "and I'm it."

Those words gnawed at her still, kept her tied to her desk when she ought to have been outside enjoying her child and her life. Later, when Gary learned how hurt she was over it and, more important, when he'd wanted her to find a job in Arizona to support them, he claimed it was all a joke, that he hadn't meant a word of it. But that was after his parents learned about the canceled dissertation at the U. of O., after they cut their fair-haired boy off from any further financial aid.

And so, in the spring of 1967, Andrew Carlisle entered Diana's and Gary's lives—insidiously almost, like some exotic, antibiotic-resistant strain of infection that ordinary remedies don't touch. Diana didn't like the man from the moment she met him at that first faculty tea, the only one to which spouses were invited. She had wanted to be there as a full participant, not as some extraneous guest. She resented what she regarded as Professor Carlisle's oily charm.

Gary, on the other hand, was captivated. Once classes started, that was all he could talk about—Professor Carlisle this and Professor Carlisle that. Sometime during that first semester, she couldn't remember exactly when, the "Professor" part was dropped, first in favor of last name only and later in favor of "Andrew."

Meanwhile, she found herself a job. Not in Tucson, where applicants outnumbered positions ten to one. She went to work in the boonies, teaching on the Papago for one of the most impoverished school districts in the entire country. The pay wasn't all that bad, and the job did come with housing, a thirteen-by-seventy mobile home parked in the Teachers' Compound at Topawa. It wounded Diana's pride to be forced to accept company housing, but with Gary in school full time, every penny counted.

At first Gary carpooled into Tucson with two other students, but then, as his days got longer, as he came more and more under Carlisle's spell, he bought himself a beater pickup so he could come and go as he liked.

Did Diana see trouble brewing? Did she read the writing on the wall? Of course not, she was too much her mother's daughter, too busy maintaining a positive mental attitude in the face of mounting disaster, too busy believing that what Gary Ladd said was the gospel. Every once in a while, the smallest splinter of doubt might worm its way into her consciousness, but she ruthlessly plucked it out. Gary was working hard, she told herself. The stack of typewritten pages on his desk grew steadily taller, offering mute testimony about work on his manuscript. Besides, Diana had interests enough of her own to keep her occupied.

There weren't any Indians living in Joseph, Oregon, when Diana was growing up. The Nez Perce had long since been exiled from their ancestral lands to the wilds of Oklahoma and back to a reservation in Idaho, but Diana had learned something about them in her reading, had discovered in books things about Chief Joseph and his loyal band of followers that would have given her father apoplexy. After all, to Max Cooper's unenlightened way of thinking, the only good Indian was still a dead Indian.

So the job teaching school on the Papago was good for Diana in more ways than one. It supported them while Gary was in school, it gave them a place to live, and it provided another avenue of attack in her unrelenting rebellion against her father. She threw herself into her work with all the enthusiasm and energy she could muster. If she was going to be a teacher for the time being, she'd be the best damned teacher the reservation had ever seen.

While doing that, she was also, unwittingly, giving Gary Ladd more and more rope—enough rope to hang himself, enough rope to destroy them both.

* * *

"Gary," she had pleaded finally. "For God's sake, tell me what's the matter!"

It was early afternoon the following Friday, a full week after he'd stayed out until broad daylight after the dance at San Pedro.

"I can't," he whimpered, "I don't know what to do."

She went to him then, held him and comforted him as she would have a small lost child or a wounded animal. She couldn't believe those frightened, despairing words came from the lips of the man she loved, from the mouth of Garrison Walther Ladd, III, someone who always had a ready answer for everything.

It had been a terrible week for Diana, a debilitating, virtually sleepless week. She alternated between bouts of fury and bleak despair over what was wrong with her husband, all the while battling her own recalcitrant body, which seemed determined to throw off every morsel of food she attempted to put in her mouth.

Gary spent the week in front of the TV set, watching everything from news to soap operas to game shows with almost catatonic concentration. He ate a bite or two of the food she brought him and sipped the iced tea or coffee, but he barely spoke to her, barely moved. With every passing moment, her sense of foreboding grew more overpowering, until she wanted to scream at the very sight of him.

Once, while he slept, she went out and examined the pickup in minute detail, looking for a clue as to what might have happened. She dreaded finding evidence that he had been in an accident, maybe a hit-and-run, but the combat scars on the Ford's battered body were all old, rusted-over wounds. In a way, finding nothing made Diana feel worse. What was the matter? she asked herself. What had panicked her otherwise self-assured husband to the point that he couldn't leave the house?

On Tuesday morning, Andrew Carlisle called to find out why Gary had missed class the previous day. Diana put her husband on the phone despite his desperately signaled hand motions to the contrary. He stammered some lame excuse about food poisoning that didn't sound at all plausible to Diana and probably not to Andrew Carlisle, either. Gary promised faithfully that he'd be in class the next day, but Wednesday came and went without him moving from the couch other than to visit the bathroom.

On Thursday evening, Andrew Carlisle himself showed up at the door. Diana was surprised to see him, amazed that he'd go so far out of his way in an attempt to talk Gary out of his stupor. She didn't like Andrew Carlisle, but she grudgingly gave the man credit. She wasn't privy to the conversation that passed between them, but she was grateful that Gary seemed in much better spirits after Carlisle left.

"What did he tell you?" she asked curiously, after the professor drove away.

"That all creative people go through black periods like this," Gary told her. "He says it's nothing unusual. It'll pass."

On Saturday morning, Diana went to the High Store for groceries. The trading post on top of the hill was abuzz with talk about the murder and the now identified victim, Gina Antone. Diana bought a newspaper and read the ugly story for herself. She was shocked to discover the victim was the granddaughter of someone she knew.

Diana worked at the school and so did Rita Antone—Diana as a classroom teacher and Rita as a cook in the cafeteria, although the two women were only slightly acquainted. Rita was known for striking terror in the hearts of children who came to the garbage cans to dump their lunch trays without first having tried at least one bite of everything on their plate.

Rita, standing guard over the garbage cans like a pugnacious bulldog and waving a huge rubber spatula for emphasis, would order them, "Eat your vegetables." Usually, the frightened Indian kids complied without a murmur. So did a few cowed Anglo teachers.

By the time Diana got back to Topawa with both the groceries and the newspaper, it was almost noon. She was in the kitchen fixing lunch when Gary turned away from the television cartoons and picked up the paper. She saw his face go ashen. The knuckles on his hands turned white.

He let the paper fall to the floor and began sobbing into his hands. She went to him. Kneeling on the floor in front of him, she begged him to tell her what was wrong. For a long time, he sat weeping with his face buried on her shoulder.

The paper lay faceup on the floor with the headlines screaming at her. Without his saying a word, she knew. Terror and revulsion took over. She drew away from him, grabbed up the paper, crumpled it into a wad, and shook it in his face.

"Is it *this*?" she demanded, not caring that her voice had risen to a shriek. "Is this what the hell's the matter?"

And he gave her the only answer she ever got from him, an agonized three-word reply that offered no comfort even while she pinned her every hope for both the past and present on it.

"I don't remember."

Not, "Of course not!" Not, "How could you say such a thing?" Not, "That's crazy!" But, "I don't remember"—a murderous kings X, as though he'd kept his fingers crossed while Gina Antone died.

The room reeled around her. Overwhelmed by nausea, she dashed for the bathroom and vomited, while her chicken-noodle soup cooked to blackened charcoal splinters on the kitchen stove.

When Diana came back out to the living room, Gary was gone. She ran to the door in time to see his pickup turning out of the Teachers' Compound onto the highway, headed for Sells. She could have driven like a demon and caught up with him on the highway, but what would she have done then, forced him off the road?

Behind her, an unearthly howl from the telephone receiver told her that the phone hadn't been hung up properly. At first, staring after the receding pickup, Diana was unable to respond.

Soon a disembodied voice echoed through the house telling her to please hang up and try again. Shaken and too spent to do anything else, she put the phone back on the hook.

Gary left the house, and she never saw him again, not alive anyway, and that last phone call, placed to Andrew Carlisle's home just before Garrison Ladd fled the house to go to his death, was one of the key pieces of evidence that linked the two men together.

Yes, Diana thought almost seven years later, going into the house in Gates Pass, closing and locking the door behind her, Andrew Carlisle was the invader here, the enemy. He had not yet set foot inside her home, but when he did, he would meet with implacable resistance, to-the-death resistance.

Rita Antone had said so, and so had Diana Ladd.

Detective Geet Farrell of the Pinal County Sheriff's Department was a cop's cop, someone who had been in the business a long time, someone who knew his way around people. Everyone in the Arizona law-enforcement community was familiar with the problems in the Pima County Sheriff's Department. At first Farrell was worried that Brandon Walker might be one of Sheriff DuShane's bad guys.

"You dragged me all the way down here with some cockamamy story, so tell me, who is this character?" Farrell asked, leaning back in the booth, eyeing Brandon Walker speculatively.

"His name is Andrew Carlisle," Walker answered. "Formerly Professor Andrew Carlisle of the University of Arizona."

Years earlier, the professor's case had been notorious, statewide. Farrell remembered it well. "If it's the same case I'm thinking about, he got himself a pretty slick plea-bargain."

"That's the one," Walker nodded. "The other guy, his student and co-conspirator, committed suicide rather than go to jail."

"Tell me about the bite."

"Like I said on the phone. One nipple was completely severed, and the key piece of evidence that could have been matched to a bite impression, the thing that would have determined once and for all who was responsible, disappeared off the face of the earth."

Farrell nodded. "You boys have a man-sized hole in your evidence room down there. Somebody ought to plug that son of a bitch." Both men knew Farrell was referring to DuShane himself and not some mythical hole.

"They ought to," Walker agreed, "but that's easier said than done."

"What makes you think Carlisle's my man?" Farrell asked.

"He was released from Florence at noon on Friday, put on the bus for Tucson. My guess is that he never made it that far."

"How'd you know about Margie Danielson's nipple?" Farrell asked. The Pinal County detective didn't play games. He had already made a favorable judgment call about the quality of his Pima County colleague.

"From two Indians," Walker answered, "an old one, a medicine man, and a younger one, too. At least I think the younger one is a medicine man. They'd heard you'd arrested an Indian."

"Arrested but not charged," Farrell agreed, "but how'd they know about that?"

"They didn't say, and I didn't ask. They were also the ones who came up with a possible connection between this case and the old one. They came to town this morning and asked me to find out whether or not Andrew Carlisle was out of prison."

"And he was," Farrell finished.

Walker nodded. "At exactly the right time. Florence released him Friday at noon."

Farrell blinked at that, as though he hadn't made the connection the first time. Noon Friday. From Florence to Picacho Peak a few hours later was indeed the right time and place. "So where is he now?"

"That I don't know. I talked to a guy named Ron Mallory who's assistant superintendent at Florence. He played real coy, acted like he had no idea where Carlisle might have gone, but the person in Records let something slip when I was talking to her. She mentioned that most of the time Carlisle was locked up, he worked as Mallory's inmate clerk, so chances are, Carlisle's got something on Mallory. He's not going to lift a finger to help us."

"Unless somebody holds his feet to the fire," Farrell said. "Now tell me, Walker, what's the real reason you're here? What's your beef? I can see how your ego might be hurt because this guy slipped off the hook once, but it seems like there's more at stake here than just the usual problem with the crook that got away."

"The other man's wife," Walker said. "The widow of the guy who committed suicide. At the time, I convinced her that we'd take care of Carlisle. All she had to do was trust the system."

"And the system screwed her over?"

"Without a kiss."

"So it is ego damage. That's something this old man understands," Farrell said with a sly grin. "I've been there, too. Finish your coffee, Detective Walker. We'll go have a look up the mountain."

Rita lay in the hospital bed and thought about her plan. It was a daring trickster plan, one both I'itoi and Coyote would have liked. She was surprised Diana had agreed so readily. After all, Diana would run the greatest risk, for she was the bait, the one Carlisle would come looking for. They would lure Carlisle to the deserted cave by Rattlesnake Skull Village and dispose of him.

Would he fall for it? Rita couldn't be sure, but she knew that people saw what they wanted to see, heard what they wanted to hear. She had already tried that once, and back home, in Tucson, she had Understanding Woman's original medi-

cine basket stored safely away among her treasures as proof that it worked.

Mrs. Charles Clark wasn't particularly nice as
she conducted the initial interview with her new
employee. The Clarks were not accustomed to
dealing with girls of dubious virtue, but Father
Mark had begged them to make an exception in
this case. Rita would be allowed to remain and
work providing her behavior was absolutely above
reproach. She must attend church regularly, do
no drinking or smoking, and have no male visitors.

There was another young *Tohono O'odham* work-
ing in the household, a slender, shy girl named
Louisa Antone. Rita and Louisa shared the same
last name, but they were not related. Rita was from
Ban Thak, while Louisa came from Hikiwoni, or
Jagged Edge.

Although Louisa was two whole years younger
than Rita, she was much more well versed in the
ways of the Clark household. Louisa explained
Adele Clark's complex housekeeping system that
allowed every room in the house to be dusted at
least twice a week. It wasn't until the third day
that Dancing Quail opened the door to what was
known as the basket room.

She remembered Father Mark saying that the
Clarks were interested in baskets, but until she
entered the sweet-smelling room, she had seen no
evidence of it. When she stepped inside, the clean,
dry smell of yucca and bear grass overpowered

her. Smelling them made her want to weep for her home, for her grandmother, and for all that was both familiar and lost to her. Tempted to cry, she forced herself to work.

Dancing Quail came from a society where baskets and livestock were signs of wealth. At home she had never seen so many baskets in one place. Many were crammed together, stacked against walls or piled haphazardly in corners, as though they'd been gathered in a hurry and no one had yet taken the time to sort them. The girl recognized some of the designs and patterns as ones from the *Tohono O'odham*, but there were baskets of many other tribes as well—Hopi, Navajo, Yaqui, even some of the hated Apache.

Slowly, savoring the smell and touch of familiar objects, Dancing Quail worked her way around the room, coming at last to a glass-enclosed case where someone had bothered to arrange the fine baskets displayed there. Cautiously, she opened one door, propped it up on its hinge, and began moving the baskets around on the shelf, gingerly dusting each basket as well as the shelf beneath it.

She had finished the first shelf and was ready to start on the next when she saw it sitting there, waiting—Understanding Woman's basket, not the crude one from the leather case upstairs, but the original one with its fine, straight seams and smooth, silky weave, the basket that had been taken from Dancing Quail's bedroll years before.

With trembling fingers, she took it in her hands and pried open the tight-fitting lid. Not only was the basket there, so were all of the things that had been inside, the sacred gifts her grandmother had given her, except for the missing geode. One at a time, Dancing Quail touched each precious item—the jagged piece of pottery with its etched turtle still clearly visible, the seashell her grandfather had brought back from the ocean, and the eagle feather Dancing Quail's father had brought to his own mother when he was still a boy.

They were all there and all perfectly safe, as though they had been waiting for Dancing Quail to find them. As she put each item back inside and carefully closed the lid, she felt Understanding Woman's spirit close beside her, guiding her.

Brandon swung by Tucson Medical Center on his way back through town. Nothing had changed with Toby Walker. Louella refused her son's offer of a ride home.

"I've got to be going then, Mom," he said.

"Going?" Louella asked vaguely. "Where?"

"I'm working," he lied. "I'm on a case."

"Oh," she said distractedly. "You go on then. I'll be fine."

"What did the doctor say?" he asked gently.

Louella's eyes filled with sudden tears. "That it's up to me," she said, "and I don't want it to be. I want somebody else to make the decision, God or someone, just not me."

She fell sobbing into Brandon's arms. He held her for several long minutes. Louella didn't ask her son to make the decision for her, and he didn't offer. It wasn't his place. "We'll just have to wait and see then, won't we?" he said.

Louella gulped and nodded. "Yes," she said. "Wait and see."

Brandon left the hospital and drove to Gate's Pass. He had waited to contact Diana, hoping to have some definite news about Carlisle's whereabouts before he told her anything. Once he talked to Mallory, there wasn't time to reach her before leaving for Picacho Peak to meet Detective Farrell.

Driving to Diana's house now, he worried about what he would say. He didn't want to alarm her unduly, but he was worried. If Andrew Carlisle was responsible for Margie Danielson's savage murder, and by now both detectives were fairly certain he was, that meant the man had somehow slipped over some critical edge. There was no telling who would be next.

A snippet of radio intruded into his thoughts, giving the first sketchy reports of a stabbing victim found dead that morning in a downtown Tucson hotel room. At least he wouldn't be called out on that case, Walker thought. The Santa Rita was well inside the city limits, so the county would have nothing to do with it. He switched off the radio and kept on driving.

Brandon heard the dog bark from inside the house as soon as he turned off the blacktop. Oh'o, as Diana called him, was a monster of an animal, a rangy, ugly specimen whose teeth could inflict real damage. Right that moment, however, Brandon Walker smiled at the dog's menacing presence. If Andrew Carlisle decided to try coming after Diana Ladd, he'd have to get past the dog first. In a fair fight, Brandon would have put money on the dog any day.

He half expected the door to open, but it didn't. Remaining out of sight, Diana spoke to him through a partially opened window. "Who is it?"

"Brandon Walker. Is it safe to get out of the car?"

"It's safe," she called back. "Bone's with me."

Brandon waited outside while she unlatched a series of locks. That seemed strange. He didn't remember seeing multiple locks on the door before, but of course they might have been there without his noticing. When the door opened, Bone sat directly behind Diana with Davy hanging on the huge dog's neck. "May I come in?" he asked.

"Yes."

He stepped over the threshold. "I've got to talk to you," he said urgently. "In private."

Diana Ladd stared up at him, her eyes fixed in turn on every aspect of his face as though examining him in minute detail. "Davy," she said, without looking away, "take Bone out back and throw the ball for a while. I'll call you in a few minutes."

The child left the room, shoulders sagging, head drooping, with the dog following dutifully behind. "What do you want to talk to me about?" she asked.

All his careful plans for telling her flew out the window. "Andrew Carlisle," he replied. "He's out."

"I know," she said. "That's why I'm wearing this."

A raw recruit would have been drummed out

of the academy for making such a mistake. It wasn't until she touched it with her hand that he noticed the gun and holster strapped to her hip. And not just any gun, either—a gigantic .45 Colt single-action revolver.

"Jesus H. Christ, woman! Is that thing loaded?"

"It certainly is," she told him calmly. "And I'm fully prepared to use it."

15

*D*IANA USHERED BRANDON into the house and showed him to a seat on the couch. The detective still worried about the gun.

"You shouldn't do this, you know," he said.

"Do what, wear a gun, protect myself? Why not?"

"For one thing, if somebody gets shot with that thing, chances are it won't be Andrew Carlisle. In an armed confrontation with crooks, amateurs tend to shoot themselves, not the other way around. For another, it's 1975. We're not still living in the Wild West, you know."

"Somebody forgot to tell the woman at Picacho Peak," Diana returned.

"You know about that, too?"

"The reservation grapevine is pretty thorough."

"And fast. Andrew Carlisle was the first thing I was coming to tell you, and Picacho Peak was the second. I've just come from there. I met with the detective on that case. His name's Farrell, Detective G. T. Farrell from Pinal County. He's a real pro. I've already pointed him in Carlisle's direction."

"I suppose that's only fair," Diana responded sarcastically, "since you're the one who helped Carlisle get off in the first place."

Diana Ladd's remark cut through Brandon Walker's usually even-tempered demeanor. "I didn't help him, goddammit!" Brandon Walker snapped. The hard edge of anger in his voice surprised them both.

"How old were you seven years ago?" he demanded roughly.

"Twenty-four."

"I was a little older than that, but I wasn't much wiser. When I told you to trust the system, I meant it, because I still did, too. I was young and idealistic and ignorant. I thought being a cop was one way to save the world. So get off your cross, Diana. You weren't the only one who got screwed. So did I."

Diana Ladd was taken aback by this outburst. In the brief silence that followed, Davy and Bone edged back into the room.

"I'm hot," the boy said. "Can I have something to drink?"

His request offered Diana an escape from Brandon Walker's unexpected anger. "Sure," she said lightly, getting up. "The tea should be ready by now. Would you like some, Detective Walker?"

He nodded. "That'll be fine."

After she left the room, Walker sat there shaking his head, ashamed of himself for lashing out at her. What she'd said hadn't been any worse than what he'd told himself time and again during the intervening years. Diana Ladd didn't have a corner on the Let's-beat-up-Brandon-Walker market. He could do a pretty damn good job of that all by himself.

With effort, the detective turned his attention to the boy who sat on the floor absently petting the dog. Davy seemed decidedly less friendly than he had been the day before. Wondering why, Brandon made a stab at conversation. "How's the head?" he asked.

"It's okay, I guess," Davy muttered.

"Does it still hurt?"

"Not much. Will my hair grow back? Where they shaved it, I mean."

"It'll take a few weeks, but it'll grow. Have the barber give you a crew cut. It won't show so much then."

"Mom cuts my hair," Davy said. "To save money. I don't think she knows how to do crew cuts."

Brandon glanced toward the swinging kitchen door. It seemed to be taking Diana an inordinately long time to bring the tea.

"Did you know my daddy?" Davy asked.

It was a jarring change of subject. "No," Walker replied. "I never met him."

"Was my father a killer?"

Brandon found the unvarnished directness of the boy's questions unnerving. "Why are you asking me?" he hedged.

"Everybody says my daddy was a killer," Davy answered matter-of-factly. "They call me Killer's Child. I want to know what happened to him. I'm six. That's old enough to know what really happened."

Brandon Walker realized too late that he'd been sucked into an emotional mine field. "What did your mother tell you?" he asked.

"That my daddy was afraid he was going to get into trouble about Gina Antone, and so he killed himself."

"That's right." At least Diana had told her son that much.

"Mom said you were the detective. Did you arrest him?"

"No," Brandon said. "By the time I got to the house, your father was already gone."

"Gone where?"

"Out to the desert."

"To kill himself? That's where he did it, isn't it? In the desert?"

"Yes."

Davy turned his immense blue eyes full on the detective's face. "Why didn't you get there sooner?" he demanded. "Why didn't you hurry and stop him? That way, I could have met him before he died. I could have talked to him just once."

Your father was a scumbag, Walker wanted to say, looking at the wide-eyed boy. Garrison Ladd didn't deserve a son like you. Instead, he said, "I did the best I could, Davy. We all did."

It is said that long ago in a small village lived a very beautiful young woman who was the daughter of a powerful medicine man. She was so beautiful that all the young men of the village liked to look at her. This made her father so angry that he made her stay in the house. If she went out, he scolded her. Whenever he found the young men of the village trying to spy on her, he scolded them, too.

In those days, Wind Man spent much of his time in that same village. One day, the young men of the village went to Wind Man and teased him and said that since he was strong enough and clever enough, he should catch the girl when she came out to get water and take her up in the air so they could all see her. At first Wind Man refused, saying that it would be wrong to do this and make her father angry, but the young men begged and pleaded, and at last that is what happened.

When the girl came out of her house to get water, all the young men in the village were watching. Holding her in his arms, Wind Man took her high up into the air, very gently carrying her around and around. Her long hair was loosened. It fell down and wrapped itself around her until it touched the ground. Then it caught up the nearby leaves and dust and carried them back into the air with her.

And that is the story of the very first Whirlwind there ever was on the desert.

Brandon Walker remembered the whirlwinds.

A fierce wind was kicking up a line of them and propelling them across the desert floor as he drove south toward Topawa for the second time. The first trip had been the day before to notify the victim's grandmother that Gina Antone was dead. The second time he returned to Topawa, he was looking for Gina's killer.

Walker was called in on the case as soon as it

was determined that the water hole in which the body had been found was in the county rather than on reservation land. A dead Indian wasn't high on Sheriff DuShane's list of priorities. As a result, Walker wasn't assigned in a very timely fashion.

The body was discovered by a pair of city-slicker hunters out shooting coyotes mostly for the hell of it, and only incidentally for the bounty paid for each stinking coyote carcass. The two men found the girl floating facedown in the muddy pond and had called the sheriff's office to report it only after getting back to town. Walker theorized that some of their hunting may have been on reservation land and they hadn't wanted to call attention to either the body or themselves until after the dead coyotes were well away from Papago boundaries.

A deputy was dispatched to the scene. Not realizing that the fence with the cattle guard took him onto the reservation and the second took him back off, he left the girl where he found her and reported that it was up to the Papago Tribal Police. Only after all jurisdictional dust settled was Brandon Walker assigned the case. By then, someone had already collected the body. He went to the scene accompanied by a tribal officer named Tony Listo and discovered the crime scene area so picked-over that there was nothing left to find.

Tony pointed Brandon in the direction of the *charco*, but he himself was reluctant to leave his pickup. "This is a bad place," he said. "People don't like to come here."

That hadn't stopped the great white hunters, Walker thought. "You mean Indians don't like to come here?"

"Yes," Listo nodded. "They sure don't."

"You're saying the girl wouldn't have come here on her own?" Brandon Walker asked.

"No, I don't think so," Listo replied.

This short exchange happened prior to the autopsy, while speculation was still rife that the young woman was nothing but a drunk who had fallen in the water and drowned. Later, after the autopsy, the rope burns on her neck and wrists among other injuries had more than borne out Listo's initial theory. Gina Antone hadn't gone to the water hole because she had wanted to but because she was forced. The other things that happened to her weren't by choice, either.

Walker left the *charco*. Following the Indian police officer's directions, he made his way first to Sells and then south to an Indian village called Topawa where the dead woman's grandmother lived in an adobe shack behind a small mission church. He went to the rough wooden door and knocked, but no one answered. He was about to leave when a vintage GMC creaked into the yard behind him. A wide-bodied old woman stepped out.

He waited by the door. "Are you Rita Antone?" he asked.

She nodded. He held out his card, which she looked at but did not take.

"I'm with the Sheriff's Department," he said. "I came to talk to you about your granddaughter."

"I know," the old lady said. "My nephew already told me."

Silent now, Brandon and the boy waited until Diana returned to the living room bearing a tray laden with glasses of iced tea and a plate of freshly made tuna sandwiches.

"We have to eat to keep up our strength," she said.

The air of false gaiety in her tone grated on Brandon's nerves. She still wore the gun. Who the hell was she trying to kid, Brandon wondered—him, her child, or, more likely, herself?

"I heard you two talking," she said, placing the tray on the table in front of the couch. "What about?"

Davy shot the detective a quick, meaningful look. "I asked him if my hair would grow back," Davy replied. "You know, the part they shaved off. He said yes."

Brandon Walker was impressed. The kid was a talented liar. They had indeed talked about Davy's hair growing back, but they had talked about a lot of other things besides. Walker was surprised that Davy didn't mention any of them. Something was going on between the boy and his mother, an undercurrent, a tension that had been missing when he had seen them on Friday and Saturday.

"How long will it take?" Diana asked, chewing a bite of sandwich and falling completely for Davy's lie of omission.

It took a moment for Brandon to reorient himself to the conversation. "To grow out his hair? A few weeks," he said. "Not much longer than that. A crew cut would help."

"I don't do crew cuts," Diana said. "I don't have clippers."

And that was the end of that. Davy took his sandwich, tea, and dog, and melted ghostlike into another room, leaving the two grown-ups in another moment of awkward silence.

"I can't get over how you've changed," Brandon said, still thinking about the gun. "Since that first time I met you, I mean."

"Murder and suicide do that to you," she responded. "They make you grow up quick. You're never the same afterward. No matter how hard you try, you can never be the same."

After watching Gary drive off and hanging up the phone, Diana stumbled blindly back to the couch and sat there for what seemed like hours, waiting for the other shoe to drop. Briefly, she thought about jumping in the car, driving into town, and looking for him, but where would she go?

Gary had mentioned lots of places where he and Andrew Carlisle hung out together, lowbrow places where Andrew said you could see slices of real life—the Tally Ho, the Green Dolphin, the Golden Nugget, the Grant Road Tavern, the Shanty. She knew the names of the bars, the joints, but she hadn't been to any of them personally and couldn't bear the humiliation of going now, of trailing after him, of being just another foolish, hapless wife asking jaded, snickering bartenders if they had seen her drunk of a husband.

Because Gary was drinking more now, she finally admitted to herself, just like her father, and she she, just like Iona, continued to stand by him for no apparent reason. She could see now that she should have stayed in Eugene, should never have agreed to come to this terrible place where she would be without resources and where he would fall under the spell of that man.

That man—Andrew Carlisle. It was easy to blame all of Gary's shortcomings on Andrew Carlisle. Diana saw the professor as a sort of evil Pied Piper, as someone who had cast a terrible spell over her husband's psyche and bent it to his own purposes.

Some of Carlisle's catchphrases whirled back through her memory just as Gary Ladd had reported them to her. "Write what you know." "Experience is the greatest teacher." "If you want to write about it, do it."

Do it? Do what? For the first time, she allowed herself to frame the question: What was Gary writing? She had never asked to look at his manuscript, had never interfered with his work. That was an act of faith on her part, a self-imposed test of her loyalty. Of course, she had passed the exam with flying colors. She was, after all, Iona Dade Cooper's daughter. How could she do anything else? She had buried her head in the sand

and refused to see anything beyond the fact that the stack of manuscript pages on his desk in the spare bedroom had grown gradually taller. That had been the only proof she'd ever required to convince herself that Gary was working, that he was doing what he was supposed to and living up to his part of the bargain.

But now, trembling with fear, Diana sprang from the couch and went looking for the manuscript. Naturally, it wasn't there. The Smith-Corona still sat on the desk in the spare bedroom, and the blank paper was there where it should have been, but the manuscript itself was gone. She had seen it earlier in the day, when she'd been straightening up the house. That could mean only one thing. Gary had taken it with him when he left.

Why? she wondered. Why would he?

Diana looked at Brandon Walker across the top of her iced tea glass. She seemed much more composed now, as though she had made up her mind about something while she was making the sandwiches.

"So why are you here?" she asked. "Why did you come all the way out here? Are you worried about me?"

"Yes," he admitted.

"And you're convinced, just like I am, that he may come looking for me?"

"Yes," he said again.

It was true, that was his concern. He could point to no concrete evidence to that effect, but all his cop instincts screamed out warnings that this woman was in danger.

She laughed aloud in the face of his obvious distress. "Me, too," she said. "At least we're agreed on that score. Now tell me, if you don't want me to wear a gun, and if you don't want me to protect myself, what do you suggest I do?"

"Leave," he said simply. "Go away for a while. Stay with friends or relatives and give us a chance to catch him. Once Detective Farrell gets going on this case, Carlisle won't be on the loose for long. He has no way of knowing that we're already onto him, and if it weren't for the Indians, God knows he wouldn't be."

"What Indians?" Diana asked.

"Two Papagos came to see me this morning, an old blind one and a younger one, an enormous man whose name is Gabe Ortiz."

"Fat Crack came to see you?" Diana said incredulously.

"His name is Fat Crack? You know him? He's evidently some kind of relative of the murdered girl."

Diana nodded. "Her cousin. He's Rita's nephew, but I can't imagine him coming to town to talk to an Anglo cop about this."

"Well, he did," Brandon said defensively, "and he brought the old blind man with him. They tipped us off early, so we're on Carlisle's trail while it's still relatively warm. When I left him, Farrell was on his way to Florence to see if he could pick up any useful information—the names of Carlisle's relatives or friends in the area, for instance, someone he might turn to for help now that he's out.

"I remember his mother hanging around town during the time when his case was about to come to trial. It seems like she was from north Phoenix somewhere, maybe Peoria or Glendale, but I don't think she had the same last name. Farrell will try to get a line on her as well."

"And meanwhile, you want me to run away and hide?"

"Right."

"Well, I won't," Diana declared stubbornly. "I'm going to stay right here in my own home. If he comes looking for me, I'll kill the son of a bitch! I'll put a damn bullet right between his eyes."

"That's premeditation," Brandon countered. "If you kill him, you'll be in big trouble."

"Too bad."

"It's a whole lot more likely, though, that you'll choke up when the time comes and not have nerve enough to pull the trigger."

"I'll have nerve enough," she replied.

She was determined, tough, and foolhardy. Brandon Walker wanted desperately to talk her out of it. He had only one other weapon at his disposal, and he didn't hesitate to use it.

"What will that do to Davy?" he asked.

Diana paused and swallowed. "Davy? He'll be fine," she said. "He'll have Rita."

"Will he? Will that be enough? People already call him Killer's Child."

Her eyes flashed with sudden anger. "How do you know that? Who told you?"

"Davy did," Brandon said, watching as shocked dismay registered on her face.

"You'd better leave now," Diana said.

Brandon Walker unfolded his long legs from the couch and got up to go, but first he stood for a moment, staring down at her.

"Think about it," he said gravely. "Davy's only a boy, Diana. How much of this do you think he can take?"

He paused at the end of the driveway and berated himself for betraying the boy's confidence, but it was the only possible means of pounding some sense into Diana's thick skull. Meantime, he looked around him in despair for other signs of civilization. No one else lived anywhere around here, for God's sake. She couldn't have picked a worse place. Help would be miles away if and when she finally needed it.

Enclosed behind the forest of cactus and with a high wall surrounding the patio and backyard area, the house had a fortresslike appearance, but appearances were deceiving. Once someone breached that walled perimeter, if the dog were taken out of the picture, for instance, the people in the isolated house would be totally vulnerable. Diana talked a good game, but Walker didn't believe for a moment that she'd actually use the gun. She would threaten, but then hesitate at the critical moment. Even veteran cops made that potentially fatal mistake at times.

But even as he worried about her, Walker was struck by the difference between Diana now—defiant and resourceful—and the way she was when he first saw her—broken and worried sick about that bastard husband of hers.

He had driven up to the mobile home in Topawa late in the afternoon of an oppressively hot June Saturday. The sky was blue overhead, but far away across the desert a red wall of moving sand topped by black thunderheads announced an approaching storm.

Diana came to the door wearing a shapeless robe. Her eyes were red, as though she'd been crying. Her face was drawn from lack of sleep and her coloring sallow and unhealthy. When he showed her his ID, she turned even paler.

"Does Garrison Ladd live here?" he asked. She nodded. "Is he home?"

"No. He's not. He's gone."

"Do you have any idea when he'll be back?"

"No."

"Are you Mrs. Ladd?"

"Yes."

"Could I come in and speak with you for a few minutes?"

She stepped aside and held the door for him to come in without asking what he wanted or why he was there. As soon as he saw the crumpled newspaper on the floor, he guessed that she already knew.

He took a small notebook from his pocket. "I'd like to ask you a few questions. Mind if I sit down?"

"No. Go ahead."

He sat while she remained standing, her arms wrapped tightly around her body as if she were desperately cold, although the cooler was turned off and the temperature was stifling. Outside, the wind kicked up, and the first few splatters of rain pelted against the metal siding.

"Was your husband home last Friday night?" he asked.

"He was out," Diana answered woodenly. "He went to a dance."

"Where?"

"One of the villages, San Pedro."

"What time did he get home?"

"Saturday. In the morning. The dance lasted all night."

"Did he go by himself?"

"No. His professor went with him, his creative-writing professor from the U., Andrew Carlisle."

"And did this Andrew Carlisle come home with your husband?"

"No. Gary came home by himself."

"How did he seem when he came home? Was he upset? Did he act as though something was wrong?"

Diana had been answering his questions as though in a fog. Now, she seemed to rouse herself "I shouldn't be talking to you," she said evasively.

Brandon played dumb. "Why not?"

"You're going to trap me into saying something I shouldn't."

"So he was upset?"

"I didn't say that he was fine when he came home. Tired from being up all night and maybe from having had too much to drink."

"He was drinking?"

"A little."

Brandon stared meaningfully at the newspaper lying on the floor, its front page crumpled into a wad. He made sure there could be no doubt about where he was looking.

"You've seen the paper," he said. "Did you know the girl?"

In the stricken silence that followed, both became aware of the steady drum of wind and rain on the outside of the trailer. For the longest time, Diana Ladd didn't answer.

"No," she said at last. "I didn't know her."

"What about her grandmother, Rita Antone? She lives just across the way a few hundred yards."

Diana nodded. "I know Rita from school, but we're not necessarily friends."

"Did your husband know Gina?"

"Maybe. I don't know everyone my husband knows."

"Why did he go to the dance?"

"Why does anyone? To eat at the feast, to drink the wine."

"Is your husband a student of Indian customs?" he asked.

"My husband is a writer," she answered.

By the time the detective finally left the house, he drove into the teeth of a raging desert storm.

Fierce winds shook the car, while sheets of rain washing across the windshield made it difficult to see. Walker had been told that the dance at San Pedro had been a traditional rain dance. It worked with a vengeance, he thought, as he slowed down to pick his way through a dip already filling with fast-moving brown water. Two miles east of Three Points, he was stuck for forty-five minutes at one of the larger dips, waiting for cascading water to recede.

He was still there when a call came over the radio telling him to turn around and go back to the reservation. A pickup truck had been found in a flooded wash off Highway 86 west of Quijotoa. When the highway patrol was finally able to reach the vehicle, they found a body inside— that of a male Caucasian with a single, self-inflicted bullet hole in his head.

That was how Brandon Walker first laid eyes on Garrison Ladd. As he told Davy years later, Garrison Ladd was dead from the bullet wound long before Walker met him.

Rita had hated living with the Clarks.

All that week, no matter what she did, the *Milgahn* woman found fault with Dancing Quail's work. She didn't work fast enough, she wasn't thorough enough, she wasn't good enough. And all that week, Dancing Quail kept silent in the face of Adele Clark's angry onslaughts, but she began planning what she would do.

"I'm very unhappy here," she told Louisa one

night as they were getting ready for bed in their stuffy upstairs room. "I must go someplace else to find work."

"My brother Gordon is in California," Louisa offered. "I could write and ask him. He might know someplace you could go."

"How far is California?" Dancing Quail asked.

Louisa shook her head. "A long way."

"How can I go there?"

"On the train, I think," Louisa answered.

"Will you write down where your brother is so I can find him?"

Louisa's eyes grew large. "You would go there? By yourself?"

"I can't stay here," Rita answered stubbornly.

Louisa wrote her brother's address on a scrap of paper, which Dancing Quail tucked inside the leather case. "What about Mrs. Clark?" Louisa asked. "What will she say?"

"She won't know until after I am gone."

Dancing Quail surprised herself when she talked so bravely, but a river of courage flowed into her from Understanding Woman's medicine basket. She was determined that once more she would have that basket as her own.

She waited impatiently for the next occasion when she would be scheduled to dust the basket room. At the appointed time, she took the other medicine basket with her, concealed under her apron. When she finished dusting, the new basket, now empty, had been exchanged for the other.

That very night important guests came to visit the Clarks and were shown through the basket room. Breathlessly, Dancing Quail waited to see if the switch would be discovered, but it was not. No one opened the glass case. The *Mil-gahn* woman either couldn't tell or didn't notice the difference in quality between the two medicine baskets.

Two days later on Thursday, girls' day, the domestic workers' traditional afternoon off, Rita declined Louisa's invitation to visit the park. Instead, she stayed behind. First she cut off her long braids, hiding the clipped hair in her leather case. Then, with her hair cut short and taking only the precious medicine basket with her, she made her way downtown. Going to one of the few stores that catered to Indians, she bought a set of men's clothing, telling the clerk she was buying it for her younger brother who was coming from the reservation to visit.

Dancing Quail took her purchases and slipped away into an alley where she donned the new clothing. At first it felt strange to be wearing stiff pants, a long-sleeved shirt, and heavy shoes, but she soon got used to it. That night, with the help of two young men, Papagos she met in the train yard, Dancing Quail headed west on a slow-moving, California-bound freight train.

It was hot on the train, and noisy, but not nearly as frightening as it had been long ago as she headed to Phoenix from Chuk Shon for the very first time. Dancing Quail told the two Indian boys she was traveling with that she was going to join her brother in California. A job waited for her there in a place called Redlands.

Each time the train slowed for a station, the Indians would jump off and hide so that when the railroad police—the boys called them bulls—checked, no one would be there. Then, as the train started up again, they would run and jump on it. Sometimes the three were alone in the car. Sometimes other travelers—mostly Mexicans but also a few other Indians—joined them.

For a long time, they rode and talked, but late that night, when the towns and stops got farther apart, Dancing Quail found herself growing sleepy. She was dozing when she felt something pressing against her. Opening her eyes she found another Papago, smelling of alcohol and very drunk, trying to unfasten her pants.

"Stop," she hissed. "Stop now."

"*Mawshch*," he whispered back. "You are promiscuous. You want it. If you did not, you would not be here."

But she didn't want it. What she had done with Father John was one thing. That she had wanted to do, but this was different. Struggling away from him in the swaying, noisy boxcar, she groped inside her shirt and found the medicine basket. She pried off the tight-fitting lid as he came after her again.

In addition to the items that had been there originally and the ones she had added from the other basket, there was now one other item—the *owij*, the awl, which Dancing Quail used to make her baskets. Her trembling fingers sought the awl, found it, and clutched it in the palm of her hand.

Her attacker reached for her again, grabbing her pants, fumbling them down over her hips, but as he leaned over her, thinking her helpless, he felt something hard and sharp press painfully into the soft flesh at the base of his throat. He grunted in surprise.

"Pia'a," she whispered fiercely. "No!"

When he didn't back off, she increased the pressure on the awl. Any moment, she would cut him, and then what would he do? Cry out? Kill her? She should have been terrified, but Understanding Woman's spirit was still strong inside her.

For a long time, they stayed frozen that way in the darkened boxcar, with him above Dancing Quail, pinning her down, and with the awl pricking his neck. Finally, he pulled away.

"Ho'ok," he said, backing off. "Monster."

But it didn't matter to Dancing Quail what he called her, as long as he left her alone. Once he was gone, she pulled her pants back up and refastened them. She lay there then, wide awake, waiting for morning, afraid to close her eyes for fear he would come after her again.

Finally, as the orange sun rolled up over the rocky, far horizon, she did drift off for a little while. She woke up with a start a few minutes later. The awl was still clutched firmly in her hand. Only later did she realize that the arrowhead had disappeared from the opened basket.

* * *

Andrew Carlisle waited until he was sure his mother was asleep before he crept out of the house. He drove until he found a pay phone at an all-night Circle K. His hand shook as he dialed the old, familiar number and then waited to see if it would ring. It had been so many years, perhaps the phone had been disconnected by now, perhaps the system no longer worked.

The telephone was answered on the third ring. "J.S. and Associates," a woman's voice said.

He plugged the required change into the phone. "I'm an insurance investigator," he said. "I'll be in town tomorrow, and I need a copy of a police report on the double. I don't want to have to wait around for it once I get there."

"Have you done business with our firm before?"

"Yes, but it's been several years."

"Are you familiar with our new location?"

"No."

"We're on Speedway, just east of the university, in a house that's been converted into offices."

Just the thought of being close to the university made Carlisle uncomfortable. He was always afraid of running into someone he knew.

"Will you be coming by in person?"

"No," he said. "Someone will be in to pick it up."

"Fine. What report is it you need?"

"The accident that happened on the Kitt Peak Road last Friday."

"Case number?"

"I don't have it with me."

"Anything else?"

"No. That's all."

"Very good. That'll be one hundred fifty dollars, cash on delivery. Please place the cash in an envelope. We'll have another envelope here waiting for you. What name should I put on it?"

"Spaulding," he said, suddenly unable to resist the joke. "Myrna Louise Spaulding. She'll be in to pick it up around noon."

"Very good. Anything else?"

"No, ma'am," Carlisle responded cheerfully. "It's a pleasure doing business with you."

Fat Crack brought Looks At Nothing home to his house where Wanda Ortiz, the younger man's unfailingly cheerful wife, served them a dinner of chili, beans, and fresh tortillas. She was mystified about her husband spending so much time with the old medicine man, but she said nothing. As a good husband and provider, Gabe was allowed his little foibles now and then.

"We will need some clay," Looks At Nothing said, "white clay from Baboquivari to make the gruel."

Fat Crack nodded. "Right. I know where to find such clay."

"And the singers?" Looks At Nothing asked.

"I know nothing at all about singers."

"The best ones for this come from Crow Hang. It will be expensive. You must feed them all four days."

Fat Crack nodded. "My aunt says she will pay

whatever it costs from her basket money. The singers can stay here at my house. Wanda will do the cooking. I will see about them tomorrow when I pick my aunt up from the hospital to take her home."

"Your wife is a good woman," Looks At Nothing said. "You are lucky to have her."

"I know," Fat Crack agreed.

They were sitting outside under the stars. Looks At Nothing lit another crooked cigarette from his seemingly endless supply. He took a puff and passed it. *"Nawoj,"* he said.

"Nawoj," Fat Crack replied.

Far away from them, across the horizon, a bank of clouds bubbled with lightning. The rains were coming, probably before the end of the week.

"You would make a good medicine man," Looks At Nothing said thoughtfully. "You understood how the enemy could be both Apache and not Apache long before I did. Perhaps I am getting too old."

"You are old," Fat Crack returned, "but not too old. Besides, in my religion I am already a medicine man of sorts, a practitioner."

"What kind of religion is this? White man's religion?"

"Christian Scientist."

"Christian I understand. This is like Father John. What is Scientist?"

Fat Crack considered for a moment. "We believe," he said, "that God's power flows through all of us."

Looks At Nothing nodded. "You are not practitioner," he insisted firmly. "You are a medicine man."

Fat Crack smiled into the night at the old man's stubbornness. "Perhaps you are right," he said laughing. "A medicine man with a tow truck."

16

*W*ITH BRANDON WALKER gone and Davy fast asleep in his room, Diana was wide awake and stewing. It had been easy to turn on the bravado when the detective was there, to act as though she were ten feet tall and bulletproof, but it was a lie. She was petrified.

Having Walker confirm that he, too, believed Carlisle was coming for them gave form and substance to a once-vague but threatening specter. Walker's fear added to Rita's as well as her own created in Diana a sense of fear squared, terror to a higher power. What before had seemed little more than a fairy tale was now disturbingly real. Brandon Walker wasn't in the business of fairy tales. Cops, particularly homicide cops, didn't joke about such things.

Diana went to bed and tried to sleep, but found herself tossing and turning, hounded by a series of waking nightmares, each more terrifying than the last. What was it like to die? she wondered. What did it feel like? Did it hurt? When her mother had died, it had been a blessing, a release from incredibly agonizing pain and worse indignity. But Diana wasn't terminally ill, and she wasn't ready to die. Not yet.

That hadn't always been the case. In those first black days right after Gary's death, she hadn't much cared if she lived or died. She was so physically ill herself that sometimes death seemed preferable. That was before she found out the cause of her raging bouts of nausea, before she knew she was pregnant—newly widowed and newly pregnant.

Max Cooper didn't come to Gary's memorial service for the simple reason that he and his second wife were neither notified nor invited. Gary's folks flew in first class from Chicago and took over. Gary's mother, Astrid, wanted a big funeral at home in her home church with all attendant pomp and circumstance. Diana respectfully demurred. All she could handle was an unpretentious and poorly attended memorial service at the faded funeral home on South Sixth. Afterward, Gary's parents left for Chicago and the real production number of a funeral, while Diana skulked back home to the reservation and shut herself up inside the trailer.

By the time the authorities finally got around to releasing the bodies, Gina Antone's funeral was scheduled two days after Gary's hurried memorial service. With no one to offer guidance, Diana Ladd spent the two days agonizing over what she should do about it. Should she go or stay away? Would her appearance be considered an admission of guilt or a protestation of Gary Ladd's innocence?

For Diana Ladd believed wholeheartedly in Gary's innocence. She believed in it with all the ferocity of a child who clings desperately to his soon-to-be-outgrown belief in Santa Claus or the Tooth Fairy. She could not yet look at who and what her husband really was. Accepting the burden of his guilt, the only option offered her by Brandon Walker, the detective on the case, would have forced the issue. Instead, she took the line of least resistance. Gary's three-word, equivocal statement transformed itself into full-fledged denial. "I don't remember," became "I didn't do it," guilt became innocence, and fiction became truth.

With all this boiling in her head, Diana peeked out between threadbare panels of drapes and looked across the muddy quagmire that separated the Topawa Teachers' Compound from the village proper. The church parking lot was filling rapidly with cars and pickups as Indians gathered to pay their final respects. It was time for Diana to make a decision, and she did.

Dressing quickly, she put on the same blue double-knit suit she had worn to Gary's memorial service, the same suit he had picked out as her going-away dress for their honeymoon. She pulled her hair back in a bun and fastened it up with hairpins the same way Iona used to wear hers. Wearing it that way made Diana look older, much older. It made her look like her mother.

Dressed in the suit, but with sandals on her feet because of the mud, Diana Ladd started across the hundred yards or so of no-man's-land, the vast gulf between the Anglo Teachers' Compound and the Indian village, between her home and Gina Antone's funeral, between Diana's past and what would become her future. Once she set foot on that path, there was no turning back.

The mission church was filled to capacity, but people in the back row shifted aside just enough to let her in. She wanted to be small, invisible, but her arrival was greeted by an inevitable and whispered notice. Everyone knew she was there. She felt or maybe only imagined the stiffening backs of people around her. She flushed, sensing that they disapproved of her presence although no one had the bad manners to say so outright.

Topawa mission itself was small and plain and reminded Diana of the church back home in Joseph, Oregon. There was no side room where Gina's mourning relatives could have grieved in private. They sat stolidly, shoulder to shoulder, in the front row next to Rita. In addition to the grandmother, there were two couples, an older one and a younger. Were two of them Gina's parents? Did they know she was here in church with them? Diana wondered. What would they do when they found out? Spit at her? Throw her out?

The service started. Gradually, Diana allowed herself to be caught up in the familiar strains of the mass, the sounds and smells of which came back from the dim reaches of her childhood.

Iona Anne Dade Cooper's daughter, Diana Lee

Bernadette, had been a devout child growing up in Joseph, but she had left the church without a backward glance in early adulthood, not only over the issue of birth control, but also over her marriage to a non-Catholic. Garrison Walther Ladd, III, the only son of staunch Lutherans, never would have consented to his child being brought up in the Catholic Church.

Somehow, in a way Gary's memorial service hadn't, Gina's funeral became a requiem for everything Diana had lost—her childhood as well as her marriage, her husband, and her mother. When the mass was over, instead of bolting out first as she had intended, she was too overcome to leave until after Rita and the others had already trudged down the aisle and were waiting at the door to greet the attendees.

There was no escape. As soon as she stood up, the people parted around her as though she were a carrier of some contagious, dread disease. And that was how she arrived in front of Rita Antone, isolated and alone, in the midst of the crowd.

The old Indian woman held out a leathery hand and grasped Diana's smooth one. The younger woman looked up and met Rita's fearsome bloodshot gaze. "I'm so sorry," Diana whispered.

Rita nodded, pressing her hand. "Are you coming to the feast?" the old woman asked.

"The feast?" Diana stammered uncomprehendingly.

"At the feast house after the cemetery. You must come. We will sit together," Rita said kindly. "You see, we are both *hejel wi'ithag*."

"Pardon me?"

"We are both left alone. You must come sit with me."

Behind them, people in line shifted impatiently. Stunned by such kindness and generosity, Diana could not turn it down. "I'll come," she murmured. "Thank you."

Detective G. T. Farrell arrived in Florence in the late evening and set about putting the Arizona State Penitentiary on notice. Farrell was a man unaccustomed to taking no for an answer. When one person turned him down, he automatically moved up to the next rung on the ladder of command and turned up the volume. By two o'clock in the morning, he had done the unthinkable—Warden Adam Dixon himself was out of bed and working on the problem. When the warden discovered that Ron Mallory's home phone was either conveniently out of order or off the hook, he sent a car to fetch him.

Ron Mallory made his way into the warden's well-lit office feeling distinctly queasy. Obviously, he should have paid more attention to the guy on the phone, the one who had been looking for Andrew Carlisle earlier, because whoever was looking for him now had a whole lot more horses behind him.

"What seems to be the problem?" Mallory asked, putting on as good a front as possible.

"Carlisle's the problem," Warden Dixon growled. "Where the hell is he?"

"Tucson, as far as I know, sir," Mallory answered quickly. "We put him on the bus to Tucson."

"Where in Tucson?"

"He had rented an apartment, down off Twenty-second Street somewhere, but that fell through the day of his release. The landlord called me while I was waiting for a guard to bring in the prisoner. The guy told me Carlisle couldn't have the apartment he wanted after all. Since he was already half signed out, there wasn't much I could do but let him go. He said he'd check in as soon as he found some other place to stay."

"Has he?"

"Not so far as I know, sir. I glanced at my messages on the way in. I didn't see anything from him, although I'll be glad to go back and check."

"You do that," Warden Dixon said. "You go check, and if you don't find it, you might consider cleaning out your desk. Come tomorrow morning, you're going to find yourself back on the line, mister. I kid you not."

In the cell-blocks? Mallory's jaw dropped. "I don't understand. What's going on?"

"I'll tell you what's going on. This detective here thinks Carlisle went on a rampage within minutes of checking out of this facility. Do you hear me? Within minutes! We've got one woman dead so far, a dame over by a Picacho Peak with her tit bitten in two. Does that ring any bells with you, Mr. Mallory? Because if it doesn't, it by God should?"

Mallory took a backward step, edging toward the door.

"Furthermore," Dixon added ominously, "you shake up whatever clerks there are on duty around here and you start them looking through every goddamned record we have for any name or address that might give this detective a lead. You're in charge, Mallory. Do I make myself clear?"

"Yes, sir. Perfectly."

"Get moving then."

Mallory bolted from the room. As he panted toward his soon-to-be-former office, he swore under his breath. If he ever got his hands around Andrew Carlisle's neck, Assistant Superintendent Ron Mallory would kill the bastard himself. Personally.

Diana fell asleep at last and dreamed about Gina's funeral, except it wasn't Gina's at all, it was her mother's. The two were all mixed up somehow. Instead of being in the mean funeral home in La Grande where Max had held the funeral in real life, with half the mourners having to stand outside the doors because there was no more room, it was in the mission church at Topawa. Even the graveside part was in Topawa.

And that, too, was like Gina's. Instead of a mortuary's canopy, four men from Joseph had stood as corner-posts holding up a sheet to provide shade while someone else, she couldn't tell who, intoned a prayer. Although he hadn't attended Iona's real funeral, one of the four sheet-holders was George Deeson, her rodeo-queen mentor, another was Ed Gentry from the First National Bank. There was Tad Morrison from Pay-and-Tote grocery, and George Howell from Tru-Value Hardware.

At Gina's graveside, an old blind man in Levi's and cowboy boots had offered a long series of interminable Papago prayers that, out of deference to Diana, the only Anglo in attendance, were translated into English by someone else. This was true in her dream as well, except instead of a blind man in cowboy boots, the main speaker was a priest praying in what seemed to be Latin. After that, they moved on to the feast.

Like the rest, this, too, was a strangely muddled mixture of Topawa and Joseph, of near past and far past, of Anglo and Indian. Instead of traditional Indian fare, the food was like the food at the Chief Joseph Days barbecue, with grilled steaks and corn on the cob, homemade rolls and fresh-fruit pies. People were dressed in their Chief Joseph Days finery, including Diana in her rhinestone boots and her coronation Stetson with its rhinestone tiara.

Diana was visiting with someone, an old lady, when her father came striding over to her, grabbed her hat, and held it just out of reach while she tried desperately to reclaim it.

"Couldn't you find something better than this to wear?" he sneered down at her, shaking the hat but still holding it well beyond her fingertips. "Did you have to come to your mother's funeral all tarted out in your hussy clothes?"

"I'm not," she said. "I'm not a hussy. I'm the queen. I get to wear these clothes. You can't stop me."

"You're not the queen," he leered back at her. "Not really. You cheated. You cheated. You cheated."

Diana woke up drenched in sweat with the

hateful words still ringing in her ears. Her father had shouted those words at her in real life and left them echoing forever in her memory, but not then, not at her mother's funeral. When was it? When had it been?

"It would sure as hell be nice if I had a little help with the chores around here of a Saturday morning," Max Cooper had grumbled. "I'm sick and goddamned tired of you getting all tarted up and taking off every goddamned weekend."

"Dad," she said, "I'm the queen, remember. I have to go. I signed an agreement saying that I'd represent Joseph in all the rodeo parades around here."

"I'm the queen," he mocked, imitating her. "My aching ass you're the queen! Like hell you are! You're no more the queen than I am. You cheated."

"Max," Iona cautioned.

"Don't you 'Max' me. How long are you going to go on letting her believe she's Little Miss Highness, God's gift to everyone? How long?"

"Max."

He turned on her then. Diana knew he wouldn't hit her. Not anymore. He'd only really come after her once after George Deeson—that "goddamned coffee-drinking Jack Mormon," as Max called him—appeared on the scene. It happened early on in the course of Waldo and Diana's training. George was just coming up the outside steps that led to the kitchen to collect his morning coffee and biscuits when all hell broke loose.

Diana never remembered what that particular fight was about and it didn't matter really. She said something to her father, and Max hit her hard across the mouth with the back of his hand, sending her spinning into the corner of the kitchen. She waited, head down, expecting the next blow, which never came. When she finally dared look, George Deeson had a choke hold around her father's collar, holding him at arm's length with a knot of fist twisted into her father's protruding Adam's apple.

"Don't you ever do that again, Max Cooper, or so help me God, I'll kill you!" George was old enough to be Max's father, and he didn't raise his voice when he said it, but Max went stomping out of the house like a whipped dog, while George calmly sat down to butter his biscuits and drink his coffee.

Evidently, Max Cooper took George at his word. He never struck Diana again, not once. Not ever, although he tried the night she came home with her clothes torn to pieces.

Later, much later, in the hospital in La Grande when her mother was dying, Diana had asked Iona about it. Why had her father called her a cheater?

"Because of George," Iona said.

"George? What did he do?"

"He bought two hundred dollars' worth of rodeo tickets the last day of the contest," Iona said. "He gave them away to a bunch of poor kids here in La Grande who couldn't have gone otherwise."

"He didn't buy them from me," Diana said. She had sold tickets until she was blue in the face, but she didn't remember selling more than one to George Deeson.

"I gave him the tickets and took the money, but they were from your ticket allocation. Even though you didn't sell them yourself, that batch of tickets put you over the top. Remember, there was only a quarter of a point difference between you and Charlene Davis."

"So Dad was right," Diana said, feeling her one moment of triumph, her rodeo-queen victory, slip through her fingers in retrospect. "I did cheat after all."

"No, Diana," Iona had said firmly, squeezing her daughter's hand despite the pain it caused her. "You've earned every damn thing you've ever gotten."

It was the only time Diana ever remembered hearing her mother use the word *damn*. As years went by, she was beginning to understand it a little. Her name, not Charlene's, had been the name on the scholarship at the registrar's office at the university in Eugene. Her name, Diana's name, was what it said on the two degrees, one from the University of Oregon and now a master's from the University of Arizona. She had earned it all, with the timely help of both George Deeson and her mother.

Lying in bed at her home in Gates Pass, Diana's eyes misted over. What would have happened to her if George Deeson hadn't driven into her life, bringing Waldo with him? Where would she be now? Married to some drunken logger in Joseph like Charlene was, or else still living in the house by the garbage dump. Would her life have been worse or better? There was no way to tell.

Her grief for George Deeson, dead now these four years, spilled over into grief for Waldo, who had broken a leg during her first semester in Eugene and had to be put down. While she was at it, she shed a tear for her mother, and finally a few for herself as well. What if Brandon Walker was right? What if she didn't have guts enough to pull the trigger? What if Andrew Carlisle killed her? What kind of legacy would she leave for her child?

Still wide awake, she thought of all those boxes sitting in the root cellar, waiting for someone to sort through them—her mother's boxes and, more than that, her husband's. Whose job was that? Who was the person whose responsibility it was to go through them, to sort the wheat from the chaff so Davy or someone else wouldn't have to do it later? There were things in those boxes that should be kept and saved for him and others that should be thrown away and never again see the light of day.

It was weeks before she could face returning to Gary's office, weeks before she could approach the desk again with its stilled typewriter and haunting stack of blank paper.

She started with the bottom drawer, thinking that would be the least painful, but of course, she was wrong. Had Gary been smart enough, he would have got rid of it, would have destroyed it, but she found the damning envelope with its University of Arizona return address almost immediately. Curious, she pulled out the sheaf of loose papers and scanned through them, recognizing at once the clumsy effort of one of her own early short stories, the one she had submitted as part of her application to the Creative Writing program.

At first she noticed only the stilted phrases, the graceless prose that flows at tedious length from the minds and hearts of beginning writers, but then her eyes were drawn to the handwritten comment at the end. "Gary," it said. "Your work here is, naturally, a beginning effort, but it shows a good deal of promise. We'll discuss the possibilities for this manuscript in greater detail once you're enrolled in the program and fully underway." It was signed, "A. Carlisle."

For a full minute, she stared down at the paper, trying to make sense of it all. Then the full weight of Gary's betrayal thundered over her, burying her in a landslide of emotion.

Gary had gained admission to Andrew Carlisle's program using her story, not his own. Not that she would have wanted to be in it after all, she thought bitterly, but the rejection had caused her to doubt her own ability, to retreat into teaching, to settle for second best rather than following her own aspirations.

Up to that very moment, in spite of everything else, Diana Ladd had grieved for her dead husband. Now she exploded in a raging fit of anger.

"Damn you!" she screamed in fury at Gary Ladd's unconcerned Smith-Corona. "Damn you, damn you, damn you!"

Having once allowed herself to succumb to anger, it never once left her. It functioned as a whip and a prod, goading her to succeed at writing no matter what obstacles might fall in her path.

Diana dropped the papers, scattering them like leaves across the desk and floor. She fled Gary's office and never returned. Only as she left for the hospital to have Davy, with the arrival of the movers barely minutes away, did she give Rita permission to go into Gary's abandoned office and pack up whatever she found there.

With the exception of appropriating the typewriter for her own, in the intervening years, Diana had never examined any of the boxes, but Rita was nothing if not thorough. Therefore, that purloined short story must still be there, carefully packed away among all of Gary Ladd's other books and papers. That story was one of the things that demanded both attention and destruction, although there were probably plenty of others. Only Diana could tell the difference. It was her job, her responsibility, and nobody else's.

"Mom?" a small voice asked from the doorway. "Are you awake yet?"

"I'm awake, Davy."

"I'm hungry. Are we going to have breakfast? We're still out of tortillas."

"We're going to have breakfast," she said determinedly, getting out of bed. "I'm going to fix it."

While Myrna Louise was making breakfast, Andrew Carlisle made a quick survey of her room. He found her extra checkbooks and the savings-account book in the bottom of her lingerie drawer, the same place where she'd always kept it, along with a fistful of twenties in hard, cold cash. The balance in both accounts was pitifully small in terms of lifetime savings for someone of her age. It was just as well she wouldn't be around to get much older, Carlisle thought. He was actually doing her a favor. Maybe she was planning to land on his doorstep when the time came, expecting her son to support her in her old age. Fat chance.

Out in the garage, he eased Jake's partially opened bag of lime into the trunk, careful not to spill any of it on Johnny Rivkin's Hartmann bag. Garden-variety lime probably wouldn't be enough to strip all the meat off the bones, but it would help kill the odor.

They had breakfast, a cheerful, family-style breakfast. Myrna Louise was careful not to fuss too much. Afterward, while she cleaned up the kitchen, Andrew loaded the car. Lida Givens, that nosy old bat from next door, came over to the fence to see what he was doing and to chat for a while. "Going on a trip?" she asked.

He nodded. "It's been a long time since Mama had a chance to get out of town. We're going to drive up past the Grand Canyon and maybe on up through the canyon country of Utah. That's always been one of my favorite places."

"Never been there myself," Lida Givens asserted. "Wouldn't know it from a hole in the ground. I much prefer California."

Andrew started for the car, then paused, snapping his fingers as if at a sudden afterthought.

"Say, are you going to be in town for the next week and a half to two weeks?"

"Reckon. Don't have any place to go at the moment. The kids are busy with their own jobs and families. They don't like me dropping in unless I give them plenty of advance warning. Why?"

"Would you mind bringing in the mail? And if you see the paper boy, tell him to put us on vacation until we get back."

"Sure thing. I'll be happy to."

"I'd appreciate it," Andrew Carlisle told Lida Givens with a sincere smile. "Living far away, it's been a real blessing for me to know my mother's in a place with such terrific neighbors."

"Think nothing of it," Lida said. "That's what neighbors are for."

Myrna Louise was delighted to get in the car and go for a ride someplace, even if it was just an overnight jaunt. Excited as a little kid, she packed a bag and had it waiting by the door for Andrew to load while she did the breakfast dishes.

Years ago, not even that long ago, she would have left the dishes sitting in the sink to rot while she went away, but not anymore. Not in her cozy little house on Weber Drive. What would the neighbors think if they happened to glance in a window and see that she'd left without doing the dishes?

She was pleased that Andrew seemed to have forgiven her for burning up his stupid manuscripts. She probably shouldn't have, really. Writing had to be a lot of work, but he seemed totally at ease this morning, whistling to himself as he loaded the car. She watched out the window as he stopped briefly to chat across the fence with Lida Givens, the lady from next door.

Thank God Andrew was making the effort to be sociable for a change, Myrna Louise thought, and thank God he hadn't done anything to dispel the Phil Wharton myth. Lida Givens had a son who was a dentist and a daughter who sold real estate out in California somewhere. It was particularly important that Andrew keep up the Phil Wharton charade with Lida Givens even if he didn't do it with anyone else.

At nine they headed for Tucson. The heat was incredibly oppressive, and the Valiant had no air-conditioning. They drove with the windows open and the wind roaring in their ears. Far to the south and east, thunderclouds edged over the horizon, but they were only teasers, hints of the coming rainy season that would bring blessed relief from some of the heat but they would bring additional humidity as well.

"Have you made any plans?" Myrna Louise shouted over the noise of the car.

It was fine for Andrew to come and visit for a day or two, but she certainly didn't want to be saddled with him on a permanent basis. She was eager to know how soon he'd be moving on.

"I'm looking for a place somewhere around Tucson, someplace I can afford, so I can get back to writing."

"Good," Myrna Louise breathed. Tucson was both close enough and far enough away.

* * *

"I don't like oatmeal," Davy complained, picking at the cereal in his bowl.

"Not even with brown sugar and raisins?" Diana asked.

Davy shrugged. "They help, I guess. I just like tortillas better. Why don't you fix tortillas?"

"I don't know how."

"Will Rita make tortillas for us when she gets home today?"

Diana thought of the huge cast covering Rita's smashed left arm. "She won't be doing that for a while," Diana said. "At least not until after her arm comes out of the cast."

"You mean we can't have any until she gets better? That could take a long time."

"Maybe I could try making some," Diana offered tentatively. "I mean, if Rita were here to coach me and tell me what to do."

Davy's jaw dropped. "Really? You mean you'd learn to make them yourself?"

"I said I'd try."

"Do you swear?"

Davy's unbridled enthusiasm was catching. This was the first sign of life Diana had seen in her son for several days. She put her hand over her heart and grinned at him. "I swear," she said.

Davy helped clear the table, then went to feed the dog, fairly skipping as he did so. He had been so strangely subdued that it pleased her to see him acting like his old self.

It was such a small thing, really, promising to

make tortillas, but it signified something else, she realized, something much more important. Promises made meant they would have to be kept, and that implied a future—a future with her in it.

Before, she had thought about sorting Gary's and her mother's things as an ending, as a means of putting her house in order in preparation for yet another catastrophe. Now, for the first time, she saw the other side of the coin. It could go either way. She might just as easily be doing it as a beginning, as a way of putting the past behind her and finally getting on with her life.

I'll do the dishes first, she thought, then I'll get started.

It is said that on the Third Day, I'itoi gave each tribe a basket. When all the women were busy learning how to make baskets, I'itoi saw that it would be good for each one to mark her baskets in a different way so they would know who had made each different basket and what it should be used for. So I'itoi brought the women seed pods from the planting, which the Mil-gahn *call devil's claw. He showed all the women how to weave the black fiber from the seed pods into their baskets to make a pattern to mark their baskets, and by each pattern, the baskets would be known.*

Now while all the women were working so hard learning to make the baskets, many of the Little People were watching as well. The birds especially, watching from a big mesquite tree, were curious about what I'itoi and the women were doing. Finally, u'u whig, *the birds, came down from the tree and stole some of the*

*fiber for making baskets. They flew back to the tree
with it and tried to make a basket of their own. But
they had not watched I'itoi closely enough, and when
their basket was finished, it slipped around and hung
upside down on the bottom of the branch.*

*When this happened, the birds began to laugh. I'itoi
heard them laughing and came to see what was so funny.
When he saw what they had done, I'itoi was very pleased.
He told the birds that they might make baskets for
themselves. He said they should call their baskets nests
and use them for homes.*

And that is why, my friend, the u'u whig, *the birds,
make nests even to this day, and all this happened on
the Third Day.*

Diana had barely moved the first stack of boxes
out of the root cellar and into the kitchen when
the phone rang. She looked at it warily, afraid of
who might be calling. Her number was unlisted,
but there were probably ways to get unlisted numbers if you knew how to go about it.

"Hello," she said.

"Diana Ladd?" questioned a strange male voice.

"Who's calling please?" she asked, while her
heart hammered in her throat and her knees
wobbled.

"My name is Father John. I'm the associate
priest, semi-retired actually, out at San Xavier
Mission on the reservation. Is Diana Ladd there?
I need to speak to her."

A priest? She didn't know any priests, not any
at all. Why would a strange priest be calling

her? Was this a trick? Was it Andrew Carlisle pretending to be a priest? She wouldn't put it past him.

"This is Diana," she said at last.

"Good. I'm sure this is all going to sound very strange," the man continued, "but I was wondering if it would be possible for me to stop by and pay you a visit?"

Pay a visit? At the house? Did he know where she lived? "Why?" she asked.

"We have a mutual friend," he said mysteriously. "Rita Antone, the lady who lives with you."

"Funny," Diana returned. "I don't recall her ever mentioning your name."

"I'm not surprised. We had a falling out years ago. I'm just now getting around to mending fences."

"Look," Diana said impatiently. "Rita isn't here. If you want to talk to her when she gets back . . ."

"It's you I need to talk to, Mrs. Ladd," the priest interrupted. "It's about Rita, but I don't need to see her. In fact, it would probably be better if I didn't. I saw her in the hospital yesterday. I'm afraid my visit upset her."

He sounded priestly. The inflections were right, the tone of voice, the attitude. "Father," Diana said, "I'm very busy right now. Couldn't this wait a few days?"

"It's a matter of life and death," he insisted. "I must see you today."

"Where?"

"I could come there."

"No," she said at once. "Absolutely not." She

wasn't dumb enough to invite a strange man into her home. "I could come out to the mission, I suppose," she suggested.

If the caller had been Andrew Carlisle posing as a priest, that would have been the end of it. Instead, he agreed readily. "Good," he said, "but would you please not bring the boy?"

"I have to bring him," Diana told him. "Rita is my only sitter. She isn't here."

"Well," he said, "all right then, but I must speak to you in private. Perhaps the boy can go over to the convent and visit for a little while. One of the nuns over there, Sister Katherine, is particularly good with children. I'm sure she would be happy to watch him for us if I ask her to. How soon can I expect you?"

"By the time we get cleaned up and ready to go, it'll probably be around an hour."

"Fine," he said. "I'll be waiting in my office, which is just behind the bookstore. Ask anyone, and they'll direct you."

Diana hung up the phone. So Father John wasn't a fake, but why would a former friend of Rita's want to talk to Diana? That was more than she could understand.

She went to the back door. Davy was swinging high on the metal swing set his grandparents from Chicago had sent as his previous year's Christmas present. On her own, Diana never could have spent that much money on a single toy.

"Come on, Davy," she called. "You have to come in now and get cleaned up."

"How come? Me and Bone are playing."

"Bone and I," she corrected firmly. "Come on. We have to go to church."

He came to the door, frowning and sulking. "To church? I didn't know this was Sunday," he said. "And why do we have to go anyway? Rita goes to church. You never do."

"Today's an exception," she said. "And it's Monday, not Sunday, so wipe that frown off your face and let's get going. If you're lucky, maybe somebody out there will be selling popovers."

"Popovers?" he asked, brightening. His mother might just as well have waved a magic wand.

"That's right. We're going to San Xavier. There are usually ladies selling popovers in the parking lot."

The very mention of popovers put Davy in high gear. Tortillas and popovers. Beans and chili. He much preferred Indian food to Anglo. Maybe she would have to break down and learn to cook Indian food after all, and not just tortillas, either.

17

*T*HEY SAY THIS *happened long ago. Cottontail was sitting next to a tall cliff when* Ban, Coyote, *saw him sitting there. Coyote was very hungry. "Brother," he said to Cottontail, "I am going to eat you up."*

"Oh, no," said Cottontail. "This you must not do, for I am holding up this cliff. If you eat me up, it will fall down and crush us both."

Coyote looked up at the tall cliff, and he was afraid that Cottontail was right. "Come over here, Coyote," said Cottontail. "You stand here and lean against the cliff. You hold it up while I go around to the back of the mountain and find a big stick to help hold it up."

"All right," said Coyote, and that's just what happened. He came over and stood beside Cottontail to help hold up the cliff. As soon as Coyote was standing there, Cottontail ran off somewhere. Coyote stood there for a long, long time, leaning against the cliff, holding it. He waited and waited, but Cottontail didn't come back.

Finally, Coyote got tired of just standing there. He thought that if he ran very fast, perhaps he could get out of the way before the cliff could fall on him. So Coyote let go of the cliff and ran as fast as he could. But when he let go, the cliff didn't fall down after all. That was when Coyote knew Cottontail had tricked him.

This made Coyote very angry. "I will follow Cottontail's trail," he said. "The next time I see him, I will eat him up."

And that, nawoj, *is the story of the first time Cottontail tricked Coyote.*

They stopped in front of an old two-story house along Speedway. "What's this?" Myrna Louise asked.

Andrew reached in his pocket and pulled out an envelope. "Run this inside for me," he said. "They'll give you another envelope."

"But what *is* this place?" she asked again.

"It's a rental agency," he said. "They're helping me find a place to live. I'll wait here in the car. Give them this and tell them your name."

Myrna Louise started to say that she was a lot older than he was, and if anyone was going to sit in the car, it ought to be her, but it didn't seem worth starting an argument when the day was going so well. She got out of the car.

Inside, behind a counter, a young woman was busy talking on the phone. Myrna Louise grew impatient standing there because the receptionist was only talking to her boyfriend. While waiting, she looked around. Nothing indicated that this was a real estate office. Shouldn't there have been signs, something that said what kinds of properties they rented?

Finally, the young woman hung up. "May I help you?" she asked.

Wordlessly, Myrna Louise handed over the envelope. The receptionist opened it, removing a blank sheet of paper that had been wrapped around a small stack of bills. She counted them out, one at a time. "And what is your name?" she asked, when she'd finished counting out $150.

"Myrna Louise Spaulding, but it's probably under my son's name, which is . . ."

"Here it is," the young woman interrupted, taking another envelope from a drawer. Myrna Louise was surprised to see her name, not Andrew's, neatly typed on the envelope. So he really had intended for her to pick it up.

"Was that a deposit?" she asked, trying to make sense of the transaction.

The young woman laughed. "You could call it that."

"Well, shouldn't you give me a receipt or something?"

"No," the receptionist replied. "That's not the way we do business around here."

Rebuffed, Myrna Louise took the envelope and went back to the car. Andrew looked decidedly unhappy. "What took so long?" he demanded. "I was afraid something had gone wrong."

"She was on the phone," Myrna Louise said.

Andrew reached out to take the envelope, but his mother placed it in her lap, letting both hands rest on it. Something was wrong with that place, she thought. "They didn't give me a receipt," she said.

Andrew laughed. "That's all right. I won't need one."

How could Andrew afford to throw away a whole $150 in cash like that and not even get a receipt? Myrna Louise wondered. She had rented houses and apartments before, and she *always* got a receipt, especially when she paid cash. Why wouldn't Andrew insist on one—unless he had lied to her and the money was for something else entirely, not for a rental at all.

Suspicion born of years of being lied to made her hands itch with curiosity about what was in that envelope. She wished she had opened it for a peek before she ever came back out to the car.

"Where are we going now?" she asked.

"To the storage unit. I want a few things from there."

"Couldn't we stop and get something to drink first?" she asked. "I'm thirsty."

Andrew sighed. "I suppose. What do you want?"

"A root-beer float would be nice. The Dairy Queen isn't far."

They stopped at a Dairy Queen, and Andrew went inside where several people were already in line ahead of him. Cautiously, keeping the dashboard between his sight line and her hands, Myrna Louise slipped a bony finger along the flap of the envelope. It came loose, tearing only a little along one edge. Inside were two pieces of paper.

She scanned through them in growing confusion. There was nothing at all about renting a house. She found herself reading some kind of police report about an auto accident. Finally, she noticed the names—Rita Antone and Diana Ladd, and someone else named David. The names of those two women were branded into Myrna Louise's memory. David had to be Diana's son, her baby. Why had Andrew paid so much money to have something about them? You'd think he'd want to forget all about them.

Hastily, she stuffed the papers back in the envelope and licked the flap. After a lifetime's worth of snooping, she knew there would be enough glue left to make the flap stick fairly well. By the time Andrew returned to the car, the envelope was once more lying innocently in her lap.

He brought the root beer to the window on her side of the car. "Here," he said, holding out his hand to take the envelope. "Let me have that before you spill something on it."

Reluctantly, Myrna Louise handed it over. She worried that he would notice the frayed flap, but he stuffed it in his shirt pocket without even glancing at it. Myrna Louise drank her root-beer float with her mind in turmoil, still trying to understand. Andrew was up to something, but what? He had paid good money for those two pieces of paper, more than he should have, but why? To get their addresses, said a tiny voice at the back of her mind. To find out where they live. Why? Why would Andrew be interested in knowing that?

For an answer, she heard only the nightmarish sound of a long-ago neighbor's cat, screaming and dying.

* * *

Brandon Walker woke up late and got ready to go to work. The house was empty. His mother had spent the night at the hospital. He had offered to bring her home, but again Louella refused. She would stay there as long as it took, she told him. He wondered how long that would be.

At the office, his clerk shook her head as he walked in the door. "You're in real hot water this time," she said. "The Big Guy wants to see you."

The Big Guy was Sheriff Jack DuShane himself. If one of the Shadows received a curt summons to the sheriff's private office, it probably wouldn't be for a pleasant, early morning social chat or a hit from the bottle of Wild Turkey from the sheriff's private stash.

"On my way," Brandon said, turning away.

"How's your dad?" the clerk asked.

"Hanging in there," he responded, "but that's about all."

Sheriff DuShane sat with an open newspaper spread out on his desk. "This is a hell of a note," he said, glancing up as his secretary escorted Brandon Walker into the room. He pointed to the upper left-hand corner of the page. "You realize, of course, that this makes us all sound like a bunch of stupid jackasses?"

"Sorry," Brandon said, "I haven't seen a paper yet this morning." Nonetheless, he had a pretty good idea about the contents of that offending article. He was sure it reported Toby Walker's unauthorized use of a police vehicle.

"You in the habit of letting your whole goddamned family use county cars whenever they damned well please?"

"It never happened before," Brandon began. "I had no idea my father would take the keys off the . . ."

"I don't give a good goddamn how it happened, but let me tell you this. If it ever does again, you're out of here, Walker. We don't need this kind of shit. Can't afford it. Lucky for you the car wasn't damaged, or you'd be on administrative leave as of right now. So keep your damn car keys in your damn pocket, you hear?"

Brandon had seen news clips of DuShane out in public charming both the media and his constituents. He wondered if those people knew that, on his own turf, DuShane was incapable of speech free of profanity.

The detective waited to see if there was anything else. DuShane didn't exactly dismiss him, but he turned back to the newspaper as though Walker had already left the room. The younger man stood there wavering, wondering if he shouldn't let DuShane know of the possible problem brewing over Andrew Carlisle.

"Well," the sheriff said. "What are you waiting for?"

"Nothing," Brandon replied, deciding. "Nothing at all."

If DuShane didn't even have the good grace to ask how Toby Walker was doing, why the hell should Brandon tell him anything? After all, it wasn't his case, not officially.

* * *

Sister Katherine met them in the office when Diana and Davy arrived at San Xavier. The nun, taking Davy under her wing with a promise of popovers, left at once. Diana was shown into a sparsely furnished office. She sat down on a rickety visitor chair facing a spare, balding old man who introduced himself as Father John.

"I hope my telephone call didn't alarm you, Mrs. Ladd," he said, "but I wanted you to understand that I consider this a matter of utmost importance."

"About Rita?" Diana asked.

He nodded. "You see, her nephew and another man, a medicine man called Looks At Nothing, came to see me yesterday. . . ."

"They came to see you, too?" she asked in some surprise. "I knew they had spoken to Brandon Walker, but why you?"

Father John seemed taken aback. "You mean they discussed this situation with someone else?"

Diana nodded. "With a detective at the Pima County Sheriff's Department. He came to the house last night and told me."

Father John folded his hands in front of him, thoughtfully touching his fingers to his lips. "How very odd," he said. "Why would a detective have any interest in Davy being baptized?"

Now, it was Diana's turn to be puzzled. "Davy? Baptized? What are you talking about?"

"About the accident, Rita's accident."

"What does that have to do with Davy?" Diana asked. "And what does his being baptized have to do with anything?"

"How long have you been here on the reservation?" he asked.

"Since sixty-seven."

"Doing what?"

"Teaching."

"Have you made any kind of study on the Papago belief system?" the priest asked.

"I'm a schoolteacher. Father John, a public schoolteacher. I don't interfere in my students' spiritual lives, and they don't fool around in mine."

"That may be where you're wrong, Mrs. Ladd," the priest said quietly. "It's my understanding that you were raised in the Catholic Church, but that you've moved away from it as an adult."

"Really, I don't see what that has to do with . . ."

"Please, Mrs. Ladd, hear me out. It is true, isn't it?"

"Yes," she answered reluctantly. "My husband was a Lutheran, for one thing, but there were other considerations as well."

"Your husband is dead," he pointed out.

"I'm well aware of that. Father, but I haven't changed my mind about the other things."

"I see," he said, nodding.

"What do you see?" Diana didn't try to conceal her growing impatience. "You still haven't told me what this is about."

"As I said earlier, it's about Dancing Quail. . . ."

"Who?"

"Excuse me. About Rita. You know her as Rita Antone. Dancing Quail was her name when she was much younger, when I first knew her. She was still a child then, not many years older than your own boy. But to get back to what I was saying about Papago beliefs, these are people with a strong spiritual heritage, you know. They have accepted much the whites have to offer while at the same time keeping much of their own. The reverse hasn't always been true."

"Meaning?"

"Meaning we Anglos haven't always been smart enough to learn from them. As a race, we've been very pigheaded, all caught up in teaching others, but not bothering to learn from our students. It's a problem I've been trying to rectify in my old age. For instance, I've learned something about Indian beliefs concerning illness and shamanism.

"In his youth, Rita's friend Looks At Nothing, that blind medicine man, probably was a victim of what the Indians call Whore Sickness, which results from giving way to the temptations of your dreams. Eye troubles in general and blindness in particular are considered to be the natural consequences of succumbing to Whore Sickness. Looks At Nothing could see as a child, but after he lost his sight in early adulthood, he went on to become a well-respected medicine man."

"Whore Sickness?" Diana repeated dubiously. "Do you really believe that?"

"Maybe I don't, not entirely, but the Papagos do, and that's the point. There's tremendous power in belief, especially in ancient beliefs, and that's what we're dealing with as far as Davy is concerned—ancient beliefs. Looks At Nothing is convinced that Rita's accident occurred because she lives in close proximity to an unbaptized baby. As such, your son is a danger to her, and will continue to be so until something is done to fix the problem."

"This is outrageous!" Diana grumbled. "It sounds like some kind of trick to trap me into coming back to church."

"Believe me, young lady, it's no trick. My concern is far more straightforward than that. In addition to the accident which has already happened, Rita is evidently suffering from what the Indians call 'Forebodings.' These pose an additional danger, a threat not only to Rita, but to Davy and yourself as well."

"So what are you saying?"

"Would you have any objections to your child being brought up in the church?"

She shrugged. "I never thought about it that much one way or the other."

"Mrs. Ladd, what I'd like to propose is this. Allow me to come give the boy some religious instruction. At his age, he ought to have some say in the matter. Once he's baptized, we can work together to solve the catechism problem and prepare him for his first communion."

Diana Ladd remained unconvinced. "This is the craziest thing I've ever heard."

Father John sat forward and hunched his meager frame over the desk. "Mrs. Ladd," he said earnestly. "I have been a priest in the Catholic Church for over fifty years. Priests are expected to live celibate, godly lives, and for most of my career, that has been true. But once, very early on, I made a terrible mistake. I fell in love with a beautiful young woman. I almost quit the priesthood to marry her, but an older priest, my superior, took matters into his own hands. He shipped her far away. Years later, I finally realized that I had a rival for her affections, a man of her own people. When she was sent away, not only did I lose her, so did he."

"This is all very interesting, but I don't see . . ."

Father John held up his hand, silencing her. "No, wait. Let me finish. Afterward, the other man, the rival, swore that he and I were enemies. I always believed that would be true until our dying day, but yesterday he came to see me here at San Xavier. We smoked the Peace Smoke, and he asked me for my help."

"The blind medicine man?" Diana asked, finally beginning to grasp the situation. Father John nodded.

"Believe me," he said, "Looks At Nothing never would have come to me for help unless he believed Dancing Quail to be in mortal danger. Naturally, I agreed to do whatever I could."

The old priest fell suddenly silent. He turned away from her and sat gazing up at the rough saguaro-rib crucifix hanging on the wall behind his desk. He averted his gaze, but not before Diana detected a telltale trace of moisture on his weathered cheek. She could only guess what telling that story had cost him, but she knew it wasn't an empty ploy. He had told her only as a last resort. Now, she sat quietly, trying to assimilate it all and understand exactly how it applied to her and to her situation.

First and by far most important was the fact that Father John, right along with everyone else, believed that Rita and she were in danger. On that score, Diana and the priest were in complete agreement, although she had difficulty accepting the idea that Davy's being unbaptized was somehow the cause of it all.

Diana's first choice of weapon to deal with the problem was a fully loaded .45 Peacemaker, but maybe a gun wasn't the only weapon she should consider using. Diana Ladd wasn't prepared to ignore anything that might prove helpful.

"When would you like to come speak to Davy?" she asked finally.

Father John's shoulders sagged with relief. He wiped his eyes, said a brief prayer of thanksgiving, and then crossed himself before turning back to face her. "Today?" he asked. "Would later on this afternoon be all right?"

Committed to action, she saw no point in delay. "Yes," she said. "That'll be fine. I'll give you the address."

As soon as they tried to leave the Dairy Queen, things started going wrong. The Valiant wouldn't start. The battery was dead. In a huff, Andrew Carlisle stalked around the parking lot looking for someone with jumper cables. Then, as they drove toward the storage unit, Myrna Louise began chattering away in her typically inane manner.

"Do you ever think about them?" she asked.

"Think about whom?"

"About those women, the ones from the reservation."

There had been times in his life when Andrew Carlisle could have sworn that his mother could read his mind. Part of her ability to do that, he discovered much later, had been related to her secretly devouring daily installments of his diary. He wondered now about the envelope in his pocket. Had she looked at the contents? If so, had she somehow guessed his intentions? He hadn't really examined the envelope when he took it from her. It had seemed all right at first glance, but he couldn't very well drag it out now and check it again in the middle of traffic.

"No," he said eventually. "They're in the past, and the past is over and done with. I've got my future to think about."

"I wonder what kind of a baby she had, a boy or a girl."

"For Chrissakes, Mama, does it matter?" he demanded, his voice rising despite his intentions of staying calm and collected, of not letting her provoke him. "Do we have to talk about this?"

"Don't yell at me, Andrew. I was only wondering. Maybe I wouldn't be so curious if I'd ever had any grandchildren of my own, you know."

Well, you didn't, he thought savagely. And you're not ever going to, either, by the time I get through with you.

"Give it a rest, Mama," he said. "I always told you I wasn't the marrying kind."

"You should have been. You're a smart man, Andrew, and smart men should father lots of babies. It's our only hope, you know. Civilization's only hope."

It was an old, old argument, one they'd had countless times before, but this time, under pressure, anxious to get on with the tasks at hand and worrying about whether or not the Valiant would keep on running, it was too much.

"Jesus Christ, Mama! Would you please just shut up about that?"

About that time, they arrived at the U-Stor-It-Here lot. There, Andrew Carlisle encountered the straw that broke the camel's back. The gate was locked. Closed and locked.

Afraid to turn off the ignition, he put the Valiant in neutral, set the emergency brake, and left it running. He swore a blue streak as he headed for the small converted RV that served as an office. The door was latched with a metal padlock and bore a hand-lettered sign that said, BACK IN FIFTEEN MINUTES.

Frustrated and fuming, he headed back toward the car. He turned just in time to see the Valiant lurch forward and knock down the gate. For a second, he thought the emergency brake must have slipped, but then, in a cloud of dust, the Valiant roared into reverse. Myrna Louise was definitely at the wheel.

"Mama!" Carlisle yelled. "Stop!"

Instead, the Valiant charged out of the driveway and shot all the way across the street, smashing into a rubber dumpster before coming to a stop. Carlisle took off after the Valiant at a dead run. He almost caught it, too, but as he reached for the door handle, the car blasted forward and careened drunkenly away, leaving him in a cloud of dust. As the car swerved crazily down the flat, two-lane roadway, Myrna Louise clipped a brown El Camino on one side of the street and a second dumpster on the other. Neither one was enough to stop her.

In fact, they barely slowed her down.

It was the last straw for Myrna Louise as well. Not the locked gate—she didn't care at all about that—but having Andrew yell and curse at her and tell her to shut up, that was just too much. It was supposed to be a fun trip for her, a vacation, he had told her. But this wasn't fun at all.

As soon as they started having car trouble, he grew more and more surly and upset. She knew from personal experience that Andrew had a vile, mean temper. Myrna Louise didn't want it turned on her. And if he was already angry with her, what would happen if he ever figured out she had looked at those two precious $150 pieces of paper?

When he got out of the car to go to the storage-unit office, Myrna Louise was still smarting. How dare he talk to her that way? No matter how old they were, children shouldn't tell their parents to shut up. How could he show her so little respect? She deserved better than that. After all, how many other mothers would have opened their homes and their arms to a son when he came dragging home from doing a stretch in prison? She gave herself high marks for being loyal and broad-minded both, for not holding a grudge, although God knows, she could have.

Myrna Louise saw Andrew turn away from the door, shaking his head in disgust with his mouth twisted into an angry grimace. He was coming back to the car, madder than ever. Seeing him like that scared her, and that's when she decided not to wait.

The keys were there, the engine already running. So what if she didn't know how to drive a car? She had been riding in them for sixty years. She had seen other people do it, hadn't she?

Sliding across the bench seat, she peered nearsightedly down at the gearshift and read the letters: *P. R. N. D. L.* The car was stopped and the needle pointed to *P.* That probably meant Park, she theorized. *R* would mean Reverse, *D* Drive, and *L* Low. Maybe she should start out in that, Low.

Cautiously, she moved the gearshift to *L,* and then put a tentative foot on the gas. The engine raced. The car rocked in place, but it didn't move forward. Something was wrong. Then she remembered—the emergency brake. Jake had always talked about the importance of using the emergency brake.

Without letting up on the gas, she released the hand brake. At once, the Valiant crashed forward into the gate, breaking the lock, knocking the gate itself loose from its hinges. She glanced in Andrew's direction. The noise had alerted him, and he was coming after her, running hard. Frightened now, desperate to get away, she shoved the gearshift to *R*, and found herself backing up at a terrifying speed. She tried turning the steering wheel, but the car went in exactly the opposite direction of what she intended. She heard rather than saw the dumpster crumple under the weight of the Valiant's rear bumper.

Andrew vaulted forward. Almost at the car, he reached out to grasp the door handle. Myrna Louise had never before seen such looks of unmasked fury distorting her son's face. What would he do to her if he caught her? Not waiting to find out, she shoved the gearshift needle over to *D*—*D* for Drive, *D* for Disappear—hit the gas pedal, and took off. She never looked back.

Slowing but not stopping at the intersection, she made it into traffic on Alvernon only because three other alert drivers managed to dodge out of her way.

It served Andrew right, Myrna Louise thought, gripping the steering wheel for all she was worth and seesawing it back and forth. Sons should never talk to their mothers that way, no matter what!

Fat Crack arrived at the hospital in Sells and found Rita sitting in a wheelchair on the front sidewalk. "Are you ready to go?" he asked.

She nodded. "I didn't like it in there. I didn't want to wait inside."

Actually, knowing his aunt's opinion about *Mil-gahn* doctors, Fat Crack was surprised she had stayed put in the hospital for as long as she had. His mother had told him that ever since returning from California, Rita had adamantly refused to visit an Anglo doctor for any reason. She would have done the same thing after the accident, too, but arriving unconscious by ambulance made refusing admission impossible.

Fat Crack helped his aunt into the truck. She winced at the high step necessitated by the tow truck's running board. "How are you?" he asked.

"All right, but the cast is heavy, and my arm aches."

"I'll try not to hit too many bumps," Fat Crack told her. "We have to stop in Crow Hang to see about the singers. Are you sure you want to start with that tonight? Wouldn't it be better to wait until you've rested some more?"

"No," Rita said. "Tonight will be fine."

At Hawani Naggiak, Crow Hang Village, Fat Crack left Rita in the truck while he went to negotiate with the singers. Rita leaned her head back against the cab window and closed her eyes. She felt weak and tired. She hadn't felt this weak since that long-ago time in California when she got so sick.

Late that September morning when she jumped off the freight train in Redlands, she asked directions and walked the eight miles out of town to the Bailey orange farm. She didn't know what else to do. Telling everyone she was going to meet her brother was fine as far as it went, but the truth was, she didn't have a brother. Gordon Antone was Louisa's brother. He didn't know Dancing Quail at all. Still, he was someone with a name, someone who would speak her language, and maybe, if she asked him, he really would help her find a job.

The sun was going down when she finally found her way to the right ranch. The people she saw working there were mostly Mexicans. When she tried asking them about Gordon Antone, they didn't understand either English or Papago.

Almost ready to give up, she tried speaking English to a young *Mil-gahn* child. As soon as she asked about an Indian, he grinned and nodded. "Sure," he said. "You must mean the chief. He's working in the toolshed." He pointed off toward a small outbuilding. "Over there."

Dancing Quail found Gordon Antone bent over a file, sharpening the edge of a hoe. He looked up as she stepped into the doorway, blocking out the sunlight and turning the place into dusty gloom.

"Are you the one they call Chief?" she asked, speaking softly in Papago.

"*Heu'u,*" he replied. "Yes."

Gordon Antone put down the hoe and file. The figure silhouetted in the doorway was that of a young male, but the voice definitely belonged to a female. "Who are you?" he asked.

"A friend of your sister's, of Louisa's. She said if I came here, you might help me find a job."

"You know Louisa? But she's in Phoenix. How did you get here?"

"On the train," Rita replied simply. "Last night. I ran away."

"You came all that way alone? From Phoenix?"

"I rode the freight train with some others."

Gordon got up and walked over to the doorway so he could see her better. "What is your name?"

"My people call me Dancing Quail, but the *Mil-gahn* call me Rita, Rita Antone."

"Your name is the same as mine."

Now that she was here, talking to Gordon, she could tell he was someone who was easy to talk to. Just being with him made her feel much better. His saying that made her laugh.

"Yes," she said. "We share the same name. I told the men on the train that you were my brother."

With her hair cut short, dressed in a boy's clothing, and grimy from travel, Dancing Quail was still a very beautiful young woman. For Gordon Antone, far from home and missing his family and friends, the real miracle was finding another person who spoke his own language. That made her more than beautiful.

"Not your brother," Gordon Antone said, "but I will be glad to be your friend."

At least Andrew Carlisle didn't lose his head. He was furious with Myrna Louise, outraged was more like it, but he had sense enough to melt into the background before all hell broke loose. The owner of the El Camino charged out of an apartment across the street and looked up and down the road in both directions, but by then Myrna Louise had disappeared around the corner.

When the U-Stor-It-Here manager showed up

a few minutes later, cops were already on the scene taking their reports. Carlisle chose that momentary confusion to reappear, walk past everyone, and head for his locker. Despite the stifling heat, he went inside his unit and closed the door. He had to think, to plan.

By now he had opened the envelope and suspected that Myrna Louise had also opened it, damn her straight to hell. So what the fuck was she thinking when she grabbed the car and took off like that? he wondered. Would she turn him in? No, that didn't seem likely. Would she know what he was up to? Maybe, maybe not. That was a tough call. After all, she was his mother, and mothers often refuse to believe bad things about their precious darlings no matter how convincing the evidence.

No, she probably wouldn't turn him in, but would she try to stop him? Damn her, she had already done that, just by taking the car. What the hell was he supposed to do now? Did she think he'd just give up? Not bloody likely. Go after her and get the car? How could he? For one thing, where would she go? Home, probably, if she could make it that far. He doubted it. The Valiant seemed to be pretty much on its last legs.

Actually, the more he thought about it, the more he decided it was just as well Jake Spaulding's car was gone. He'd have to get a new one, and that might be inconvenient at the moment, but for what he was planning, he couldn't risk using an undependable vehicle. No, what he needed was a new car. Not necessarily brand new, but certainly different—"reliable transportation," as they say in car dealer's parlance. Once he had another vehicle, he'd figure out some way to make his plan work anyhow. Not only for Diana Ladd, but also for Myrna Louise. As of now, she was on his list twiceover.

It pissed him off that she'd got away clean like that, but he'd get even for that eventually. His main problem now was one of time. How long before she would open the trunk and discover what was in it? If she did that, maybe she'd turn him in after all. He'd have to move forward, probably a whole lot faster than planned.

Standing there waffling back and forth, he was startled by a knock on the door. His heart went to his throat. Damn! The gun was still in the car along with Myrna Louise.

"Yes?" he called.

"Police," a voice answered.

His hands trembled as he went to open the door. As soon as he did so, he shoved his hands in his pockets. The two uniformed cops he had seen earlier stood outside, both holding clipboards.

Carlisle concentrated on keeping his voice neutral and calm. "What seems to be the trouble, Officer?"

"We're investigating the broken gate," one of them said. "A car smashed through it. Next it took off and bashed the El Camino across the street. You came not long after that. Did you happen to see anything out of the ordinary?"

Carlisle shook his head. "Nope," he said. "I didn't see a thing."

The cops apologized for disturbing him and left. It took a while for his breathing to settle back down, to get his mind back to the problem at hand. First and foremost, he thought, he had to have another car.

Focused on solving that one problem, he prepared to leave his storeroom, but first he rummaged around until he found the bulky box that contained not only his first draft of *Savage*, but Garrison Ladd's manuscript as well. It was a good thing that hotshot detective had never found either one. Carrying the box, he locked the door and walked toward the street. The cops waved to him as he passed, but that was all. They didn't really notice him, and he was careful to do nothing that would attract their attention.

In his search for Andrew Carlisle's mother, Detective Farrell had struck out completely. The apartment complex in Peoria where Myrna Louise Taylor had been living at the time of her son's trial was such a transient place that it turned out to be a total dead end. She had evidently moved on from there more than three years earlier. The manager had been on duty for only six months. The complex's group memory didn't stretch back any further than that.

Stymied and discouraged, Farrell trudged back to his car where the steering wheel, door handles, and seats were all too hot to touch. He turned on the car's air-conditioning full blast, but it made very little headway. Gingerly fingering the controls on his radio, he called in to check for messages.

There were several, but the only one he paid any attention to was from Ron Mallory. The assistant superintendent at the Arizona State Prison was anxious to keep his cushy job. He was doing everything possible to cooperate with Farrell's investigation.

Instead of heading straight out of town, Farrell drove to Metro Center, the nearest air-conditioned mall, and went inside to use a pay phone. "What's up?" he asked when he finally had Ron Mallory on the line.

"I've got a name for you," Mallory said. "I had to ask more than once, but when I finally got his attention, Carlisle's ex-cellmate came up with his mother's new last name, Spaulding. It was something else before that. She remarried a year or two ago."

"Anything else besides last name? Location maybe? Husband's first name?"

"Sorry. The last name was all I could dredge out of this guy. I was lucky to get that much."

"You're right," Farrell agreed. "It is progress. I can't expect the whole case to be handed to me on a silver platter."

Myrna Louise made it home in one piece. That in itself was no small miracle. She got the hang of steering fairly well, although she tended to run over curbs going around corners. Her worst problem was keeping steady-enough pressure on the gas pedal. She constantly sped up and slowed down. For the last sixty miles, she held her breath for fear of running out of gas. She didn't dare go to a gas station and turn off the motor. What if she couldn't get it started again? All she could think of was how much she wanted to be home, safe in her own little house.

If God got her home all in one piece, she promised, she'd never ask him to do anything for her again.

18

A S DIANA AND Davy returned home from San Xavier, Fat Crack's tow truck was parking in the front drive. Diana was momentarily concerned about the presence of a strange vehicle, but Davy was ecstatic when he caught sight of Rita. He was ready to leap from the car well before it stopped.

"Be very gentle with her, Davy," Diana cautioned. "She had surgery, you know. She has stitches, too."

"On her head?"

"No, on her tummy."

"I'll be careful," Davy promised, scurrying toward the truck. Reaching the door just as Fat Crack handed Rita down, Davy stopped short, daunted at first by the huge Indian's presence. Then, remembering who the man was, he stepped forward. "Hi," he said shyly to Fat Crack.

Davy's first instinct was to throw himself at Rita, but remembering his mother's warning, he hung back until Rita raised her good arm and beckoned him to her. He hugged her gingerly around the waist while she patted the top of his head. The gesture activated his "On" switch. With a grin, he jumped away from her and pointed to the shaved spot on his head.

"See my stitches?" he boasted. "How many do you have? Can I see them?"

Rita smiled and shook her head. "No, you can't see them, and neither can I. I'm too fat." She laughed, and so did Fat Crack.

During this exchange, Fat Crack pulled several loaded hospital-issue plastic bags from the truck. "I'll take these inside," he said.

Fat Crack went on ahead. Rita limped after him with Davy holding tightly to her good hand. Diana waited at the front door, holding it open. "Welcome home," she said.

"Thank you."

There was a strange formality between the two women, as though neither knew quite how to behave in the presence of Rita's blood kin. "Do you want him to take your things out back?" Diana asked.

Rita nodded. "I'll go, too. I want to rest."

Davy started to follow her, but Diana called him back. "You and the dog go outside and play," she said. "Rita's tired."

His face fell in disappointment, but Rita came to Davy's rescue. "It's okay. They can both come along. I missed them."

Despite DuShane's ass-chewing, Brandon still hung around the office. He wanted to be there in case his mother called, and he didn't want to miss any messages from Geet Farrell. He took the time to read the *Arizona Sun* cover to cover, including both the brief account of Toby Walker's ill-fated joy-riding incident, and the much longer front-page article about the brutal stabbing of Johnny Rivkin, a well-known Hollywood costume designer, knifed to death in his downtown Tucson hotel room.

Brandon read about the bloody Santa Rita murder with a professional's interest in what was going on, to see what his competition at Tucson PD was doing on the case. He routinely read about homicides committed in the city in case something in the killer's MO coincided with one of his unsolved county cases. In this instance, nothing rang a bell.

Several times he was tempted to call Diana Ladd to check on how she was doing, but each time he reconsidered. He'd been summarily thrown out of the woman's house both times he'd been there. She wasn't exactly keeping the welcome mat out for him. Brandon Walker knew he was a dog for punishment, but Diana Ladd dished out more abuse than even he was willing to take.

Every time he thought about that exasperating woman, he shook his head. He wanted so much to make her see reason, to help her understand the error of her ways. It was crazy for her to hole up in that isolated fortress of hers and wait for disaster to strike. Supposing her idea did work. Supposing Andrew Carlisle showed up, and she somehow managed to blow him away. What would happen then? Maybe Carlisle would be dead; but so might she. Whatever the outcome, Walker was convinced an armed confrontation would irreparably harm Davy.

Diana didn't realize that her son was a fragile child, Brandon decided. Women always thought their male offspring tougher than they were in actual fact. Davy needed something from his mother, something he wasn't getting. Brandon couldn't tell quite what it was, but he sat there thinking about it, wishing he could help.

Gradually, as time passed, a plan began to form in his mind. He would help, after all, whether or not Diana Ladd wanted him to, whether or not she even knew it. As soon as Brandon got off work that afternoon, he would take the county car home, borrow his mother's, stop by the hospital long enough to check on his parents, and then head out for Gates Pass. He'd lie in wait outside Diana's house all night long if necessary. If Andrew Carlisle actually showed up out there, he'd run up against something he didn't expect—an armed cop rather than some wild-eyed latter-day Annie Oakley packing a loaded .45.

In fact, the more Brandon Walker thought about the idea, the better he liked it. As a cop, he had behaved responsibly in doing what he could to talk Diana Ladd out of her foolhardy scheme. But since she was too hardheaded to give up, Walker would use her as a magnet to draw Andrew Carlisle to him. Diana might be the tender morsel necessary to lure Carlisle into the snare, but Brandon Walker would be the steel-jawed trap.

* * *

Diana went into the kitchen to fix herself a glass of iced tea. The one dusty box she had carried in from the root cellar still sat on the kitchen table. Diana looked at the box and sighed. "There's no time like the present," she said aloud, quoting one of Iona's old maxims.

Squaring her shoulders, she found a butcher knife and attacked the aging layers of duct tape that sealed the box shut. The labeling may have been done by Francine, her stepmother, but the profligate use of duct tape was Max's specialty. Diana remembered the stack of boxes he had brought down to the car on the morning she left for school in Eugene.

Some of the other girls in her class had got real cedar chests for high school graduation, "hope chests" they called them. When Max came with the boxes, Diana had no idea what they were.

"Those aren't mine," she said. "I can't take all that stuff."

"Your mother says you're taking it," Max said sourly.

She left, taking the boxes with her. It wasn't until she was unpacking in her tiny apartment over the garage that she discovered Iona had made a hope chest for her, too, one in cardboard not cedar, but with hand-embroidered tea towels and napkins, crocheted doilies and tablecloths, a brand-new service-for-four set of Safeway-coupon Melmac dishes, and a heavy hand-pieced quilt. There were a few pots and pans, some cheap silverware, and a brand-new percolator.

Opening each box was an adventure, a reprise of a dozen Christmas mornings. Cloth goods were neatly ironed and folded, the edges crisp and straight. Glassware—there was even some of that—was individually wrapped in store-bought tissue paper.

One at a time, as she took out each item and admired each bit of handiwork, Diana wondered how and when her mother had managed to amass such a treasure without arousing Diana's suspicions. After opening the last box, she rode her bike over to the Albertsons' and called home from the grocery-store pay phone.

"What's wrong?" Max demanded when he heard her voice. "Long distance calls cost money. Did you get in a car wreck, or what?"

"Nothing's wrong," Diana told him. "Just let me talk to Mom."

But when Iona came on the phone, Diana was so overcome with emotion that she could barely speak. "When did you have time to make all that stuff, Mom? It's wonderful, but how did you do it?"

For years, Diana kept her mother's answer buried in the furthest reaches of her memory. Now, it came back to her. "Love always makes time," Iona had said.

Remembering those words now left Diana awash in a sea of guilt. Love always makes time. Measured against her mother's performance, Diana's relationship with Davy seemed a gigantic failure. She was too busy with her own concerns and ambitions to pay attention to Davy's day-today needs. Stung by guilt, she was still so busy justifying her continued survival in the face of both her mother's death and her husband's suicide that she forgot to pay attention to the quality of that survival. Luckily for her and for Davy, Rita was there to take up the slack.

I'll do better, Diana promised herself. If I live long enough, I swear I'll do better.

She peeled the final layer of tape from the box, releasing the lid. In moments, Diana went from remembering her cardboard "hope chests" to what could only be called hopeless chests, from boxes filled with promise to ones packed with crushed dreams and dashed hopes. That's all Iona Dade Cooper's boxes contained.

All the while the unopened boxes are stored in the root cellar, Diana had imagined them packed with her mother's few prized possessions, the treasures arranged with the same loving care Iona had used to pack the boxes she sent to Eugene. Except those boxes held no treasures. What was stowed there hardly qualified as personal effects.

Francine Cooper had gone through her new husband's house, Iona's house, packing up only what she didn't want—the inconvenient onion chopper with its broken blade, the battered metal pie tins Iona used only as a last resort when the season's current crop of fruit—pumpkin in the fall, mincemeat in the winter, rhubarb in the spring, and fresh peach in the summer—had swamped her supply of good Pyrex pie plates. There were ragged hot pads and oven mitts, not the good ones Iona had used for company meals and church dinners, but the old ones she had used only for canning, and that, by rights, should have been thrown out with the trash long before they were stuffed into boxes.

Resolutely now, Diana ripped open the tape on each succeeding box. One rattled ominously as soon as she picked it up. At the bottom of that one, she found the smashed remains of the only really nice thing Iona Dade Cooper had ever owned—a Limoges salt-and-pepper-shaker set she had inherited from her own Grandma Dade— clattered brokenly around in the bottom of the box without even a paper towel as protection against breakage.

Grim-faced, Diana set a few things aside on the table to keep. The rest was swept into a waiting trash can. Only in the bottom box, the heaviest one, did Diana strike gold. There were books in there—the whole frayed green set called My Book House from which Iona had read her daughter countless fairy tales and poems and fables.

Seeing the books, Diana felt a flash of recognition. From these volumes, she had gained her love of reading, her fascination with the written word. She pulled out each book individually, thumbing through the pages, glancing at the familiar illustrations, remembering her favorite stories, wishing Davy knew them the way she did.

And then, in the very bottom of the box, stuffed in hastily perhaps so Max wouldn't see, was the real treasure, the one item of her mother's that Diana had really wanted and had counted lost—

her mother's well-worn Bible. Reverently, she picked it up. One corner of the cover had been permanently bent back. She opened the book gently, trying to smooth out the wrinkle.

As she did so, a paper fell out. Picking it up, she found it was actually three papers, welded by age into a tightly folded, brittle mass. Carefully, she undid them. The outside was a letter. Folded into that were two other pieces of paper—a yellowed newspaper article and a small, flower-covered funeral program dated August 16, 1943.

She glanced at that first, wondering whose it was—Harold Autry Deeson. Harold Deeson? Who was he? She had never heard of anybody by that name, although she read right there on the program that Harold's parents were George R. and Ophelia Deeson.

George had a son? Diana wondered. How come she never knew about him? How come nobody ever mentioned him by name?

She turned to the newspaper article. The paper was brittle and flaked apart in her hand, but it was from the *La Grande Herald* on August 11, 1943, and it told how Harold Autry Deeson, only son of George R. and Ophelia Deeson, had died in a one-car crash on the highway halfway between Wallowa and Enterprise. Heading back to base at Fort Lewis, near Seattle, after being home for a weekend, Harold's car had slammed into the highway embankment and then skidded across the road, ending up in the river. There was no clue as to what caused the accident, although the sheriff theorized that he may have braked to avoid hitting an animal that had wandered onto the road or else he had fallen asleep. Either way, Harold Autry Deeson was dead on impact.

Reading through the account of the accident, the whole picture of Diana's family history suddenly shifted into focus. She started crying long before she ever picked up the letter. It was little more than a note, but Diana knew instinctively what was written there—not exactly, not the details, but the general outline.

"Dearest Iona," Harold had written in a hastily scrawled, immature hand. "Thank you for tonight. I don't care what my mother says. You may be Catholic, and my mother's Mormon, but that doesn't matter, not to me, and it's not a good enough reason for us not to be together.

"I can't make it home from Seattle again for at least a month, but when I do, we'll run away together to La Grande or Pendleton, or maybe even all the way to Spokane. If we come back married, no one will be able to do anything about it, not even my mother. Please be ready. Love, Harry."

Diana let the paper drift from her hands onto the table. She didn't need to count on her fingers. Max and Iona Cooper were married in September of '43. She was born in May of '44. No wonder George Deeson had brought her Waldo. George Deeson had been her real grandfather, but why hadn't someone told her the truth?

Under normal circumstances, Davy would have fought tooth and nail at any suggestion of a nap, but that day, when Rita lay down on her old-fashioned box spring mattress with its frail metal headboard, Davy climbed up onto the bed, while Bone settled down comfortably on a nearby rug. Because of the cast, Rita lay on her back with her arm elevated on pillows. Davy nestled in close to her other side and fell sound asleep.

Davy slept, but Rita didn't. She looked around the room, grateful to be home, glad to have survived whatever the *Mil-gahn* doctors had dished out. To be fair, Dr. Rosemead was a whole lot different from the first white doctor she'd met, an odd-looking little man with strange, rectangular glasses and huge red-veined nose who had been called in for a consultation when she first got sick in California.

The Baileys hadn't needed another girl-of-all-work, so Gordon found her a job at a farm a few miles up the road. There, barely a month later, she began to feel tired. A cough came on, accompanied by night sweats. She tried to hide the fact that she was sick, because she didn't want to risk losing her job and being sent home, but finally, when the lady found her coughing up blood, she sent Rita to bed and summoned the one itinerant doctor who treated the valley's Indian and Mexican laborers.

Dr. Aldus was his name, and Rita never forgot it, no matter how hard she tried. He came to see Dancing Quail in the filthy workers' shack where she lay in bed, too sick to move. He examined her and then spoke to the foreman who waited in the background to take word to the farm owner's wife.

"We'll have to take the baby," the doctor said. "The girl may live, but not the baby. Go bring my things from the car. Ask the cook to set some water boiling."

The doctor came back to the bed and loomed over Dancing Quail. "It's going to be fine," he said. "Everything's going to be okay."

Those were the exact same words Dr. Rosemead had used all these years later, but with Dr. Aldus, everything was definitely not okay. His breath reeked of alcohol. He swayed from side to side as he stood next to her bed.

"No," Dancing Quail pleaded, struggling to get up. "Leave my baby alone," but he pushed her back down and held her pinned until the foreman returned, bringing with him the doctor's bag and a set of thick, heavy straps. Somehow the two of them strapped her to the bed frame, imprisoning her, holding her flat. The doctor pressed an evil-smelling cloth to her face. Soon Rita could fight no longer.

She woke up much later, once more drenched in sweat. The straps were gone. She felt her flattened belly and knew it was empty. She was empty. The straps were gone, and so was her baby.

She cried out. Suddenly, Gordon was there, leaning over her in the doctor's stead, his broad face gentle and caring. "Why didn't you call me?" he asked, speaking in Papago. "Why didn't you send someone to tell me you were sick so I could come take care of you?"

Rita couldn't answer. All she could do was cough and cry.

* * *

Around four, Rita shook Davy. "Wake up," she said. "Fat Crack will come soon and I must be ready."

Davy sat up, rubbing his eyes, "Ready for what? Where are you going?"

"To Sells. For a ceremony."

"What kind of ceremony? Do you have to leave again? You just got here."

"It's important," she said. "The ceremony's for you, Olhoni."

His eyes widened. "For me? Really?"

She smiled. "Really. The singers will start tonight. On the fourth night, you will be baptized. A medicine man will do it."

"A real medicine man? What will he do?"

"Don't ask so many questions, Little One. You will see when time comes. He will baptize you in the way of the *Tohono O' odham*. Have you spoken to the priest yet?"

"Priest?" Davy returned. "Oh, the one out at San Xavier?" Rita nodded. "Mom saw him, this morning. She said he was coming to see me today, this afternoon, I guess. I don't know why."

Rita sighed in relief. Father John had asked, and Diana had consented. "I do," she said. "Listen, Olhoni, you must listen very carefully. You are very old not to be baptized, not in your mother's way and not in the Indian way, either. Most people are baptized when they are babies. This is not good, so we are going to fix it. I asked Father John to speak to your mother, because where the Anglo religion is concerned, it is better for

Mil-gahn to speak to *Mil-gahn*. Do you understand?"

Davy nodded seriously, but Rita doubted she was making sense. "When Father John comes to see you, do whatever he asks."

"But what will he ask?"

"He will speak to you of the *Mil-gahn* religion, of your mother's religion."

"But I thought you said a medicine man . . ."

"Olhoni," Rita said sternly. "You are a child of two worlds, a child with two mothers, are you not?" Davy nodded. "Then you can be a boy with two religions, two instead of none, isn't it?"

Davy thought about it a moment before he nodded again.

"So tonight," Rita continued, "whenever Fat Crack comes to get me, I will go out to Sells and be there for the start of the ceremony. I will return during the day, but each night I must go again. On the fourth night, the last night, you will come, too. Either your mother will bring you, or I will come back for you myself."

"Will there be a feast?" he asked.

"Yes, now get up. I need your help."

Davy scrambled off the bed. "What do you want, Nana *Dahd*?"

"Over there, in the bottom drawer of my dresser, there is a small basket. Bring it."

Davy did as he was told, carrying the small, rectangular basket back to the bed. "What's this?" he asked.

"My medicine basket."

As he handed it to her, something rattled inside. "What's in it, Nana *Dahd*? Can I see?"

With some difficulty, Rita had managed to pull herself up on the side of the bed. Now, she patted the mattress, motioning for Davy to sit beside her. "You'll have to." She smiled. "I can't."

Davy worked at prying off the tight-fitting lid. It was a testimony to Understanding Woman's craftsmanship that even after so many years, even with the repairs Rita had made from time to time, the lid of the basket still fit snugly enough that it required effort to remove it. When it finally came loose, Davy handed the opened basket back to Rita.

One at a time, she took items out and held them up to the light. After looking at each one, she handed it to Davy. First was the awl, the *owij*, Rita called it. Davy knew what that was for because he had often watched her use the sharp tool to poke holes in the coiled cactus to make her baskets.

Next came a piece of pottery.

"What's that?" Davy asked.

"See the turtle here?" Rita asked, pointing to the design etched into the broken shard. Davy nodded. "This is from one of my great-grandmother's pots, Olhoni. When a woman dies, the people must break her pots in order to free her spirit. My grandmother kept this piece of her mother's best pot and gave it to me."

Next she held up the seashell. "Grandfather brought this back from his first salt-gathering expedition, and this spine of feather is one my father once gave to his mother when he was younger than you are now. The clay doll was used for healing."

Next, Davy saw a hank of black hair. "What's that?" he asked.

"It's something we used to use against the *Ohb*, the Apaches," Rita explained. "Something to keep our enemies away."

At the very bottom of the basket were two last items—a piece of purple rock and something small made of metal and ribbon.

"What are those?"

"A spirit rock," Rita answered, holding up the fragment of geode. "A rock that's ordinary on the outside, but beautifully colored on the inside."

"And that?" he asked.

"That is my son's," she said softly, fingering the frayed bit of ribbon. "Gordon's. His Purple Heart. The army sent it to me after the war."

"What war?"

"The Korean," she said.

"Did your son die, too?" Davy asked.

"I guess," she answered. "He joined the Army during World War II and stayed in. He never came home after Korea. The Army said he was missing, but he's been missing for twenty-six years now. I don't think he's coming home. His wife, Gina's mother, ran off some place. With no husband, she didn't want a baby. I took care of Gina the same way I take care of you."

Rita looked down at the little cache of treasure lying exposed on the bedspread. "Put them all back for me now, Davy. I want to take them with me."

One at a time, with careful concentration, Davy put Rita's things back in the basket then he fitted the lid on tight.

"I've never seen this basket before, have I?" he asked, handing it back to her.

She took it and slid it inside the top of her dress, where it rested out of sight beneath her ample breast and above her belt. "No, Olhoni. You have to be old enough before you can look at a medicine basket and show it proper respect."

"Am I old enough now?"

"You have not yet killed your first coyote," she said, "but you are old enough to see a medicine basket."

By four o'clock that afternoon, Carlisle had set up camp on the rocky mountainside overlooking Diana Ladd's home in Gates Pass. Using Myrna Louise's cash, he had bought an AMC Matador from a used-car dealer downtown who claimed to be "ugly but honest." So far that seemed to be true of the car as well. The layers of vinyl on the roof were peeling off and the paint was scarred, but the engine itself seemed reliable enough.

He had constructed a rough shelter of mesquite branches. The greenery not only provided some slight protection from the searing heat, it also offered cover from which he could spy on the house below without being detected. Sitting there with his high-powered binoculars trained on the house, he watched the comings and goings,

counted the people he saw, and planned his offensive. During the long hours, he had to fight
continually to stave off panic. In all his adven-
tures, this was the very first time things had gone
so totally wrong. He bitterly resented the fact that
his own mother was the main fly in the ointment.

In taking the Valiant, Myrna Louise had complicated his life immeasurably. For one thing, she
had forced him to spend some of his limited cash
on a new vehicle. More seriously than that, Margie Danielson's gun was still in the trunk of the
car Myrna Louise had stolen right out from under his nose. So was Johnny Rivkin's suitcase, for
that matter—the bag containing the clothing and
wigs Andrew Carlisle had planned to use for his
getaway.

But far more serious than all the others put
together was the loss of time. Everything had to
be compressed and hurried, without opportunity
for the kind of careful planning Andrew Carlisle
considered to be the major prerequisite for getting away with this particular murder. Instead of
having days to work out the logistics of his attack
against Diana Ladd, it would have to be done in a
matter of hours. He would have to retrieve the
damning evidence from his mother either before
or after the main event.

Carlisle knew that his mother hated staying in
hotels, and she had severely limited resources
besides. Like an old war-horse, she would, in all
likelihood, head directly back to the barn, unless
of course the cops picked her up for reckless driving somewhere along the way. The very thought

of that possibility caused his heart to beat faster. Damn that woman anyway! He'd teach her to interfere.

A door opened in the yard below. He trained his binoculars on a long-legged Diana Ladd. Tanned and wearing shorts and a tank top, she emerged from the back of the house carrying a tall plastic trash can that she emptied into a rusty burning barrel at the far end of the yard. Then, using a series of matches, she set fire to the contents of the barrel and stood watching them burn.

While she tended the fire, a huge black dog gamboled up to her and dropped a tennis ball at her feet. Obligingly, the woman picked it up and threw it across the yard. The dog raced off at breakneck speed to retrieve it. They played like that for several minutes, When the woman went inside a short time later, so did the dog, still carrying the ball and leaving Andrew Carlisle sitting alone on the mountain, pondering this newest wrinkle in his well-laid plans. That dog would have to go, he thought. He worried about the gun she was wearing. Someone might have warned her. Why else would Diana Ladd be walking around with a leather holster strapped to her hip?

Of the two, the gun and the dog, the dog was really far more serious. Surprise could take away any advantage having a weapon gave her, but the dog could bark and rob him of the initiative. Andrew Carlisle thought about the problem for some time, considering the issue from every angle like a scientist dealing with some small but pesky detail that stands in the way of completing a major project. When the idea finally came to him, he acted on it at once.

Sticking to the thin cover as much as possible, he made his way down the mountainside and back to the Matador, which he had left parked at a shooting-range parking lot half a mile away. Once in the car, he headed for the nearest grocery store. Cheap hamburger was easy to find in any part of town, but liquid slug bait wasn't. For that, he would have to go a little father afield to a top-notch nursery halfway across Tucson proper.

He hurried through traffic, careful not to speed, not calling any undue attention to the all-too-distinctive red-and-black car. A nice white Ford would have been better, but the Matador's price was right. Besides, he didn't expect to keep it for long.

Driving was easier than sitting on the mountain watching the house. It calmed his nerves. The more he thought about it, the more determined he was that he would be careful. Just because he'd been forced to telescope his plans didn't mean he had to blunder around or make any more costly mistakes. Letting Myrna Louise slip away was bad enough, but if things worked out the way he hoped, he'd soon have her back in hand.

They say it happened long ago that a woman lived near the base of Baboquivari Mountain with her husband and her baby. During the day, the husband would go to work in the fields that were close to the village. After working hard in the fields, he often did not

want to make the long trip home, so he would stay in
the village and visit with friends. This made the woman
sad, but she stayed with her baby and waited for her
husband, who did not come home.

One night, when the woman was all alone, she heard
Ban, *Coyote*, call, but this was not the usual call of Coyote, so she went out to look for him. It was very dark. At
first she could not see, but finally she saw his eyes, glowing like coals in the firelight. He was a large old Coyote,
but even when she came close to him, he did not move.
At last she came close enough to see that he was lying
beside a pool of water.

"Brother," she said, for this was when the Tohono
O'odham, *the Desert People,* still knew I'itoi's lan-
guage and could speak to the animals. "Large Old
Coyote, why did you call to me?"

"I came to this pool to drink the water," he told her.
"This rock shifted and trapped my foot. Will you help
me?"

So the woman moved the rock, but by then the Large
Old Coyote's foot was so badly injured that he still could
not walk. So the woman fed him and watered him and
nursed him back to health. She called him Old Lame
Coyote.

In the evening, when the woman's husband did not
come home and she was very lonely, Old Lame Coyote
would tell her news of the desert—where to find honey,
when the rains would come again, where the best piñon
nuts could be found. In this way, the lonely woman and
Lame Old Coyote became good friends.

Once she got out of the car, it was all Myrna
Louise could do to make it into the house and

down the hall to her room. Without taking off her clothing, she fell sideways across the bed. She was no longer angry with Andrew, and she hoped by now that he was over being angry with her. It was too bad that whenever they spent any time together, they always ended up quarreling.

She was awakened by a knock on the door, and there was Lida, from next door, holding the newspaper and two pieces of mail.

"Back so soon?" Lida asked. "From the way Phil talked this morning, I thought you'd be gone for at least a week. I already told the newspaper boy to stop delivery, just like Phil said, but he had to deliver today's and maybe tomorrow's. Here's your mail. I picked that up, too. No sense leaving it for someone to go snooping through."

Myrna Louise stared blankly. Lida's words made no sense. She had stopped the paper and was collecting the mail? What was going on? "I'm sorry, Lida," Myrna Louise said. "I'm not feeling well."

"No wonder you came back. I was afraid the kind of trip Phil was planning would be too much for you. Driving to the Grand Canyon isn't my idea of a picnic."

Grand Canyon? Myrna Louise thought. Who's going there? It was more than Myrna Louise could stand. "You'll have to excuse me, Lida, I've got to go back and lie down."

Brandon Walker took off right at five. He drove straight to the house. He parked the Galaxy and pocketed the keys, then he drove his mother's

Olds to the hospital. Louella was sitting in the ICU waiting room. Brandon had planned to stay at the hospital for only a few minutes, but as soon as he saw his mother's ravaged face, he knew there was trouble.

She ran to him and buried her head against his shoulder. "I'm so glad you're here," she sobbed. "I've done what the first doctor said, I've turned off the machine. The nurse told me I could go in now and wait, but I'm afraid to be there alone. Stay with me, Brandon, please. Stay until it's over."

What could he do, tell his mother he had a prior commitment? Taking Louella gently by the shoulders, he looked down into her grief-stricken face. "I have to make a phone call," he said.

"You won't leave me, will you?"

"No, Mom," he said, shaking his head. "I'll be right back."

19

SORTING THROUGH IONA'S boxes was all
the emotional baggage Diana could handle
for one day. Gary's would have to wait. When she
finished, she carried the garbage outside, dumped
it, and set fire to the trash barrel. As she stood
there watching it burn, she felt a peculiar satisfaction, the lifting of a lifetime's burden.

Diana watched the flames lick through Iona's
ancient oven mitt and understood at last why her
mother considered herself "damaged goods," why
she had stayed with Max Cooper no matter
what. Iona owed him. He grudgingly lent Iona
the use of his name for her baby, for Diana, thus
saving Iona's family and reputation from savag-
ing by Joseph's sharp-tongued scandalmongers,
but Iona paid a heavy price for that dubious
privilege, paid with every waking and sleeping
moment of her life.

The flames in the burning barrel soared higher,
kicking up and over the surrounding metal. In the
leaping flames, something else caught fire, something more than just Francine Cooper's useless

castoffs. Max Cooper's hold on his supposed daughter was being consumed as well. At last Diana grasped why Max had despised her so, why he had hated her and berated her for as long as she could remember. She understood now why he had so resented the rodeo-queen escape hatch that a resourceful Iona, with George Deeson's timely help, had managed to open for her.

But knowledge brought with it an ineffable sadness. If only she had known the truth earlier, while there was still time to ask her mother about her real father or maybe even ask George Deeson himself. Would he have told her, if she had asked him on one of those endless Saturday mornings when it had been just the two of them out in the corral with Waldo? Would things have been different if she had known the old man was really her grandfather?

What was it the Bible said? "The truth will set you free." Was Diana Cooper Ladd free now? Maybe. She felt lighter than she had in years. As the flames charred through the debris, not only did Max lose his grip on her, so did the past.

Just then, Bone dashed up and dropped a tennis ball at her feet. With a laugh, she ruffled the dog's shaggy head, then threw the ball for him as hard as she could. Eagerly, he raced off after it, returning with it, prancing and proud, tail awag.

"You funny old dog," she said, and threw the ball again.

Over and over she threw the ball. Over and over he brought it back. It surprised her to find that each time Bone retrieved the ball, the silly, pointless game made her laugh. Laughter felt good, and so did the hot sun on her back.

"Come on, Mister Oh'o," she said at last when the dog was panting so hard his scrawny sides shook. "Let's go inside, cool off, and figure out what's for dinner."

After their naps, Davy and Rita entered the main house to the surprising but familiar smell of baking tortillas. In the kitchen, they found Diana struggling with stiff wads of tortilla dough, waxed paper, and a rolling pin. A stack of misshapen tortillas sat on a platter next to a smoking electric griddle. The tortillas were amazingly ugly—thick in some places, punched full of holes in others. Some were more than slightly burned, but for a first attempt, they weren't too bad.

Rita touched one of the balls of dough still sitting in a mixing bowl, on the countertop. "A little more shortening next time," she suggested. "Then you can pat them out by hand instead of using a rolling pin."

"Mom, did you make these all by yourself?" Davy asked wonderingly. "Can I have one?"

"If you're brave enough," Diana told him. "They're pretty pitiful."

Slathering a load of peanut butter on one side, Davy tried a bite and diplomatically pronounced the tortilla "almost as good as Rita's." With a second peanut butter-covered tortilla in one hand and a plain one for Bone in the other, Davy and Oh'o went outside to play.

Rita sat down beside the kitchen table and

watched Diana work. The Anglo woman seemed self-conscious under the Papago's scrutiny, but she kept on rolling the dough and tossing the resulting crooked sheets onto the waiting griddle.

"While I was just lying there in Sells," Rita began, "I was thinking about how you helped me after Gina died, when people wanted me to leave because I was bad luck."

"Forget it," Diana said determinedly. "What they thought doesn't matter. I've been delighted to have you with me. With us," she added.

"But it does matter," Rita returned. "I thought I was leaving there just to go somewhere and die, but helping you and taking care of Davy gave me back my luck. It made me young again. The other day, the doctors said I was dead in that ambulance, but thinking about Davy made me want to live, made me want to come back."

Diana Ladd put down the rolling pin and brushed hair from her sweat-dampened face, leaving a white smudge of flour on her face.

"Rita, Davy has always been as much yours as he is mine. You're the one who's spent all the time with him, who's taught him things, and taken care of him. If you're worried about the Indian baptism, don't be. Father John told me about it this morning when I saw him at San Xavier."

"He did?"

Diana nodded. "He explained the whole thing."

"Good," Rita said. "You don't mind?"

"No. How could I mind? When will it happen?"

"Because of the . . ."

Rita paused, groping for the proper word. What

she felt coming toward them was far more serious than mere danger. Weak as it sounded, that
was the only *Mil-gahn* word she could think of to
express the problem. Diana Ladd would not understand the word *ohb.*

"Because of the danger to us all," Rita continued, "the baptism ceremony starts tonight. It will
continue for four days and nights. Four nights
from now, we go to Sells for the last night of singing and for the feast. On that night, the medicine
man feeds the child's parents gruel made from
corn and clay."

Diana made a face. "That sounds even worse
than my tortillas, but it won't kill me, will it?"

Rita smiled. "No, it won't kill you."

"What about you?" Diana asked. "You said parents. I'm only one. Will you eat the gruel with me,
Rita? The two of us can be Davy's parents together."

The offer came from a generous heart and
caused a dazzling smile to suffuse Rita's worn
face. She looked twenty years younger. "Yes, *nawoj,*" she said softly, "we will eat the gruel together."

Just then, out in the yard, Bone started up a
noisy racket. They heard him scrabbling over the
high stone wall just as Davy burst in through the
back door.

"A car's coming," Davy announced. "Oh'o
went after it. I couldn't stop him."

Dusting the flour from her hands, Diana hurried to the window and looked out. An unfamiliar late-model Buick was easing into the driveway,

while Bone, up to his usual tricks, attacked the front tires for all he was worth. Diana recognized Father John before he rolled down the window. "Oh'o," she called sharply. "Here."

With one final offended woof, the dog abandoned his attack and came to the porch, where Diana let him into the house. "It's Father John," she told Davy. "Take Bone back outside and keep him there while I bring the company into the house."

Father John entered the house warily, holding his hat in front of him. "That's quite some dog you've got there," he said. "Are you sure it's safe?"

"Believe me, Bone's exactly the kind of dog we need at the moment," Diana returned, "but don't worry. Davy took him outside. Would you care for something to eat?"

"No, no thank you. I just came to speak to the boy."

"Something to drink then. Iced tea?"

"Tea would be fine."

Diana started for the kitchen but paused when she found the kitchen doorway blocked by Rita's stocky frame. The old woman stood staring at the priest. Eventually, Rita moved aside and let Diana pass, but she did so without taking her eyes away from Father John. For a long moment, the two old people faced one another in awkward silence.

When Father John had invaded the hospital room in Sells, it had been without Rita's knowledge or permission. The man who came there was the same one who had abandoned her years earlier, the one who had caused her to be sent away in disgrace. But now, by helping with Davy, Father John had redeemed himself somewhat in the old woman's eyes. She no longer saw him through a cloud of bitterness.

The old woman broke the silence. "Thank you for helping with Davy."

Father John nodded. "*Nawoj,*" he said. "Friend, it is nothing." He moved into the room. At once his eyes were drawn to the large basket hanging on the wall over the couch, a plaque actually, two-and-a-half to three feet in diameter. Schooled in the subtle aesthetics of Papago Indian basketry, the priest immediately recognized the superior workmanship in the rare yucca-root basket. The red design, a finely woven rendition of the traditional Papago maze, spread out in the four sacred directions. At the top stood the square-shouldered Man in the Maze.

Father John studied the basket for some time before turning to Rita. "You made this?" he asked. She nodded. "Understanding Woman taught you well," he continued. "It is very beautiful."

Back on the rocky mountainside with a Styrofoam meat package full of poisoned hamburger, Andrew Carlisle thanked his lucky stars that he had taken the precaution of climbing up to reconnoiter one last time before approaching the house. While he watched in dismay, the crazy dog set up a frenzied roar of barking and then vaulted over the fence to attack an approaching car. Carlisle couldn't believe it. The ugly mutt charged the front tires of the still-moving vehicle as if he were going to tear them apart.

Christ! How had the dog done it? That stone wall had to be at least six feet tall, and it hadn't slowed him down one damn bit. Carlisle knew that if he tried approaching the house on foot, the dog would have him for lunch, so the problem was finding a way to get the poison to the dog without losing either an arm or a leg in the process.

Through binoculars trained on the household below, Carlisle saw the woman hustle the dog inside while a man, who appeared to be a priest, got out of the car and started for the house. The man went in the front door, while the dog and the child came out through the back. The boy left the dog pacing in unhappy circles on the rear patio. Clearly, the dog wanted in. If he was generally an inside dog, it wouldn't be long before someone relented. Carlisle realized he would have to act quickly.

Carlisle's first problem was to lure the dog out of the fenced backyard. Having witnessed the frenzied attack on the Buick, that didn't seem difficult. Carlisle figured just showing his face would be enough to provoke the dog into another battle. The trick was maintaining enough of a safety margin to make escape possible.

Carlisle hiked back down to the Matador and drove as near the house as he dared, stopping just beyond a sharp curve that concealed the car from anyone inside the house. After turning the car around so it faced back in the opposite direction,

Carlisle took the slug-bait-laced meat with him and walked to the middle of the roadway. First he dropped chunks of meat in a wide pattern over the pavement; then, lying down flat on the rocky shoulder, he whistled one short, sharp burst.

At once, the dog responded with a fit of barking. Carlisle whistled again, and the dog barked again. Someone came to the back door. Diana herself emerged from the shadow of the patio and surveyed the area, using one hand to shade her eyes from the glare of the setting sun. Carlisle kept his head low to the ground and prayed that no other traffic would appear on the road.

Satisfied there was nothing amiss, Diana spoke to the dog. "Quiet, Bone. It's all right. Be still."

Carlisle heard her voice floating up to him from below. The very sound of it was enticing. Hearing her voice, combined with the knowledge that he was almost within touching distance of her, gave him an instant erection and made his breath come in short, harsh gasps. If you only knew, little lady, he thought, stifling an urge to laugh. The dog's smarter than you are.

Below him, the sliding glass door slammed shut behind her as Diana Ladd returned to the house. For a moment, Carlisle was afraid she might have taken the dog with her. He breathed a sigh of relief when he peered over the bank and saw that the dog was still pacing restlessly in the yard below, still staring up in his direction. He whistled again.

"Come here, little doggie," he whispered under his breath. "Nice little doggie. Come and get it."

This time, the dog made no sound at all. He simply leapt over the wall and came crashing up the embankment.

Carlisle waited until the last possible moment before making his dash for safety. He had spread the meat over a wide segment of the roadway so the dog would be sure to find it. Now, he ran straight through the meat to his car so the dog— Bone was a funny name for a dog—following his scent, would be led directly to the poison.

Carlisle jumped into his Matador and drove away, hoping against hope that his plan had worked.

After that, I'itoi struck the water with his stick. The bank broke, and the water from the lake and from all the oceans ran together. And then I'itoi, who can make himself either very large or very small, climbed into the basket he had made, and Ban, Coyote, climbed into his hollow cane, and the waters began to rise.

Soon the waters rose high enough to wash them away. I'itoi told Ban to follow him to the west, but Coyote did not listen, and the waters continued to rise. Soon all the villages on the flat were covered with water and the people drowned.

The people who lived near Giwho Tho'ag, Burden Basket Mountain, saw the water coming. They hurried to the highest part of the mountain, thinking they would be safe, but as the water came up, the mountain split in two, and all the people were drowned.

In another part of the valley, a very powerful medicine man led his people up to the highest mountain and told them that there they would be safe. As the water rose, the medicine man sang a powerful song, and the mountain rose higher and higher. The water rose and fell, rose and fell until it had risen and fallen four times.

Then the Indians on the mountain were happy, because everything in nature goes by fours, and they thought that now they would be safe. The medicine man said that there would be a great feast and the people began to get ready—some cooking, some grinding corn.

Now it happens that the people had with them on the mountain only one gogs, one dog. The people sent Dog down the mountain to see how high the water was. Dog went to the edge of the mountain, and then he stretched himself and came back. "The water is going down," Dog said. "It will not rise again."

And right then, at that very moment, as Dog spoke, all the people on the mountain were turned to stone. They changed to stone just as they were when Dog spoke—some cooking, some eating, and some grinding corn. If you go to the place called Superstition Mountain, you can see them to this day.

And that is why, nawoj, *my friend, you must never permit a dog to speak to you, for if you do, you may be turned to stone.*

Davy and Father John were talking quietly at the kitchen table; Rita had returned to her room. After cleaning the kitchen, Diana had barely started reading the newspaper in the living room when the dog whined and scratched at the front door.

"How did Bone get back out front?" Diana asked irritably as she hurried to let him in. She was worried that he might make a dash for the kitchen and scare Father John. Instead, the dog plodded in slowly, shambled past her without even looking up, and walked directly into the opposite wall with a resounding thump.

"Oh'o," she said, alarmed, "what's the matter with you?"

Bone stood splayfooted, long tail tucked between his legs, head down. He swayed drunkenly. Davy, hearing the concern in Diana's voice, called from the kitchen. "Mom, what is it?"

"I don't know. Something's wrong with Bone. I let him inside, and he walked straight into the wall."

Davy hurried into the room followed by a still-apprehensive Father John. The dog, who had once seemed so ferocious, now showed absolutely no interest in attacking the priest. Instead, he put one tentative foot in front of the other and tried to walk, only to fall down flat on his belly.

"That dog's been poisoned!" Father John announced decisively. "I've seen it before. We've got to get him to a vet."

"Poisoned?" Diana repeated. "How can that be?"

"Look at him. I had a dog die of poisoning once. He came inside acting just like this. The vet said that if I'd brought him in right away, he might have saved him. There's no time to lose."

Uncertain what to do, Diana glanced at her

watch. A quarter to six. The vet's office would close in fifteen minutes. Rita reappeared just then. "What's wrong?" she asked.

"It's Oh'o. Father John thinks he's been poisoned. We'd better load him in the car. Davy, Rita, come on. We'll all go."

Rita shook her head. "Fat Crack will be here soon. You go on. If we all go, Davy and I will just be in the way. We'll wait here. I'll call Dr. Johnston and tell him you're coming."

On the floor between them, Bone's body shook convulsively. One look at the suffering animal convinced her. "All right," Diana said. "You stay here."

Diana knelt beside the quaking dog. "Bone, come," she ordered. With a whimper, the dog tried valiantly to get up, only to stumble and collapse once more. Diana attempted to pick him up by herself, but he was well over one hundred pounds of dog, far more than she could lift or carry.

"Father John, would you help me load him into the car?"

"Of course."

Lifting together, they raised Bone off the floor and carried him outside. "My car's out back," Diana said, heading that way.

"No," Father John corrected. "We'll take mine. It's closer."

They reached the car and eased the stricken animal onto the backseat. As Diana straightened up, she found that Davy had followed them and was starting to climb into the car with Bone. Diana stopped him. "You stay here with Rita," she ordered. "If she has to leave before I get back, you can go along with her."

Davy, close to tears, barely heard her. "Is Oh'o going to die?" he asked.

"I hope not, but I don't know," Diana answered grimly. She climbed into the car and closed the door behind her while the priest started the engine. Before driving out of the yard, Father John stopped the car beside the distressed child and rolled down his window.

"Remember how we were talking about prayer a while ago?" the priest asked. Davy nodded. "Would you like me to pray for Bone?"

The boy's eyes filled with tears. "Yes, please," he whispered.

"Heavenly Father," the priest said, bowing his head. "We pray that you will grant the blessing of healing to your servant, Bone, that he may return safely to his home. We ask this in the name of the Father, of the Son, and of the Holy Ghost. Amen."

"Does that mean he'll be all right now?"

Father John shook his head gravely. "When God answers prayers, He can say either yes or no. Right now, it's too soon to tell. You keep on praying while we take him to the vet, okay?"

"Okay," Davy said, his voice quavering. "I will."

Andrew saw the priest and the woman drive away in a hurry. The dog was with them in the car. They were probably taking the mutt to a vet. Maybe it would work, but he doubted it. He had put enough slug bait in that hamburger to choke a horse. This was, however, one very large dog.

Carlisle turned back toward the house in smug satisfaction and saw the boy walk dejectedly back into the house. Everything had worked like a charm, just the way he'd planned it. The boy was as good as his. It was stupid of Diana to leave him there alone, but that was her problem. Diana was gone, and the boy was unprotected, and Andrew Carlisle wanted Davy in the very worst way.

Sliding down the mountain, not caring now whether or not he stayed out of sight or made too much noise, Andrew Carlisle started toward the house. He had spent seven long years waiting for this moment. Now that it was finally starting, he could barely contain himself. Diana Ladd was going to make it all worthwhile.

At ten minutes to six, when the phone rang in the house on Weber Drive, Myrna Louise was waiting. She had gone out to the car to bring in her suitcase from the trunk and had subsequently discovered everything hidden there—her bankbook, her blank checks, the gun, the bag of lime, and the luggage with someone else's name on it. She didn't bother to open the luggage. It had been stolen from someone else as surely as her own savings-account book had been stolen from her. And her cash, too, as she discovered moments later.

For half an hour now, she had sat quietly in her rocking chair, wondering what it all meant. She had already assimilated the idea that Andrew, her own son, had meant to kill her, would have killed her, if she hadn't taken the crazy notion into her head to drive off in the car. Sure knowledge of Andrew's murderous intentions had shocked her at first, but initial shock had worn into fuming anger.

Now, she sat rehearsing what she would say to him when Andrew finally called her, as she knew he would. She had considered turning him in herself but decided against it. Someone else would have to do the dirty work, not her, not his own mother. But if the cops happened to come to her house looking for him, she wouldn't raise a hand to stop them.

Constantly rephrasing her speech, she decided to tell Andrew that if he ever came near her again, if he ever darkened her doorstep or wrote her a letter or even so much as tried to contact her by phone, she would see to it that he rotted in prison for the rest of his natural life. How did that sound?

Andrew had finally stepped beyond Myrna Louise's considerable threshold of tolerance. Having once reached the end of her rope, she determined to no longer have a son. She would declare him null and void. As far as she was concerned, Andrew Carlisle would cease to exist.

So when the phone finally rang, it was his voice she expected to hear on the other end of the line, whining and blathering. Instead, the voice was that of a total stranger.

"Is Andrew there?" the man asked.

Myrna Louise's heart skipped a beat as she tried

to conceal her disappointment "Who's calling, please?" she asked guardedly.

"A friend of his," the man said. "Is he there?"

"Not right now. May I take a message?"

It sounded as though the person on the other end of the line let out a long sigh, but Myrna Louise couldn't be sure.

"No," he said. "That's all right. I'll call back later."

He hung up—slammed the phone down in her ear, actually. She hung up, too, sitting there for a long time afterward with her hand still resting on the receiver. She wished it had been Andrew on the phone so she could have had it out with him once and for all, but it wasn't. For that she would have to wait a little longer.

The human body isn't quite like anything else, Brandon Walker thought. People talk about pulling the plug, but just turning off life-sustaining machines doesn't necessarily mean it's over, doesn't mean the person gives up the ghost and dies the way a light goes off when you disconnect a cord from the socket. It wasn't that simple. Nothing ever is.

The machines had been silenced for over an hour now, but Toby Walker stubbornly clung to life, persisting in breathing on his own much to the doctor's surprise and dismay. His blood pressure was gradually falling, but there had been no marked or sudden change.

Nurses looked in on them every once in a while, respectfully, as though conscious that their presence was now an intrusion, not a help. Their concern focused on the two nonpatients—a woman quiet at last, worn out from continual weeping, and a man, the son, whose narrow jaw worked constantly, but who sat beside his dying father stiff and straight, dry-eyed and silent.

Brandon Walker had forgotten he was a cop in all this, forgotten that there was another duty calling. Sitting there, he was nothing but a grieving son, a lost, abandoned, and nearly middle-aged child, facing his own bleak future in a universe suddenly devoid of its center, an unthinkable world where his father didn't exist.

The three people waited together in a room where the silence was broken only by the old man's shallow breathing. No words were necessary. They had all been spoken long ago, and Brandon was convinced that in that broken shell of a man on the bed, there was no one left to listen.

Detective G. T. Farrell was well outside his Pinal County jurisdiction. He should have contacted the local law-enforcement agencies, either Maricopa County, or, in this case, the Tempe Police Department to ask for backup, but that would have taken time. Farrell knew in his gut there was no time to lose. He was propelled forward by the common force that drives all those who pursue serial killers—the horrifying and inevitable knowledge that time itself is the enemy.

Refusing to be rushed, Farrell had systematically worked the problem, marching down the

Spaulding column in the phone book, calling each number in turn, always asking for Andrew—a first name Andrew—rather than giving out any further information. He had tried Spauldings in Phoenix proper. Next he worked the suburbs. Halfway through that process, a frail-sounding old woman answered the phone.

As soon as he asked for Andrew and heard the sharp, involuntary intake of breath, he knew he had hit pay dirt. Even while he talked to her, making sure his voice on the phone stayed calm and noncommittal, he was frantically tearing the page with her name on it out of the book. This was no time for scribbling notes.

But once in the car, Farrell couldn't risk lights or siren. That would have raised too many unpleasant questions had anyone stopped him. He drove only as fast as the traffic would bear.

A resourceful man who always carried a selection of maps in his car, Geet headed East on Camelback in the general direction of Tempe, using crosstown stops at lights and the usual rush-hour slowdowns to locate the exact whereabouts of Weber Drive and to pinpoint the address in his *Thomas Guide*. Farrell figured it would take him about forty-five minutes to get there. His actual elapsed time was thirty-eight minutes flat.

Getting out of the car on Weber Drive half a block away from the address, he patted his holster and felt the reassuring presence of his .38 Special. It was possible that the old woman had lied and that her son had been right there in the room with her all along, but Farrell doubted it.

The old woman didn't sound as though she was that glib or that fast on her feet. She wasn't that capable a liar. At least Geet Farrell fervently hoped she wasn't.

Taking a deep breath, Farrell opened the gate, strode up the long walkway, and rang the doorbell. Almost immediately, he heard movement inside the small house. He swallowed hard to calm himself as the door opened and an old woman peered nearsightedly out at him through a screen door. "Yes?" she asked.

Carefully, using deliberate gestures, he brought out his badge. "I'm a police officer," he said, holding it up to the screen so she could see it. "I'm looking for Andrew Carlisle."

The woman squinted at the badge without reading it. "He isn't here," she said.

"Could I talk to you then? Are you his mother?"

"For the time being," she answered.

Farrell wondered what that meant. He wondered, too, if she recognized his voice from the phone. If so, her next question gave no hint of it. "What do you want with him?"

"We want to ask him some questions, that's all," Farrell answered. "There are a few matters we need to clear up."

"Me, too," the old woman added, opening the screen door, motioning him inside. "I have some matters I'd like Andrew to clear up for me, too."

Something in the woman's injured tone suggested a switch in tactics from investigator to sympathizer, from potential enemy to ally. "What kind of matters, ma'am?" Farrell asked innocently.

"He stole my money, for one thing," she answered with ill-concealed fury, "my money and my bankbooks. Then, when he saw I was leaving, he was so angry that I think he would have killed me if he could have gotten close enough, but I fooled him. I drove away all by myself. I drove all the way here. Can you believe it? Andrew never thought I would, and neither did I. After all, I'm sixty-five years old and had never driven a car before in my life, but I did. So help me I did. I wouldn't have done it, either, if he hadn't treated me so badly."

"Maybe you ought to tell me about it, ma'am," Geet Farrell said. "This could be important."

Davy was surprised when he saw the bald-headed man standing outside the glass patio door. The man was wearing funny brown-colored clothes, the kind with plants painted on them, that soldiers sometimes wore in the movies.

"Nana *Dahd*," he called. "Someone's here."

Davy expected the man would wait outside until Rita came to the door to talk to him. Instead, he shoved the door open and stepped inside.

"Who are you?" Davy demanded. "What do you want?"

"You," the man answered. "You're what I want."

The man lunged for him. Davy tried to dart out of the way, but the man was too quick. He caught Davy by one arm, spinning him around. He swung the child up in the air and held him two feet off the ground.

"You were talking to somebody, kid. Who was it? Where are they?"

"I'm right here," a woman's voice said behind him. "Don't hurt him."

"Nana *Dahd*," the boy complained. "He just came right in the house. He didn't even knock."

Suddenly, the man's arm clamped tight around Davy's throat, choking off his air. He kicked and fought, but he couldn't get away. The last thing he heard before he blacked out was the man saying, "I don't have to knock, because as long as I have you, I own the place. Isn't that right, old woman?"

Davy didn't see Rita's answering nod. It was true. As long as he had Davy, Andrew Carlisle could have anything else he wanted.

Around the Pinal County Sheriff's Department, Detective Geet Farrell had a considerable reputation as a ladies' man. With men he could be tough and hard-nosed as hell, but with women he gentled them along until even the bad ones offered to give him the shirts off their backs.

Slowly but urgently, Geet Farrell worked Myrna Louise Spaulding. He didn't rush her, but he didn't allow any unnecessary delays, either. Within minutes, he had talked her into showing him the contents of the battered Valiant's packed trunk. He recognized Johnny Rivkin's name as soon as he saw the tag on the luggage, but he didn't let anything betray his exultation. Because it was too soon. He needed to know more.

So he led the garrulous old lady through her

entire day, encouraging her to remember everything from the moment she woke up until he himself had arrived on her doorstep.

Myrna Louise loved having an appreciative audience. She warmed to the telling and was totally engrossed by the time she got to the part about going into the office in Tucson to pick up those mysterious papers with those two women's names on it. Only then, as she was telling the detective about the papers, did she fully allow herself to know what those two names meant, what Andrew was really going to do. It hit Detective Farrell at the same time, like a fierce, double-fisted blow to the gut.

"Where is he now?" he demanded savagely. All gentleness disappeared from the man, transformed instantly into a single-minded intensity that was frightening to see.

"I don't know," Myrna Louise whimpered. "I don't have any idea."

"We've got to find him. Where was he when you left him?"

"I already told you. At the storage unit. In Tucson."

"Can I use your phone?" he asked.

"Yes," she whispered, barely containing the despairing sob that rose in her throat. "Go ahead. Help yourself."

20

*D*R. JOHNSTON, *THE* vet, was guardedly optimistic about the dog's chances for survival as he sifted a pinch of yellow powder into Bone's eyes. "This is apomorphine," he explained, "an emetic. It gets into the bloodstream through the conjunctival sacs. It'll make him barf his guts out within minutes. He's certainly exhibiting all the classic symptoms of slug-bait poisoning. Where'd he pick it up?"

"I don't know," Diana said. "He was fine just twenty minutes or so earlier when we put him outside. He came back in acting drunk. He could barely walk."

The vet shook his head. "You've got a neighbor who hates dogs."

"I don't have any neighbors," Diana started to say, and then stopped. A chill ran down her spine. Perhaps this was it, she thought, the beginning of what Rita called the wind coming to the windmill, the reason she was wearing a gun.

"You'd better go on out now, Diana," Dr. Johnston warned. "Bone is going to be one miserable dog here for a while, but if we caught it as soon as you say, he should pull through. I'd like to keep him overnight, though, if you don't mind."

But Diana did mind. She dreaded the idea of going home without the dog. Bone was her first line of defense. She glanced at her watch. It wasn't dark yet and wouldn't be for some time, but once it was, she wanted the dog with her.

"I'd rather wait, if it's not going to be too long."

"Suit yourself," Dr. Johnston said. "It won't take long, but it isn't going to be pretty."

Half an hour earlier and 120 miles away, Pinal County homicide detective Geet Farrell had considered his options and hadn't liked any of them. He tried calling Brandon Walker directly, but there was no answer, either at his office or at home. Farrell refused to waste any more time in stationary phoning, but he didn't want to abandon his questioning of Myrna Louise Spaulding, either. There might be more she could tell him, details he had so far neglected to ask.

Farrell flung the phone back on the hook. "You do know what he's up to, don't you?"

Myrna Louise nodded. "I do now."

"I'm going to try to stop him," the detective continued grimly. "Will you help? I'll need you to come with me."

"Yes," Myrna Louise answered, rising unsteadily to her feet. "I'll do whatever I can. Just let me get my purse."

They left Weber Drive in a spray of gravel and headed for I-10. Once across the Pinal County line, Detective Farrell switched on lights and sirens and drove like a bat out of hell. They sped south on the Interstate through the hot desert evening, while Farrell's mind grappled with the problem on three different levels.

First, he dealt with the car, navigating with fierce concentration. Second, he played radio tag, trying to get a good enough connection to be patched through to someone in Tucson who could actually help him. Third, he listened to Myrna Louise Spaulding's seemingly endless story.

It wasn't until a Pinal County dispatcher hooked him up with the counterpart dispatcher in Pima, a guy named Hank Maddern, that Farrell finally felt as though he was talking to somebody real, someone with a sense of urgency.

"What can I do for you, Detective Farrell?" Maddern asked. "Brandon Walker told me to expect your call."

"Where is he?"

"At the hospital. His father's dying."

"I'm sorry as hell to hear it, but this can't wait. You've got to get him on the phone for me."

"Why?"

"Tell him we've got trouble. Tell him it's bad. I just don't know how bad."

"It could take some time," Maddern cautioned. "They're in the ICU at Tucson Medical Center. Can anyone else help?"

Considering what Myrna had told him about Carlisle's illegal purchase of police records and what Farrell himself knew about the graft and corruption in the Pima County Sheriff's Office, the detective was leery about bringing in any more players whose loyalty might be questionable. Maddern sounded like the genuine article, but Farrell remained skeptical. Someone high in DuShane's administration had helped Andrew Carlisle at least once before. It might very well happen again.

"I don't want to have to brief someone else if it isn't necessary," Farrell hedged. "Try getting through to Walker. I'm just now passing Picacho Peak. If you can't reach him within a matter of minutes, then we'll have to do something else."

By six-thirty Wanda Ortiz, Fat Crack's wife, was finishing the last batch of tortillas. She had started out early that morning by making six dozen tamales, a big vat of pinto beans, and another of chili. With a dozen preparations left to do before the singers arrived, she was hot, sweaty, and tired. She was also annoyed.

She was annoyed because her mother-in-law, Juanita, had refused to lift a finger to help her. Real Presbyterians didn't participate in pagan baptisms, Juanita had archly informed Fat Crack when he had gone to his mother's house asking for help. She wouldn't lend her support to Looks At Nothing's crazy idea, not even as a favor for her own sister.

So Wanda had done all the cooking herself, not complaining, but with a layer of very un-Christianlike anger seething just beneath her seemingly placid surface. This was Wanda's second church-related battle with her mother-in-law in less than a month. The first had been over whether or not Juanita's grandchildren would attend Presbyterian Daily Vacation Bible school. Juanita had won the skirmish hands down since the Presbyterian church also happened to own the reservation's only swimming pool.

There were times, Wanda thought, slapping the last tortilla on the griddle and picking it off with nimble fingers, that she wished all the Anglo missionaries would go back where they came from. Even Fat Crack's Christian-Science studies sometimes provoked her.

Wanda was still nursing her grudge when Looks At Nothing pounded on the door with his walking stick. She wasn't especially happy to see him, either. At that particular moment, the Indian medicine man was more trouble than all the others put together.

"What is it?" she asked curtly, wiping her hands on her apron.

"Where is your husband?"

"Taking a nap. He has to stay up all night with the singers. He wanted to sleep before going to get Rita."

"We must go now," Looks At Nothing said urgently. "It's started."

Wanda shook her head. Gabe had given her strict orders not to wake him up until seven. He had spent the whole afternoon dragging a stalled BIA road grader out of a sandy wash, and he had wanted to sleep as long as possible. Looking at the agitated old man, Wanda wondered if perhaps he was crazy in addition to being blind.

"No," Wanda replied. "Nothing has started yet. It's too early. The singers don't come until nine."

"Not the singers," he snapped. "The *ohb*. We must go quickly, or it will be too late."

In Dr. Johnston's waiting room, Diana Ladd alternately sat and paced while Father John thumbed through a worn pet-food catalog. She berated herself for leaving Rita and Davy home alone, for being stupid about waiting for the dog, for not accepting Brandon Walker's offer of help. When Dr. Johnston's receptionist got up to leave, Diana asked to use the phone.

The phone at home rang nine or ten times without anyone answering. That in itself wasn't alarming. When Rita was out in her room, she and Davy sometimes didn't hear the phone ringing.

Just as Diana started to hang up, Rita answered. "Hello."

"Rita, it's me. Diana. Is everything okay there?"

"Okay?" Rita's voice seemed distant, hollow. "Yes. Everything here is okay."

"Bone's still with Dr. Johnston," Diana rushed on. "We're waiting for him. We'll be home as soon as we can. Did Davy tell you he can go with you if you have to leave before I get home?"

"No," Rita replied. "He didn't tell me, but that's good."

Diana hung up, too preoccupied to think it odd that Rita had answered the phone instead of Davy. Without leaving the desk, Diana decided to swallow her pride and call Brandon Walker. The least she could do was let him know what had happened and ask for his advice, but he wasn't in. With a frustrated sigh, Diana sat back down. It was probably just as well. What she and Rita planned for Andrew Carlisle should be kept totally secret. If she talked to Brandon Walker, she might accidentally let something slip.

Father John glanced at her. "The dog's going to be fine," the priest said reassuringly, misreading her agitation as concern for Bone. "We got him here so soon after it happened that I'm sure he'll be okay."

Diana nodded but said nothing. According to Rita, things were still all right at home, but with Andrew Carlisle on the loose, the dog was really the least of her worries. She sat there wishing she'd left the .45 at home with Rita.

"It's taking so long," she said, glancing at her watch for the second time in less than a minute.

"Some things can't be rushed," Father John replied.

Diana started to argue and then thought better of it. What Father John didn't know wouldn't hurt him. If he thought she was only worried about the dog, so be it.

Now that he was actually inside Diana Ladd's house, Carlisle felt downright invincible. His plans were working perfectly. Still holding the boy, Carlisle ordered the old woman to sit down on the couch. She did so at once. Her immediate compliance gratified him. Carlisle was sure that holding the boy hostage would work exactly the same magic on Diana Ladd. With Davy in jeopardy, she would have to submit to his every demand, give him whatever he wanted when and how he wanted it.

The phone blared, startling him so that he almost dropped the child. He held the knife to Davy's throat. "Answer it," he growled at the old woman. "Try anything funny and the boy dies."

Clumsily, Rita heaved herself off the couch and hobbled over to the phone. Carlisle nodded with satisfaction at her curt answers. As far as he could tell, she made no attempt to pass along any secret messages.

"Who was it?" he asked when she put the phone back in the cradle. "Diana Ladd?" The old woman nodded. "What did she say?"

"She'll be back soon."

"Good," he said. "We'll be waiting, won't we? Pull the cord out of the wall."

The old woman hesitated as though she didn't understand him. He brandished the knife over the now fully awake boy. Seeing the knife, the boy regarded him through terrified eyes, but he made no effort to fight.

"I said pull it out," Carlisle repeated. "No more phone calls." Rita yanked the phone cord from its receptacle, and Carlisle smiled. "Good. Now, back on the couch." He almost laughed aloud at the way the old woman jumped to do his bidding. He was enjoying having them all by the short hairs.

Carlisle knew firsthand how abject submission works. If he had learned nothing else, his tormentors in Florence had taught him that lesson well. He had seen how, in order to avoid pain, victims can become so eager to please that they transform themselves into willing participants in their own destruction. The old woman's reaction was a textbook case. Diana Ladd's would be as well.

With the younger woman, though, he would have to be careful. Pacing would be everything. He would have to restrain himself in the beginning and not go too far. The kind of dehumanizing submission he wanted from her would take time and effort and a certain amount of finesse.

There were those in the prison community who took the position that raping a rapist qualified as poetic justice and maybe even as a kind of aversion therapy. Well, Andrew Carlisle was here to tell those jokers that it hadn't worked out that way for him. Physical violation hadn't "cured" him at all. Instead, it had only added fuel to his Diana Ladd bloodlust, given him something else to blame her for. He'd spent years planning every move of his campaign against her. He wouldn't settle for anything less than total capitulation. He looked forward to having Diana Ladd crawling naked on the floor before him. He wanted to see her on her hands and knees, subject to his every whim. He wanted the pleasure of hearing the bitch beg.

Carlisle sat the boy down on one end of the couch and ordered him to stay still while he tied up the old woman. Busy with the twine, Carlisle found he was having difficulty concentrating. His whole body pulsed with eagerness for the coming confrontation. What would happen in those first crucial minutes? he wondered. Would she fight or give in at once? Would the very sight of him strike terror in her heart? Would she guess what was in store for her? He didn't think so. The others hadn't, why should she?

For the first time, Carlisle considered whether or not she'd bring the priest back with her. He hoped not. Carlisle was not a religious man, nor was he terribly superstitious, but the idea of killing a priest lacked appeal. Not only that, he was reluctant to expend his energies on any side issue that might dull his appetite for the main course.

"What are you going to do?" the old woman asked, intruding rudely into his thoughts. He didn't answer immediately. Finished tying her one good hand to the cumbersome cast, he went to work binding her swollen ankles together, hobbling her like a horse with the short lengths of twine he had cut up and brought along for that express purpose. Advance planning was everything.

"Whatever I want," he replied nonchalantly. "I'm going to do whatever I want."

Diana was about to call home again when Dr. Johnston returned to the waiting room. It was almost seven, a whole hour after the veterinarian's office had been scheduled to close.

"I think we're over the hump now," Dr. Johnston said. "He's been one sick puppy, but I believe he's going to be okay. Plenty of rest, plenty of liquids. Tell Davy not to overtax him for the next few days. He's probably through the worst of it, but we'd better cover your car seat with some old blankets, just in case."

Dr. Johnston's assistant, a burly teenager named Scott, carried the ailing dog back out to Father John's car and laid him gently on a layer of hastily assembled blankets. With a huge sigh, the dog put his chin on his front paws and closed his eyes.

"Call me in the morning," Dr. Johnston said, "and let me know how he's doing."

Diana replied with a grateful nod. "I'll call first thing."

"That was weird," Scott said as Father John's Buick pulled out of the office parking lot.

"What's weird?" Dr. Johnston asked.

"How come that lady was wearing a gun?"

"A gun? Was she really?" Dr. Johnston sounded startled. "I was so concerned about the dog that I never even noticed."

The old woman sat silently at one end of the couch. Carlisle ordered Davy to the opposite end, where he began tying the boy up as well. He wanted his prisoners relatively immobile but easily transportable when necessary, because Carlisle had no intention of playing out his whole game in Diana Ladd's house.

It was fine for the first major skirmish to take place here. Invading Diana's private territory and bloodying her there was an essential part of his psychological warfare against her. But after that, after he'd humiliated her and established a pattern of absolute control, then he would take his prisoners to the cave, to Gary Ladd's own special cave, for dessert.

Carlisle theorized that the isolated cave by what had once been Rattlesnake Skull Village was eminently suited to his purposes. No one, not even that wise-ass young detective, had ever figured out that the cave, not the *charco*, had been the actual scene of Gina Antone's last moments on this earth.

During the pretrial proceedings, Carlisle had made absolutely sure that no one knew of the existence of Gary Ladd's manuscript with its whining references to the cave. Once he left three more bodies there to rot, he would have all the more reason to see that Gary Ladd's crude manuscript disappeared off the face of the earth. Too bad Myrna Louise hadn't thrown that in the burning barrel instead of *Savage*. She would have been doing something useful for a change.

He thought longingly about the cool, dark cave, about how the timeless limestone walls would swallow up whatever agonized sounds his particular brand of pleasure might wring from his captives. In that dusky cave, with the added luxury of total isolation, no one would interrupt him or interfere with the process. There, once and for all . . .

Carlisle had tried explaining that same thing to Gary Ladd years before, the morning after their little debacle, but the man had been hysterical when he learned the girl was dead, astounded that things had got so far out of hand while he slept.

Even then, things would have been fine if Ladd hadn't lost his nerve and gone back later to move the body so she could have a proper burial. The fool dumped her in a water hole, for God's sake, thinking people would be stupid enough to believe she had drowned. With the rope burns around her neck and her nipple bitten off? What the hell kind of dumb-ass idea was that? And then, a week later, if Carlisle hadn't stopped him, Ladd would have gone to town and confessed for both of them, taking his tell-tale manuscript with him. Thanks a lot, buddy, but no thanks.

Carlisle shivered at the tantalizing memory, letting his imagination travel back to the cave, remembering that long-ago desert night and the girl. Despite her objections, he had coaxed her into that huge and immensely silent place. He had started a small fire—for light he had told her—but light wasn't all the fire was for, not at all. He had other plans for those burning twigs and coals.

To begin with, she had liked being tied up, giggling drunkenly as he bound her, thinking it nothing but some kind of kinky game. Gradually, as she learned the terrible truth, her tipsy laughter changed, first to fear and then to terror and dread as the tenor of the night changed around her. Carlisle hadn't much liked her screaming when it finally came to that. Screaming showed a certain lack of delicacy and finesse on his part. He much preferred the small, animal-like whimpers of pain and the begging. God, how her begging had excited him! Even though it was in a language he didn't speak, he had understood her well enough. He hadn't stopped when she asked him to, of course, but he had understood.

And all the while that jackass of a Gary Ladd was dead drunk in the pickup. When he did wake up finally, after the fun and games were all over, Carlisle managed to convince Gary that he, too, had been an active participant in all that had gone before, that being too drunk to remember was no excuse.

"But she's dead," Ladd had protested, as though he couldn't quite believe it. Of course she was dead. Carlisle had always intended that she would be, that was the whole idea, wasn't it? But Gary Ladd was far too cowardly to value or take advantage of what he was learning, and he hadn't been smart enough to keep his mouth shut, either.

Carlisle shook himself out of what was almost a stupor and found he was sitting on the floor in front of Diana Ladd's couch. Both the boy and the old woman were tied up, although he didn't remember finishing the job. They were both watching him with strange expressions on their faces. Had he blacked out for a moment or what?

These episodes were beginning to bother him. It had happened several times of late, and it scared the shit out of him. Was he losing his mind? He'd come back to himself feeling as though he'd been asleep when he knew he hadn't been. Sometimes only seconds would have passed, sometimes whole minutes.

He inspected the knots. They were properly tied, but he had no recollection of doing it. Somehow it seemed as though his body and his mind functioned independently. He'd have to watch that. It could be dangerous, especially in enemy territory.

"Who are you?" the boy demanded.

Carlisle looked hard at the child, recognizing some of Gary Ladd's features, but the boy had a certain toughness that had been totally lacking in his father.

"Well, son," Carlisle said in a kind tone that belied his words, "you can just think of me as retribution personified, a walking, talking Eye-for-an-Eye."

Davy Ladd frowned at the unfamiliar words, but he didn't back off. "What does that mean?"

Andrew Carlisle laughed, giving the boy credit for raw nerve. "It means that the sins of the fathers are visited on the sons, just like the Good Book says. It also means that if you don't do every single goddamned thing I say, then I use my trusty knife, and you and your mother and this old lady here are all dead meat. Do you understand that?"

Davy nodded.

The room was quiet for a moment when suddenly, sitting there, looking him directly in the eye, the old lady began what sounded like a mournful, almost whispered chant in a language Carlisle didn't recognize. He glowered at her. "Shut up!" he ordered.

She stopped. "I'm praying," she said, speaking calmly. "I'm asking I'itoi to help us."

That made him laugh, even though he didn't like the way she looked at him. "You go right ahead, then. If you think some kind of Indian

mumbo-jumbo is going to fix all this, then be my
guest. But I wouldn't count on it, old woman.
Not at all."

"Why did you do it?" she asked.

"Do what?"

"Why did you kill my granddaughter?"

Prosecutors and lawyers and police tend to limp
around questions like that. Carlisle wasn't accustomed to such a direct approach. It caught him
momentarily off guard.

"Because I felt like it," he said with a grin.
"That's all the reason I needed."

A while later, Coyote followed the trail to where Cot-
tontail was sitting. "Brother, you tricked me back there,
and now I really am going to eat you up."

"Please," said Cottontail, "don't eat me yet. I don't
want to die until I have seen a jig dancer one last time.
Do this for me and then you may eat to your heart's
content."

"All right," said Coyote. "What do you want me
to do?"

"Come with me over here," said Cottontail. "First I
will plaster your eyes shut with pitch. Then, when your
eyes are shut, you will hear firecrackers popping. When
that happens, you must dance and shout. When the
dance is over, then you may eat me."

So Cottontail plastered Coyote's eyes shut with pitch,
then he led him into a cane field. When Coyote was in
the middle of the field, Cottontail set fire to it. Soon the
cane started crackling and popping. Coyote thought
these were the firecrackers Cottontail had told him
about, so he began to dance and shout. Soon he began

to feel the heat, but he thought he was hot because he was dancing so hard. At last, though, the fire reached him, and burned him up.

And that, my friend, is the story of the second time Cottontail tricked Coyote.

From the sound and cadence of that softly crooned chant, someone listening might have thought Rita Antone was giving voice to some ancient traditional Papago lullaby. It included the requisite number of repetitions, the proper rhythm, but it was really a war chant, and the words were entirely new:

"Do not look at me, little Olhoni.
Do not look at me when I sing to you
So this man will not know we are speaking
So this evil man will think he is winning.

"Do not look at me
When I sing, little Olhoni,
But listen to what I say.
This man is evil.
This man is the enemy.
This man is ohb.
Do not let this frighten you.

"Whatever happens in the battle,
We must not let him win.
I am singing a war song for you,
Little Olhoni. I am singing
A hunter's song, a killer's song.
I am singing a song to I'itoi

Asking him to help us.
Asking him to guide us in the battle
So the evil ohb *does not win.*

"Do not look at me, little Olhoni,
Do not look at me when I sing to you.
I must sing this song four times
For all of nature goes in fours,
But when the trouble starts,
When the ohb *attacks us,*
You must remember all the things
I have said to you in this magic song.
You must listen very carefully
And do exactly what I say.
If I tell you to run and hide yourself,
You must run as fast as Wind Man.
Run fast and hide yourself
And do not look back.
Whatever happens, little Olhoni,
You must run and not look back.

"Remember it is said that
Long ago I'itoi made himself a fly
And hid himself in the crack.
I'itoi hid in the smallest crack
When Eagle Man came searching for him.
Be like I'itoi, little Olhoni.
Be like I'itoi and hide yourself
In the very smallest crack.
Hide yourself somewhere
And do not come out again,
Do not show your face
Until the battle is over.

Listen to what I sing to you,
Little Olhoni. Listen to what I sing.
Be careful not to look at me
But do exactly as I say."

The song ended. Rita glanced at Davy, who was looking studiously in another direction. He had listened. He was only a boy, one who had not yet killed his first coyote, but she had trained him well. He would do what he'd been told.

In the gathering twilight, Rita glanced at the clock on the mantel across the room. Seven o'clock. Fat Crack must come for her soon, because the singers were scheduled to start at nine. The very latest he could come was eight o'clock, an hour away.

One hour, she thought. Sixty minutes. If they could stay alive until Fat Crack got there, they might yet live, but deep in her heart, Rita feared otherwise. As he tied them up, she had looked into Andrew Carlisle's soul. All she saw there were the restless, angry spirits of the dead Apache warriors from Rattlesnake Skull Village. They had somehow found this *Mil-gahn*'s soul and infected it with their evil. Andrew Carlisle was definitely the danger the buzzards had warned her about, the evil enemy who Looks At Nothing said was both *Ohb* and not *Ohb*, Apache and not Apache. And although the process had been started, Davy was still unbaptized.

The man sat on the floor in front of her, unmoving, seemingly asleep although his eyes were open. She had heard of these kinds of Whore-Sickness trances before, although she herself had never witnessed one. She knew full well the danger.

Looking away from their captor, Rita stared over her shoulder at the basket maze hanging on the wall behind her. She remembered the ancient yucca she had harvested to find the root fiber to make it. *Howi*, a yucca, an old cactus, had willingly sacrificed itself that Diana Ladd might own this basket.

And, suddenly, Rita knew that I'itoi had heard her song and sent her a message even without the use of Looks At Nothing's sacred smoke. She would be like the plant that had given up its life so I'itoi's design could spread out from the center of the basket. Davy Ladd had become the center of Rita Antone's basket. She would be his red yucca root.

"Whatever you're going to do," she said softly, "the boy should not see."

Andrew Carlisle seemed startled, as though she had peered into his brain and read the secret plans written there. "Do you have a better idea?"

Rita nodded. "There's a root cellar," she said. "Off the kitchen. Put the boy in there. I will stay with him."

"A root cellar?"

Carlisle sounded almost disbelieving. He had been worried about how to handle the growing number of hostages in case the priest showed up as well, but now here was the old lady helping out, solving the problem for him. Carlisle knew all about root cellars. There had been one in his grandmother's home, a place where he'd been left on occasion for disciplinary purposes. A root cellar would do nicely.

He rushed into the kitchen to see for himself, worried now that Diana might return before he was ready. And the old lady was absolutely right. Except for a stack of musty old boxes and a few canned goods, there was nothing else there.

Back in the living room, he grabbed the boy and carried him into the root cellar. Then he hauled the old woman to her feet and helped her shuffle along. With both prisoners safely stashed inside the room, he slammed the door shut and locked it with the old-fashioned skeleton key that was right there in the lock. For safekeeping, he put the key in his boot along with his hunting knife. Smiling to himself, Carlisle hurried back to the living room and stationed himself out of sight behind the door.

Actually, the more he thought about it, the more he liked the idea of having those first few minutes with Diana all by himself—just the two of them, one on one, sort of a honeymoon. He pulled a whetstone from his pocket and began to sharpen the blade of the hunting knife. It wasn't necessary—the blade was already sharp enough, but it gave him something to do with his hands while he waited.

The dog had already had two accidents in the priest's car between Dr. Johnston's office and the driveway. Diana was embarrassed. The vet had been right all along. She should have left Bone there overnight to recuperate.

"I'm sorry about your car, Father," she apologized.

"Don't worry about it," Father John said, driving into the yard and stopping in front of the house. "These things happen. Would you like him inside?"

Diana shook her head. "I don't think so. There's no sense taking him inside and having him be sick in there as well. If you can, take him on out to the back patio, while I work on cleaning up this mess. Ask Davy to fill his water dish with fresh water and take it out there for him."

The vet had sent the ailing Bone home on a borrowed leash. Using this, Father John coaxed the now-docile dog through a gate at the side of the house and into the backyard. Meanwhile, Diana dealt with the lingering physical evidence of the dog's illness, removing soiled blankets from the priest's car and draping them over the wall for a quick hosedown.

She was surprised that Davy wasn't waiting on the porch to greet them, but she was so busy cleaning up after the dog that the idea never quite surfaced as a conscious thought. Leaving the windows open to let the car air out, she started into the house.

With his heart hammering in his chest, Carlisle watched the car pull into the driveway. Damn! The priest was there. What the hell should he do now?

The man and woman in the car spoke briefly, then the priest got out, opened the door, and bent into the backseat. What was he doing? Getting the dog? Goddamn! The dog was back, too? What the hell kind of constitution did that dog have?

For a moment, Carlisle vacillated between following the man and staying to keep an eye on Diana Ladd. At first he couldn't understand what was going on, but then, when she pulled the blankets out of the car and turned on the hose, he realized he was getting another chance. There was time to do both. He headed for the kitchen at a dead run.

Father John left the dog resting on the dusky patio and rose to go into the house. Seeing no sign of Rita or Davy, he stepped up to the sliding patio door, which had been left slightly ajar.

"Hello," he called. "Anybody home?"

Hearing no answer, he crossed the threshold and turned to close the door behind him just as something heavy crashed into the back of his skull.

The root-cellar door flew open. From the darkened kitchen, something heavy was thrown in with them before the door slammed shut again. Davy felt with his feet and realized it was a person lying flat on the floor, someone who didn't move when Davy touched him. At first the child was afraid it might be his mother, but finally he realized the still body belonged to Father John.

"It's the priest," he whispered to Rita.

Before locking them in, Carlisle had warned they would die if they made noise, so Davy and Nana *Dahd* spoke in subdued whispers.

"Try to wake him up," Rita said.

Davy moved closer to the man and nudged him, but the priest didn't stir. His labored breathing told them he wasn't dead. "He won't wake up," Davy said.

"Keep trying," Rita told him.

Diana stepped onto the porch and turned the doorknob. Suddenly, with no warning, the door gave way beneath her hand, yanking Diana into the house.

Before she could make a sound, before she could reach for the handle of the .45, iron fingers clamped down over her face and mouth. The razor-sharp blade of a hunting knife pressed hard against the taut skin of her throat.

"Welcome home, honey," Andrew Carlisle said. "You're late. It's not nice to keep a man with a hard-on waiting."

Diana shook her head wildly, struggling to escape, but he ground his punishing fingers deep into the tender flesh of her face. "Oh, no, you don't lady. Make one sound, and everybody dies. Starting with you."

21

SO I'ITOI WENT to see Gopher Boys, who guard
the gates of those who live below. "I need people to
come help me," I'itoi said. "I have people from the East
and the West, from the North and the South, who will
help me fight Evil Siwani. Are there any people here
who will help me fight my enemy?"

"First," said Gopher Boys, "you must sing for four
days to weaken your enemy. After that, come again, and
we will open the gates."

Meanwhile, Evil Siwani worried about how many
warriors I'itoi would bring with him, so he sent Coyote
to see. Coyote ran to the top of Baboquivari and looked
down just as Gopher Boys opened the gates. The people
who would help I'itoi started coming out, more and
more of them all the time.

It is said that long ago, if Coyote didn't like something, he could laugh and change it. So Coyote laughed
and said, "Will these people never stop coming?" Right
then the hole in the earth slammed shut, and no more
people came out.

Coyote ran back to tell Evil Siwani that I'itoi was
on his way with many warriors. Wherever there were

people who heard about the coming battle, they were happy to join forces with I'itoi. Finally, I'itoi's warriors camped for the night just a little way from Evil Siwani's village. I'itoi called his people together.

"Whoever kills first in the morning will have first choice of the place he wants to live."

She wanted to scream, but she couldn't, not with his hand clamped over her face, crushing her cheeks and nostrils together, cutting off her ability to breathe. Carlisle had grabbed her from behind. She felt his hot breath on the back of her neck.

"Take the gun out of the holster," he ordered, "nice and easy. Hold it by the handle with your thumb and forefinger. We're going to walk over and put it down on the table, very carefully."

Where are Davy and Rita? she wondered. Where is Father John? If he was still out behind the house, he might come in and help. . . .

The blade of the knife pressed against her skin. "I don't want to cut you, baby. Blood's real messy for what I have in mind, but I will if I have to. Don't try me. The gun. Now!"

Faint from lack of oxygen, she thought maybe that was all he intended—strangling her, but then he eased his pincerlike pressure, allowing her to gulp desperate mouthfuls of air.

"The gun!" he repeated.

She reached for it silently, cursing Brandon Walker as she did so. He had been right, damn him. She'd never had a chance to touch the gun, to say nothing of using it. All having the gun had done was to make her stupid, to give her a false sense of security.

She removed the gun from its holster and held it as she'd been told. With Carlisle clutching her from behind, they glided from door to table like a pair of grotesque waltzing skaters.

"That's better," he muttered once the .45 was resting on the tabletop. "Much better. Now turn around and let me look at you."

"Where's Davy?" she asked, without turning. "What have you done with Davy and Rita?"

His voice rose menacingly. "I gave you an order, goddamnit! Turn around." He grabbed her by one shoulder and spun her toward him. The abrupt motion threw her slightly off balance. She almost fell, but he caught her by one wrist and held her upright. The knife seemed to have disappeared into thin air, but as soon as his powerful fingers closed around her wrist, Diana knew he didn't need the knife. Not really. His hands alone were plenty strong enough.

"Where's Davy?" she asked again, trying to keep her voice steady, trying not to let it expose her rising terror.

He grinned back at her. "Where's Davy?" he mocked. "Where do you think he is? What will you give me if I show him to you? A kiss maybe? A piece of tail?"

Carlisle's tone was light and bantering, but Diana's wrist ached from the punishing pressure of his fingers. She knew then, with a sinking heart, that strangling wasn't it. Carlisle would never let her off that easy.

Someone seeing the frozen tableau from outside the window might have thought the man and woman to be lovers standing face to face, might have imagined them holding hands and exchanging endearments in preparation for a romantic kiss. The man was smiling. Only a glimpse of the woman's stricken face betrayed the reality of their desperate life-and-death struggle.

"Let me go!" She started to add, "You're hurting me," but she didn't. Life with Max Cooper had taught her better than that. In an uneven contest where defeat is inevitable, she had learned to show no reaction at all, to deny her tormentor his ultimate gratification—the perceptible proof of his victim's pain.

"You know you're going to give me whatever I want, don't you?" he leered at her, relentlessly pulling her closer. Steeling herself, she refused to shrink away from him, refused to cringe, but even as she struggled against him, she was beginning to fear the worst—Davy and Rita were dead. They had to be. If not, they would have given her some sign, some reason to hope.

"One way or another," Carlisle continued, "like it or not, I'm going to have you six ways to Sunday, little lady, so you could just as well get used to the idea, lay back and enjoy it, as they say. Now tell me, how's it going to be, hard or easy?"

She didn't respond.

"That was a joke," he said, laughing. "Didn't you get it?"

By then, their lips were almost touching. For an answer, she brought her knee up and rammed it into his groin. Stunned, he doubled over, grabbing himself, groaning with pain. Momentarily, he let go of her hand, giving her the chance she needed. Dodging backward and to one side, Diana groped for the handle of the .45.

The gun was a mere three feet away, but it could just as well have been three miles. She picked it up and used both hands to pull back the hammer, but before she could aim or pull the trigger, Carlisle tackled her, slamming her hard against the wall, knocking the wind from her lungs, forcing her hand up into the empty air overhead. The gun discharged with an earsplitting roar, blasting a hole in the stucco ceiling before he knocked it from her hand and sent it whirling across the room.

"That's going to cost you, bitch!" he snarled. "That cute trick is really going to cost you."

He came after her then in a blind heat of rage, tearing the clothes from her body, sending her sprawling. They crashed to the floor together with him on top, using Diana's body to cushion his own fall. The back of her head bounced off the Mexican tile. A kaleidoscope of lights danced before her eyes. The room swirled around her while she drowned in a sea of despair. Davy's dead, she thought. My son is dead. . . .

By the time she could see again or breathe or move, resistance was useless. Carlisle was on her, inside her, pounding away.

Davy was still trying to waken the priest when the root cellar was rocked by the roar of gunfire.

Frightened, the boy cringed against the wall. No one had to tell him what the sound meant. That terrible man, that *ohb*, was out there with his mother, trying to kill her. Maybe he already had. Out in the living room, braced by Nana *Dahd*'s secret song, it had been easy to pretend to be brave, but now cowardly tears sprang to his eyes.

"Don't let him kill my mommy, Nana *Dahd*," he sobbed. "Please don't let him."

"Quiet!" Rita ordered.

Davy was startled by the harshness in Nana *Dahd*'s voice. Never had she spoken to him so sharply. "Listen. Come help me with the medicine basket. I can't get it out by myself."

Davy scrambled over the priest's prone form. He felt around Rita's body until he located the medicine basket still hidden beneath the ample folds of her dress. The basket was too large to slip out without first unfastening some of the buttons.

"Hurry," she urged as he struggled in the dark with the buttons and the slippery material. When the basket came free, it popped out and fell to the floor. "Find it," Rita ordered. "Take off the lid and give me the *owij*."

Davy groped on the floor until he found the basket with its tight-fitting lid still securely closed. After some struggle, he finally pried open the lid and fumbled inside until his fingers closed around the awl.

"Here it is," he said.

"Good. Put it in my good hand, then come close. Hold your hands steady and as far apart as you can."

"What are you going to do?" he asked.

For an answer, she poked at the twine around his wrists with the sharp point of the awl, the same way she had poked it through thousands of strands of coiled cactus. Pulled taut, the twine cut sharply into Davy's wrists. The child yelped with pain.

"Quiet," she commanded. "Don't make a sound, Olhoni, no matter how much it hurts." He bit his lip to stifle another cry.

"Once we are free," Rita continued, "we must stand on either side of the door and be absolutely silent. When the door opens, the *ohb* will be there. He will expect us to be tied up just as he left us. When he does not see us, he will step into the cellar. I will try to hit him with my cast or stab him with the *owij*. We will have only one chance. You must not wait to see what happens. Like I said in the song, you must run somewhere and hide."

"But what about you and my mother?" Davy whispered.

"No matter what happens, you must stay hidden until morning, until someone you know comes to find you."

Looks At Nothing sat hunched forward in the speeding tow truck as though by merely peering blindly ahead through the windshield he could somehow remove all obstacles from their path. "How soon will we be there?" he asked.

Fat Crack was driving flat out, red lights flashing. "Fifteen minutes," he said, not daring to take his eyes from the road long enough to check his watch. "Ten if we're lucky."

For a time, there was no sound in the cab other than the wind rushing through the open windows. "We will probably have to kill him, you know," the old man said finally. "Before it's over, one of us may kill the *ohb*. Have you ever killed before?"

It was a startling question, asked in the same manner Looks At Nothing might have inquired about the weather, but this was no rhetorical question, and it demanded a serious answer. "No," Fat Crack replied.

"I have," Looks At Nothing continued. "Long ago. When I worked in the mines in Ajo, I accidentally killed a man, another Indian. Afterward, there was no one to help me paint my face black, no one to bring me food and water for sixteen days. That is one of the reasons I'itoi took away my sight. If you are the one who kills the *ohb*, I will bring you food and water. If I do, will you bring it to me?"

As a child, Fat Crack had heard stories of how ancient Papago warriors who killed in battle were forced to remain outside their villages, purifying themselves by eating very little and by praying for sixteen days until the souls of those they killed were finally quiet. This was 1975. He was driving a two-ton tow truck, not riding a horse. After-battle ceremonies should have been a thing of the past, but they were not. Looks At Nothing was absolutely serious, and Fat Crack could not bring himself to deny the medicine man's request.

"Yes, old man," Fat Crack replied. "If you kill the *ohb*, I will bring food and water."

Louella Walker left Toby's bedside long enough to use the rest room down the hall. When she returned, she touched Brandon's shoulder. Although his eyes were wide open, he jumped as though wakened from a sound sleep. She nodded toward the door, and he followed her into the hallway.

"What is it?" he asked.

"There's a phone call for you at the nurses' station."

He seemed dazed. "A phone call? For me?" he asked vaguely.

She nodded. "Over there."

Watching him go to the phone made her heart ache. He looked much as his father had looked years earlier—the same impatient gestures, the same lean features. But Brandon was almost a stranger to her. She had expended so much energy and concentration denying what was happening to Toby that she had totally lost touch with her son.

Putting down the phone, he turned back toward her with his face contorted by anger or grief, Louella couldn't tell which. She wondered who had been on the phone. From his look, the news must have been as bad or worse than what was going on beyond the swinging door of her husband's room.

"Brandon," she said, reaching out to him. "What's wrong?"

He pushed her hand aside and shook his head. "Nothing," he said irritably. "It's work."

"Don't lie to me," Louella flared. "It isn't nothing. It must be important. I can see it in your face."

To her dismay, Brandon exploded in anger. "You're right. It is important. Terribly important, but what the hell am I supposed to do? I can't be in two goddamned places at once!"

With her child of a husband far beyond help, Louella searched her heart for strength enough to once more be a mother to her child. "It's all right, Brandon," she said, giving his shoulder a reassuring pat. "You do what you have to. Your father and I will stay right here. We'll be fine until you get back."

As Davy's hands came free, Rita's heart overflowed with thanks to Understanding Woman for giving her granddaughter the *owij*, for teaching Dancing Quail to be an expert with it. There was no tool Rita knew better, nothing she had held in her hands longer.

At once she reached down and went to work on the twine binding Davy's feet. It was important that he be totally free and capable of running, even if her own knots were still securely tied.

Breathing shallowly, the priest lay still, while no sounds at all came from the rest of the house. The ominous silence filled the old woman with misgiving. She knew some of what had been done to Gina, and she hated to think what that *ho'ok*, that monster, might be doing to Diana. Whatever it was, at least Davy wouldn't see, not if he followed her directions and did as he'd been told.

The twine around Davy's legs tugged free at last. Rita turned her attention on her own bindings. With one arm in a cast, it should have been much more difficult, but her craftsman's fingers quickly learned the secrets of Andrew Carlisle's crude knots, which melted apart beneath the probing point of her awl.

With Davy quaking beside her, Rita began to pray. First she addressed I'itoi, asking that the boy and his mother both be granted strength and courage. Then she spoke to Father John's God, asking that the priest be spared from dying there on the root-cellar floor. Finally, to comfort herself as much as the boy, she took up the refrain of her song, crooning softly in the darkness.

> *"Remember what I say, Little Olhoni,*
> *You must run swiftly and not look back.*
> *That is the only way to help your mother.*
> *That is the only way to help me.*
> *Be like I'itoi, little Olhoni.*
> *Hide in a crack and do not come out."*

"Get dressed," he whispered in her ear, snapping her head back with a savage pull on her hair that loosened some of it from the roots. As tears sprang to her eyes, the ghost of an elusive memory fluttered briefly, but she couldn't capture it. It required all her mental stamina to resist the temptation to cry out. Earlier, sinking his teeth deep into the tender flesh of her breast, he had elicited one involuntary gasp of pain. She had sensed his excited, eager response. She was grimly determined not to let it happen again.

Carlisle let go of her hair, and she fell limply back to the bed. "I said move!"

Diana had lost all sense of time. She might have been battling with him for minutes or hours or days. After his first, frenzied attack, he had dragged her from the living room to the bedroom, where he had assaulted her again. Survival instinct warned her to obey his commands, but her body refused. Bruised and bloodied, her flesh functioned at a level that was somehow beyond whatever further violation Andrew Carlisle could inflict.

Davy's dead. The words ran through her head like a broken record. Davy's dead, and so is Rita. Grappling with catastrophe, Diana lost all will to carry on. Whatever happened to her no longer mattered.

Carlisle grabbed one ankle and twisted it until Diana was forced onto her back. She lay naked on the bed while he feasted his eyes on her. He particularly admired the series of angry bruises around her swollen nipples. He congratulated himself for his self-restraint for being able to let go once he had fastened his teeth on her. He was saving the nipples for later.

He enjoyed the look of wary watchfulness in her eyes. She must be wondering, dreading to learn what might come next. He regretted that he couldn't get it up again right that minute, but there was plenty of time. He would show her that, hard-on or not, he was still full of surprises.

Her gritty silence annoyed him. Diana Ladd was one tough cookie, but he knew she wouldn't be able to deny him forever. He'd find her weakness eventually. In the face of his carefully focused efforts, she wouldn't always keep quiet. When the agonized sounds finally escaped her lips, they would be music to his ears. You'll come around, he thought, smiling down at her.

Carlisle had begun the complicated process of subjugation. Having once established dominance, it was important to consolidate his control, to show Diana Ladd exactly who was boss.

Stepping from the foot of the bed to the side of it, he reached down and yanked ruthlessly on the exposed mound of auburn pubic hair, pulling out a handful of the stiff, curly stuff. She winced and gritted her teeth, but again she refused to cry out. Damn her! She was deliberately spoiling his fun.

He moved to the head of the bed and stood looking down at her, hoping that she'd shrink away from him and try to get away, but she lay beneath his gaze without moving, staring brazenly back at him, daring him to hit her.

And so he did, slapping her hard across the face. He smiled at the rewarding droplet of blood that appeared almost instantly at the corner of her mouth. Maybe now he'd start getting through to her. He hit her three times in all—twice open-handed and once with the back of his hand. He didn't have to put much effort into it. The blows were gratuitous, stinging slaps, administered mechanically and without emotion, calculated more to humiliate than hurt.

Andrew Carlisle hit the woman primarily for effect and for his own amusement. He hit her because she dared stare back at him. He hit her because he could. It never occurred to him that hitting her was a tactical blunder. That thought never crossed his mind.

Diana tasted blood in her mouth where a tooth had cut through her cheek. She focused on the salty taste, and that, combined with the teeth-rattling blows, shocked Diana out of her stunned lethargy and forced her to remember that other man who had once hit her like this, who had pulled her hair out by the roots. The sudden surge of memory galvanized her in a way Carlisle couldn't possibly have foreseen or predicted. It rekindled the spark of her old anger, relit a raging fire that lost hope had almost extinguished.

Without a word, she sat up.

"Get dressed," he ordered again, flinging a pair of shorts and a tank top in her direction. "Wear these, but no shoes. I like my serving women dressed but barefoot."

She stared blankly at the clothing. They weren't what she'd been wearing before. Those, torn from her body in his initial fierce attack, still lay in a heap on the living-room floor.

Carlisle leered at her from the doorway, savoring the marks he'd left on her sore and naked body, but she refused to turn away from him while she dressed. "Hey," he said jokingly, "except for a few stretch marks here and there, you've got a pretty good bod. Anybody ever tell you that?"

A flush of embarrassment crept up her face. She said nothing. He came over to where she sat on the edge of the bed and shoved the muzzle of the gun hard into the tender flesh of her already bruised breast.

"Don't you have any manners at all?" he demanded. "Didn't your mother teach you that when someone pays you a compliment, you're supposed to say thank you?"

"Thank you," she murmured.

"That's better. Now, get moving. We're going to the kitchen. I want you to fix me some dinner or, better yet, breakfast. Sex always makes me hungry. How about you?"

Without answering, she started for the kitchen at once, hoping he would read defeat and submission in her every action. But Diana Ladd knew she was fighting him again, and Andrew Carlisle was far too pleased with himself to notice.

There were two sounds in the room—the priest's breathing and the mouse-like twitchings of Rita's *owij* picking at the twine. Davy wished Bone were there. He longed for the dog's comforting presence, but Bone was at the vet's or dead now, too, along with everybody else.

Forbidden to make a sound, Davy thought about what Rita had told him, for him to run away, to find a crack, to hide. A crack.

He thought about cracks, about the jagged one

in the lumpy plaster beside his bed. He always examined that crack in great detail when he was supposed to be taking a nap, wondering if it had grown bigger or smaller since the last time he saw it. But a fly could never hide in there. Davy couldn't even put his thumbnail in it. Flies were bigger than that.

A crack. The verse came to him, singsong, the way he had heard it at school. "Step on a crack, and you'll break your mother's back." But that was a sidewalk crack. Again, not big enough.

There was Fat Crack, but he wasn't a crack at all. He was a person.

Then, finally, Davy remembered the cave he and Bone had found, the chimney in the mountain behind the house. Now that he thought about it, maybe that cave wasn't a cave at all. It was a crack—a crack in the mountain. That was where he would go, where he would run to hide if he ever got a chance.

Suddenly, there were voices on the other side of the door. Davy's heart pounded, wondering how soon the door would fly open again, how soon before he would have to make his dash for freedom.

At first, Davy heard only the man's voice, talking on and on, but then he heard another voice, that of a woman, softer and higher. Straining, he recognized his mother's voice. She wasn't dead after all.

Rita had finally managed to free herself. Davy tugged at the old woman's hand, wanting to tell her the news, but she laid her fingers on his lips, warning him to silence. Carefully they moved into position. A sliver of light had appeared under the door. They used that as a guide.

They stood on either side of the door for what seemed like forever. Eventually, the smell of frying bacon came wafting into Davy's nose. It was a long time since he and the Bone had shared their last tortillas. The smell of that frying bacon filled Davy's nostrils and made his mouth water. His feet itched. He needed to go to the bathroom. Davy began to doubt that the door would ever open. He fidgeted a little, but Rita clamped her good hand down hard on his shoulder, poking him painfully with the awl in the process. After that, he stood quietly and waited.

A hundred yards or so from the turnoff, Fat Crack doused the lights and parked the truck. He had kept the lights flashing almost the entire way, but as they neared the house, he turned off everything, flashers and headlights included.

"Now what?" he asked, shutting down the ignition and parking the truck just beyond a curve that concealed the house from view.

"We go down there and try to take him by surprise."

"Good luck," Fat Crack returned. "What about the dog?"

"Dog?"

"Rita has a huge dog named Oh'o. When I was here earlier, he almost bit my leg off."

"He must be inside," Looks At Nothing said.

Right, Fat Crack thought. Sure he is. Famous

last words. With a disgusted shake of his head, the younger man hurried around to the passenger side and helped Looks At Nothing climb down. Moving as quietly as possible, they headed for the driveway that led down to the house. The dark made no difference to the blind medicine man, but when they stepped off the pavement, Fat Crack had some difficulty negotiating the rocky terrain.

They'd gone only a few steps when Fat Crack saw, a mile or so away, the approaching headlights of another vehicle. That other car worried him. What if Looks At Nothing was wrong? What if the *ohb* was only now coming to the house, only now beginning his attack? If he drove up right then, they would be trapped in the open driveway with no means of retreat or defense.

"I have my stick," the old man was saying. "What will you use for a weapon?"

"A rock, I guess," Fat Crack replied. "I don't see anything else."

"Good," Looks At Nothing said. "Get one."

Fat Crack was bent over picking one up when he heard the dog. This time there was no warning bark, only a hair-raising, low-throated growl. The night was black, and Bone was a black and brown dog, totally invisible to the naked eye. Fat Crack straightened up and looked around, expecting to fend off an all-out attack. Instead, Looks At Nothing spoke forcefully into the darkness.

"Oh'o, *ihab*!" the medicine man commanded. "Bone, here!"

To Fat Crack's astonishment, the dog obeyed at once, materializing out of the brush beside the road. He went directly to the old man, tail lowered and wagging tentatively.

Preoccupied with the dog, they failed to notice the other car again until it braked at the head of the drive. Too late Fat Crack tugged at Looks At Nothing's arm, trying to pull him down the hill toward the meager cover of a mesquite tree.

All the way from TMC, Brandon had cursed himself for being in his mother's car instead of the Galaxy, for being cut off from all communications. If only he had talked to Maddern again, they might have coordinated some kind of game plan. As it was, the only thing he'd thought to tell Hank was for him to call Diana and warn her.

He reached down and checked the .38 Smith & Wesson Special in his ankle holster. Police officers were required to be armed at all times. Ankle holsters were the only feasible choice when wearing ordinary clothing.

Brandon's car sped over the top of the rise and roared down the long canyon road. Ahead and to the right, he could see lights glowing peacefully in the windows of Diana Ladd's solitary house. Maybe he and Farrell were pushing panic buttons for no good reason.

Walker slowed and switched on his turn signal. As his tires dropped off the hard surface onto the dirt driveway, the headlights caught two shadowy figures dodging into the underbrush ahead of him. Walker felt a rush of adrenaline. He had surprised them, caught them in the act.

He jammed on the brakes, cutting the motor,

turning off the lights. Expecting gunfire, he ducked down on the seat and drew his weapon. Heart pounding, he lay there waiting, with the desert night still and expectant around him.

Two of them, he thought. So who had that bastard Carlisle brought along with him? Whoever it was, Brandon thought, they're going to get more than they bargained for. Not only was he here, Geet Farrell was on his way with plenty of reinforcements. In addition, there was that godawful dog. If those two jokers ran into Bone out there in the dark somewhere, they'd have yet another rude awakening.

Carlisle scrounged through the refrigerator and came away with a pound of bacon and half a dozen eggs, which he handed over to Diana. "Bacon, crisp. Eggs, over easy. Toast. Orange juice and coffee. Think you can handle that, honey? You know, if you're a good-enough cook, maybe I'll keep you around awhile. We'll play house, just the two of us—cooking and fucking—and not necessarily in that order. What do you think of that?"

Diana said nothing. Carlisle, enamored with the sound of his own voice, didn't notice. While he continued with his rambling monologue, Diana gathered what she needed for cooking—frying pan, salt and pepper shakers, the spatula. What would happen if she turned on the gas in the oven and didn't light it? Would enough propane accumulate to cause an explosion, or would the oven just come on eventually when the gas seeped out far enough to reach the pilot lights on top of the stove? Anything was worth a try. Diana turned on the control.

She worked mechanically, trying not to think about Rita and Davy. That would divert her, take her mind away from the problem. She put a few pieces of bacon into the frying pan, started the fire under it, and loaded coffee and water into the percolator.

Still talking, Carlisle had meandered into a long self-pitying dissertation about prison life. "Do you know what they do to people like me in places like that?" he was saying. "Do you have any idea? Answer me when I speak to you."

"No," she said, "I have no idea."

A spatter of hot fat leaped out of the frying pan as she turned the bacon, stinging Diana's wrist. She jumped back, but the pain on her bare wrist gave her the beginning glimmer of an idea. Quickly, she dumped the rest of the pound of bacon into the frying pan and turned up the heat.

"How do you like your eggs?" she asked.

"I already told you. Over easy, same as I like my women. Get it?" He laughed. "Pay attention, girl. You pay attention to everything I say, and maybe I'll let you hang around a little longer."

She nodded, knowing it was a lie, and stirred the sizzling bacon, willing the fat to render out of it, welcoming the painful spatters that found their way to the bare skin of her arm and wrist.

"That was Gary's problem, you know," he continued offhandedly. "He didn't pay attention. That's why I had to get rid of him."

Trying to shut him out, Diana almost missed Carlisle's throw-away admission. Then, when she did understand, the what of it if not the how, she fought off the temptation to react. It was still too soon.

Ducking down on the seat to make himself less of a target, Brandon waited for the bark from Bone that would signal the dog's attack or at least alert those in the house to their danger. The expected bark never came.

"Damn," Walker muttered. The dog was probably inside the house, sleeping on the job. The detective lay there and tried to strategize. He had to assume that both his opponents were armed and dangerous. Two-to-one odds aren't very good, especially for a cop dealing with crooks who may not care that much if they live or die.

He considered honking the horn to alert the people in the house of the impending danger, but that might do more harm than good. If Diana came outside to see what was going on, she might possibly fall into the wrong hands. What if the crooks took off with her before help arrived?

Finally, Walker hit on the only strategy that seemed feasible. He would attempt to make his way to the house undetected. Once inside, he and Diana could probably hold the bad guys off long enough for help to arrive and catch them in a cross fire. Once the decision was made, Walker moved to put it into action.

Closing his eyes so the overhead light wouldn't rob him of night vision, he eased open the passenger door and quickly dropped to the ground. The door closed behind him with a dull thud, and he scuttled silently off into the desert, swinging wide and hoping to make it to the side of the house before Carlisle and his pal realized what he was up to.

The bacon turned to hard, brittle curls in the pan, but an oblivious Andrew Carlisle continued talking. "There are tools for rape, you see, things you wouldn't normally think about, but in prison you have to use whatever's handy. You'd be surprised what people get off on. This gun, for instance. What would you think if I crammed that all the way up inside you? Would it make you come? The metal gun sight might bother you a little, don't you think?"

Diana's stomach lurched with dread, and the hand holding the wooden spatula trembled uncontrollably.

His voice rose in pitch. "Look at me when I speak to you. I asked you a simple question. What would you think of it?"

She looked. He was grinning at her, holding the .45, fondling it, sensually stroking the long barrel with his fingertips. "I wouldn't like it," she said.

"Wouldn't you?" he asked, eyeing her speculatively. "I think you would. Maybe after I eat, we could have a lesson. I'll show you how it works right here on the kitchen table. Mr. Colt has a permanent hard-on for you. I think he'd enjoy it."

He paused, as if waiting for Diana to comment. When she didn't, he bent over and pulled something out of the top of his boot. She saw him out of the corner of her eye and trembled to think that he had retrieved his knife, which he would use on her as well, but when he straightened up, he wasn't holding the knife at all. Between his fingers was a key—a familiar, old-fashioned skeleton key.

"Or maybe, little Mama," he added with a malicious grin, "since you don't think you'd like it, maybe I should bring that kid of yours out here and cram it down his throat or maybe up his ass a couple of inches. How much could he take? How much could you? What would you do then, Diana? Would you ask me to stop? Would you beg me to do it to you instead of him? Would you crawl on your hands and knees on the floor and kiss my feet and beg?"

A shock of recognition sent needles and pins through her hands and feet. Davy wasn't dead after all. He was alive and in the root cellar. There was still hope, still a chance.

Suddenly, frowning, Carlisle stood up. "Hey, wait a minute, aren't you burning the bacon?"

Putting the key down on the table and retrieving the gun, he started toward the stove. When he was three steps away, Diana grabbed the overheated handle of the frying pan and heaved it full in his face. Pieces of blackened bacon clung to his skin wherever they landed. He screamed as fiery-hot fat burned through his clothing, sealing it to his skin.

Diana dodged to one side as the gun roared to life, shattering the window behind her.

* * *

Walker, riveted by both the ungodly scream and the gunfire, knew his worst nightmare had come true. Somehow his opponents had made their way inside and were firing guns. Someone was hit and dying.

Forgetting about cover, Walker charged toward the house himself, circling around the thicket of gigantic prickly pear and coming up on the front porch from the opposite direction. He tried the door handle and found it locked. He tried kicking it, but the stout old door didn't give way. The windows all had screens. From inside the house, Walker heard the sounds of an ongoing battle, but off to the side of the porch, the detective caught sight of movement.

"Stop," he shouted, but two shadowy figures simply disappeared into the darkness beyond the porch. Two of them, he thought. Some inside and at least two still out here. How the hell many of them are there? Walker wondered grimly.

In silent pursuit, he moved sideways off the porch. At the side of the house, he encountered only a massive wall with a tall wooden gate. He tried the gate, but it appeared to be latched from the inside.

Through a nightmare of searing pain, Andrew Carlisle tried to wipe the clinging grease from his face and eyes. He could see nothing. I'm blind! he thought furiously. The bitch blinded me!

He slipped on the greasy floor and crashed into the table, banging it into the wall before managing to right himself. With superhuman effort, he pulled himself above the terrible pain.

"I'll kill you," he whispered hoarsely. "So help me God, bitch, I'll kill you if it's the last thing I do!"

Diana watched in horror as Carlisle attempted to wipe the blistering grease from his skin and eyes. Pieces of his face seemed to melt away with his hand, dissolving like the water-soaked Wicked Witch of the West in the *Wizard of Oz.*

"I'll kill you," Carlisle muttered over and over. It was a chant and incantation. "I'll kill you."

Somehow he still held Diana's .45. Frozen with fear, Diana stared at the weapon, waiting for the death-dealing explosion that would end her life, but for some strange reason Carlisle didn't seem to be pointing it at her. He turned around and around, like a child playing blindman's bluff.

"Where are you, bitch?" he demanded. Only then did Diana realize that he couldn't see. The bacon grease had blinded him.

Holding her breath for fear the sound might betray her whereabouts, Diana glanced around the room, looking for an escape hatch or place to hide. On the floor beside the up-ended table, she spied the fallen key to the root cellar. As soon as she saw it, she dived for it, even though Carlisle was between her and the key.

Hearing movement, Carlisle lunged in her direction. They collided in midair and crashed to the floor together. The force of the blow knocked the .45 from Carlisle's hand. It spun across the floor, coming to rest at the base of the sink. Of the two, he was far stronger, but being able to see gave Diana a slight advantage. Twisting away, she eluded his grasp and retrieved the key. She scrambled toward the root-cellar door and was almost there when his powerful fingers clamped shut around her ankles.

She kicked at his fingers, but her bare feet had no effect on the hands inexorably dragging her away from the door. She fought him desperately but despairingly, realizing she was no match for him, that it was only a matter of time.

Dimly, Diana became aware of Bone's frantic scratching on the sliding glass door. If only she could let him into the house. Maybe, with the dog's help . . .

Suddenly, for the barest moment, Carlisle let go of her. She scrambled away from him, and this time managed to shove the key into the lock before he grabbed hold of her again. She tried to push him away only to have a smarting pain shoot across her hand and up her arm. Shocked, Diana looked at her arm and hand as blood spurted out. Carlisle had his knife again. This time she knew he would kill her with it. There would be no escape.

Stymied by the latched gate, Brandon Walker dropped back and then vaulted over the barrier, which seemed to be covered by a layer of wet blankets. Inside the yard, he landed on something soft and yielding, something human. His added weight brought the other man down. They fell to the ground as one and grappled there briefly until he glimpsed Fat Crack's face in the pale starlight.

"Fat Crack!" Walker exclaimed. "What the . . ."

"It's the detective," Fat Crack said simultaneously.

From deeper in the yard came Looks At Nothing's commanding voice. "We must hurry! Come," he ordered.

Fat Crack let go at once, and they both struggled to their feet. In the melee, Walker had dropped his .38 Special. They wasted precious seconds searching for it. At last Fat Crack found it and gave it back.

"If you're out here," Brandon whispered, "who's in there?"

"The *ohb*," Fat Crack answered. "It's the *ohb*."

Faced with her bloodied arm and inarguable evidence of her own mortality, Diana resolved that even if she died, somehow her son would live. Once more Carlisle's fingers locked onto her ankle. Once more he dragged her toward him and toward the raised knife he held above his head, waiting to plunge it into her.

She searched desperately for something to hold onto, something to give her purchase on the slippery floor. Suddenly, her flailing hands encountered heat—the still fiery-hot frying pan. Ignoring the blistering handle, she picked it up and drove it with all her strength toward Andrew Carlisle's forehead.

* * *

He couldn't see it, but Carlisle felt the super-heated frying pan whizzing toward him. He drew back in panic, holding up his arms in an attempt to ward off the blow. The frying pan missed his skull but struck his hand, knocking the knife away from him. While he groped blindly for it, he heard her scrabbling away from him again. Weaponless except for his bare hands, he crawled after her.

Partway across the room, something rushed past him, making for the outside door. He turned to it as if to follow.

The momentary respite gave Diana one more chance. This time she made it all the way to the root-cellar door. Still on her knees, she reached up and turned the key in the lock. Before she could move out of the way, the door banged open, knocking her backward into the wall.

At the sound of the second gunshot, Davy almost burst into tears. Once more Rita shushed him. "Ready now," she whispered. "When the key turns, open the door and run."

"I'll kill you," the man was saying over and over outside the door. "I'll kill you."

Davy's heart leaped to his throat. His mother was still alive. Would she be when the door opened? He crossed his fingers and tried to remember how to pray.

The key filled the lock. The tiny keyhole-shaped patch of light disappeared, but the key didn't turn. The door didn't open.

Again they waited. Davy heard another sound now—the Bone, scratching frantically at the back door, wanting to be let in. Oh'o was home, but he couldn't get inside to help them.

And then, miraculously, the key did turn. Davy shoved the door with all his might, flung it open, and dashed outside. In the middle of the room, he encountered a man—at least it looked like a man—crawling toward him on his hands and knees. This terrible apparition, its face a misshapen mass of bloodied blisters, must be the *ohb*.

Pausing long enough for only one look at that terrifying visage, Davy turned and raced for the sliding glass door.

The pain was terrible, beyond anything he could have imagined, but what was worse, Carlisle feared Diana Ladd had escaped. He started toward the door.

"Where are you, bitch?"

"Here," Diana responded from someplace else in the room. "I'm behind you." To decoy Davy's safe escape, she wanted Carlisle's attention focused solely on her.

"Where?"

"Right here," she answered again, and it sounded as though she was laughing at him.

Doggedly, like an unstoppable monster from an old B-grade movie, Andrew Carlisle whirled and came crawling toward her, but before he made any progress, something heavy landed on his back. Horrified, he felt a dog's inch-long canines plunge into the back of his neck.

* * *

Too stunned to move and trying to stem the flow of blood from her own arm, Diana could do nothing but watch. The dog was everywhere at once, huge jaws snapping. He leaped up and backward and sideways, always staying just out of the man's reach. Finally, Bones's jaws closed over Carlisle's wrist.

While the man howled in inhuman rage, the dog shook his massive head. Bones crunched in Carlisle's mangled wrist. Tendons and nerves snapped like so many broken rubber bands.

Arm upraised, *owij* in hand, Rita emerged from the root cellar ready to do battle. She, too, stood transfixed, watching the man struggle to escape the attacking dog. Trying to save his mangled wrist, Carlisle attempted one last kick. The dog let go of the hand and pounced on the foot. As the dog's jaws closed once more, Carlisle folded himself into a fetal position.

Rita remained where she was for a moment, surveying the room, while Carlisle sobbed brokenly. "Get the dog off me. Please, get him off."

The Indian woman pocketed her *owij*. It was no longer needed. Across the room, she saw both the knife and the gun. She hurried at once to retrieve them. Only when she had them both firmly in her possession did she speak to the dog.

"Oh'o, *ihab*." The dog came to her side at once, wagging his tail, waiting to be petted. "Good *gogs*," she crooned, patting his shaggy head. "It's over."

Rita turned from the dog and placed the gun

in Diana's lap. "Here," she said. "If you wish to shoot him, now's your chance. Do it quickly."

Diana looked from Rita to the stricken form of Andrew Carlisle, who lay sobbing on the floor in a widening pool of his own urine. Finally, Diana looked down at the gun and shook her head.

"No," she said. "I don't have to now. It wouldn't be self-defense."

A radiant smile suffused Rita's weathered old face. "Good," she said. "I'itoi would be proud of you."

Behind them, Brandon Walker burst into the room. Bone turned to fend off this new attack, but before he could, the oven door blew its hinges with a resounding thump, knocking the dog to the floor.

Crying and laughing both, Diana knelt beside Bone and cradled his massive head in her lap. The dog looked up at her gratefully and thumped his long tail on the floor. He wasn't hurt, but it had been a hard day for a dog. He didn't want to get up.

Detective Farrell and Myrna Louise arrived just ahead of a phalanx of police cars dispatched by Hank Maddern at the Pima County Sheriff's Department. For the first time in her life, she refused Andrew's summons when he asked for her. Stone-faced and without getting out of the car, Myrna Louise watched while her son was loaded into a waiting ambulance. Ironically, he was taken first. Of all the injuries, his were deemed the most serious.

But not serious enough, Myrna Louise thought bitterly, not nearly serious enough. If she'd been lucky—and she had never been lucky where her son was concerned—Andrew would have died. Someone would have put a bullet through his wretched head and taken him out of his misery, the way they used to do with rabid dogs.

After that, another stretcher came out of the house with someone strapped to it. The old Indian woman—what was her name again—limped heavily along beside the stretcher and climbed into the waiting ambulance to ride to the hospital, although she herself didn't seem to be hurt.

A few minutes later, Myrna Louise recognized Diana Ladd. She, too, was carried past the detective's car to an ambulance, with a man walking along beside her. Thank God they weren't dead, Myrna Louise thought gratefully. She never could have lived with herself if that had happened.

Myrna Louise sat there quietly, knowing that eventually it would be her turn to answer questions. What would she say about Andrew when they asked her? Tell the truth, she thought. And what would happen when the neighbors on Weber Drive found out that Andrew Carlisle was her son? Would they still speak to her?

Myrna Louise sighed. She could always move again, she supposed. She'd done it before. Maybe she'd get herself one of those U-Hauls. What did they call that, "an adventure in moving"? She'd drive herself far away and start over again, somewhere where nobody knew her.

But first, she thought, she'd have to get herself

a driver's license, and maybe even a pair of glasses.

Davy sat in the crack and waited. That's what he would call it from now on, I'itoi's crack. He wondered how it would feel to be a fly and to go back down to the house. He would be able to see what was happening, but nobody would know he was there. He wanted to know and yet he didn't. He was afraid to know.

His mother was still alive when he ran past her, and so was Nana *Dahd*, but were they still? He couldn't tell. Bone had wanted to come with him, but he had ordered the dog to stay. Now, he wished he hadn't. Why didn't Bone come looking for him? Why didn't someone else?

While he watched, a string of cop cars came streaming down the canyon road, lights flashing. It looked like a parade, except it wasn't. There were no floats, no marching bands. The police cars were all going to his house. What would they find there? Would his mother still be alive?

When he first reached the cleft in the rock, he was panting, out of breath, afraid that the terrible man was right behind him. Now, as more time passed, he wondered who would come for him. Nana *Dahd* had been very specific about that. She had told him he must wait until morning, wait for someone he knew.

He shifted his body. The sharp rocks behind his back were growing uncomfortable. What if they forgot all about him and nobody came? Maybe he'd end up living there forever. How long was forever, anyway?

Three more sets of flashing lights came down the winding road and pulled in at the driveway. How many police cars did it take? he wondered. What was happening? He kept thinking his mother would come for him or Rita, but the longer it went without anyone coming, the more he was afraid they were dead.

What happened to you after you were dead? That was one of the things he was supposed to talk about with Father John the next time he saw him. Davy thought about Father John lying there so still on the root-cellar floor, and he thought about what the priest had said as they were leaving to take Bone to the vet.

How had that prayer gone? Davy squeezed his eyes shut and concentrated, trying to remember the exact words.

"In the name of the Father, of the Son, and of the Holy Ghost."

The Father he could understand, and he could understand the Son, but who was the Holy Ghost? Maybe, thought Davy, the Holy Ghost was I'itoi. So he bowed his head, just as he had seen Rita do, just like Father John, and he said a prayer for his mother, for Nana *Dahd*, for Father John, and also for Oh'o. He finished by praying, "In the name of the Father, of the Son, and of I'itoi. Amen." It sounded a little different, but Davy was sure it meant the same thing.

Just then, as he finished the prayer, he heard a

rock go scrabbling down the face of the cliff. He drew back inside the rocky cleft, making himself as small as possible, holding his breath, afraid that somehow the *ohb* had managed to escape and was coming after him.

He listened. Clearly now, he could hear footsteps coming closer and closer, as though whoever was coming knew the path to the crack, as though they knew all about Davy's secret hiding place.

"Olhoni?" Someone was calling his name, his Indian name, but it wasn't Nana *Dahd*. Who could it be then? No one else called him that. The voice wasn't familiar, and Nana *Dahd* had given him strict orders to wait for someone he knew.

Then, suddenly, Bone thrust his spiked head into the entrance to the crack and covered the boy's face with wet, slobbery kisses. Behind the dog, a man's face peered in the small opening.

"Olhoni? Are you in there?"

Weak with relief, Davy let his breath out. It was Fat Crack. "*Heu'u*," he answered. "Yes."

"Come on, boy," the Indian said, gently moving the dog aside. "An old man and I are waiting to take you to the hospital."

Hospital? The word made Davy's heart hurt. "Is my mother all right?" he asked. "Is Nana *Dahd*?"

"Your mother is hurt, but not bad," the Indian said quietly. "Rita went with Father John. Come on. Everyone will be better once they know you are safe."

As soon as Davy was outside the cave, Bone careened around him in ecstatically happy circles, but the boy was not ready to play. This was still far too serious. What he had lived through that day was anything but a game.

"What about the *ohb*?" Davy asked. "Is he dead?"

"No, *nawoj*," Fat Crack replied. "The *ohb* isn't dead, but he didn't win. He's in the hospital, too. Your dog almost bit his hand off. Rita wouldn't let him."

"She should have," Davy said angrily. "What will happen to him now?"

Fat Crack shrugged. "The *Mil-gahn* will send him back to the *Mil-gahn* jail, I guess."

"Will he get out again?" Davy asked.

"Who knows?" Fat Crack said, shaking his head. "That, Olhoni, is up to the *Mil-gahn*, isn't it."

Epilogue

*W*ANTING TO BE the first to kill, Rattlesnake crept close to Evil Siwani's camp, so the next morning, when the battle started, Rattlesnake killed first, and he chose the place that is now called Rattlesnake House.

When the battle was finally over, Evil Siwani was dead, and his house and all his people had been destroyed.

So I'itoi told the warriors who had helped him that they should choose where they wanted to live. Some people wanted to be farmers, and they went to live by the river. Since then they have been called Akimel O'odham, or the River People.

Some of the warriors were hunters, so they went to live near Waw Giwulk, which means Constricted Rock and which the Mil-gahn call Baboquivari. There they found plenty of mule deer to hunt and lots of other good food to eat. The people who stayed there have been called Tohono O'odham, or the Desert People.

And that is the story of how the Desert People emerged from the center of the earth to help I'itoi battle the Evil Siwani, and how they came to live here in this desert *country where,* nawoj, *my friend, they still continue to live even to this day.*

The feast was well under way. In four days' time, word had got around the reservation that Rita Antone's luck had changed for the better. The ritual singing had been well attended, and the feast was a rousing success. The expense was more than Rita alone could have managed, but someone else was helping to defray the cost. Eduardo Jose, the bootlegger from Ahngam, whose grandson, Lucky One, had recently been released from the Pinal County Jail, was more than happy to help out.

Rita had spent two days sitting at Father John's bedside at St. Mary's Hospital. Now, she sat at the head of the long oilcloth-covered table in the feast house at Sells. Davy, his face still bearing telltale traces of red chili, sat on one side of her. Diana Ladd sat on the other.

Shyly, a girl of sixteen or seventeen sidled up to Rita's chair, hanging back a moment before daring to say what she had come to say. "I remember you," she said almost in a whisper. "You used to make us eat our vegetables."

Instantly, Davy's ears perked up. "Wait a minute. You, too? I thought I was the only one."

Rita laughed. "No," she said. "I try to get all children to do that. Gordon taught me to eat my vegetables when I was sick in California."

"Gordon your son?" Davy asked.

"No. Gordon my husband. I was very sick, and he and Mrs. Bailey, the *Mil-gahn* lady he worked for, told me that if I ate all my vegetables, it would make me better, and it worked. I'm still here, aren't I?"

They all laughed at that, even Diana.

In four days, that was the first time Davy had heard his mother laugh, so maybe now she would be all right, just like Detective Walker said. He had told Davy it would take time, that the *ohb*, Carlisle, had hurt her badly, but that if they were very careful of her, she would be okay.

The boy looked around, noticing for the first time that the men had all disappeared.

"Where's Fat Crack?" he asked.

Rita shrugged. "Out by the truck, I guess."

Davy promptly set off to find him.

The four men gathered in an informal group around the hood of Fat Crack's tow truck. The medicine man tried to explain Whore Sickness to the detective. He told him it was Staying Sickness and not the bacon grease that had caused Andrew Carlisle's blindness. This was all quite strange to Brandon Walker, although he tried to listen with an open mind.

No one was surprised when Looks At Nothing opened his leather pouch and pulled out one of his cigarettes. Walker watched with renewed amazement as once again the old man flicked open his Zippo lighter and unerringly lit the cigarette.

Upon hearing Brandon would be driving the boy and the two women out to the reservation for the baptism feast, Hank Maddern had warned his friend about not being sucked into some strange kind of peyote ritual. Brandon had quickly put Hank's worries to rest.

"Believe me," he said. "Tobacco is the only thing in that old man's cigarettes, and it's not very damn good tobacco, either."

Looks At Nothing took a deep drag, said, "Nawoj," and then passed it along to Father John. The priest had spent three full days in the hospital being treated for a concussion, but he had convinced the doctor that he had to be dismissed in time to go to a feast in Sells on Friday. The doctor had grumbled, but in the end he had let the old man have his way.

The cigarette passed from the priest to Fat Crack to the detective, and back, at last, to the medicine man. Far to the west, a thundercloud rose over the desert. Periodically, lightning lit up the cloud's billowing interior, but the rains had not yet come. The California river toads still slept quietly in their hardened mud beds.

"He is a good boy," Looks At Nothing said, "but I am worried about one thing."

"What's that?" Father John asked.

He was sure it would be some complaint that the other part of the bargain, the *Mil-gahn* baptism, was going too slowly, but he had only just got out of the hospital that very afternoon. Davy Ladd was scheduled to be baptized during the eleven o'clock mass at San Xavier the day after tomorrow. What more did the old man want?

But Looks At Nothing's objection had nothing to do with that. "Edagith Gohk Je'e," he said, calling Davy by his new Indian name. "One With Two Mothers, this boy, has too many mothers and not enough fathers.

"There are four of us," Looks At Nothing continued, "and all nature goes in fours. Why could we not agree to be father to this fatherless boy, all four of us together? We each have things to teach, and we all have things to learn."

As soon as Brandon heard the words, he knew Looks At Nothing was right. No matter how much Rita Antone and Diana Ladd loved Davy, they could not be his father. A lump caught in Brandon Walker's throat as he listened. Fatherless himself for three days now, Brandon Walker felt for Davy Ladd almost as much as he hurt for himself.

It grew quiet in the circle. No one said aloud that he would or would not accept the assignment. That was a foregone conclusion. The decision had been made for them long before they were asked. Looks At Nothing had decreed it so, and that was the way it would be.

Davy himself came running up just then. "What are you guys doing?" he demanded. "I looked around the feast house, and you were all gone."

"We were talking," Brandon Walker said.

"What about?"

"You."

"About me? What were you saying?"

"That somebody needs to take you into Tucson for a haircut," Brandon said, affectionately ruffling Davy's hair, but being careful about the stitches.

"You mean it?" Davy asked. "Honest? To a real barber?"

"That's right," Brandon Walker replied with a slight grin. "You see, Davy, mothers don't give crew cuts. Barbers do."

Here's a sneak preview of
J.A. Jance's new novel

QUEEN OF THE NIGHT

Available now
wherever books are sold

Prologue

*T*HEY SAY IT *happened long ago that a young Tohono O'odham woman fell in love with a Yaqui warrior, a Hiakim, and went to live with him and his people, far to the South. Every evening, her mother, Old White-Haired Woman, would go outside by herself and listen. After a while her daughter's spirit would speak to her from her new home far away. One day, Old White-Haired Woman heard nothing, so she went to find her husband.*

"Our daughter is ill," Old White-Haired Woman told him. "I must go to her."

"But the Hiakim live far from here," he said, "and you are a bent old woman. How will you get there?"

"I will ask I'itoi, the Spirit of Goodness, to help me."

Elder Brother heard the woman's plea. He sent Coyote, Ban, to guide Old White-Haired Woman's steps on her long journey, and he sent the Ali Chu Chum O'odham, the Little People—the animals and birds, to help her along the way. When she was thirsty, Ban led her to water. When she was hungry, The Birds, U'u Whig, brought her seeds and beans to eat.

After weeks of traveling, Old White-Haired Woman

finally reached the land of the Hiakim. There she learned that her daughter was sick and dying.

"Please take my son home to our people," Old White-Haired Woman's daughter begged. "If you don't, his father's people will turn him into a warrior."

You must understand, nawoj, my friend, that from the time the Tohono O'odham emerged from the center of the earth, they have always been a peace-loving people. So one night, when the Hiakim were busy feasting, Old White-Haired Woman loaded the baby into her burden basket and set off for the North. When the Yaqui learned she was gone, they sent a band of warriors after her to bring the baby back.

Old White-Haired Woman walked and walked. She was almost back to the land of the Desert People when the Yaqui warriors spotted her. I'itoi saw she was not going to complete her journey, so he called a flock of sha-shani, *black birds, who flew into the eyes of the Yaqui and blinded them. While the warriors were busy fighting* shashani, *I'itoi took Old White-Haired Woman into a wash and hid her.*

By then the old grandmother was very tired and lame from all her walking and carrying.

"You stay here," Elder Brother told her. "I will carry the baby back to your people, but while you sit here resting, you will be changed. Because of your bravery, your feet will become roots. Your tired old body will turn into branches. Each year, for one night only, you will become the most beautiful plant on the earth, a flower the Mil-gahn, *the Whites, call the Night-Blooming Cereus. The Queen of the Night."*

And it happened just that way. Old White-Haired Woman turned into a plant the Indians call ho'ok-wah'o *which means witch's tongs, but on that one night in early summer when a beautiful scent fills the desert air, the Tohono O'odham know that they are breathing in* kok'oi 'uw, *Ghost Scent, and they remember a brave old woman who saved her grandson and brought him home.*

Each year after that, on the night the flowers bloomed, the Tohono O'odham would gather around while Brought Back Child told the story of his grandmother, Old White-Haired Woman, and that, nawoj, my friend, is the same story I have just told you.

April 1959

Long after everyone else had left the beach and returned to the hotel, and long after the bonfire died down to coals, Ursula Brinker sat there in the sand and marveled over what had happened. What she had allowed to happen.

When June Lennox had invited Sully to come along to San Diego for spring break, she had known the moment she said yes that she was saying yes to more than just a fun trip from Tempe, Arizona, to California. The insistent tug had been there all along, for as long as Sully could remember. From the time she was in kindergarten, she had been interested in girls not boys, and that hadn't changed. Not later in grade school when the other girls started drooling over boys, and not later in high school, either.

But she had kept the secret. For one thing, she knew how much her parents would disapprove if

Sully ever admitted to them or to anyone else what she long suspected—that she was a lesbian. She didn't go around advertising it or wearing mannish clothing. People said she was "cute," and she was—cute and smart and talented. She suspected that if anyone learned that the girl who had been valedictorian of her class and who had been voted most likely to succeed was actually queer as a three-dollar bill, it would all be snatched away from her, like a mirage melting into the desert.

She had kept the secret until now. Until today. With June. And she was afraid if she left the beach and went back to the hotel room with everyone else and spoke about it, if she gave that newfound happiness a name, it might disappear forever as well.

The beach was deserted. When she heard the sand-muffled footsteps behind her, she thought it might be June. But it wasn't.

"Hello," she said. "When did you get here?"

He didn't answer that question. "What you did was wrong," he said. "Did you think you could keep it a secret? Did you think I wouldn't find out?"

"It just happened," she said. "We didn't mean to hurt you."

"But you did," he said. "More than you know."

He fell on her then. Had anyone been walking past on the beach, they wouldn't have paid much attention. Just another young couple carried away with necking; people who hadn't gotten themselves a room, and probably should have.

But in the early hours of that morning, what was happening there by the dwindling fire wasn't an act of love. It was something else altogether. When the rough embrace finally ended, the man stood up and walked away. He walked into the water and sluiced away the blood.

As for Sully Brinker? She did not walk away. The brainy cheerleader, the girl who had it all—money, brains, and looks—the girl once voted most likely to succeed would not succeed at anything because she was lying dead in the sand—dead at age twenty-one—and her parents' lives would never be the same.

1978

As the quarrel escalated, Danny covered his head with his pillow and tried not to listen, but the pillow didn't help. He could still hear the voices raging back and forth, his father's voice and his mother's. Turning on the TV set might have helped, but if his father came into the bedroom and found the set on when it wasn't supposed to be, Danny knew what would happen. First the belt would come off and, after that, the beating.

Danny knew how much that hurt, so he lay there and willed himself not to listen. He tried to fill his head with the words to one of the songs he had learned at school: Put your right foot in; put your left foot out. Put your right foot in and shake it all about. You do the Hokey Pokey and you turn yourself around. That's what it's all about.

He was about to go on to the second verse when he heard something that sounded like a firecracker—or four firecrackers in a row, even though it wasn't the Fourth of July.

Blam. Blam. Blam. Blam.

After that there was nothing. No other sound. Not his mother's voice and not his father's, either. An eerie silence settled over the house. First it filled Danny's ears and then his heart.

Finally the bedroom door creaked open. Danny knew his father was standing in the doorway, staring down at him, so he kept both eyes shut—shut but not too tightly shut. That would give it away. He didn't move. He barely breathed. At last after the door finally clicked closed, he opened his eyes and let out his breath.

He listened to the silence, welcoming it. The room wasn't completely dark. Streetlights in the parking lot made the room a hazy gray, and there was a sliver of light under the doorway. Soon that went away. Knowing that his father had probably left to go to a bar and drink some more, Danny was able to relax. As the tension left his body, he fell into a deep sleep, slumbering so peacefully that he never heard the sirens of the arriving cop cars or of the useless ambulance that arrived too late. The gunshot victim was dead long before the ambulance got there.

Much later, at least it seemed much later to him, someone—a stranger in a uniform—gently shook him awake. The cop wrapped the tangled sheet around him and lifted him from the bed.

"Come on, little guy," he said huskily. "Let's get you out of here."

June 2010

It was late, well after eleven, as Jonathan sat in the study of his soon-to-be-former home and stared at his so-called "wall of honor." The plaques and citations he saw there—his "Manager of the Year" award along with all the others that acknowledged his exemplary service were relics from another time and place—from another life. They were the currency and language of some other existence where the rules as he had once known them no longer applied.

What had happened on Wall Street had trickled down to Main Street. As a result his banking career was gone. His job was gone. His house would be gone soon, and so would his family. He wasn't supposed to know about the boyfriend Esther had waiting in the wings, but he did. He also knew what she was waiting for—the money from the 401 K. She wanted that, too, and she wanted it now.

Esther came in then—barged in really—without knocking. The fact that he might want a little privacy was as foreign a concept as the paltry career trophies still hanging on his walls. She stood there staring at him, hands on her hips.

"You changed the password on the account," she said accusingly.

"The account I changed the password on isn't a joint account," he told her mildly. "It's mine."

"We're still married," she pointed out. "What's yours is mine."

And, of course, that was the way it had always been. He worked. She stayed home and saw to it that they lived beyond their means, which had been considerable when he'd still had a good job. The problem was he no longer had that job, but she was still living the same way. As far as she was concerned, nothing had changed. For him everything had changed. Esther had gone right on spending money like it was water, but now the well had finally run dry. There was no job and no way to get a job. Banks didn't like having bankers with overdue bills and credit scores in the basement.

"I signed the form when you asked me to so we could both get the money," she said. "I want my fair share."

He knew there was nothing about this that was fair. It was the same stunt his mother had pulled on his father. Well, maybe not the boyfriend part, but he had vowed it wouldn't happen to him— would never happen to him. Yet here it was.

"It may be in an individual account but that money is a joint asset," Esther declared. "You don't get to have it all."

She was screaming at him now. He could hear her and so could anyone else in the neighborhood. He was glad they lived at the end of the cul-de-sac—with previously foreclosed houses on either side. It was a neighborhood where living beyond your means went with the territory.

"By the time my lawyer finishes wiping the floor with you, you'll be lucky to be living in a homeless shelter," she added. "As for seeing the kids? Forget about it. That's not going to happen. I'll see to it."

With that, she spun around as if to leave. Then, changing her mind, she grabbed the closest thing she could reach, which turned out to be his bronze Manager of the Year plaque, and heaved it at him. The sharp corner on the wood caught him full in the forehead—well, part of his very tall comb-over forehead—and it hurt like hell. It bled like hell.

As blood ran down his cheek and leaked into his eye, all the things he had stifled through the years came to a head. He had reached the end— the point where he had nothing left to lose.

Opening the top drawer of his desk, he removed the gun, a gun he had purchased with every intention of turning it on himself. Then, rising to his feet, he hurried out of the room intent on using it on someone else.

His body sizzled in a fit of unreasoning hatred. If that had been all there was to it, any defense attorney worthy of the name could have gotten him off on a plea of temporary insanity, because in that moment he was insane—legally insane. He knew nothing about the difference between right and wrong. All he knew was that he had taken all he could take. More than he could take.

The problem is that was only the start of Jonathan's problems. Everything that came after that was entirely premeditated.

*P*IMA COUNTY HOMICIDE detective Brian Fellows loved Saturdays. Kath usually worked Saturday shifts at her Border Patrol desk job, which meant Brian had the whole day to spend with his girls, six-year-old twins, Annie and Amy. They usually started with breakfast, either sharing a plate-sized sweet roll at Gus Balon's or eye-watering plates of chorizo and eggs at Wags.

After that, they went home to clean house. Brian's mother had been a much-divorced scatter-brain even before she became an invalid. Brian had learned from an early age that if he wanted a clean house, he'd be the one doing it. It hadn't killed him, either. He'd turned into a self-sufficient kind of guy and, according to Kath, an excellent catch for a husband.

Brian wanted the same thing for his daughters—for them to be self-sufficient. It didn't take long on Saturdays to whip their central area bungalow into shape. In the process, while settling the oc-casional squabble, being a bit of a tough task-master, and hearing about what was going on with the girls, Brian made sure he was a real presence in his daughter's lives—a real father.

That was something that had been missing in Brian's childhood—at least as far as his biological father was concerned. He wouldn't have had any idea about what fathers were supposed to be or do if it hadn't been for Brandon Walker, Brian's mother's first husband and the father of Tommy and Quentin, Brian's half brothers.

Brandon, then a Pima County homicide detective, had come to the house each weekend and dutifully collected his own sons to take them on non-custodial outings. One of Brian's first memories was of being left alone on the front step while Quentin and Tommy went racing off to jump in their father's car to go somewhere fun—to a movie or the Pima County Fair or maybe even the Tucson Rodeo—while Brian, bored and lonely, had to fend for himself.

Then one day a miracle had happened. After Quentin and Tommy were already in the car, Brandon had gotten out of the car, come back up the walk, and asked Brian if he would like to go along, too. Brian was beyond excited. Quentin and Tommy had been appalled and had done everything in their power to make Brian miserable, but they did that anyway—even before Brandon had taken pity on him.

From then on, that's how it was. Whenever Brandon had taken his own boys somewhere, he had taken Brian as well. The man had become a sort of super-hero in Brian's eyes. He had grown up wanting to be just like him and it was due to that, in no small measure, that Brian Fellows was the man he was today—a doting father and an experienced cop. And it was why, on Saturday afternoons after the house was clean, he never failed to take his girls somewhere to do something fun—to the Randolph Park Zoo or the Arizona Sonora Desert Museum. Today, as hot as it was, they had already settled on going to a movie at Park Mall.

Brian was on call tonight. If someone decided to kill someone else tonight, he'd have to go in to work, but that was fine. He would have had his special day with his girls, well, all but one of his girls, and that was what made life worth living.

Brandon Walker knew he was running away. He had the excuse of running to something, but he understood that he was really running from something, something he didn't want to face. He would face it eventually because he had to, but not yet. He wasn't ready.

Not that going to see G. T. Farrell was light duty by any means. Stopping by to see someone who was on his way to hospice care wasn't Brandon's idea of fun. Sue, Geet's wife had called with the bad news. Geet's lung cancer had been held at bay for far longer than anyone had thought possible, but now it was back. And winning.

"He's got a set of files that he had me bring out of storage," Sue had said in her phone call. "He made me promise that I'd see to it that you got them—you and nobody else."

Brandon didn't have to ask which file because

he already knew. Every homicide cop has a case like that, the one that haunts him and won't let him go, the one where the bad guy got away with murder. For Geet Farrell it had been the 1959 murder of Ursula Brinker. Geet had been a newbie ASU campus cop at the time her death had stunned the entire university community. The case had stayed with him, haunting Geet the whole time he'd worked as a homicide detective for the Pinal County Sheriff's Department and through his years of retirement as well. Now that Geet knew it was curtains for him, he wanted to hand Ursula's unsolved case off to someone else and make his problem Brandon's problem.

Fair enough, Brandon thought. *If I'm dealing with Geet Farrell's difficulties, I won't have to face up to my own.*

Geet was a good five years older than Brandon. They had met for the first time as homicide cops decades earlier. In 1975, Brandon Walker had been working Homicide for the Pima County Sheriff's Department, and G. T. Farrell had been his Homicide counterpart in neighboring Pinal. Between them they had helped bring down a serial killer named Andrew Philip Carlisle. Partially due to their efforts Carlisle had been sentenced to life in prison. He had lived out his remaining years in the state prison in Florence, Arizona, where he had finally died.

It turned out Brandon had also received a life-long sentence as a result of that case, only his had been much different. One of Carlisle's intended victims, the fiercely independent Diana Ladd, had gone against type and consented to become Brandon Walker's wife. They had been married now for thirty plus years.

It was hard for Brandon to imagine what his life would have been like if Andrew Carlisle had succeeded in murdering Diana. How would he have survived for all those years if he hadn't been married to that amazing woman? How would he have existed without Diana and all the complications she had brought into his life, including her son, Davy, and their adopted *Tohono O'odham* daughter, Lani?

Much later, long after both detectives had been turned out to pasture by their respective law enforcement agencies, Geet by retiring and Brandon by losing a bid for reelection, Geet had been instrumental in the creation of an independent cold case investigative entity called TLC, The Last Chance, started by Hedda Brinker, the mother of Geet's first homicide victim. In an act of seeming charity, Geet had asked that his old buddy, former Pima County sheriff, Brandon Walker, be invited to sign on.

That ego-saving invitation, delivered in person by a smooth-talking attorney named Ralph Ames, had come at a time when, as Brandon liked to put it, he had been lower than a snake's vest pocket. He had accepted without a moment of hesitation. In the intervening years, working with TLC had saved his sanity if not his life.

All of which meant Brandon owed everything to Geet Farrell, and that was why, on this amazingly hot late June afternoon, he was driving to

Casa Grande for what he knew would be a deathbed visit.

The twin debts Brandon Walker owed G. T. Farrell were more than he could ever repay, but he hoped that taking charge of Ursula Brinker's file and tilting at Geet's insoluble windmill of a case would help even the score. Just a little.

NOVELS OF SUSPENSE BY
NEW YORK TIMES BESTSELLING AUTHOR

J.A. JANCE

Featuring Sheriff Joanna Brady

DAMAGE CONTROL
978-0-06-074678-0

Cochise County sheriff Joanna Brady has to investigate
an apparent double suicide that an autopsy suggests
may be something different.

DEAD WRONG
070-0-00-054091-3

A corpse is discovered in the desert with the fingers
severed from both hands—the body of an ex-con who
served twenty years for a murder he claimed not to remember.

EXIT WOUNDS
978-0-380-80471-9

As she probes the macabre death of a loner and her
17 dogs, Sheriff Brady soon finds herself beleaguered by the
victim's family, an angry mob of animal rights activists and
an underground bigamist colony.

PARTNER IN CRIME
978-0-06-196171-7

The Washington State Attorney General's office thinks this
investigation is too big for a small-town *female* law officer
to handle, so they're sending Sheriff Joanna Brady some
unwanted help—seasoned detective J.P. Beaumont.

www.jajance.com

Visit www.AuthorTracker.com for exclusive
information on your favorite HarperCollins authors.

Available wherever books are sold or please call 1-800-331-3761 to order.
JB 1010

NOVELS OF SUSPENSE BY
NEW YORK TIMES BESTSELLING AUTHOR

J.A. JANCE

Featuring Sheriff Joanna Brady

DESERT HEAT
978-0-06-177459-6

TOMBSTONE COURAGE
978-0-06-177461-4

SHOOT/DON'T SHOOT
978-0-06-177480-5

DEAD TO RIGHTS
978-0-06-177479-9

SKELETON CANYON
978-0-06-199895-9

RATTLESNAKE CROSSING
978-0-06-199896-6

OUTLAW MOUNTAIN
978-0-06-199897-3

DEVIL'S CLAW
978-0-06-199898-0

PARADISE LOST
978-0-380-80469-6

www.jajance.com

Visit www.AuthorTracker.com for exclusive
information on your favorite HarperCollins authors.

Available wherever books are sold or please call 1-800-331-3761 to order.

JB1 1010

Masterworks of suspense by
New York Times bestselling author

J.A. JANCE

FEATURING J.P. BEAUMONT

JUSTICE DENIED 978-0-06-054093-7
Beau and his girlfriend (and fellow cop) Mel Soames investigate a deadly conspiracy that's leading them to lofty places they may not be allowed to leave alive.

LONG TIME GONE 978-0-380-72435-2
The vicious slaying of his former partner's ex-wife is tearing at J.P. Beaumont's heart as his friend is the prime suspect.

PARTNER IN CRIME 978-0-06-196171-7
Retired homicide detective J.P. Beaumont is sent to Bisbee, Arizona, to supply some unwanted help for local Sheriff Joanna Brady.

BIRDS OF PREY 978-0-380-71654-8
A pleasure cruise toward the Gulf of Alaska is no escape for J.P. Beaumont, as death is a conspicuous, unwelcome passenger.

BREACH OF DUTY 978-0-380-71843-6
Beaumont and his new partner Sue Danielson are assigned the murder of an elderly woman torched to death in her bed.

NAME WITHHELD 978-0-380-71842-9
Nobody is grieving over the death of a biotech corporation executive whose numerous criminal activities included illegally trading industrial secrets ... and rape.

FIRE AND ICE 978-0-06-123923-6
Two cases, one in Seattle, one in the Arizona desert, are drawing Beau once more into Brady country.

Visit www.AuthorTracker.com for exclusive information on your favorite HarperCollins authors.

Available wherever books are sold or please call 1-800-331-3761 to order.
JAN 0410

MASTERWORKS OF SUSPENSE BY
NEW YORK TIMES BESTSELLING AUTHOR

J.A. JANCE

Featuring Detective J.P. Beaumont

UNTIL PROVEN GUILTY
978-0-06-195851-9

INJUSTICE FOR ALL
978-0-06-195852-6

TRIAL BY FURY
978-0-06-195853-3

TAKING THE FIFTH
978-0-06-195854-0

IMPROBABLE CAUSE
978-0-06-199928-4

A MORE PERFECT UNION
978-0-06-199929-1

DISMISSED WITH PREJUDICE
978-0-06-199930-7

MINOR IN POSSESSION
978-0-06-199931-4

PAYMENT IN KIND
978-0-380-75836-4

WITHOUT DUE PROCESS
978-0-380-75837-1

FAILURE TO APPEAR
978-0-380-75839-5

LYING IN WAIT
978-0-380-71841-2

Visit www.AuthorTracker.com for exclusive
information on your favorite HarperCollins authors.

Available wherever books are sold or please call 1-800-331-3761 to order.

JAN1 0611